Praise for the Works of Annie England Noblin

Sit! Stay! Speak!

"A warm, emotionally grounded story that will delight fans of Mary Kay Andrews and contemporary women's fiction."

—*Booklist*

"Readers of Debbie Macomber will enjoy poet and nonfiction author Noblin's first novel. It's an enjoyable story full of laughter, tears, and just plain fun."

—*Library Journal*

"Noblin's fish-out-of-water story combines food, family, suspense, and romance into one delightful read . . . a comfort read that's perfect for a summer night. The dog-centered plot will earn points from all animal lovers. A cozy read that's full of dogs, romance, and small-town charm."

—*Kirkus Reviews*

"*Sit! Stay! Speak!* by Annie England Noblin is a must read for any animal lover."

—Fresh Fiction

Just Fine with Caroline

"*Just Fine with Caroline* is all heart. Annie England Noblin knows how to make characters come to life. I was completely charmed on my trip to Cold River."

—Stephanie Evanovich, *New York Times* bestselling author of *Big Girl Panties*

"Fans of Mary Kay Andrews and Debbie Macomber will adore this warm and lighthearted tale of self-reliance, small town gossip, and second chances."

—*Booklist*

Pupcakes

"Noblin's tale of self-discovery, populated with a colorful cast of characters, is both lighthearted and life-affirming. Readers are in for a sweet treat." —*USA Today*

"Fans of Noblin's canine-themed tales (*Sit! Stay! Speak!*; *Just Fine with Caroline*) will beg for more." —*Library Journal*

"*Pupcakes* is the sweetest story I have read this year and I was hooked from the first to the last page. Annie England Noblin is obviously a dog lover . . . and her story is sweet, funny, and touches the heart." —*Fresh Fiction*

The
Sisters Hemingway

Also by Annie England Noblin

Pupcakes
Just Fine with Caroline
Sit! Stay! Speak!

The
Sisters Hemingway

A Cold River Novel

Annie England Noblin

wm

WILLIAM MORROW
An Imprint of HarperCollins*Publishers*

P.S.™ is a trademark of HarperCollins Publishers.

HarperCollins books may be purchased for educational, business, or sales promotional use. For information, please email the Special Markets Department at SPsales@harpercollins.com.

FIRST EDITION

Designed by Diahann Sturge

Chapter opener art © Daleen Loest / Shutterstock, Inc.

Library of Congress Cataloging-in-Publication Data has been applied for.

ISBN 978-0-06-267451-7

19 20 21 22 23 LSC 10 9 8 7 6 5 4 3 2 1

For Brittany

The
Sisters Hemingway

PROLOGUE

Rachael Hemingway watched the clouds gather overhead as she raced along the gravel path leading her away from her house. It was quiet, too quiet; not even the birds were chattering in the trees above her. If she hadn't known better, she would have guessed it was winter instead of a mild spring day.

She knew what was coming.

Her eldest daughter, Hadley, was safe at her boyfriend's house; at least, that's what Rachael hoped. She hadn't spoken to her since their argument earlier that afternoon. Moments ago, she sent her two younger daughters, Pfeiffer and Martha, to the cellar with the old transistor radio, forbidding them to leave. It was Mary, Rachael's youngest, she'd set off to find.

When Mary first turned up missing, Rachael hadn't thought much of it. Mary often disappeared into the woods beyond their farm. Their land bordered part of the Missouri National Forest, and Mary, quiet, dark, and thoughtful, loved the solitude of the thickest parts. At twelve years old, Rachael's youngest daughter was so unlike her sisters. She was a force in her own quiet way, it was true, not unlike the storm that was surely coming to these

Ozarks Hills, and that was what Rachael loved about her most. She was so like her father, Matthew Hemingway. He'd been different, too, not from here, probably that was what attracted Rachael to him in the first place.

It wasn't until Mary hadn't come home, not even for dinner, that Rachael began to worry. It wasn't until she was frying chicken in her mother's cast-iron skillet that she realized Mary must've overheard the argument between herself and Hadley. She'd likely been listening through the vent in her room, as it carried the sounds and smells of the kitchen right up to the second floor. Rachael couldn't be sure exactly what Mary heard, but she knew now that it was probably enough. By the time she pulled on her boots and tied back her hair, the clouds were rolling in, thick and heavy, bringing with them the emotions she'd been carrying around with her all day long, and she knew it was a bad sign.

The wind picked up, and Rachael wished she'd brought along a jacket. She was sure Mary had neglected to bring one with her when she left the house that afternoon. Mary never thought of things like that—necessities such as coats or mittens or even shoes, for that matter.

When the rain started, Rachael picked up her pace, running through the forest, calling out for her daughter. Her voice was lost in the wind, and the branches scratched at her bare legs as she ran, but she didn't let up, not even for an instant. If she could get to the white oak tree at the center, the oldest and tallest of all the trees in the forest, she knew she would find Mary.

Mary asked her once how old she thought the tree might be, if she had to guess. Rachael had stared up at it, as it was well over one hundred feet tall, and not known the answer.

"I'm not sure," she said. "But it's very old."

"Ten years?" Mary asked. She was scarcely six at the time, and she must've thought ten years old sounded quite grown up.

"Much older than that," Rachael replied, trying not to laugh. It hurt the little girl's feelings when her mother laughed at her questions.

"Fifty years?"

"Older."

"A hundred years?" Mary asked, her eyes wide. "Mama, do you think this tree could be a hundred years old?"

Rachael nodded. "I think this tree may be a hundred years old or more," she said. "It's been here a very long time."

"Isn't there a way to tell how old the tree is?" Mary asked.

"Not without cutting it down," Rachael said. "The only way to tell how old a tree really is, is to cut it down and count the rings inside."

"Rings?"

"Around the bark." Rachael made a circling motion with her hand.

"But that will kill the tree," Mary stated.

"It would," Rachael agreed.

"Maybe I could just ask the tree," Mary said, tilting her head to one side the way she often did when she was thinking hard about something.

"You could try."

Mary let go of her mother's hand and stepped closer to the tree. She touched her fingertips to the jagged bark and closed her eyes, whispering something that Rachael couldn't quite hear. After a few moments, she fell back into place next to her mother.

"She says she's awfully old," Mary said. Her dark eyes were two shadows. They could see, Rachael knew, what others could not. "She's so old that we wouldn't believe her even if she told us."

Rachael laughed at that. She couldn't help it. She had to laugh to keep from being unnerved. Mary might've been a child, but Rachael never had any doubt that the tree was speaking to her that day, a spring day in March much like this one, when she'd been just six years old.

Now all Rachael could think about was getting to that tree. "Mary!" she shouted, the rain pelting against her face. "Mary!"

That was when Rachael saw her, right where she knew she'd be, her skinny arms wrapped around the tree, hanging on for dear life. Her hair was clinging to her face, and her jeans were ripped and bloodied at the knee.

"Mama!" Mary called when she saw her, not daring to let go. "Mama, I'm here!"

"Mary," Rachael gasped, grabbing on to her. "Mary, we have to go. Now!"

"No!" Mary tightened her grip. "No, I won't leave her."

"The tree will be fine. Its roots are deep," Rachael said. "It's been through storms worse than this."

"You're a liar!" Mary screamed.

"I'm not lying," Rachael replied, her voice hoarse from screaming through the wind and the rain and the forest. "The tree will survive."

"You lied about everything," Mary said. "I'm not going."

Rachael closed her eyes to steady herself. There wasn't time for this argument. Not now. "We have to go," she said again.

"No!"

"Please!" Rachael grabbed at her daughter's arms, tearing them away from the tree. "We won't make it back if we don't hurry."

Mary dug her fingernails farther into the bark, but it was no use. Her mother tore her away and dragged her from the tree while she shrieked, "Please don't make me leave! Please!"

Rachael half dragged, half carried her daughter through the thicket, the storm upon them now, unrelenting. They were too far out into the country for the sirens, but Rachael knew they must be sounding in town, and she said a silent prayer that her other three daughters were safe.

When they got to the gravel road just beyond the house, they continued to run, Mary no longer having to be dragged, too terrified of the storm to protest. The rain came down in slanted sheets, and the sky was lit up with shades of green. Rachael saw the neighbor's old rusted cattle gate, sliding along the road beside them as if it were floating down a river of dust. She knew the twister was behind them, moving far faster than they could ever run, and she knew there wasn't time to make it to the cellar before it was upon them.

"Mama!" Mary stopped dead in her tracks and turned around to face what was coming. "Mama, it's here!"

Rachael was in awe. In her fifty years on this earth, she'd never seen anything quite like it. The sheer magnitude of the storm overwhelmed her, and she was stuck in place for an entire lifetime before she felt Mary pulling on the sleeve of her rain-soaked T-shirt.

"Come on," Rachael said, hurrying Mary down into the ditch. "Get down."

"Mama."

Rachael got down on top of her, covering as much of her

daughter's fragile body as she could, wrapping her arms around her. "I love you," she managed to say before the wind knocked the breath out of her and the noise of the moment was there, on top of them, all the while, the great white oak tree, by now the very oldest in the entire forest, could do nothing but stay rooted into the ground as the rest of the world was carried off without it.

CHAPTER 1

Pfeiffer

P FEIFFER HEMINGWAY IGNORED THE DOORBELL. INSTEAD, she rolled over on the couch to face the back cushions. No good could come of answering the doorbell. Not now. There had been a time, in the not-so-distant past, when the sound of the doorbell meant delight. When there was someone standing outside her expansive Chelsea apartment, it meant there had been a package delivered or it was Benny with the takeaway pad thai or her friends were there to pick her up for a night out.

Now when the doorbell rang, it just meant there was someone standing there waiting to take something away from her. This time, she assumed that there were people here for her couch. After all, it was the only piece of furniture left. The only thing she owned that had not been repossessed in recent months. The last time the furniture men had tried to take it, she'd sat there in her nightgown with a can of Mace, bits of pad thai stuck to the corners of her mouth as she ordered them to *try it*.

Still, the doorbell persisted.

"Go away," she muttered, pulling the blanket up over her head.

"Pfeiffer Francine Hemingway, you open this door right now!"

Pfeiffer sat up. She knew that voice. "Seth?"

"Open the door, Pi."

Pfeiffer flung off the blanket and stalked to the door. "What do you want, Seth?"

"To make sure the smell emanating from your apartment isn't your decomposing body," he replied. "Let me in."

"Fine," Pfeiffer said, unlocking the dead bolt and pulling open the door. "Come in."

"Jesus Christ," Seth whispered when he stepped inside. "What in the hell happened in here?"

"Unemployment."

"Pi, that was nine months ago."

"Two hundred and seventy-two days ago," Pfeiffer replied. "Apparently, that's how long it takes to drain a savings account."

"Have you even applied for another job?" Seth asked, leading her over to the couch and sitting her down. "Surely you've got a lead or two."

"If I had any leads, don't you think I'd be out pursuing them instead of hiding in a ratty nightgown on my couch?" Pfeiffer asked. "Nobody will have me. No one."

Seth sighed, pushing his glasses farther up his nose. "Well, you can hardly blame them."

In fact, Pfeiffer did blame *them*. She did blame Henry Brothers Publishers for firing her after almost a decade as an editor, after almost a decade of finding bestsellers for them, and after a decade of making them money. Sure, she'd made a mistake. In fact, she'd made the worst mistake an editor could make: she'd passed on a future bestseller.

She had been, of course, the one to send the agent of the aforementioned author an email, tartly telling her that her client ought not to quit her day job. That had been just a few weeks before editors at five other houses got ahold of the book and began a frenzied bidding war, causing the author's name and title of the book, *Aurora's Artifacts,* to be the most sought-after prospect since the Harry Potter series—not the first Harry Potter book. No, not that one. An editor had once told J. K. Rowling not to quit her day job, too.

It didn't take long for the Henry Brothers to figure out Pfeiffer's grievous error, and matters only got worse after that damned email made its way around the publishing world. In less than twenty-four hours, she'd become a pariah. No one, not even her oldest friends—save Seth—would return a text message. The next day, Pfeiffer Hemingway, senior editor, had been told not to let the door hit her where the good lord split her, and just like that—she was out of a job. Nobody, not even the lowest of the lowest publishing houses, would touch her.

"You're taking a risk being here," Pfeiffer said, eyeing the empty room wildly. "Did anybody see you?"

Seth rolled his eyes. "It's not like there's a hit out on you," he said.

"Might as well be," she grumbled. "Nobody will hire me."

"Give it time."

Pfeiffer opened her arms wide. "Does it look like I have any more time? The only reason I still have this couch is because I look half-rabid, and the men from the furniture store were afraid to get too close for fear I'd bite."

"I have it on good authority that you *do*," Seth replied with a wink.

"Shut up," Pfeiffer replied miserably, a smile creeping onto her lips despite herself. "I'm serious. What am I going to do? I'm out of money. Out of friends. Out of a job. I'm screwed, Seth, and you know it."

"Maybe it's time to consider another line of work," Seth said in earnest.

Pfeiffer sighed, pushing her wild, strawberry curls out of her face. "I don't know how to do anything else," she said.

"When you first showed up here in the city, you said you wanted to be a writer," Seth replied.

"But I ended up editing other writers instead," Pfeiffer replied. "I'm better at that. At least I used to be."

Seth patted her knee. "Wow, that's hairy," he muttered to himself before saying, "What about going home?"

"Home?" Pfeiffer blinked up at him. "Home? I *am* home. Well, at least this is home until the end of the month."

"You know what I mean, Pi."

Pfeiffer sat back, exposing both of her hairy knees. If this had been nine months ago, she would rather have died than let Seth or anyone else know she even *had* hair on her knees, let alone any other part of her body. But today was today and not nine months ago, and indeed, she did know what Seth meant. He meant that maybe she should go back to her childhood home.

To Missouri.

To the Missouri Ozarks.

To Cold River.

Pfeiffer winced at the thought. "I haven't been home in almost two decades," she said at last. "I can't go home."

Seth looked at her, very serious for what seemed like a long time. "Pi, honey, how long have you had your cell turned off?"

Pfeiffer shrugged. "A couple of weeks, probably."

"Well, you got a call at the office today—several calls, in fact—from your sister Hadley. I finally had to promise that I'd deliver a message to you personally."

Pfeiffer sat up a little straighter. "What are you talking about?"

"I don't really know how to tell you this," Seth said, scratching at his perfectly coiffed head. "But your aunt Beatrice is dead."

"What?"

"Dead," Seth repeated. "Your sister said it happened yesterday."

Pfeiffer sighed. Hadley. She always knew everything first. *Maybe,* Pfeiffer thought, not for the first time, *it's because she was born first.* It had long been a suspicion of Pfeiffer, the second sister, that the oldest sister knew everything first, and it was her responsibility as the oldest sister to hold that information over her younger sisters for all eternity. It had been nearly a year since she'd talked to Hadley, and nearly five years since she'd seen her, despite the fact that Hadley lived in Washington, D.C., which really wasn't that far away from New York. Pfeiffer didn't like Hadley's husband, and she didn't like the person Hadley became around her husband, and so instead of wasting her time arguing about it, she found it best to keep her mouth closed and stay in New York. Their relationship was tenuous on a good day, and today was not a good day.

"She said she would be on the first flight home tomorrow morning," Seth said. "Red-eye from D.C."

"Did you tell her I don't work at Henry Brothers anymore?" Pfeiffer asked. She couldn't stand the thought of Hadley or Martha learning that she'd been fired.

"Of course not," he said. "You know I wouldn't do that to you."

Pfeiffer eyed her friend and former colleague. He looked uncomfortable, like he would do anything to get out of her barren apartment and away from her shabby-without-the-chic appearance. She bit at the corner of her lip and then said, "Seth, do you still have that old car? The one you drove here from Nebraska?"

Seth's eyes darted around the room, as if he thought at any moment spies from Henry Brothers might pop up out of nowhere. "You promised never to speak of . . . Nebraska."

"Oh, come on," Pfeiffer said, standing up to stretch. "Everybody knows you weren't *born* inside the Kate Spade on Fifth."

"Well, they at least have the decency not to *say that*," Seth said with a sniff. "What do you want with my car?"

"I need to borrow it," Pfeiffer replied. "I can't afford a plane ticket, and I can't let Hadley pay for a plane ticket, because then she'll know I lost my job."

"And you think showing up in a 1994 LeBaron won't out you?"

"I'll figure something out between here and Cold River," Pfeiffer said.

"I know," Seth replied, reaching out to touch her leg again and then thinking better of it. "You always do."

"Can I borrow your phone?" Pfeiffer asked. "I should probably call Hadley."

Seth stood up and worked his hand down into the pocket of his jeans. "Here."

Pfeiffer eyed her friend. "Could your jeans be any tighter?"

"If I keep eating the scones at work, the answer is yes," Seth replied.

Pfeiffer rolled her eyes and shuffled back into her empty bedroom to call her sister. She pressed the numbers into the phone and waited. Hadley answered on the first ring.

"Hello?"

"Hadley?" Pfeiffer asked, even though she knew who it was. "It's Pfeiffer."

"I've been trying to get ahold of you," Hadley said. "What is going on? You aren't at work. Your phone is out of service."

"My phone isn't out of service."

"That's the message I get when I call."

Pfeiffer sighed. "I'm having some trouble with it," she said. "I'll have it fixed soon."

"And why haven't you been at work?" Hadley continued. "I've never known you to take more than half a day off in all the years you've been at Henry Brothers."

"I had some time coming," Pfeiffer said simply. "I took it."

"That doesn't sound like you."

"I didn't call you so we could play twenty questions," Pfeiffer replied.

"That sounds more like you," Hadley replied. "I guess you got the message about Aunt Beatrice?"

"Just now."

"We need to go home."

"Why?" Pfeiffer wanted to know.

"Because that's what you do when someone dies," Hadley replied. "You go home and go to the funeral. I mean, really, Pfeiffer. I thought you of all people would want to go to the funeral. She loved you best, after all."

And there it was. What Pfeiffer had been waiting for. "She didn't love me best," she said. "I just understood her."

"I didn't?"

"Look, Hadley," Pfeiffer said. "Can we just not fight about this?"

There was a long pause on the other end of the line. "So are you coming or not?"

"Yes," Pfeiffer replied. "I'll be there."

"Good," Hadley said. "Oh . . . and Pi?"

"What?"

"I don't know what's going on with you, but I'm going to find out."

CHAPTER 2

Martha

MARTHA COULD SMELL THE COW SHIT EVEN BEFORE SHE crossed over the Ozark County line. She hated cows. They were big, dumb animals with mournful eyes and jittery dispositions. She'd been kicked by one once, in June, just after her eighth birthday, and broken her arm. Her mother said she'd been lucky it was her arm and not her head, but her sister Pfeiffer had muttered that Martha's head was the hardest part of her body, anyway, so why not?

Martha gripped the steering wheel as her Tesla Model S careened around the curves of the Missouri foothills. She'd written her first songs about this place. She'd closed her eyes and imagined it here a million times after she first moved to Nashville, longing to sit down on the front porch of her mother's house in Cold River and listen to the crickets and mosquitoes join in with the hum of her guitar.

But that had been nearly sixteen years ago, before she'd become a runaway, before the cockroach-infested apartment in an ugly part of Nashville, before she'd gotten her first record deal, and certainly before she'd met, married, and been divorced by Travis Tucker. And, of course, before she'd spent the last six months in rehab.

Martha always thought her return home would be triumphant. She thought she'd arrive on a giant tour bus with Travis in tow, and she'd step out, glamorous and beautiful. She'd flip her golden hair over one shoulder, carrying her golden albums, and be presented with a key to the city.

Instead, she was driving back from Nashville by herself. Still glamorous and golden, yes, but the shine slightly dulled with age and cigarette smoke. She hadn't had a number one album in nearly three years, and it appeared she never would now that her husband and record label had dumped her all within the last year. Yep, the Nashville press had really had a field day with all of that. Her agent, the only person she'd told the doctors at the facility she would talk to, told her all about it. Later that month, she was served with the divorce papers and then a certified letter from her label. It's a good thing, she thought, that she was already in rehab, because all of that bad news certainly would have driven her to commit herself.

Martha rounded the corner just on the edge of town and rolled up her window so that nobody would be able to see her through the tint. The house where she'd grown up was on the other side of Cold River—a hundred and forty acres and a farmhouse plopped down somewhere in the middle. She wondered idly if her sisters, Hadley and Pfeiffer, were already there. She'd spoken to Hadley on the phone briefly, but the only words that stuck were "Aunt Bea" and "dead." She'd been half-asleep when her sister called, and now she reached back into the far recesses of her brain to recall their conversation.

It was no use. Martha's memory was rotten. It had not been a kick from a cow but a fall from an apple tree that had seen to that. The whiskey in the years following didn't help matters much. Her last fight with Travis, the one just before he'd walked out, had been about whiskey. Well, it was more about her *drinking* the whiskey than anything else, but hell, what else was she supposed to do on a tour bus *alone*? Travis sure hadn't been spending any time with her.

Martha saw a man on a horse trotting along on the side of the road, a typical sight in Cold River. No, this was certainly *not* the first place she thought she'd visit after rehab. She'd been envisioning a beach with white sand, her white bikini, and . . . well, something nonalcoholic that tasted fruity. Instead, she slowed down to move around the ambling horse and then sped up once again as the man atop the horse tipped his hat to her in her rearview mirror.

CHAPTER 3

Martha

T EN MINUTES LATER AND MARTHA WAS OUTSIDE OF COLD River, eyes squinted to find the county road where she turned to get to the farm. It'd been so long, she could scarcely remember if it was on the right or left side of the road. The number, however, she remembered—County Road 1957. It was the year her mother had been born, and she and her sisters always joked that it meant her mother was as old as the dirt on the road they traveled.

As she made the turn, on the right, as fate would have it, she noticed a car sitting in the middle of the road, seemingly abandoned. The car was placed so that Martha couldn't get around it from either side without driving into the ditch.

Annoyed, she threw the Tesla into park behind the car and got out. Upon closer inspection, she realized that there was smoke coming from the hood. Farther down the road, she saw the outline of a person moving away from where she stood and toward the farm.

"Hey!" she shouted, running after them. "Hey! Your damn car is in the middle of the road!"

The person didn't stop, didn't turn around.

"Hey!" Martha continued her stride, feeling the rocks beneath her flip-flops digging into the soles of her feet. "Stop!"

Finally, the person in front of her halted and turned on her heel to face Martha. The person, a woman, had her hands on her hips; one long, lean leg jutted out in front of her, as if she were ready for a confrontation.

Martha blinked and then blinked again. The person standing half a football field away from her was one of her sisters. She ventured closer. "Pfeiffer?"

"Martha?"

Martha trotted up to her sister, arms flung out to embrace her before she remembered a millisecond too late that her sister didn't, under any circumstances, hug. Her fingertips brushed at the sleeves of Pfeiffer's red cardigan instead. "Is that *your* POS broke down in the middle of the road?"

Pfeiffer straightened herself and brushed a speck of red clay mud off her pencil skirt. *"No,"* she replied, her tone haughty. "It's my assistant's. You know I don't have a car."

"Or a valid license," Martha muttered.

Pfeiffer shot her sister a look. "I *borrowed* it."

Martha craned her neck around to look back at the car. It wasn't Pfeiffer's style at all and had clearly seen better days. "Why didn't you just fly in?" she asked. "You could have rented a car at the airport."

Pfeiffer shrugged, rolling her eyes at the same time, an indication that she was bored with the conversation. "I thought it might be fun to drive, you know, clear my head."

"You?" Martha asked. "Have fun?"

"Anyway, I don't have cell service out here," Pfeiffer replied, ignoring her sister. "I thought maybe the house might still have a landline, and I could call to have that monstrosity towed."

Martha followed along after her. "Do you have a key?"

"I figured I could just use the one underneath the mat."

"Pfeiffer," Martha said, catching up to her, "what makes you think that mat will even still be there?"

"It'll be there."

Martha wasn't so sure, but she wasn't about to argue. Of the three sisters, Pfeiffer was most often right, and she liked to remind Martha and Hadley of this on a regular basis. As the younger sister, Martha didn't mind it so much. That was just what older siblings did, she assumed. But she did wonder sometimes if Hadley minded, since she was the oldest. Hadley was mild-mannered, for sure, but something about Pfeiffer always brought out the worst in her.

"Do you think the old place will look the same as always?" Martha asked.

Pfeiffer stopped in her tracks and stared over at Martha. "*You* certainly don't look the same."

It wasn't a compliment, Martha could tell. It was, however, true. "I look better," she said indignantly. She hadn't seen her sister in five years, not since the last time she'd flown to D.C. to see Hadley. The two of them practically had to force Pfeiffer to visit, playing on her duty to them as a sister. But she and Pfeiffer still talked on the phone every few months, and although their conversations were superficial, at least it was a conversation. Martha was used to being the go-between when it came to her sisters, but she wished more than anything that she didn't have to be. She always thought that when they grew up, they'd be best friends. But when Hadley married Mark, all of that changed. Mark's job as a congressman kept Hadley busy all the time, and Pfeiffer's dislike for him kept her from Hadley.

Pfeiffer, unaware that Martha was deep in thought, pointed down at her sister's feet. "Couldn't you afford a better pair of footwear than flip-flops?"

Now it was Martha's turn to roll her eyes. It was true, she was still wearing flip-flops, but they were more expensive flip-flops than the dollar-store ones she'd worn as a child. They *were* Marc Jacobs, after all. Her hair was blond now, and it suited her. Her blue eyes were blue, thanks to the help of colored contacts, and her V-neck tank top accentuated her cleavage, the very first thing she'd bought and paid for when her debut album went gold. "I doubt anybody would recognize me now," she said. "Flip-flops or not."

"Everybody will notice you," Pfeiffer retorted. "You're famous, remember?"

"I am," Martha said, remembering herself.

"How was rehab?"

"Sober." Martha sighed.

"That's a good thing, right?"

"I don't know." Martha gave her sister a sly smile. "Do *you* like to be sober?"

Ahead of them, the James farm loomed. The house, the second to be built by the James family after the first one burned in 1900, was a turn-of-the-century farmhouse. It was nothing special as far as houses go, as the ancestral Jameses had been Quakers and not much interested in making a statement of wealth or frivolity. It was a standard two stories, and with the exception of the time the sisters' mother got the notion to paint it a pale pink like the houses she'd seen on the beaches of Florida, it was nearly always painted white. But it had a sprawling and inviting front porch, which had always been Martha's favorite part of the house.

Now, as they neared the property, Martha saw that the front porch appeared to be sagging, just like the rest of the place. It was as if someone had gone and sucked all of the air, all of the life, out of it.

"I can't believe Aunt Bea let it go like this," Pfeiffer said. She put one foot atop the crumbling, concrete steps. "She was so particular."

"I know," Martha muttered.

Their aunt, unlike their mother, hadn't liked a messy home. She started cleaning when the sun came up, and she didn't stop until the sun went down. She even set out a list of chores every morning with each of the sisters' names on it. They couldn't leave the house or do anything else until the chores were done. Martha hadn't minded so much, enjoying a clean house, and neither had Hadley. But Pfeiffer hated it. She'd sit up in her room for hours and hours, refusing to do anything their aunt wanted them to do. It was a battle of wills every day, and Pfeiffer never won. Still, Pfeiffer and their aunt shared a special bond that the other sisters didn't. It was an understanding, Martha guessed, because they were just so much alike.

"Found the key," Pfeiffer huffed, straightening herself up from bending down to search under the mat. "Same mat and everything."

Martha looked down at the faded mat lying at the foot of the door. Once upon a time it had read "Welcome" in big, bold letters. Now the lettering was gone, and what was left was a lumpy, beige mass surrounded by a thick layer of dirt. "Great," she replied halfheartedly.

Pfeiffer wiped the key off on her skirt and stuck the key in the lock. "Hey," she said. "It's open."

"What?" Martha stepped closer to her sister. "What do you mean?"

"I mean it's unlocked, dummy," Pfeiffer said, impatient. "You think Hadley is already here?"

"I didn't see another car," Martha replied.

"Me either."

"Only one way to find out," Martha said, stepping past her sister and pushing the front door open.

"What if there's somebody in there?" Pfeiffer asked, hanging back.

"We're not in New York City," Martha replied. "The worst that could happen is that a couple of raccoons got inside and are going through the trash cans."

"I have no interest in being attacked by a raccoon," Pfeiffer said, her slender hands, their mother's hands, on her hips.

"Remember Renaldo?" Martha asked, stepping through the threshold and into the house. "How he used to wait outside by the door in the morning for Mom to feed him?"

Renaldo had been the family's pet raccoon. He'd been injured as a baby, run over on the highway and left for dead. The girls' mother stopped when she saw a flash of movement as she drove by, and rescued him from his fate. They'd nursed him back to health, and when he got old enough, their mother released him into the forest, and their youngest sister, Mary, had cried all night. The next morning, however, Renaldo was back, clearly not happy about having been turned out. From then on, they took turns feeding him in the morning. After their mother died, the girls never saw him again.

"I wonder what happened to poor, old Renaldo," Pfeiffer mused. "I still think about him sometimes, you know."

Martha was touched by this display of humanity from her sister. It didn't often make an appearance. They'd lost their father, mother, and sister, all before they'd become adults. Pfeiffer's way of dealing with it was to close herself off from everyone, even more than she already had. It was a wonder she hadn't stopped speaking completely like their aunt.

"I'm sure he ran off with the woman of his dreams," Martha replied. "I bet they had lots of tiny raccoon babies."

"Kits," Pfeiffer reminded her.

"Yes," Martha said. "Kits."

The two women took in their surroundings. The house, if one could still call it that, was a shambles. Everything, including the peeling wallpaper, was covered in what looked like an impenetrable layer of dust. There were sheets covering all of the furniture in the living room, but even they were dirty and moth-eaten. The floors, original hardwood and once their aunt Bea's pride and joy, looked as if they might splinter with every step.

"Oh my God," Pfeiffer whispered. "What *happened* here?"

"Hadley did say that Aunt Bea was pretty bad there at the end," Martha replied. "Of course, I doubt she would let anyone know it. We sure didn't know it."

"I didn't even know she was sick until I got the call that she'd died," Pfeiffer said, walking around the living room, her face scrunched up as if she were about to cry. "Did you?"

Martha shook her head. "No."

Above them, there was a creak in the floorboards that made both of them jump. Pfeiffer put her finger to her lips and pointed toward the stairs. "Do you think someone is up there?" she whispered.

"Who?" Martha mouthed.

Pfeiffer shrugged and motioned for her sister to follow her.

The noises coming from the upstairs sounded like furniture or something equally heavy was being dragged across the floor—obviously a feat too large for a group of raccoons, even rabid ones. *A gaze,* Martha reminded herself as she crept up the stairs. *A group of raccoons is called a gaze.* She wasn't sure why she was thinking about that right then, but she knew that if she and her sister survived the next few minutes, and she happened to use the wrong term in the future, Pfeiffer would be more than happy to correct her.

She was so lost in her thoughts that she didn't see that Pfeiffer had stopped in front of her, and Martha charged right smack into her, causing her sister to fly forward, face first into the closed door of their childhood bedroom.

"Ow!" Pfeiffer exclaimed. "Ow, shit!"

There was blood on Pfeiffer's hands when she finally pulled them away from her face, just in time for the door to swing open and for a face to be staring back at them, the lines in his face cavernous, his eyes filled with equal parts worry and confusion. "Pfeiffer? Martha?" the man asked, cocking his head to one side. Then, noticing the blood pouring out of Pfeiffer's nose, he said, "Lord have mercy, child! What have you done?"

"We thought you were a robber," Pfeiffer said through gritted teeth.

"Or a raccoon," Martha replied, shrugging when her sister shot her a look.

"We best get you downstairs," the man said, taking Pfeiffer by the arm and leading her down the steps. "There are some clean washrags in the kitchen."

Rufus Crowley was the caretaker at the James farm. He'd been there ever since forever, and there weren't many memories on the farm that didn't involve him. He'd been old back then, and Pfeiffer and Martha used to take bets on how old he was and in what year he would die, much to the vexation of their eldest sister, Hadley.

"You shouldn't talk like that," Hadley would say. "Old Crow hears everything, you know. You wouldn't want for him to put a curse on you."

The rumor around Cold River was that Rufus Crowley's mother had been a witch, just as her mother before her, and her mother before her. The Crowleys lived on the farthest outskirts of town, past even the clannish and unpredictable Cranwell family, in a clapboard shack at the river's edge. Townsfolk often went to Mother Crowley for advice and healing medicine, and for advice on any troubles they were too embarrassed to discuss in the company of each other. Of course, these were just stories now, as she'd passed on years and years before any of the girls were born, leaving her only son, a man everyone called "Old Crow," even when he'd been a young man.

Martha, however, suspected that Old Crow had never, ever been young. Their mother hadn't liked that nickname, and made them call him "Mr. Crowley" in her presence, although they'd all called him "Old Crow" behind her back. Good-natured and kind, Old Crow never seemed to mind.

"Let me have a look at it," Crowley said, easing Pfeiffer down into one of the cracking kitchen chairs.

"Is her nose broken?" Martha asked.

"You'd like that, wouldn't you?" Pfeiffer asked, a single trail of blood sliding down from her nose and into her mouth so that her teeth showed the faintest hint of red when she spoke.

"I would not," Martha protested, although she was trying desperately to hide a smile. She didn't relish that her sister was hurt, not at all, but she had to admit that seeing Pfeiffer even the slightest bit undone did give her more pleasure than it should have.

"Oh, it's not as bad as all that," Crowley replied, dabbing at Pfeiffer's nose with a wet rag. "It ain't broken. Just a bit busted."

"What's the difference?" Pfeiffer asked, her eyes closed in an attempt to ward off the throbbing she was beginning to feel now that the shock was wearing off.

"Won't be needin' no doctor," Crowley replied. "Though you may have a couple of shiners in the mornin' below them eyes."

"Great."

"I really am sorry," Martha offered, reaching out to touch her sister on the arm, but she jerked away from her grasp. "I didn't mean to. I swear."

"Of course ya didn't," Crowley agreed. "What are you two doing here, anyway? Nobody told me you was comin'."

"Alice Beacon called Hadley," Martha replied. "She said the family night was tonight, and I guess the funeral is tomorrow morning."

Crowley nodded, handing over the cloth to Pfeiffer. "Mrs. Beacon and the ladies of the auxiliary planned the whole thing," he said. "I reckon your aunt saw fit to leave it to them in the end."

For a moment, Martha saw a flicker of hurt cross through

Crowley's eyes. He and Aunt Bea had been friends since they were children. "Were you around?" she asked. "To help her?"

Again, Crowley nodded. "I were," he said. "She had trouble getting around the last few years."

"She never told us," Pfeiffer replied.

"She wouldn't have wanted to bother ya none," Crow said. "You know how she was."

Both Pfeiffer and Martha knew how their aunt was. Technically, Aunt Bea was their great-aunt, the younger sister of their grandfather. They hadn't known her as children. Their mother told them that she'd run away from home at seventeen and never come back. She told them something traumatizing must've happened to her, because she stopped speaking, to anyone, after she left. In fact, according to their mother, their aunt never spoke to another living soul again. The sisters never believed her, but when she arrived on their doorstep the day after their mother and sister were killed in the storm, they found out she'd been right. Bea never said a word to them, but she was always able to make her point clear. The social worker referred to it as "selective mutism," as she'd been able to speak at one point in her life and for some reason made the choice to be silent. They were told that it was severe anxiety that kept their aunt from talking, but Martha always thought it might be something else. Despite this, she was their only surviving family, and without her, she and Pfeiffer would have been sent to foster care. Martha was grateful to her for keeping the sisters together.

Martha blinked, pushing away these thoughts, and looked to Pfeiffer for what to say. She wished Hadley were there. She always knew what to say in situations such as these. She would have found a kind word to say about their dead aunt, instead of standing there awkwardly like the two of them were doing, staring at Crowley and the lines on his face.

"I'm sorry the place looks as shabby as it does," Crowley continued when both women remained silent. "Your aunt wouldn't let me do much, save for a bit of work here and there."

"She always cared so much about keeping the place looking nice," Pfeiffer replied, still holding the cloth to her nose.

"It was hard on her without any of you youngin's here to help her," Crowley said. "She had rheumatoid arthritis, and it hurt her to walk."

"She could have told us," Martha replied.

"No, she couldn't," Crowley said.

"You know what I mean," Martha replied. "She could have written us a letter or something. We would have come home if she needed help."

"Would ya?"

Martha and Pfeiffer shared a look. It wasn't like they would have refused. They'd loved their aunt. She'd come and cared for them at a time in their lives when they were utterly alone. But their years of being scared little girls were over the second they left Cold River. Besides, their aunt's letters put off any offers to visit. In them, she often wrote that she wanted the girls to live their lives away from the farm, away from Cold River. She wouldn't visit them, and they didn't visit her. That was the way things were, and Martha never thought to question it. She knew what Crowley meant, however. Neither of them—neither she nor her sister—had any desire to come back to Cold River. It was where they were from, but it hadn't been home in a long time.

"Is anybody up here?" came a new voice from the other end of the hallway.

All three of them turned to stare at the woman before them, silhouetted in the doorframe, slim and perfect. She looked as if she'd materialized out of the beams of light coming in through the dust-covered windows rather than like a road-weary traveler. Her clothes were not rumpled like Martha's. Her hair was not undone and frizzy like Pfeiffer's.

"Hadley!" Martha exclaimed. "When did you get here?"

"Just now," Hadley replied. "What happened?"

Pfeiffer removed the cloth from her nose and stood up. "Martha happened," she said.

Martha wasn't sure if she should reach out and hug her oldest sister. Instead, she got caught halfway between a hug and handshake and stood there awkwardly for a few seconds before pulling her hand back down to her side and averting her gaze.

Hadley shot a quizzical look at her youngest sister but said nothing. Instead, she turned her attention to Crowley. "I'm glad to know you've been here taking care of the place," she said. "The last time I got a letter from Aunt Bea, she said you were absolutely invaluable to her."

Crowley stood up a little straighter. "I did what I could, Miss Hadley."

"She did lead me to believe things were in better shape than they are," Hadley admitted. "I guess I shouldn't be surprised."

"Well," Crowley said, backing away from the three women slowly as if he were a lone, fat chicken and the sisters were cats licking their lips and ready to pounce. "I'd better go and get meself cleaned up before the family night tonight."

"At Macri's?" Hadley asked. "Six o'clock, right?"

"The only funeral home in town," Crowley replied, giving her a rare smile. "I reckon I'll be seeing y'all there."

It wasn't a question, more of a command, and Old Crow took his leave, bounding down the stairs, muttering to himself the litanies of a man who was happy to have made his escape.

Chapter 4
Hadley

ADLEY ASSUMED SHE WOULD BE THE FIRST TO ARRIVE AT the house, as she had been first in birth and in nearly everything else in her life since. Of course, she knew Mr. Crowley (she refused to call him "Old Crow" as her sisters did) would be there. She'd spoken to him over the last few months, when her aunt was in the final stages of death. Hadley offered more than once to come down to Cold River and stay with her, but Aunt Bea declined every time. In truth, Hadley had been relieved when her aunt wrote back to say that she didn't need any help. Hadley assumed Mr. Crowley was all the help her aunt needed, and that was partly because she'd forgotten how old he was. In her mind, he was at least twenty years younger than he really was.

He *was* old, though, and there likely wasn't much he could do to keep the place up like he'd done when she and her sisters were children. They'd scared him even then, her sisters. Pfeiffer's razor-sharp tongue and Martha's beauty were a lethal combination when they were together and had someone cornered. Her sisters would have something to say about the fact that she'd been speaking with both their aunt and Mr. Crowley and not bothered to tell them. They'd think she was keeping secrets from them, as if they were still ten, eight, and six years old, stairstepped siblings, hiding in the woods beyond the fields.

For a moment, Hadley allowed herself to pretend they *were* that age again, instead of grown women, now thirty-eight, thirty-six, and thirty-four. She closed her hands tighter around her Louis Vuitton carryall and remembered a time when neither she nor her sisters would have known what a Louis Vuitton was, back to a time when it was perfectly acceptable to have skinned knees and flyaway curls rather than a chic bob and legs ravaged by costly electrolysis.

"Hadley?"

Hadley blinked away the memories to find Martha staring at her, her thick eyelashes catching each other as she blinked. "What? What is it?"

"Pfeiffer went downstairs to use my phone. Her car stalled on the dirt road."

"I saw," Hadley replied. "I had to ask my driver to drop me off right there. He wasn't too happy to do that, let me tell you."

"Your driver?"

Hadley sighed. "Mark hired him. Wanted to make sure I didn't have to drive myself from the airport."

"Oh," Martha replied. "Good old Mark."

"Yes, well . . ." Hadley trailed off.

She and Mark had been married for the last fifteen years. They'd met when she'd been invited to a graduation party in Columbia, Missouri, after her friend finished law school. Hadley was taking some time off from her education degree and had been working nonstop for nearly a year. She'd been eager for a night out with her friend, and when Mark introduced himself as a recent law graduate, she'd been enamored with him. He was incredibly competitive, with his eye on a seat in the United States Senate, and Hadley had been desperate to get out of Columbia and the mounds of debt she was piling up. Another year of work as a waitress, and she'd have to move back to Cold River with her aunt. Mark had been a way out, and she'd jumped at the opportunity.

"Mark couldn't come with you?" Martha asked, breaking Hadley out of her thoughts.

"He's working on his campaign strategy," Hadley replied. "Just another year and a half before the next election."

"Right," Martha replied, rolling her eyes. "Well, anyway, Pfeiffer is going to call a tow. I guess we'll have to wait for that before we can leave for the funeral home."

"Don't you have a set of jumper cables in that shiny, new Tesla I saw parked behind Pfeiffer's car?"

"No," Martha said. "I don't know. I hadn't thought to check. Besides, the hood was smoking. I doubt the car needs to be jumped."

"It needs to be junked," Hadley said, a faint smile crossing her lips. "But don't you dare tell your sister I said that."

Martha bit at her bottom lip to keep from returning her sister's smile. "Something is going on with her," she said.

"What do you think it is?" Hadley asked.

"I don't know." Martha shook her head, crossing her arms across her chest. "But she's being even more sarcastic than usual."

"How could a person possibly be more sarcastic than Pfeiffer?"

"I didn't think it was possible either. I think her phone is turned off," Martha said. "Says her number is no longer in service."

"I got the same message," Hadley replied. "I thought maybe she'd switched numbers and didn't tell us."

"Wouldn't be the first time," Martha grumbled.

"I called her work, too," Hadley continued. "When I couldn't get her on her cell. That Seth person kept putting me off. Wouldn't give me much information."

"She's never wanted us to know much about her life," Martha said. "I don't know why not. Everybody under the sun knows about our lives."

"You should have let her handle that book deal of yours," Hadley scolded. "I'm sure she's not forgiven you."

"That was three years ago!" Martha replied. "And Henry Brothers offered me way less money than the other publisher. They thought I'd take it because Pfeiffer's my sister."

"How little they know the Hemingway sisters," Hadley said, arching her eyebrow just enough to be noticeable. "Come on, let's go downstairs. We need to get that car towed and ourselves ready for tonight."

"Fine," Martha said. "But I'm just staying until the funeral on Friday. I've got to be back in Nashville by the weekend."

"That suits me," Hadley replied. "I need to be back in D.C. by the weekend. Mark's got a function on Saturday night, and I simply must be there."

"Simply must?"

"Yes," Hadley said, turning her back on her sister. "I'm his wife, and it's important for me to be there, cocktail in hand, smiling to meet the donors."

"I guess not much has changed in politics since 1950," Martha replied, following after her. "I didn't realize that it was a constant episode of *Mad Men* out there."

"I do what he asks," Hadley said simply, feeling Martha's eyes on her. Of late, that statement was less than true, but right now she couldn't bring herself to say so. It wasn't the right time, anyway, as they should all be thinking about their aunt.

"Maybe if I'd done more of what Travis asked, he wouldn't have divorced me," Martha muttered.

"Travis is a self-centered child," Hadley replied.

"I don't think Mama would have liked him," Martha said. "Or Mark, for that matter."

"Mama's not here," Hadley said, trying not to let on that she agreed with Martha. "We did the best we could."

"Don't you think we ought to get hotel rooms in town tonight?" Martha asked once they were all back downstairs. "There is no way we can stay here."

"Why not?" Pfeiffer wanted to know.

Martha stamped her feet on the hardwood floor, causing a cloud of dust to rise up beneath her shoes. "*This* is why."

"You're afraid of a little dust?" Pfeiffer asked.

"We'll be lucky if this house doesn't fall in on us before we make it outside," Martha said. "I'm getting a hotel room."

"Well, I'm staying here," Pfeiffer replied, crossing her arms over her cardigan. "It'll be fun. Like an adventure."

"An adventure where everybody gets tetanus," Hadley grumbled.

"Oh, come on," Pfeiffer said. "It will probably be the last time we stay here."

"Fine," Hadley replied. "Have it your way." She threw up her arms in defeat and moved away from her sisters into the kitchen.

"I usually do," Pfeiffer replied.

"Great!" Martha said, clapping her hands, which only sent more particles of dust circling around them. "The three of us together again."

They stood there, close, but not touching, each careful to keep her thoughts behind her teeth. They hadn't been together in this house for a long time, and Hadley was sure that it was bringing up memories for each of them that they didn't want to revisit. For so many years, this place brought joy. For so many years, they were as close as sisters could be, but all of that was gone with one terrible storm, and Hadley didn't know how they could ever set things right.

CHAPTER 5
Hadley

THERE WAS ONLY ONE FUNERAL HOME IN ALL OF COLD River, and it was located on the same street as most of the churches in town, with the exception of Second Coming Baptist, which resided in a building that had once been a short-lived nightclub. Their aunt singularly refused to attend *any* church, reformed nightclub or otherwise, and so her friends and the ladies of the auxiliary had commissioned a Methodist minister from their own congregation for the service. It was odd for a woman of Aunt Bea's age to refuse to go to church, and that fact wasn't lost on the people of Cold River. As a girl, like all members of the James family, their aunt had attended the Methodist church. But when she moved back from St. Louis, she refused to go, and it was a rebellion in which the sisters reveled, no longer compelled to get up early in the morning and wear their Sunday best.

The first time members of the church came out to check on them, their aunt let them in and listened calmly to all the reasons why she ought to bring her orphaned nieces back into the fold. When they'd finally run out of reasons, their aunt looked at Pfeiffer and nodded, which was a cue for Pfeiffer to say, "Thank you very much for your time, but we'll worship the lord from the living room on Sunday morning."

Despite protests from the elders, Pfeiffer got up and showed them the door. Once it had been closed and locked behind them, their aunt got up and baked a chocolate cake, allowing the sisters to have cake for breakfast, and they stayed in their pajamas all day watching Molly Ringwald movies on their old, blurry television set. It was a day that Hadley remembered well, but she hoped that none of the elders of the church did.

The older women watched the sisters as they approached. *They* had everything planned, and they eyed Hadley, Pfeiffer, and Martha as if they were strangers from a foreign land rather than grown-up versions of the girls they'd once been—the girls all of the Cold River Ladies Auxiliary had known since birth.

They met the sisters at the door of the funeral home with waxy smiles and lipstick settling into the creases just beyond their lips.

"And I thought we looked like the Witches of Eastwick," Pfeiffer muttered as they approached.

"The movie was better than the book," Martha shot back, knowing full well that a reference to *any* movie being better than the book would get a rise out of her sister.

"At least you don't have two black eyes," Pfeiffer replied.

"Be quiet," Hadley replied through gritted teeth. "You both promised to be on your best behavior."

"Girls!" Anna Graham, the president of the auxiliary and Aunt Bea's closest friend, said. "I was starting to think you wouldn't make it."

Martha looked down at her phone. "It's only half-past six," she said.

"I hardly recognized you," another one of the women replied. She was staring straight at Martha's chest. "You've changed so much since the last time I laid eyes on you."

"Thank you for taking care of the arrangements," Hadley said. "We all three appreciate it so much."

"It's the least we could do," Ellen replied. "Besides, we know how busy you girls are nowadays."

"I wish she'd stop calling us *girls*," Pfeiffer said, just loud enough for her sisters to hear. "We're women."

Hadley gave Pfeiffer a sharp jab in her side. "We are all quite a ways from Cold River now, it's true," she said.

"Shall we go inside?" Anna offered. "I know you'd like to pay your respects."

"We'd like that," Hadley replied.

Anna and Ellen led them inside, past the man at the door in the woolen suit too hot for August, and past the book of names of visitors. Hadley wanted to stop for a moment and scan the list, but the older women marched right past it and into the big room, where a crowd was gathered.

"Your aunt didn't want an open casket," Anna said, gesturing to the front of the room, where a large, rose-gold casket sat, half of the top propped open, the top of their aunt's face just visible from where they stood. "She wanted to be cremated, but we talked her out of that."

"Then why is the casket open?" Pfeiffer asked.

"The funeral home misunderstood the instructions," Anna replied, a slight tone of annoyance in her voice. "By the time we realized, people were coming in. And how would that look? Running up to slam a coffin lid down in the middle of a crowd?"

The room grew quiet as they entered. It was as if by opening the door and walking inside, they'd let out all of the air. Hadley knew most of the faces she saw, but it would take her a moment for the names to come back to her. Names were her specialty. It was one of the reasons Mark insisted she attend every event with him, political or otherwise. She could whisper the name of a man they'd met once in a coffee shop on their morning walk through the city, and Mark could say that man's name and make him feel as if he were the most important person in the world. He had charm, her husband. He'd do well here tonight, and Hadley felt a twinge of longing for him that she hadn't expected, even though she knew it was far too late for any of that. It had been a long time since they were even in the same room, let alone out in public, together.

Hadley smiled at the faces she recognized and even the few she didn't. They all smiled back, and many came to her with an embrace and kind words. A few of them, mostly the older women closer to her aunt's age, made thinly veiled references to the fact that Hadley and her sisters never visited. Hadley glanced over at her sisters. Pfeiffer and Martha were sticking closely together, careful not to get any closer to Aunt Bea than they had to.

"Would you like to go up and see your aunt?" Anna asked, gesturing to the front of the room.

"Oh . . ." Hadley trailed off. In fact, that was the very last thing she wanted to do. "I suppose so."

Hadley motioned to her sisters, but they pretended not to see

her. Instead, she let Anna and Ellen take each one of her arms
and lead her to the front. The carpet in the mourning room was
a deep burgundy, and she felt her heels sinking deep down into
it with each step. As they neared the casket, she prayed for the
carpet to instead be quicksand and swallow up more than just
her expensive heels. She wished *she* could be swallowed; that
way she wouldn't have to face what she knew was coming.

"Doesn't she look beautiful?" Anna asked, glancing down at
Hadley's dead aunt, her eyes so full of love that they threatened
to overflow with it.

Hadley cleared her throat, struggling to find her voice. "She
does," she replied.

Aunt Bea did look quite lovely. Her long, white hair surrounded
her face. They'd left it loose, Hadley supposed, to honor the
style in which she always wore it. Aunt Bea's hair had been
white as long as she'd known her, but she'd seen pictures of her
with long chestnut hair that fell in soft, loose curls all down
her back, the same color and texture as Pfeiffer's. Their aunt's
hair was her crowning glory, and even though it had been
completely white by the time she came to live with them, it
was still beautiful.

The last time Hadley had seen a dead body was at the funeral of her mother and youngest sister. She was eighteen at the
time. Both of their caskets had been open, which drew many
more visitors than usual, because everyone was interested to see
how a springtime tornado could pick up two people in one spot
and place them in another miles away without a single scratch.
When Pfeiffer overheard two girls in her high school class gos-
siping about it in the hallway, she'd flown into a rage, scratching
one of them across the face, and had to be restrained by Aunt

Bea, who'd arrived only days before and was completely out of her depth with the teenagers. She'd pulled Pfeiffer outside and tried to calm her down, but instead, Pfeiffer took her anger out on their mother's station wagon, denting the hood in several places. Their aunt hadn't said a thing about it, but Hadley always wondered if in that moment their aunt Bea didn't ask herself if she hadn't made a huge mistake agreeing to take care of them.

Hadley remembered watching the scene unfold with a kind of serenity she hadn't understood at the time. She didn't feel rage like Pfeiffer did. She didn't feel abandoned like Martha did. All she knew was that her mother and her baby sister, Mary, were both dead.

Their mother's name had been Rachael, and she liked to say that she and Mary were two slices of bread in a sandwich, the top the oldest and the bottom the youngest, holding in the rest of the family, and although Mary joked that her older sisters were bologna and smelly cheese and mustard, their mother said they came together to make something delicious, something perfect, something whole, and something made for each other.

The day of their funeral, all Hadley had been able to think about was how their wholeness had been broken, their perfection torn apart, and now she and her sisters were alone in the world without a proper beginning or ending. She knew, of course, that the unraveling had started long before that.

As Hadley thought about this, about the last time she'd stood in this exact same spot, she felt tears prick at her eyes and her shoulders began to shake. For all her embarrassment, she couldn't hold it in.

"There, there, honey," Anna said. "Don't cry. It's going to be okay."

"She had a good, long life, your aunt," Ellen told her. "Come here and have a seat."

Hadley did as she was told. She wasn't crying for her aunt, not really. She was crying for all of them—for all the years they'd spent without their mother and sister, and for all the ways their aunt couldn't fix it.

"Thank you," Hadley said when Ellen handed her a handkerchief. She was oddly comforted to see that somebody actually still carried those. It smelled like lavender and something else she couldn't identify. Mothballs, maybe.

She glanced over at her sisters just in time to see two younger women approach Martha, eyes wide. Her sister was, after all, quite famous. She'd been less successful over the last few years, it was true, without a hit record or even a new single for the radio. Most of the attention Martha got lately was about her divorce, which had been splashed all over the place, and Hadley was sure everybody in Cold River knew and had an opinion about it. Hadley knew how much Martha had loved Travis, even though Martha wouldn't admit it, not even to her—maybe especially to her. Despite all of this, though, her sister was a star. There was no doubt about it. She'd be back on top soon; Hadley knew it.

"I can't believe you're here!" one of the girls in the room squealed in Martha's face. "I told Katie you would be. I mean, it is your aunt's funeral, after all."

"Are you Katie?" Martha asked, unperturbed and turning her attention to the other girl.

"Yes," the girl replied. "And that's Kelly."

"Sisters?" Martha asked.

"Yes," they said in unison.

"You look alike," Martha replied.

Kelly gave Pfeiffer a sweeping gaze before she said, "You don't look anything like your sister."

"You don't think so?" Martha asked.

The girls shook their heads.

"Well," Martha replied, "we used to look so much alike as kids, people thought we were twins."

"It's true," Pfeiffer said. "That was before . . . you know . . . the reconstructive surgery on my face."

"What?" Kelly gasped. "You had reconstructive surgery?"

"No," Martha cut in, giving Pfeiffer a sidelong glare. "She's just being silly."

"Oh," Katie said, visibly relieved.

"So," Kelly continued. "Did you really go to rehab because Travis Tucker dumped you?"

"I better go and collect my sisters," Hadley said to Anna, standing up. "It looks like they're starting to get in over their heads."

She hurried over to Martha and grabbed her arm. "I'm sorry to interrupt, ladies, but my sisters and I really need to be going."

"Aw," Katie replied. Then her eyes brightened. "Are you coming to the potluck after the funeral tomorrow?"

"I don't think so," Hadley replied.

"I need to get back to Nashville," Martha added.

"To record another album?" Kelly asked. "We've been waiting forever!"

"Oh, please stay!" Katie said, her voice on the edge of a squeal. "Please, please!"

"It would be nice if you girls could stay afterward," Anna cut in, approaching them. "I think your aunt's friends would really appreciate it."

Hadley looked at Pfeiffer, hoping she would speak up, but she only shrugged. She'd always been the one to say the things nobody else wanted to say, and Hadley couldn't imagine her actually wanting to stay in Cold River any longer than she had to.

"Okay, why not," Hadley said at last. "I'm sure we can work it out."

"Well, then it's settled," Anna said. "You girls don't have to bring anything other than yourselves. We'll see you tomorrow."

Hadley watched Anna leave, Katie and Kelly in tow. She felt a sense of relief wash over her. "Do you think we can leave now without anybody thinking we're bad people?"

"I'm pretty sure they all already think that," Pfeiffer replied. "Well, not Martha. Everybody loves her. She's just so pretty."

"Shut up," Martha replied. "At least nobody is asking *you* about your recent divorce or stint in rehab."

"Not yet," Pfeiffer replied, a wry grin on her face.

"Why didn't you speak up when you had the chance about the potluck?" Hadley asked Pfeiffer. "I figured you'd say something."

"I don't care to stay," Pfeiffer replied.

"Really?"

"Really."

Hadley glanced around the room, gauging the crowd to decide upon their safest exit strategy.

Martha caught her and asked, "See anybody else you know?"

"Only half the town."

"That's not what I mean."

Hadley knew that wasn't what her sister meant, but aside from the teenage girls fawning all over Martha, girls who'd probably come with their grandmothers simply because they knew Martha would be there, Hadley hadn't seen anyone under eighty years old all night. "I haven't seen *anyone*," she said.

"I really thought he'd be here," Martha said.

"Why?"

Martha sighed. "Oh, come on, Hadley."

"I haven't seen him in twenty years," Hadley replied.

"We haven't seen any of these people in twenty years," Martha replied, pursing her lips. "I just thought he might turn up for old time's sake."

"To our ancient aunt's family night?"

"If it might be a chance to see you."

"That was a long time ago, Martha," Hadley said. "A very long time ago."

"You two were pretty fast and furious, if I remember correctly," Martha said.

"What would you know about that?" Hadley asked. "You were fourteen years old."

"I knew a lot more than you thought," Martha replied, taking her sister's arm and steering her toward Pfeiffer. "I knew a lot more than you thought."

CHAPTER 6
Pfeiffer

A LTHOUGH SHE'D NEVER ADMIT IT, PFEIFFER WAS GLAD that her sisters had agreed to spend the night at the farm. She hadn't wanted to stay by herself. In fact, she hadn't wanted to stay at all, but she'd used any hotel money she had to get Seth's junk towed. It was why she'd also agreed, with little fight, to go to the potluck the next morning after the funeral. She knew her sisters would have to know eventually that she was without both a job and a home, but she didn't suppose they had to know just yet. The longer she could prolong her stay at the farm, the longer she had to figure things out.

"I made up the beds in our old rooms," Hadley said, coming down the stairs. "But I'm afraid that Pfeiffer's mattress is a little worse for the wear."

"It's fine," Pfeiffer said, shrugging. "I'll sleep down here on the couch."

"You're quite agreeable tonight," Hadley replied, sitting down next to her.

"I just hate sharing a room with you," Pfeiffer said with another shrug. "You snore."

"I do not!" Hadley protested.

"You do," Martha said, setting a bottle of whiskey and a bottle of Coke on the coffee table in front of them. "You always have."

"Where did you get that?" Hadley asked.

"The whiskey?" Martha replied. "I got *that* from Aunt Bea's liquor cabinet. You know, the one Mama used to keep all her sewing supplies in. The Coke I bought from a gas station before I got into town."

"I thought you stopped drinking," Hadley said.

"I did," Martha replied with a shrug. "Six months sober. Girl Scout's honor. But that doesn't mean you all have to abstain on account of me."

Pfeiffer glanced from one sister to the other. Hadley was staring at Martha as if she didn't quite believe her. Hadley could always sniff out a liar, *especially* if one of the liars was one of her sisters. Her stare was like a truth serum, and neither Pfeiffer nor Martha was ever able to keep anything to herself once Hadley made her mind up to get their secrets out of them.

"Didn't they teach you at . . . at the *facility* that you should keep yourself away from temptation?" Hadley asked.

"You mean the rehab *facility* that cost me ten thousand dollars a week?" Martha asked.

Pfeiffer, who'd already poured herself a shot of whiskey, was now choking on it. "Rehab cost you ten thousand dollars a week?"

Martha nodded, unscrewing the cap of the Coke. "Yep, and it was money well spent, too," she said, looking pointedly at Hadley. "Would I like to have a drink? Yes. Always. Will I have a drink? No. I won't."

"I just don't know if we should drink in front of you," Hadley said.

"Oh, leave her alone," Pfeiffer heard herself say. Her throat was burning, and she poured herself another. "She's a big girl. If she says she can handle it, she can."

"Fine," Hadley replied. "But I'm not having any."

"More for me," Pfeiffer replied.

"I can't believe you," Hadley said, crossing her arms over her chest.

"What?" Pfeiffer asked. "I'm not the one who set out the whiskey. I'm not the one who is an alcoholic." She glanced over at Martha. "No offense, of course."

"None taken," Martha replied. "It's really okay. I got it out so that I could get it over with. If I hadn't, I would have been looking at that cabinet the whole time I was here wondering what's inside. Now I know, and I know I don't need it."

"See?" Pfeiffer said, shoving her glass into Hadley's face. "I'm helping her."

Hadley pushed Pfeiffer away and stood up. "I'm going to bed," she said. "I'll see you in the morning."

"Aw, don't be like that!" Pfeiffer called after her, but it was too late. Hadley was already upstairs and the slamming bedroom door was her response.

"You shouldn't push her buttons like that," Martha said once they were alone. "You know how wound up she can get."

"She's acting like our mother," Pfeiffer replied, rolling her eyes. "And she's not."

"She's the closest thing we have now," Martha said.

"She pushes my buttons, too, ya know," Pfeiffer continued. "It's not like she's innocent."

"It's not a competition," Martha reminded her, taking a sip of her Coke. "I think we *all* need to remember that we're all we have left." She glanced around the house. "This house is all we have left."

They'd all grown up in this house—this sprawling farmhouse on acres upon acres. It had been in their mother's family for generations, and they'd lived there with her, and their father, and each other. And then, the August Pfeiffer was six, their father died.

The way Pfeiffer remembered it, he'd been fine one day and dead the next. He'd been her blond, scruffy, farmer daddy and then he was gone. Of course, now she knew that her father had been sick for a long time—months, maybe even a whole year, before he died. It was cancer, first in his pancreas and then his liver. Then it was everywhere else, and one night her mother carried her into a hospital room to say good-bye.

Pfeiffer had been scared. The man before her, tucked into the bed, didn't look like her father. He was pale, skeletal, and worst of all, he was bald. Pfeiffer had seen her father only one other time without facial hair—when he'd shaved for church one Sunday morning. He came down the steps of the house and sauntered out to their truck so casually that she knew the man walking toward her *had* to be her father, but he didn't *look* like her father, and so she began to cry. He'd held her in his arms and told her that he was, in fact, her daddy, her real daddy, and he promised her he'd never shave again.

And he hadn't. Until that night in the hospital. Now all of his hair was gone, on his head as well as his face, and Pfeiffer again cried. He'd motioned for her mother to bring her closer, despite her howling, and set her down on the bed beside him.

"My best girl," he'd said to her in his daddy voice. The voice he used just for her. "Don't be scared."

"Matthew," her mother said, gently chiding him. "You need to rest. We can come back."

But Matthew Hemingway shook his head and lifted his hand, now thin and frail, to the top of Pfeiffer's head. "She's all right, Rachael," he said.

In that moment, Pfeiffer *had been* all right. She stopped crying and curled up next to her father on the bed and fell asleep. She hadn't woken even when her mother came to retrieve her sometime in the night, and by the next morning, her father was gone.

After that, they continued to live on the farm, and her mother hired help from among the local men, usually Old Crow. Aunt Bea hadn't come down for the funeral, instead sending that letter along with some money for the burial. She'd always been good to her niece and great-nieces in that way. She provided for the family when Rachael couldn't, which was often after Matthew died.

Their father hadn't been from Cold River. Matthew Hemingway found his way to the small Ozarks town when he'd run out of gas on his way from Memphis, Tennessee, to Springfield, Missouri, where he always claimed to have relatives nobody ever met. Their mother told them that the people in town were immediately suspicious of a man with the strange last name and no connection to the famous author with whom he shared it. He'd gotten a job at Cranwell Station running the gas pumps and then as seasonal help with Rachael's daddy on the farm. That was when seventeen-year-old Rachael met twenty-year-old Matthew, and, according to Rachael, fell madly in love. Nobody was happy about it, especially Rachael's mother, Maryann James. But then Aunt Beatrice sent a letter to Maryann, and everything changed. Rachael told the story often, and even though she never really knew what was in that letter, as her mother burned it in the fireplace soon after receiving it, Rachael told her daughters that she was forever in her aunt's debt, because she knew it was that letter that changed her mother's mind. Aunt Beatrice might not use her voice, but that didn't mean her opinions weren't always heard, loud and clear.

Pfeiffer knew after her father's death that her mother wanted to leave Cold River, but she hadn't wanted to uproot her children, especially Mary. Mary had been so much like their father. She was dark and quiet, and she had a way about her that made people fall in love with her, despite the fact that she was so different. It was the same trait that eventually allowed the town of Cold River to fall in love with their father and treat him as one of their own. Pfeiffer figured that it would have been difficult for their mother to pack up four children and leave the safety of the town she'd known her whole life, and she didn't blame her for it. In fact, she was grateful.

Even after their father's death, the Hemingway sisters lived a happy and comfortable life. Their mother was an artist when she wasn't farming and baking goods to sell at the farmers market, and she devoted every second she had free to them.

Still, everything changed when their father died. Their mother wasn't as happy. She didn't sing or dance around the house anymore. She didn't smile as much, and money was always tight.

One morning, Pfeiffer and Hadley overheard their mother talking on the phone to one of her friends. She was crying, her voice barely audible above the sobs. "I can't do this anymore," she was saying. "I can't do this without him."

There was a pause, and then their mother said, "I can't ask my aunt for any more money. It's not right."

Another pause.

"I don't know what we're going to do. She won't help me if we don't live here. That's what she said in her last letter," Rachael said. "She wants someone here to take care of this place, but we're barely scraping by."

Pfeiffer felt something clench inside of her stomach. She felt sick, the way she felt when she'd eaten too much Halloween candy or that time Hadley dared her to swallow watermelon seeds. Beside her, Hadley sucked in air and clenched her hands together tightly.

The girls crept back to their room in time to pretend to still be asleep when their mother came to wake them. They never spoke about that day again.

"Well," Martha said, draining the last of her Coke, "I think I'll go on to bed."

Pfeiffer took a final swig from her glass, draining the contents. "Are you going up there to try to make nice with Hadley?"

"No."

"Yes, you are," Pfeiffer told her. "You know, I'm just as good as Hadley when it comes to sniffing out a liar."

"Again, it's not a competition," Martha replied. "Just promise me that you'll at least *try* to be nicer to her tomorrow, okay?"

Pfeiffer sighed. "Fine."

"Say it."

"I'll try to be nicer to Hadley tomorrow."

"And if you're not nice," Martha continued, "I'll blame any relapse I might have on you."

"I can just see the headlines now," Pfeiffer replied. "'Ugly Sister Forces Beautiful Sister into the Waiting Arms of Jim Beam.'"

Martha laughed. "Stop it," she said. "I just think we need to be nice to each other, that's all. And the only way I've ever been able to get you to listen to me is to threaten you."

Pfeiffer knew her sister was right. She *did* need to try to be nice. She wanted to tell Martha exactly what she'd been going through these last months—the loss of her job, of her life . . . of everything. If anybody understood recent misery, it would be Martha. She poured herself another drink and said, "I'm glad you gave this stuff up, but damn, I have to admit I like it."

"You like it enough to lose a husband over it?" Martha asked.

"I don't know," Pfeiffer replied. "I don't know much about husbands in general, but I can't say I ever really liked that one of yours."

"He wasn't all bad," Martha said.

"No?"

"Don't believe everything you read."

"I never do."

"Not even the things you publish?"

Pfeiffer sucked in her breath and hoped her sister hadn't noticed the second of hesitation she'd allowed to pass over her face before she said, "I deal in fiction, mostly."

Martha stood up and stretched. "Long day tomorrow, especially if I'm going to get back to Nashville before it gets too dark out."

"So you're leaving tomorrow, then?" Pfeiffer asked. She hadn't known what she expected, really. Of course Martha would go home. So would Hadley. *She* was the only one who didn't have a home to go back to.

"That's the plan," Martha replied. "I need to get back in the studio, get back to work, if I ever want anyone to talk about anything other than my train wreck of a life."

Pfeiffer was thankful that her own train wreck of a life wasn't as public as Martha's. That was something, at least. "You could write new songs here," she said.

Martha laughed. "Can you sell books from here?"

Pfeiffer shrugged. She honestly hadn't thought about it. "I guess I could."

"I doubt your publisher would like that too much," Martha replied. "Besides, there isn't a damn thing here I want to write *or* sing about."

"It would be a nice hideout, in any case," Pfeiffer said.

"I don't need to hide out," Martha said. "I need to be back in the damn spotlight, in a fabulous dress looking like a skinny Missy Lion."

"Suit yourself."

"Are you sure you'll be okay down here by yourself, Pi?"

Pfeiffer wasn't sure. But she didn't want to say it. What she wanted to do was have several more glasses of whiskey and pass out on the couch. "I'll be fine," she said. "Leave the bottle."

Martha raised her eyebrow but obliged. "See you in the morning," was all she said.

For a moment, Pfeiffer thought about how it used to be with her sisters, about when they were close as children and teenagers. She thought about the way they'd all slept together the night of their mother's and sister's funeral, her bed and Hadley's pushed

together in the middle of the room to accommodate their bodies. They'd huddled there, thigh to thigh underneath the covers,
awake but not speaking. They'd continued sleeping that way for
weeks until their aunt found out and insisted that they sleep
in their own rooms, forcing Martha into the room she'd once
shared with Mary. Pfeiffer could hear Martha crying at night
when she thought everyone else was asleep, but the girls were
scared, and they didn't want to do anything that might anger
their aunt, worried that she'd find a way to split them up. Of
course, Bea never would have attempted anything like that, but
the damage was already done. Losing their father cracked the
foundation, but losing their mother and sister caused it to crum-
ble entirely.

Aunt Beatrice, for her part, remained silent, as always. She
didn't force the girls to talk about their loss the way the social
worker had. She was a quiet presence in the house, and Pfeiffer
realized, looking back, that she was probably just as scared as
they had been.

Pfeiffer always thought that once she and her sisters left Cold
River, their aunt would resume her life in St. Louis, but she
didn't, and it puzzled Pfeiffer. All those years she refused to
come home, and now she refused to leave. She refused to sell the
farm, staying all the way out there alone, with only Old Crow to
keep her company. She didn't drive and rarely went into town,
and of course, she didn't speak to anyone.

Pfeiffer poured herself another drink and stood up to scan the
room. Her aunt sure had let the house fall into disrepair. If she
couldn't get around to fixing things herself, why wouldn't she just
hire someone else besides Old Crow, who was older than she was?
It didn't make sense.

Of course, their aunt had been incredibly private. She wouldn't even write about her life before the age of seventeen. That was the year Aunt Bea left for St. Louis and began work in one of the factories there. She'd written to their mother that she liked the work because nobody expected her to talk. She'd shown them pictures of her time there, but for the most part, Aunt Bea's room and all of her belongings were strictly off-limits. The sisters hadn't liked that—being told there was an entire room in their own house where they could no longer go. The room was no longer a sanctuary, no longer a safe space, but a cold and shut-off part of their lives that they weren't allowed to touch.

Pfeiffer studied herself in the mirror hanging on the wall by the staircase. The room was dark and the image she saw was warped and grimy, but she could still see the outline of her face. She looked like her mother's side of the family—like the James women who came before her. Her sisters favored their father; even now, with her bleached hair and plastic surgery, Martha still looked like Matthew Hemingway. Mary had looked like him, too—a smaller and darker version. At least, Pfeiffer *thought* Mary looked like their father. She couldn't remember now; so many of those memories were as fuzzy as the mirror. Where her sisters were soft, Pfeiffer was hard. Where her sisters' noses turned up, Pfeiffer's was straight. Where her sisters were tall, with rounded hips and breasts, Pfeiffer was short and as angular as a line.

It wasn't that Pfeiffer hadn't tried to be like her sisters. She *had*. All her life she'd tried. She'd tried to soften up, to be less sarcastic. She'd tried to smile and be polite. She'd watched her sisters and her mother with the same kind of curiosity one feels when visiting a museum. But no matter how hard she tried, she couldn't make it work. She couldn't *be* like them. She felt staccato around them—a menace.

Maybe she was too much like her aunt, and that was why she'd felt safe with her. Aunt Bea always seemed to know what Pfeiffer was thinking. She hadn't tried to cajole Pfeiffer into compliance. She hadn't scolded her for her sharp tongue. She'd just smiled and patted the seat next to her, allowing Pfeiffer to rest her head on her shoulder when nobody else was looking. Maybe Pfeiffer hadn't gone home to visit like she should have. Maybe she should have fought her aunt to be there. Despite that, however, her aunt's presence had been a comfort to her, even all the way in New York City. Now that she was gone, Pfeiffer felt more alone than she had in a long time, an orphan for always, because the people she loved always seemed to die before she got the chance to tell them good-bye.

Turning away from the mirror, she downed the whiskey in one gulp and sat back down on the couch to pour another. It was going to be a long night.

Chapter 7
Pfeiffer

In the dream, Pfeiffer was eight years old. She and her sisters were at the creek below their house, searching for tadpoles and crawdads. Mary was four, already so dark-eyed and thoughtful. She rarely spoke unless she had to. In this dream, though, she was chatty, jubilant because Hadley was carrying her on her hip and pointing out the different kinds of birds in the trees.

"Is Old Crow a bird?" Mary asked.

Hadley laughed. "No, he's just a man," she replied.

"An old, old man," Mary said.

"He's not so old," Hadley said, trying to keep her face stern after her fit of laughter. "And you should always be kind to him, okay?"

Pfeiffer looked up from the stream, a crawdad dangling between her thumb and forefinger. "He turns into a bird at night," she said.

"He does not!" Hadley protested. "Don't listen to her, Mary. She's just trying to scare you."

"He does so," Pfeiffer replied. "He turns into that old black crow on the tree branch outside your window. You've seen him, right?"

Mary shook her head back and forth, eyes wide. "No!"

"Well, he's there," Pfeiffer continued. "Watching you to make sure you're being good. Because if you're not, he'll peck your eyes out!"

"That's enough!" Hadley started. "You're scaring her!"

Pfeiffer threw the crawdad at Hadley, causing her to drop Mary onto the ground. Mary pitched forward, landing on her knees. She started to cry, and when she sat up, there was blood trickling down one of her knees.

"Ouch!" Mary groaned, covering her knee with her hands. "Ouuucchhh."

Hadley turned to glare at Pfeiffer. "You're awful," she spat. She bent down and picked Mary up off the ground and cooed to her, "Shhh, it's okay. Don't worry. Let's go home and get you cleaned up."

Pfeiffer stood there for a moment watching them go, ambling over to where her sisters had been standing to search for the crawdad. She found it, struggling in the grass, wriggling its back half from side to side in an effort to scurry back to the creek. She knew she could pick it up and take it back or let it find its way itself. Either way, it would be fine. Instead, she lifted up her foot and pressed down on the little creature, hard, until she heard the inevitable crunch.

She waited to feel something, anything, about what she'd just done—but she didn't. All she felt was numbness in her lips and fingertips that she couldn't explain and a small, low buzz in the back of her brain. Everything else muted, turning a taupe color against the brilliant blue of the Ozarks skyline.

Pfeiffer opened her eyes, expecting to see the high, white ceilings of her apartment in New York City. Instead, she was staring up at cobwebs and exposed beams. It was then that she realized that she was in her childhood home and that the buzzing in her head was the alarm on her phone, vibrating on the coffee table.

She reached to turn off the alarm and swung her legs over the side of the couch. To her surprise, her feet didn't hit the hardwood floor. Instead, they hit something warm. And furry. And lumpy. Pfeiffer pulled her feet back up and shoved them under the blanket, hanging her head down to see what she'd just touched.

It was a dog.

A snoring dog.

Pfeiffer looked around the room, wondering if she was still dreaming. Her head was fuzzy and throbbing from the whiskey, so she knew she had to be awake. *How had a dog gotten into the house?* she wondered. Surely she would have noticed if one of her sisters had come with a dog the day before. Should she just shoo it off? Was it going to attack her if she woke it? Could she escape the couch without it noticing? How did the damn thing get inside to begin with?

That's when she remembered the opening in the front door— the one her mother had made for Renaldo the raccoon all those years ago. Looking down at the dog again, she wasn't sure how an animal that big had managed to get inside an opening made for a raccoon, but it had to be the only way it had gotten inside.

As Pfeiffer stared down at the sleeping animal, Hadley appeared at the top of the staircase. She stopped halfway down, one of her delicate hands gripping the banister. "Is that . . . is that a *dog*?" she asked.

Pfeiffer nodded. "Yes," she whispered.

"You let a dog into the house?"

"I didn't *let it in*," Pfeiffer whispered. "I woke up, and there it was, snoring on the floor."

"How did it get here?"

"I don't know."

Hadley proceeded down the stairs, not taking her eyes off of the dog. "Do you think we should wake it up?"

Pfeiffer shrugged. "Think it might try to bite us?"

"I don't know," Hadley replied. "It doesn't look vicious."

"Its face looks melted," Pfeiffer said.

It was true, the dog's long face looked like a puddle on the floor, its jowls moving ever so slightly with each snore. It was a basset hound, Pfeiffer realized. It was the kind of dog, along with beagles, that were common out in the country. It could have come from any one of the neighbors' houses.

"Wake it up," Hadley demanded.

Pfeiffer sighed. It was too early for her sister to be making demands of her. She opened her mouth to protest, and then remembered what she'd promised Martha the night before. "Fine," she said.

She reached down and rubbed her hand across the dog's back. It didn't even stir. Next, she scratched its ears. Still nothing. Finally, Pfeiffer got out of bed and crouched down on the floor next to it and lifted its head slightly. The dog's eyes fluttered open and then rolled to the back of its head.

"Is it dead?" Hadley asked.

"No," Pfeiffer replied, standing up. "It's breathing."

"What are we going to do with it?" Hadley wanted to know.

Pfeiffer shrugged. "I'm leaving it right where it is," she said. "I have to get ready for the funeral."

"You can't just leave it," Hadley replied, her hands on her hips. "You have to make it go outside."

"It's not my dog," Pfeiffer retorted. "I don't have to do anything. If you want it to go outside, do it yourself."

Pfeiffer ignored Hadley's glare as she traipsed up the stairs. As she went past Martha's room, she noticed the door was cracked open a bit. When she looked inside, she didn't see her. Figuring she'd missed her opportunity for the use of the bathroom, she turned around to go back downstairs when something caught her eye from inside the other bedroom. It was Martha, sound asleep on Pfeiffer's bed. Well, the bed that had once been Pfeiffer's. Technically, nothing in this house had been hers for a long, long time.

Her sister was sprawled out on her back, her blond hair splayed out around her. Pfeiffer could see a little bit of dark coming in at the roots—the dirty dishwater of Martha's natural color. Her limbs were tanned and toned, and her eyelashes, clearly false, fluttered a little when Pfeiffer accidentally brushed against the door, and it gave an annoyed, underused groan.

Martha sat up, blinking. "Who's there?" she called. "Hadley?"

"It's only me," Pfeiffer said, stepping inside the bedroom. "I didn't mean to wake you up."

"It's fine," Martha replied. "I meant to get up an hour ago and go for a run."

"A run?"

Martha nodded. "You know, exercise?"

"I know what exercise is," Pfeiffer replied. "I just don't do it unless I have to."

"Not all of us can stay skinny without it," Martha said. She sounded annoyed, but a grin was creeping across her face. "So did you get some sleep?"

"A little," Pfeiffer admitted. "I had some crazy dreams, though."

"Me too," Martha replied. "I think it's being back here in this old house. It's stirring up a lot of . . . memories."

"Memories I don't think any of us want to think about," Pfeiffer muttered. "I mean, I know we all talk about how we would have come for visits if Aunt Bea hadn't told us no, but I don't think that's true."

Martha looked up at Pfeiffer. "Why would any of us want to come back here?" she asked. "Everybody we've ever loved has died in this damn town."

Pfeiffer sat down next to her. "My therapist told me two years ago that I needed to go home and confront my *demons*," she replied. "I told her I didn't have any demons. Just a lot of dead relatives."

"I never tried therapy. I guess I should have," Martha said.

"Sure you did," Pfeiffer said. "Pretty sure Jack Daniel's did more for you and cost less than my therapist."

Martha laughed. "Do you remember when Travis's grandmother died a few years ago?"

Pfeiffer nodded.

"Well, after the funeral, I made some terrible joke about death—remember like we used to do after Mom and Mary died?"

"We had to make jokes," Pfeiffer said. "It was the only way to deal with such an awful thing happening to us."

"Well," Martha continued, "I don't remember what it was, but I thought maybe he'd think it was funny. Maybe he'd be able to smile even though he was heartbroken," she said. "But he didn't laugh. In fact, he told me I was insensitive and didn't speak to me for three days."

"Not everybody appreciates our humor," Pfeiffer admitted. "The only people I ever felt like I could talk to about that time are you and Hadley."

"But we don't talk," Martha said. "Not like we used to."

"No," Pfeiffer agreed. "We don't."

"Do you think Hadley's ever talked to anyone else about it?" Martha asked.

"Absolutely not," Pfeiffer replied, a grin pasted across her face. "She's pretty tightly wound."

Martha eyed her sister skeptically. "Have you two already been into an argument this morning?"

Pfeiffer avoided Martha's gaze. "Not exactly."

"Pfeiffer!"

"It wasn't my fault!" Pfeiffer protested. "I woke up, and there was this *dog* on the floor beside the couch."

"A dog?"

"Yeah. A big, old basset hound."

"How did it get inside?" Martha asked.

"I think through Renaldo's old pet door," Pfeiffer replied.

"Did Aunt Bea have a dog?"

"I don't think so."

"Weird."

"Anyway," Pfeiffer said, "Hadley told me to make it go out-side, like I'd personally invited it inside to pass out on the floor. I told her if she wanted it gone, she could do it herself."

"You know she's allergic to dogs," Martha replied.

Pfeiffer scrunched up her face and said, "She is not. That's just what she always said because she didn't want to be the one to feed Daddy's cattle dogs."

"I didn't mind," Martha said. "I love dogs."

"Come on," Pfeiffer said. "We better get ready to go to this funeral, or Aunt Bea will haunt us for being late."

"Don't say that!" Martha replied. "She really might, you know."

"Ghosts don't exist," Pfeiffer replied. "And anyway, she'd be too old to catch us now."

"Ghosts do exist," Martha said. "And if Aunt Bea is going to haunt anyone, it's sure as hell going to be you!"

The sisters dissolved into a fit of giggles, and for the first time in a long time, Pfeiffer remembered just how good it felt to laugh.

"I really need to get ready," Martha said. "It takes me forever."

"Go on ahead," Pfeiffer replied. "I can wait."

"Are you sure?"

Pfeiffer nodded. "All I need to do is brush my teeth and straighten my hair. I know you've got a whole MAC counter in that bag of yours. So go ahead."

"You want to borrow some makeup?" Martha asked, getting out of bed and stretching.

Pfeiffer wrinkled her nose. "No," she replied. "Foundation gives me a rash."

"Well, a little lip gloss and mascara never hurt anybody."

"Go," Pfeiffer said, pointing toward the open door. "Before I change my mind."

"Whatever," Martha replied, turning around. "Just trying to help you out."

Pfeiffer rolled her eyes. She'd never managed to master makeup, and to be honest, she was glad. It took up so much time. All she needed was a bit of ChapStick, and she was good to go, but her sisters were always trying to get her to wear more. She didn't like makeup. She didn't like the way it made her skin feel or covered the smattering of freckles across the bridge of her nose—her favorite feature.

She stood up and walked out into the hallway. She walked past the bathroom, a 1950s addition to the house, when their grandparents moved in with their mother to take care of the farm and their grandfather Charlie's aging parents. She stopped when she got to Aunt Bea's room. It was at the far end of the hallway, the opposite direction from the stairs, and Pfeiffer didn't know why her feet led her there. She raised her fist to knock, and then dropped it back down to her side when she realized that there wasn't any need to knock—not anymore. Instead, she pushed the door wide open and stepped inside.

The room looked much like it had when it belonged to her mother and both of her parents before that. She figured it probably hadn't changed too much throughout the years, with the exception of paint on the walls and different pictures hanging on them.

There was a queen-sized bed pushed against the far end of the wall with a wrought-iron headboard and frame. The mattress was covered with a lavender quilt, probably handmade by her aunt. There was a matching oak dresser and nightstand,

and the closet door was open, revealing all of Aunt Beatrice's clothing.

Pfeiffer walked over to the bed and sat down. It smelled like the perfume their aunt always wore, Gardenia by Park & Tilford. Pfeiffer wasn't sure how her aunt managed to find the scent, since she was sure it had been out of production for years, but nonetheless, that's what she smelled like. There was a nearly empty bottle of it on the nightstand, along with two photo albums and a notebook that Pfeiffer had never seen before.

Glancing around the room, as if her aunt might walk in at any moment, Pfeiffer took the albums off of the nightstand and set them in her lap. Gingerly, she opened the first one, and was surprised to see baby pictures of her mother. The first few pages were full of her; from the time she was born up until the time she was two or three years old. She'd been a beautiful baby, with sweet round cheeks and a headful of white-blond hair. Towheaded, is what her mother had called it. Her hair stayed that blond for all of her life, and their mother said that many babies outgrow it, like Pfeiffer and her sisters had.

The next pages were more photos of her mother as she grew up. There were school pictures and birthday party pictures, and at the end . . . a wedding picture of her mother and father. Pfeiffer paused, spreading her fingers across the photo. They were both so young, and they both looked happy. She wished she could pull the picture out and take it with her, but it felt wrong to tear it from the album where it'd lived for so many years. Reluctantly, she turned to the last page and saw a picture of herself with her sisters, the last photograph of their whole family, when Mary had been an infant.

She remembered that photo. They'd had it professionally

taken, and their mother complained about how much it cost, but their father insisted. It was July, and so hot outside that she'd cried when her mother made her wear tights underneath her dress, and Hadley slapped her hands in the car when she tried to take them off. That was the reason she was scowling while everybody else, even her baby sister, was smiling.

Pfeiffer shut the album and closed her eyes. She didn't want to think about any of that right now, even though she knew she should be grateful for the memory. She put the album back on the nightstand and looked down at the other one. It was much older, and the pages were even yellower than the first one. When she opened it, the spine gave a tired sigh as if the album might break apart right there in her hands.

The photos stopped at Aunt Bea's seventeenth birthday party; there were two pages of Bea and what appeared to be several of her friends all dressed up and sitting daintily at a table in the kitchen—the same table that was still in the room at that moment. In the photographs, Aunt Bea's eyes were bright, despite the fact that the pictures were faded. She was smiling, and she looked happy. She was so far away from the version of Aunt Bea that Pfeiffer knew that Pfeiffer brought the album up close to her face for better inspection.

As she did so, something slipped out from between the pages and fell onto her lap. Pfeiffer set the album aside and looked down. It was a brooch composed of two tarnished hearts. It was cheaply made, Pfeiffer realized, and not something someone would keep for monetary value, which meant that her aunt had likely kept it because it held sentimental value of some kind.

Pfeiffer turned it over in her hands, looking for an inscription and finding none. She wondered if a man had given this piece of jewelry to her aunt. As far as Pfeiffer knew, her aunt had never come close to getting married. Aunt Bea didn't talk about her relationships, and that was mainly because she didn't seem to have many. The thought of Aunt Bea being in love seemed strange to her; still, someone had given her the brooch, and Aunt Bea had seen fit to keep it for all these years.

"Pfeiffer!" Martha called from the other end of the hallway. "I'm done in the bathroom. It's all yours!"

Pfeiffer shoved the brooch back into the album. "I'm coming," she said. She stood up and placed the albums back on the nightstand. As she did so, the dog ambled into the room, and in her effort to shoo it away, Pfeiffer got her foot tangled in the bedskirt and tripped. She put her hands out to catch herself, grabbing onto the nightstand in the process. It came toppling over with her, landing on top of her in a heap on the floor.

"What's going on up there?" Hadley called. "Are you all right?"

"Damn dog," Pfeiffer managed from beneath the nightstand. She sat up, pushing the pieces of splintered wood off her. Both the lamp and the bottle of perfume lay broken beside her. Next to them, covered in shards of glass and old perfume, was a black leather-bound notebook. It had the letters *BAJ* embossed on the front. Pfeiffer picked it up, holding her nose as the ancient scent of Gardenia invaded her nostrils.

"Pfeiffer!" Hadley called again. "What is going *on* up there?"

"I'm fine!" Pfeiffer hollered. "I'll be right down."

Pfeiffer stood up, careful to avoid any broken glass, and wincing at the small piece of splintered wood lodged in the palm of one of her hands. In the other hand she still held the journal. The dog looked up at her with its mournful eyes and then plopped itself down onto the rug at the foot of the bed. Looking over her shoulder to make sure neither of her sisters was standing in the doorway, she sat down next to the dog and opened the journal.

Beatrice
January 14, 1948

Today I turned 17 years old. Now that it's past midnight, I can write it and not be telling a fib. I've never been able to sleep the night before my birthday. I love birthdays more than anything else in the world. Mama stayed up late baking me a German chocolate cake, and Daddy went to town and bought me mittens and a scarf, my first-ever store-bought, as a present. When I told him that I planned to stay inside this year for my party, because I'm practically a woman and too old for the outside games we usually play, he looked sad. Every year he clears out a special place in the yard for games. We all drink hot chocolate and warm ourselves by the fire, running in and out of the house each time our legs have thawed out enough to move. But not this year. This year, I want a luncheon with my three best girlfriends.

I want to dress up and drink tea. I want to talk about boys and giggle about things Mama calls "foolhardy." I'm not sure I know what that word means, but Mama uses it to describe everything I like.

Daddy's new farmhand stopped to talk to me while I was outside feeding the chickens yesterday.

His name is Will, and he's 25. He comes from some place back east. I can't remember the name of the town right now. But he says that their winters are ten times as cold and that they catch lobster in big traps, fresh from the Atlantic Ocean. He knows more about anything than any boy I've ever met. Rufus Crowley doesn't like him, but I think that's just because he's jealous. Mama says he's got a crush on me, but he's my friend. Besides, I don't want to live on a farm for the rest of my life, and that's all Rufus could ever offer me.

Last night, just as I was about to fall asleep, I heard a thump against my window. At first, I thought maybe a bat had flown into the side of the house, but then I heard it again and again, and I knew not even a bat could be that stupid.

When I opened the window to check, I saw Will standing down there in the dark. He lives in an old tenant shack on the edge of our property, and I'd never seen him out this late before. I asked what he was doing, and told him he better hush up or he was going to wake Daddy, and I knew Daddy wouldn't be happy to find Will staring up at me while I was wearing nothing but my nightgown.

He called to me to come outside. Luckily, Mama and Daddy sleep heavy and they were all the way on the other side of the house. My brother, Charlie, lives in town with his wife, Maryann, and so there was nobody awake to keep me from going down to meet him, even though I knew I shouldn't.

I went downstairs, careful to skip the squeaky step toward the bottom. I found my boots and buttoned my jacket around my nightgown. I know I probably should have changed my clothes, but I didn't want to take a chance that Will might think I was ignoring him.

It was so cold, and Will wasn't wearing a jacket. I asked him what he was doing, and he said of course he'd come to see me. He said he remembered it was almost my birthday, and he'd come to give me a present. I wished Anna could have been there—she would have been so jealous. The only boy to ever give her a present was Marty Walters, and it was a rock shaped like a toad.

Anyway, he pulled a package out of his pocket, all wrapped up pretty and tied in twine with a bow. He told me to open it, and so I did. My hands were so cold, I didn't think I could do it, but when I did, I gasped. It was a brooch with two hearts on it, and it shone in the moonlight like nothing I'd ever seen before. Will said I should pin it to my dress at my birthday party so that when he was working, he could come in for a drink and see me wearing it. I told him I would.

We decided to keep our meeting a secret, because Daddy wouldn't like it if he knew. I don't think Mama would mind so much. She seems to like Will. But Daddy says he's lazy and that if he doesn't start working harder, he's going to send him right back to where he came from.

*I told Anna about Will, because I tell her every-
thing, and she agreed to tell Mama and Daddy, and
anybody else who asks, that she gave me the brooch.
Maryann says all women ought to have a secret or
two, and for now, Will is mine.*

Pfeiffer closed the journal and held it on her lap for a long
moment. She wished she could stay and read more, but she knew
that her sisters would be up looking for her, and for some reason,
she didn't want to share what she'd just found. She tucked the
journal between the mattress and box spring and allowed herself
to stroke the length of the dog's back. It let out a sigh and rested
its head on her lap.

"Come on," she said, standing up. "Let's go."

To her abject surprise, the dog followed her down the hallway, down the stairs, and right out the front door. She, Hadley,
and Martha watched it trot away, down the dirt road and out of
sight.

"What just happened?" Hadley asked, her coffee cup halfway
to her lips.

"I don't know," Pfeiffer replied. "But I'm pretty sure I don't
believe it."

CHAPTER 8
Pfeiffer

Cars lined the street of the Methodist church, people in their Sunday best streaming inside the wooden double doors to the front entrance of the sanctuary. The last time Pfeiffer went through those doors was for a wedding when she was seventeen. The name of the bride escaped her now, but she'd been the daughter of one of her mother's friends, just a couple years older than she. Pfeiffer remembered the groom and how his face had been mottled and pitted with acne, and it had reminded her of a scene in a high school play rather than an actual wedding.

"There are tons of people here," Hadley said. "Way more than were there for the family night."

"I know," Martha replied. Her voice was barely above a whisper as they entered the sanctuary. "I didn't realize Aunt Bea had so many friends."

"We've been gone a long time," Pfeiffer said. "I guess anything is possible."

"She did grow up here," Martha added.

It was true; they often forgot that their aunt grew up in Cold River. She'd moved away to St. Louis long before the children were born, but the farmhouse had been in the family for generations. The only reason they lived there to begin with was that there was no one to take care of it except their mother.

From the front of the sanctuary, Anna was waving at them. "Y'all come on down here. We've saved seats for the family."

Pfeiffer rolled her eyes. The last thing she wanted to do was sit at the front. "I've never seen so many old people in one place," she said, and was immediately shushed by Hadley. "What? I was just commenting."

"Well, don't," Hadley replied as they took their places next to Anna.

Pfeiffer fought the urge to stick her tongue out at Hadley, realizing just how juvenile a reaction it would have been. Besides, her sister was no longer paying attention to her, as she was staring straight ahead at the front of the sanctuary, where the now-closed casket of their aunt had been placed.

Beside her, Martha was also sitting still and staring straight ahead. Pfeiffer wondered if she was the only one who felt fidgety, as if she just might jump right out of her skin as everyone sat chaste around her. She slid her hands underneath her legs in an attempt to keep still, and when the organ music started, she was relieved to have something else to listen to besides the sound of her own breathing.

Pfeiffer closed her eyes and thought about New York. She wondered what everyone in that great city was doing. She wondered if her former colleagues were gulping copious amounts of coffee and slogging over slush piles as they complained about their workload. She wondered if someone was at this moment discovering the next *New York Times* bestseller and congratulating herself on her find. She wondered about the editor who'd taken her place—a fresh, new set of eyes hungry for praise and not yet sarcastic in her replies to literary agents and writers.

She wondered, too, about her apartment. She'd dropped the keys off at the super's office before she left when she knew he would be out. The only thing left in that apartment was the couch, which, despite its expensive fabric, had managed to look grubby against the gleaming hardwood of her bare floors. Surely the furniture men had come and taken it away by now, having been alerted by the super of her sudden disappearance while she still owed months in rent.

The pastor, a younger man with a clean-shaven face, droned on and on about how Beatrice James had been an absolute pillar of the community. He talked about her good works in the community and how much she loved Cold River. As the pastor continued to talk, Pfeiffer realized that much of what he was saying was generic—it could have been written about anybody, and she began to wonder how much anybody really knew her aunt. She'd been such a quiet, unassuming woman. She kept to herself on the farm, and with the exception of the ladies' auxiliary meetings, she never went anywhere Crowley couldn't drive her.

Pfeiffer couldn't help but wonder the same thing about herself. She had never been able to make friends the way most people did. Most of her socializing took place at work, with colleagues. When she lost her job, nobody but Seth even bothered to call. He was probably her only true friend, and she didn't know if he would still want to be friends with her once she told him that she'd practically ruined his car.

She thought about her aunt's journal. Even though Bea was dead, it still felt a bit wrong to be reading something so personal that belonged to someone else. Always before, at work, she'd had permission to read the things other people wrote. Pfeiffer had never heard her aunt speak. She didn't know what her voice sounded like, but reading the journal gave her a sense of the young woman her aunt had been, and there was something almost comforting about it.

She looked over at Anna, who was sitting on the other side of Hadley, and she wondered if she was the same Anna her aunt mentioned in her journal. Surely, she had to be. She wondered, too, what happened to the man named Will who had worked on the farm—she knew that her aunt never married, so something must've gone wrong in their relationship. Maybe the journal would tell her something. The thought gave her a buzz of excitement, and she made a mental note to ask Anna more about Aunt Beatrice later, and she wished, not for the first time, that she'd been there when her aunt died. She should have been there, she knew, and it was one of many regrets Pfeiffer knew she'd live with for the rest of her life.

CHAPTER 9
Martha

MARTHA WAS RELIEVED WHEN THE SERVICE WAS OVER. She stood in the receiving line with her sisters and allowed people she barely knew or remembered to kiss her cheek and tell her how sorry they were. Some of them, mostly the younger people, told her how much they loved her music. Kelly and Katie were both there, and Martha was glad they'd been ushered away before either of them had a chance to mention rehab or Travis or anything else they'd likely read in *Star* magazine.

"Honey," a middle-aged woman in a Chanel-style suit asked when she reached Pfeiffer, "what happened to your face?"

"I got hit with a door," Pfeiffer replied grimly.

Martha had to stifle a giggle. Pfeiffer did indeed have two black eyes, and for once in the last fifteen years, people were paying more attention to her sister than they were to her. Pfeiffer, for her part, did not seem to be enjoying the attention.

"You sure that's what happened?" the woman asked, raising

her eyebrow. "My cousin's daughter looked just exactly like that when her husband caught her with his brother at the Ramada Inn. Took three people to restrain him."

"I'm sure," Pfeiffer replied, her teeth gritted together so tightly she looked like she had a serious case of lockjaw.

"You think that big publisher you work for up there in New York might be interested in a story like that?" the woman continued. She was holding up the line now, and people behind her were starting to grumble. She didn't seem to notice. "My cousin is writing a book, you know."

"No," Pfeiffer replied. "I didn't know."

"Think you'd have time to take a look at it?"

Martha braced herself for her sister's response. She'd seen Pfeiffer in action when presented with a request to read an unsolicited manuscript. She was never cruel, but she always told whoever was asking that on no uncertain terms would she entertain working on a manuscript not presented to her by a literary agent—an agent she already knew.

Instead, Pfeiffer took a deep breath and said, "Maybe."

"Oh, Janice will be so happy to hear that," the woman said. "I'll have her look you up on Facebook. She's got her own page and everything."

Martha stole a glance at Hadley, wondering if she'd caught this decidedly un-Pfeiffer-like display of benevolence, but beside her, Hadley was rigid, her gaze focused on something or someone at the back of the line. A few inches shorter than her sister, Martha had to stand on her tiptoes to see on what it was her sister was concentrating.

Toward the back of the crowd, there was a man standing a head above the rest. His sandy hair was falling slightly over his eyes, making him appear younger than he actually was, but Martha knew him immediately. His name was Brody Nichols, and he'd once been the love of Hadley's life. In fact, Martha couldn't remember much of her childhood without Brody. He'd once been like a brother to her.

The line lurched forward, and Brody came closer to them. Martha could feel Hadley's breath become raspy beside her, and she snuck a glance up at her sister. She'd probably thought when he wasn't at the funeral home the night before that he wouldn't be at the funeral today, but Martha knew better. He'd always managed to turn up wherever Hadley was.

"Hello, Martha," Brody said, suddenly standing in front of her. "You're certainly all grown up."

Martha grinned and reached up to hug him. "So are you."

"I'm old," he whispered.

"Not so old," she replied.

Martha was about to say something else when she realized Brody's attention had already turned to Hadley. He was standing in front of her, his smile lopsided, as if he wasn't sure if he ought to be smiling at all. It might've been because it was a funeral after all, but Martha thought it probably had more to do with the stricken look on Hadley's face.

"How are you, Hadley?" Brody asked. "I mean, besides your aunt being dead."

Martha stifled a giggle. Brody always did have a way with words. He'd always known how to make her and her sisters laugh. It was one of the things she most appreciated about him.

At last, Hadley pasted on a smile and said, "Hello, Brody. It's so good of you to come today."

"Yes, very *good*," Pfeiffer chimed in, rolling her eyes at Hadley's sterile greeting. "You'll have to excuse my sister. She's been stuck in Washington, D.C., greeting the wives of dried-up politicians for far too long."

"Not all of them are dried up," Hadley said, defensive.

"You're certainly not dried up," Brody replied; this time, his whole face lit up in a smile. "You look just the same as the last time I saw you."

Martha watched as Hadley's grimace gave way, and she finally relaxed. Martha had never known exactly what happened between the two of them. She'd just been fourteen the summer they broke up—the same summer her mother and sister died—and in some ways, the loss of the relationship between the two of them—Brody and Hadley—felt like a death as well. Martha wondered what he'd been up to all these years.

As if reading her mind, Brody said, "I'm sorry I can't stay for the potluck, but I've got to get back to the farm. We've got a broken-down tractor and nobody else to fix it."

"The farm?" Hadley asked. "What farm?"

"I bought the old Richmond place a few years ago," he replied. "Been trying to make a go of it ever since."

"You're a farmer now?" Pfeiffer asked.

"Not all of us can be big-shot book editors in New York City," Brody said. "Some of us have to get our hands dirty to make a buck."

"Editing is dirty enough," Pfeiffer muttered.

"Oh, I'm sure," Brody replied. "Just not the same kind of dirty, I reckon."

"Where's your farm?" Martha asked, not anxious to hear any more about books.

"Just about five miles down the road from yours," Brody

replied. "I offered to help your aunt out with the house and the yard a few times, but she always said no. Now that the farm is yours, my offer still stands. It needs some work, from what I've seen."

"It's not ours," Pfeiffer said.

"It's gotta be yours now," Brody said. "Nobody else on this earth she could have left it to."

The sisters shared a look.

"She wouldn't leave it to us," Hadley said quickly. She glanced between Martha and Pfeiffer. "I just figured it would go to auction or something."

"Why would it go to auction?" Brody wanted to know. "When your aunt has three real-life heirs here to take care of it."

Hadley opened her mouth to reply, but Martha cut her off. "It looks like the line is getting pretty backed up. It was good to see you, Brody."

Brody nodded. "I guess that's my signal." He reached out and cupped Hadley's elbow with his hand. "It was nice to see y'all, too. And I truly am sorry about your aunt Beatrice."

"Do you think Aunt Bea really left us the farm?" Martha whispered once Brody had ambled off.

"I don't know," Hadley replied, smiling at another familiar face.

"What will we do if she did?" Martha continued. "There's nobody else to leave it to, like Brody said."

"Let's not talk about it here," Hadley said.

"Brody looked good, don't you think?" Pfeiffer asked, her gaze sliding over to Hadley. "I swear, he hasn't changed a lick in twenty years."

"He's a farmer now," Hadley replied. "That's changed."

"It's an honest way to make a living," Pfeiffer said.

"His dad can't be too pleased," Hadley said. "He always used to say that Brody was going to be a veterinarian. Remember?"

"I remember," Martha chimed in. "I guess he never did take over his dad's practice. From what I hear, Amanda is the vet now."

Martha had been a friend of Brody's younger sister, Amanda. She'd been at family dinners when Dr. Nichols would come in, still dirty and bloody from helping a farmer pull a calf, waxing poetic about the miracle of birth. "It's the same for all animals," he'd say, winking at the girls. Martha thought it was pretty gross, but not any worse than Mrs. Nichols's meat loaf.

"Let's go," Pfeiffer said. "We're finally at the end of the line."

"Should we go say good-bye to her?" Hadley asked, turning her head slightly toward the front of the sanctuary and the coffin.

"I think we should," Pfeiffer replied.

"It almost seems wrong not to," Martha said.

"Don't you feel like we should?" Hadley asked again, as if trying to convince herself. "Just for a minute?"

"I do," Martha said, even though it was the last thing she wanted to do. She held up her hand for the pallbearers to give them a moment, and then she followed her sister. "What are you going to say to her?"

Hadley shrugged. "I don't know."

Martha looked down at the now-closed casket. She hadn't been brave enough to walk this close the night before. In fact, she'd wanted to leave with Pfeiffer, but she couldn't abandon Hadley. So much of her wished she'd just stayed back in Nashville, despite how hard it was there for her right now. At least she could have gone back into a studio, any studio, and tried to record. In rehab, the only thing besides clothes she'd taken with her was her guitar. She'd written fifteen new songs during her stay there, and some of them, she thought, were pretty good.

Her aunt hadn't liked it when she played music. Aunt Bea liked things to be quiet, which was no easy task when there were three teenage girls living underneath the same roof.

After both of her sisters left for college, Martha came home one day to find all of her musical instruments locked away in the attic. Aunt Bea left her a note to say that the music gave her headaches. Unlike her sisters, it wasn't in Martha's nature to protest, so she went back to her room, pulled out a miniature bottle of whiskey her twenty-three-year-old boyfriend bought her, and began to plot her escape. The day she left home, her aunt was supposed to go into town with Old Crow to buy groceries. But for some reason, Old Crow was held up, and when Martha's boyfriend pulled into the drive, Aunt Bea had gone outside expecting it to be Old Crow. She'd sat down on the front porch and watched Martha leave, her bags packed, with her boyfriend. She hadn't made a sound.

Martha knew that her aunt had left home at around the same age, and she always wondered if Bea saw in her that day the same desperation she'd felt when she herself left home, the very same home, as a teenager. And now, like her aunt, here she was back in Cold River, the one place she'd always said she'd never revisit.

"I bet she was pissed about that open casket last night," Pfeiffer said, finally breaking the uneasy silence that had fallen over them. "Can you imagine what she would have said?"

"She wouldn't have said anything," Hadley replied.

"You know what I mean."

"Now I bet if she haunts anybody, it'll be Anna and the rest of her friends," Martha said, a small smile ticking up her face.

"She can haunt me," Pfeiffer said quietly, her hand outstretched to touch the smooth surface of the casket.

Martha wanted to reach out and hug her sister. She remembered the way Pfeiffer hung back from the crowd, away from other people, even as a child. "Let's go," she said, taking her sister's hand. "It's time."

Pfeiffer nodded, stepping in front of her sisters to hurry out ahead of them.

Martha glanced over at Hadley, who looked like she might start crying. Martha didn't think she could stand it, so she said, "Brody looked good, huh?"

Hadley turned away from her. "He did."

"When was the last time you spoke to him?"

Hadley shrugged. "I guess before I left."

"You didn't keep in touch at all?"

"I didn't see a reason to," Hadley replied. "I met Mark my first semester at Missouri State. He wouldn't have liked me to keep in touch with an old boyfriend."

Martha wrinkled her nose. She'd never liked Mark. He was such a politician. In the entertainment industry, she'd met more than her fair share of fake people, but Mark just about took the cake. Nothing about him was genuine, most especially, Martha suspected, his affection for Hadley. "Is there anything Mark likes?" she asked.

Hadley didn't answer, and Martha wondered if Mark and Hadley even liked each other. Martha thought back to the day the two were married. Although the memory was fuzzy thanks to the free-flowing tequila fountain, she remembered her sister hadn't looked very happy as Martha watched her walk down the aisle. It could have been because Pfeiffer refused to come, pretending that her new job as an editor's assistant kept her busy, but both Martha and Hadley knew that probably wasn't true. Martha and Pfeiffer always expected that Hadley and Brody would get married. Hadley probably expected it, too. But like so many things, the death of their mother and sister changed all that.

"Let's go," Hadley said finally. "We're going to be late."

THE SMELL OF food permeated the fellowship hall and wafted down the corridor. Martha could feel her stomach grumbling. She hadn't eaten any breakfast, and the two cups of coffee she'd poured down her throat that morning were no longer doing the trick.

"I'm starving," she whispered to her sisters.

"Me too," Pfeiffer replied.

"You should have eaten breakfast," Hadley said. "Honestly, you two are old enough to know better."

"You should have let us stop at McDonald's after the graveside," Pfeiffer shot back.

"Then you'd ruin your appetite for the potluck," Hadley replied. "Now be quiet; it's time to pray."

Martha bowed her head and nudged Pfeiffer to do the same. Pfeiffer sighed, but complied, and Martha couldn't help but smile that Pfeiffer still resisted Hadley's mothering after all these years. She supposed it was because the two were so close in age that Pfeiffer was so defiant, but that was only partly true. Pfeiffer hadn't liked being told what to do by anyone, ever. She disliked being scolded by her older sister even more.

From the corner of her eye, Martha could see Hadley glancing around the room.

Brody wasn't there, and Martha couldn't tell if her sister looked relieved or disappointed. She'd always wondered what happened between the two of them, but Hadley stayed tight-lipped about the entire thing. Even after all these years, Martha knew if she asked what happened, she'd get the same answer, or nonanswer, that she always got.

The prayer ended, and Martha moved hungrily to the spread in front of them, foods glossy with steam. She remembered these potlucks as a child, and she remembered how she would greedily hedge her way to the front of the line so she could load her plate before anyone else got the chance to take what she herself wanted.

Now, however, her hunger was different. She couldn't remember the last time her stomach felt full. She couldn't remember the last time she hadn't had to worry about gaining an extra five pounds and some ridiculous Internet troll making fun of her supposed weight gain while she ran around sweating her ass off onstage. What she looked like was important.

At the funeral, she'd glanced around and noticed all the older women sitting in the pews. Most of them were visions of southern elegance—smartly dressed in appropriate funeral attire, their lipstick subdued to a nude or pink color for the occasion, instead of the signature Mary Kay red that women of a certain age were wont to wear. She wondered, fleetingly, if any of them ever looked in the mirror and mourned their youth. If they remembered the day that their hair became too gray to cover or if they noticed each new line forming on their faces. Martha herself had started getting Botox treatments when she was twenty-five, the night after an interviewer on the red carpet of an awards show had described her as a "country-music veteran" and an "inspiration to younger, aspiring artists."

"Hurry up," Pfeiffer said behind her. "I'm starving, and you're holding up the line."

"Sorry," Martha mumbled, taking one of the paper plates offered to her by an older lady she sort of recognized. She hurried past the fried chicken and corn casserole and opted for a wilting salad while jealously watching Pfeiffer load up on carbs and help herself to a huge glass of sweet tea.

"Is that all you're going to eat?" Pfeiffer asked, following her to a table toward the back of the fellowship hall. "All this great food, and you're going to eat a salad?"

"It's all I want," Martha replied, trying not to salivate at the delicious smell that wafted toward her from Pfeiffer's plate.

"A chicken leg isn't gonna hurt."

"I don't eat meat," Martha said. "I haven't eaten meat for nearly ten years."

Hadley's lunch looked similar to Martha's, except that she had a small portion of meat on her plate. Martha knew that Hadley's choices weren't due to metabolism, but because she believed that *ladies* didn't like to appear hungry in public. The thought made Martha want to grab an entire chicken with her teeth.

As she sat there, envisioning chewing something other than lettuce, a man in a suit approached them. Martha looked up at him, her fork poised at her mouth.

"Excuse me, ladies?"

Hadley swallowed her iced tea and said, "Yes?"

"My name is Luke Gibson. I'm the attorney for Ms. Beatrice James's estate," the man said. He gave them a broad smile, showing off a brilliant set of white teeth. "May I sit down?"

Hadley motioned for him to sit next to her. "By all means."

"You don't look like the Luke Gibson I remember," Pfeiffer said, her mouth full of baked beans. "You should be like ninety years old by now."

Luke cleared his throat. "You're thinking of my grandfather. I've taken over his practice," he said.

"It's nice to meet you, Mr. Gibson," Hadley said, shooting a sidelong look at Pfeiffer. "How is your grandfather?"

"Dead, actually."

Hadley's mouth formed a silent O at the same time Pfeiffer snorted beans through her nose. Ignoring Pfeiffer, Hadley said, "Oh, Mr. Gibson. I'm so very sorry for your loss."

Luke's mouth turned up in a small smile, his hazel eyes twinkling. "I'm not. The old man was a bastard. He never said much, but what he did say wasn't very nice."

"Our aunt didn't speak . . . ever," Pfeiffer managed to say in between wiping her mouth. "That's probably why the two of them got along."

A smile twitched on Luke's face before he said, "I know now isn't the appropriate time, but I need to meet with you three to discuss your aunt's estate."

"Why?" Pfeiffer wanted to know. "Surely she didn't leave anything to us."

"She left it all to you."

The sisters shared a glance, and Martha caught Hadley's polite smile faltering.

"What do you mean, she left it all?" Martha asked. "All of what?"

"Everything," Luke said. "The house, the land, and all of her worldly possessions. I can't say there's much money to be had, not anymore, but whatever she died with is yours now."

"She really thought we'd want it?" Hadley asked, more to herself than anyone else.

Luke shrugged. "You are her only family left on this earth. It makes sense."

"We haven't been back in years," Hadley replied, and then, her face full of guilt, she said, "Not even to see her."

"She didn't want us back," Pfeiffer replied quickly. "It wasn't like we didn't try."

Martha bowed her head in an attempt to keep from looking at the faces around the table. She knew that both of her sisters had tried to come home and visit their aunt, but she, for her part, hadn't.

"Well, we can discuss everything later this week. What day would be suitable for you all?" Luke stood, smoothing out an imaginary crease in his suit. "I'm in the office nine to five every day of the week."

"We're leaving this afternoon," Martha said.

"It'll be easier if we can work this out in person," Luke replied. "Discuss it among yourselves, and let me know. Here's my card." He placed a rectangular card on the table in front of them and moved off.

Hadley, Pfeiffer, and Martha stared after him.

"What do we do now?" Martha wanted to know. "We're all supposed to leave this afternoon."

"We could still leave," Hadley replied. "He said it would be tough to sort it out electronically, but not impossible."

"I'm staying," Pfeiffer said, putting down her fork. "What's so urgent that we can't stay an extra day?"

"Uh, because we all have jobs and lives?" Hadley retorted.

"You have a job?" Pfeiffer replied. "Where?"

Hadley's face reddened. "I have responsibilities in D.C."

"That's not the same thing as a job."

"It's close enough."

"No," Pfeiffer said, "it's not. And I'm sure that your *husband*, the illustrious congressman, can handle things by himself for a week or two while we get this all sorted out."

This time, Hadley didn't even attempt to hide her annoyance. She glowered over at Pfeiffer. "I'm sure he *can*."

"What about you, Martha?"

Martha glanced at her two sisters. The last thing she wanted to do was run interference between the two of them for any amount of the foreseeable future. But when she thought about returning home to her empty house, when she thought about trying to write alone, she felt tears pricking at her eyes and had to swallow to make them go away. "Fine," she said. "I guess I can stay for a couple of extra days."

"Pfeiffer," Hadley said, setting her gaze squarely on her sister. "Are you sure Henry Brothers won't mind if you take more time off?"

"Of course they won't mind."

"Don't you need to call them and ask?"

Now it was Pfeiffer's turn to look uncomfortable. "I'll call them later," she said.

Hadley fished her phone from her purse and handed it to Pfeiffer. "Why don't you call now?"

Pfeiffer took the phone and shoved her chair away from the table. Everyone turned around to stare at her as the force of her movement knocked the chair onto the concrete floor of the fellowship hall. Ignoring them, she stalked outside with Hadley's phone.

"Why did you do that?" Martha asked.

Hadley shrugged. "I wanted to see what she'd do."

"Why?"

"Have you ever known Pfeiffer to go more than five minutes without checking into the office?" Hadley asked. "She hasn't mentioned it once since she got here. She doesn't have her laptop. She doesn't have her briefcase full of paperwork. She doesn't even have a *phone* with her."

"You're right," Martha said. She sat back in her chair and eyed what was left of the food on Pfeiffer's plate. "What do you think is going on?"

"I don't know," Hadley replied, pushing the plate closer to Martha so that her sister could discreetly grab a piece of corn bread. "But I can guarantee you that whatever it is, she doesn't want us to know about it."

"Then maybe we should leave it alone," Martha replied, tearing off a piece of a roll and popping it into her mouth. It tasted so good; she fought the urge to moan with pleasure.

"Not a chance," Hadley replied, crossing her arms across her chest. "Not a chance."

CHAPTER 10
Hadley

Back at the house, Hadley sat on the front porch in one of the ancient rocking chairs. She'd been afraid it might collapse as she sat down on it, but aside from the groan the chair let out when she began to rock back and forth, it was surprisingly sturdy.

The chairs had been sitting on that front porch for as long as Hadley could remember. In fact, they'd been there for longer than Hadley or any of her sisters had been alive. Their mother told them they'd been a wedding present from Mr. Crowley when she got married to their father, Matthew. Each chair had their parents' names and wedding date carved into the wood. She remembered when she'd been about four or five, she'd taken one of her father's pocketknives out of her parents' bedroom and carved her own name next to theirs. Afterward, fearing she'd be in trouble, she'd hidden in the woods behind the house for two hours until her mother, who was frantic and terrified, found her.

"What on earth are you doing out here?" her mother asked,

panic written all over her face. "You know you're not supposed to be out here alone, and it's starting to get dark."

Hadley burst into tears and told her the whole story, pleading with her not to call the police and have her arrested for vandalism.

Her mother, trying not to laugh, asked her where she'd even learned that word, and Hadley told her that a television detective used it when he arrested a teenage boy for spray-painting the side of a building.

"Honey," her mother said, stroking Hadley's hair, "nobody is going to have you arrested. But why did you do it?"

"I wanted my name next to yours and Daddy's," Hadley said, wiping her runny nose on her sleeve.

After that, each of the Hemingway sisters carved her own name into the rocking chairs, just as soon as she was old enough to wield a pocketknife. Hadley stood up and crouched down beside the chair, running her fingers over the wood to find the names. They were all there—Rachael and Matthew Hemingway first, and then Hadley, Pfeiffer, Martha, and Mary. She stopped when she got to Mary's name, pressing her fingertips over it and closing her eyes, trying to remember her sister's face.

"Hadley?"

Hadley jerked her head up, falling over onto her backside. Pfeiffer was standing over her with her hands on her hips. "You scared the life out of me," Hadley said, struggling to stand up.

"What are you doing down there?"

"Nothing," Hadley said. "I was just getting ready to call Mark."

"Has he called at all since you got here yesterday?" Pfeiffer asked.

Hadley narrowed her eyes at Pfeiffer. "He doesn't need to call," she replied. "He knows where I am."

"I figured he would at least call to make sure you were safe," Pfeiffer continued.

Hadley pulled her phone out of her pocket, somewhat disappointed to see that she actually had service. "So," she said, "what did your boss at the publisher say when you told her you'd need another few days?"

"She said it was fine," Pfeiffer replied, her tone breezy.

"Really?" Hadley asked. "Because the last time I asked you to take a few days off for a vacation in Vermont last year, you told me that you simply couldn't."

"If you'd been dead," Pfeiffer replied, "I'm sure she wouldn't have minded."

Hadley opened her mouth to reply, but Martha's voice wafted out from the kitchen. "Pfeiffer," she called. "Come here!"

Hadley watched her sister go back inside, and then she walked toward the end of the porch and dialed Mark. The call went to voice mail, and she tried again, and then again. Finally, she pulled the phone away from her ear and stared at it. Frustrated, she typed in a text message.

Need to stay in CR for a few days.

Almost immediately Mark responded with a thumbs-up emoji, and Hadley had to resist the urge to throw her phone across the porch. He'd obviously seen her missed calls and chosen not to answer. He couldn't even muster the energy to text her back a single word. She wondered where he was and whom he was with, but she didn't want to think too hard about it. The years of her marriage to Mark had taught her that much, at least. Their marriage was always more of a business contract than a holy union, and that meant that Hadley was on a need-to-know basis. And most of the time Mark thought she didn't need to know.

"Hadley?" Martha appeared on the porch, her brow furrowed.

Hadley shoved her phone into her pocket and forced a smile. "Hey," she said.

"Everything okay?"

"Everything's fine."

"Still no word from Mark?"

"I just got a text," Hadley replied. She felt her smile falter. "He's okay with me staying a few extra days."

"Pfeiffer just got off the phone with that lawyer. We'll go in tomorrow morning to discuss the estate," Martha said. "Did you know the landline still works?"

"No," Hadley replied absently, still thinking about the stupid thumbs-up emoji she'd gotten from Mark. "You think the number's still the same?"

Martha shrugged. "Why do you think Aunt Bea kept a phone that she never used?"

"I have no idea."

"Are you sure everything is okay?" Martha asked. "You seem . . . preoccupied."

For a moment, Hadley considered telling her sister the truth. But even if she wanted to tell her, she didn't know what she'd say. Instead, she said, "I'm fine. I'm just trying to wrap my head around the fact that all of this is ours."

"What are we going to do with it?"

"We could sell it. I figure that's what we'll have to do," Hadley replied.

Martha was quiet for a moment and then said, "Aunt Bea wouldn't want us to do that, you know?"

"I know," Hadley said. "But Aunt Bea had to know that we wouldn't want to live here. Hell, she didn't even want us to come back for a visit."

"We could fix it up and rent it out," Martha offered. "I know the place needs some work, but surely we could do enough to make it more livable. And we could ask Brody to help."

"No," Hadley replied with more force than she intended.

"No, what?" Pfeiffer asked, stepping out onto the porch with her sisters.

Hadley shot Martha a look before she said, "We were just talking about what to do with the house."

"I guess we could sell it," Pfeiffer replied, echoing Hadley.

"It's been in the family for more than a hundred years," Martha said. "If Aunt Bea wanted us to sell it, she wouldn't have left it to us."

"Let's just wait until we meet with Mr. Gibson tomorrow," Hadley replied. "We don't even know what we've got yet."

"I've got heartburn," Pfeiffer said.

"Well, maybe you should stop being so salty," Martha replied, a small grin appearing on her face.

Pfeiffer burst out laughing, and for a moment, Hadley caught a glimpse of how it used to be, when they'd all lived together. When they were the Hemingway sisters with their names carved into a pair of old rocking chairs on the porch.

"Do you two think the kitchen stove works?" Hadley asked,

shoving her phone inside her pocket. "I thought maybe I'd cook us some dinner."

"With what food?" Martha wanted to know. "I don't think anything in the pantry is edible."

"I could run in to the supermarket," Hadley replied.

"It takes nearly half an hour to get into town. You won't be running anywhere," Pfeiffer said. "But I won't argue with you if you want to cook. I'm already hungry again."

"Of course you are," Martha said. "You're always hungry."

"So are you," Pfeiffer replied, looking pointedly at Martha. "Don't pretend like you're not."

Martha rolled her eyes but didn't disagree. "Will you see if they have any veggie burgers?" she asked.

Hadley nodded. "Sure. Can I borrow your car?"

"Let me grab the keys," Martha replied.

Hadley felt her phone vibrate in her pocket, and she pulled it out hopefully, frowning when she saw a text not from Mark, but from a friend she'd been planning a ladies' luncheon with, letting her know they were going to have to change the venue. Before she placed the phone back in her pocket, she scrolled through the call list and saw a New York number she didn't recognize. It must be Henry Brothers, she thought, but she made a mental note to call the number back later just to check.

"What is it?" Pfeiffer asked. "Mark not thrilled about you staying here for a few days?"

"Oh, he doesn't care," Hadley replied before she had time to think about her response.

Pfeiffer raised an eyebrow.

"I mean, he's perfectly capable of taking care of himself," Hadley finished. "As you reminded me so tactfully earlier today."

Just then, Martha emerged from the house with the car keys. "Here you go," she said, handing them to Hadley. "Will you check to see if they have sparkling water?"

"At Joe's Grocery and Go?" Hadley asked, raising her eyebrow.

"You could go somewhere else," Martha replied.

"Joe's is closest."

"The tap water is *brown*," Martha said.

"I'll find you something, I promise," Hadley said.

"As long as it's not brown, I'll be happy," Martha replied. "Otherwise, I'll be forced to drink whiskey."

"Whiskey is brown," Hadley said.

"But water shouldn't be."

Hadley rolled her eyes and turned on her heel to make her way to Martha's car. She had to admit that she was excited to drive the sleek, new Tesla. Her own car, despite the fact that she and Mark had no children, was a BMW station wagon. It was nice, but it was still a station wagon, and most of the time she had a hired driver. She'd wanted to drive herself to Cold River, but Mark insisted she take a plane, and he'd hire someone to pick her up at the airport. She wondered fleetingly if that was because he hadn't wanted her to have the freedom of her own vehicle—to be able to drive anywhere she wanted, especially back to D.C., without notifying him first.

Hadley climbed into the car and started it up, allowing the purr of the engine to drown out any more thoughts of Mark or his ulterior motives. For now, at least, she was in Cold River, she was home, and despite the grim circumstances for which she'd come, she was going to try to enjoy her freedom as long as it lasted.

CHAPTER 11
Hadley

JOE'S GROCERY AND GO SAT RIGHT ON THE EDGE OF TOWN, just off the dirt road from the farm. It had been there ever since Hadley could remember. She didn't even know who Joe was, but she figured he was a long-dead relative of the Beard family, who'd always owned the store, as there was a picture of a bespectacled man with a cigar hanging out of his mouth in the entryway, along with the first dollar the store ever earned.

Hadley was glad that the store was still there. So much of Cold River hadn't changed a lick since the last time she was there, and it was a comfort to her. She knew that Pfeiffer and Martha hated the slow pace when they were younger, but despite her life in D.C., the truth was that Hadley preferred the leisurely atmosphere.

She smiled absently at the vaguely familiar faces she passed in the aisles, looking for hamburger buns, and sparkling water for Martha. She found the buns, but no sparkling water and settled instead for diet ginger ale. As she was trying to decide between

Swiss and American cheese, she heard someone clear their throat behind her. She turned around to see Brody standing there.

"Hello, Hadley," he said, a wide grin on his face.

Too startled to think, she replied, "What are you doing here?"

Brody laughed. "I live here."

"Oh," Hadley replied. "I mean, obviously."

"Obviously."

Hadley stared at him. She couldn't help it. It'd just been so long. There were little creases in the corners of his blue eyes, and his skin was tanner than she remembered, probably from working outside on his farm, but other than that, Martha was right, he did look good, and he looked exactly the same as he had nearly twenty years ago.

"Looks like you're gonna be in town for a few days," Brody said, eyeing her cart and breaking the awkward silence that formed between them.

"You were right about my aunt," Hadley replied. "She left everything to us. My sisters and I will be here, at least until we can figure out what to do."

"What do you mean?" Brody asked.

"Well, we could sell the property as is or pay someone to fix it up and sell it," Hadley replied, rattling off the possibilities she'd already considered. "We could break up the land and sell it separate."

"You're going to sell?"

"We haven't decided," Hadley admitted. "But I don't know what else we'd do with the place."

"But it's your house," Brody said. "You grew up there."

"It hasn't been my house since my mother died," Hadley replied, feeling the heat rise in her cheeks.

"You know what I mean."

Hadley was about to respond that *no,* she *didn't* know what he meant, when a skinny girl with glasses and freckles across the bridge of her nose appeared behind Brody.

"Daaaad," she said, her tone annoyed. "You were supposed to meet me over by the dog food."

Hadley glanced between Brody and the girl. *"Dad?"*

"Hadley, I'd like you to meet my daughter, Lucy," Brody said, placing a hand on the girl's shoulder. "Lucy, this is Mrs. Hadley . . ." He stopped.

"Lawrence," Hadley replied, sticking out her hand to Lucy. "I'm Hadley Lawrence, but I used to be Hadley Hemingway."

"It's nice to meet you, Mrs. Lawrence," Lucy said.

Hadley smiled, impressed. "It's nice to meet you, too, Lucy."

"So did you just move here or something?" Lucy asked.

"No," Hadley said, almost laughing. "I'm just here for a few days."

"Me too," Lucy said.

Hadley gave Brody a questioning look before she said, "Oh?"

"Her mother and I divorced a few years ago," Brody explained. "Melissa moved to Little Rock, and Lucy finds it *much* more appealing in the big city than she does down here."

"My stepdad has a pool," Lucy whispered. "And my dad has . . . well, he has hay. And cows."

"You used to love the cows," Brody replied.

"That was years ago, Dad," Lucy said, rolling her eyes. "I'm not a little kid anymore."

"So you keep reminding me."

Hadley saw the smile playing on Brody's lips, but she also noticed his eyes darkening the way they always did when he was hurt. Without missing a beat, she said, "We have a pool in D.C., but we don't use it much. I think it's kind of a silly luxury."

"Your kids don't like it?" Lucy asked, incredulous.

"I don't have any children," Hadley replied. She could feel Brody's eyes on her, but she couldn't bring herself to meet them. Having children had always been something she and Mark talked about—something Hadley always said she wanted.

"I'm never having kids," Lucy replied, breaking the silence, her arms planted firmly across her chest.

"She has a lot of opinions, this one," Brody drawled, shrugging his shoulders.

"Gee, I wonder where she gets it?" Hadley looked pointedly at Brody.

Lucy tilted her head up at Hadley and regarded her carefully. "You look familiar. Have we met before?"

"I don't think so," Hadley replied. "But my husband is a United States congressman. Maybe you've seen me on television or something standing next to him."

"No, that's not it," Lucy said. "But I know I've seen you before. I swear I have."

Hadley thought about it. "My sister is Martha Hemingway. Maybe you're thinking of her."

"Your sister is Martha Hemingway?" Lucy squealed. "My friends and I all *love her.*" Then, turning to her father, she said, "Daaaad! You didn't tell me you had famous friends!"

Brody shrugged again. "You never asked."

Lucy rolled her eyes again, and Hadley began to wonder if she and her father had the eye-rolling and shoulder-shrugging routine down to an art. "Is she here, too?" Lucy asked hopefully.

"She is," Hadley replied. "I'm sure she'd love to meet you before you go back to Little Rock."

"Really?"

"Of course," Hadley replied.

"See, I told you it wouldn't be so bad these next couple of weeks," Brody said to Lucy.

"No thanks to you," Lucy muttered, but she was smiling.

"Go on and get Ollie some treats," Brody said. "I'll be right there in a sec."

Lucy sighed, but didn't protest. "Will you really tell your sister about me?" she asked Hadley.

"I'll tell her as soon as I get home," Hadley replied. "And I'll get with your dad to work out the details before either one of you leaves."

"Thank you!" Lucy exclaimed, and for a moment, Hadley thought the girl might actually hug her.

"You're welcome."

Lucy turned to walk away and then stopped, whipping her head around so that she could face Hadley once again. "I know where I've seen you," she said.

"Oh, really?" Hadley asked. "Where?"

"My dad's hunting cabin," Lucy replied. "Your picture is on his dresser. But you were *a lot* younger."

"Go on and get those treats," Brody said. "Hurry up, now."

Hadley stared at Brody, wishing she could see her face in a mirror. She didn't know if she looked horrified or pleased, but she figured it was probably something in between. "So you have a—"

"Hunting cabin," Brody finished. "Yep. In Missouri, over by Bakersfield."

Hadley nodded. "Why Missouri?"

Brody shrugged. "Bought it cheap."

"That's the only reason?" Hadley wasn't sure if she was still talking about the cabin, but for whatever reason, she couldn't stop herself.

"Who knows why I do what I do," Brody replied. "But thanks for telling Lucy you'd introduce her to Martha. You just made her entire year."

"Did you really never tell her you knew Martha Hemingway?" Hadley asked.

"Why would I tell her?" Brody asked. "It's not like I thought I'd ever see Martha again . . . or you," he finished.

Hadley slid her gaze back down to her cart, the handle of which she was gripping so tightly that it was beginning to hurt. "I always meant to call you," she said.

"But you never did."

"No," Hadley replied. "I never did."

"You know I had to find out you were married on television?" he asked, his eyes darkening once again. "On television. Like I was some kind of stranger."

Hadley swallowed. Her throat felt thick. "I didn't think you'd want to know."

"Did you think I'd storm in and stop your wedding?" he asked. "That I might pull a Garth Brooks and show up in boots and ruin your black-tie affair?"

Hadley wanted to laugh at Brody's use of "friends in low places" to describe himself, but she could tell he was serious. Besides, it wasn't as if the thought hadn't crossed her mind. The way they'd left things, the two of them, hadn't exactly been friendly. In fact, it had been downright ugly. "Well, what about you?" she said, finally. "You went off and married *Melissa Mitch-ell*, for God's sake."

"How do you know I married Melissa Mitchell?" Brody wanted to know. "I could have married any Melissa."

"Lucy looks just like her," Hadley shot back. "And besides, of course you married her. She always had a thing for you."

"Well, we aren't married anymore."

"I'm sorry," Hadley replied. She tried to regain her compo-sure. She'd always hated the way she just said whatever popped into her head when she was around Brody. "I didn't mean it."

"Yes, you did," Brody said. "I guess I better go help Lucy with the dog food. I'll be in touch about bringing her out to see Martha, okay?"

Hadley nodded. "I'll, uh . . . I'll see you later."

Brody waved at her as he pushed his cart away. Hadley stared after him, unsure what to think. She should have known she couldn't avoid him while she was here—Cold River was far too small for that. Of course, she never really thought she'd be in Cold River again. She felt like she was eighteen and watch-ing him leave her at the airport, the fight they'd had all the way from Cold River to Springfield as fresh in her mind now as it was then. He'd wanted her to stay, and she'd told him she couldn't. He'd wanted to marry her, and she'd told him no. She wondered if the ring he'd tried to give her was the same one he'd given to Melissa. She wondered why he still had her senior photo on his dresser in his hunting cabin.

Hadley shook her head. She didn't want to think about that. She didn't want to think about any of it. She wanted to get the food she'd come for and go back to the farm. Twenty years was a long time, and she hoped that Brody had forgotten their awful fight and everything that led up to it—especially everything that led up to it.

She pushed her cart forward and headed in the opposite direction from Brody, and, not for the first time, wished she, too, could just forget.

CHAPTER 12

Pfeiffer

BY THE TIME MARTHA AND PFEIFFER WERE FINISHED cleaning the kitchen, they were both dirty and sweaty. Martha's hair was covered in so much dirt it looked like she'd been dropped headfirst into a hole, and Pfeiffer had somehow managed to ruin a perfectly good pair of Kate Spade flats.

"I don't know that we've even made a dent," Pfeiffer said, wiping a hand across her forehead. "But I guess now we can eat and cook in here without catching some sort of fatal disease."

"Oh, it's not that bad," Martha replied, pulling out her ponytail and shaking her head. "It's dingy, but not dirty."

"Don't you miss being in your five-thousand-square-foot mansion in Nashville?" Pfeiffer asked. "You know, where the oven wasn't manufactured in 1974?"

Martha laughed, but the amusement didn't quite reach her eyes. "I don't live in a mansion," she said. "And sure, I like the stainless steel and the marble countertops in my house, but it's no fun being in my kitchen alone. I don't even know where all of the pots and pans are. Travis used to do most of the cooking."

"I've always stored makeup in my stove," Pfeiffer replied. "I don't think I've eaten anything in the last decade that hasn't come from a takeout box."

"No point in cooking for one person."

Pfeiffer shrugged. She'd never minded being alone. In fact, until recently, when she'd found herself out of her job, her apartment, and her friends, she'd actually preferred it. "I guess you're right."

"Now, Hadley's kitchen," Martha said, wiping the dirt from her hands onto her jeans. "*That's* a kitchen."

Pfeiffer had to agree. The one time she'd seen Hadley's kitchen, nearly five years ago, she'd wanted to buy a sleeping bag and move into one of the cupboards. It was three times the size of her entire apartment. It wasn't as modern-looking as Martha's, but its French country feel was the perfect place for a glass of wine and gossip.

"I wonder if she ever even uses it," Pfeiffer said. "You know, the last time I was there . . . well, which I guess was the same time you were, I don't think I ever saw Mark. Not even at night."

"Well, he does work a lot," Martha said.

"He's a United States congressman," Pfeiffer scoffed. "He doesn't even work half as many days as we do."

"They've always had a strange relationship," Martha agreed.

"I don't think they even like each other," Pfeiffer continued. "And have you noticed how weird she's being about him right now?"

"Maybe she just doesn't want to talk to you about Mark, because she knows you hate him," Martha said.

"I don't hate him," Pfeiffer replied. "I just think, as I've always thought, that Hadley could do better."

Martha raised a dust-smudged eyebrow. "That may be the nicest thing you've ever said about Hadley."

"Shut up."

"No," Martha said. "It's true. Maybe you should say nice things *to* her sometimes."

"I don't think she'd like it if I told her that her husband wasn't good enough," Pfeiffer replied. "You know how she is. She wants everything to be perfect."

"Brody was perfect," Martha said.

"He was."

The screen door slammed, and Hadley huffed in, her arms full of plastic bags. "I honked the horn," she said, out of breath. "Did you not hear me?"

Pfeiffer and Martha looked at each other. "No," they said in unison.

Hadley plopped the sacks down onto the kitchen table and looked around the room. "Well, at least it's clean in here."

"The stove works," Martha said.

"So does the microwave, miraculously," Pfeiffer added.

"It was probably more dusty than dirty," Hadley said. "I mean, it's pretty clear Aunt Bea didn't come down here much, but I think she tried to keep up."

"This old place got to be too much," Martha agreed.

"She should have sold the place and moved out," Hadley continued. "It would have been better than letting it fall into disrepair."

"I don't understand why she didn't sell it," Pfeiffer said.

"She must have liked it at least a little bit, to stay here even after we all left," Hadley said.

"I guess so," Pfeiffer agreed. Her thoughts strayed back to the journal, and she wondered if she ought to tell her sisters. They had the right to know, yet still, something held her back.

"I still can't believe we're all that's left of the family," Martha said, pulling hamburger buns and ketchup out of the plastic bags. "And seriously, who uses plastic bags anymore?"

"Cold River," Hadley replied. "I didn't think I'd be here long enough to go shopping, so I didn't bring any of my shopping bags with me."

"There's a whole drawer full of plastic bags," Pfeiffer said. She motioned to one of the cabinets behind her. "I guess Aunt Bea thought she'd use them again or something."

"Remember how Mama used to take cloth bags with her when she went shopping?" Martha asked. "Everybody looked at her like she was nuts."

"She was ahead of her time," Hadley agreed.

"I always thought Mama would have done better in a city," Pfeiffer replied. "She never really fit in here."

"Who knows where Mom would live now . . ." Hadley said, turning her back to her sisters and lighting the propane stove. "If she were still alive."

Pfeiffer glanced over at Martha, who was pretending to rummage through the plastic bag drawer. Although Hadley never spoke ill of their mother, sometimes she said things that reminded Pfeiffer of the fight Hadley and their mother had the night their mother and little sister were killed. Hadley never spoke about it, and Pfeiffer and Martha knew better than to ask. The memories of that time were so difficult for all of them, Pfeiffer didn't see any reason to dredge up a long-ago disagreement that probably had more to do with Hadley's short skirts than anything else. That was one subject Pfeiffer would never broach with her sister—there was a difference between irritating Hadley and being flat-out cruel.

"You bought ginger ale?" Martha asked, sorting through the bags.

"It was the closest I could find to what you wanted," Hadley said. "And then I ran into Brody and forgot about it. I'm sorry."

"You saw Brody?" Martha stopped her rummaging. "Who cares about the stupid ginger ale? Tell us all about it!"

Hadley shrugged. "There's not much to tell, really."

"Bullshit," Martha replied.

Hadley turned around to look at Martha, the look on her face frozen between shock and amusement. "Really, we just exchanged pleasantries and then I met his daughter."

"Wait," Pfeiffer said. "He has a *daughter*?"

"Yes," Hadley replied, turning back to the stove. "Her name is Lucy."

"So he's married?" Pfeiffer asked.

"Not anymore," Hadley said.

"Who's Lucy's mom?" Martha asked.

"Melissa Mitchell."

Hadley's back was turned, but Pfeiffer could tell that her sister was gritting her teeth as she said the woman's name. They'd not been friends in school. In fact, if Pfeiffer remembered correctly, Melissa did everything she could to make Brody and Hadley break it off with each other. It had been all Pfeiffer could do not to knock her teeth out during home economics when they'd been made partners during the Valentine's Day bake sale.

"Really?" Martha asked. "Melissa Mitchell?"

"Yes," Hadley replied, her back still turned and her teeth still gritted. "But their daughter seems sweet enough. And she's apparently your biggest fan. She wants to meet you."

"Who does she look like?" Pfeiffer interrupted. "Brody or Melissa?"

"I don't see why that matters," Hadley said. "But I guess she looks like Melissa. She has Brody's eyes, though."

"I'd love to meet her," Martha said, shooting a look at Pfeiffer. "Maybe one day this week, you know, before we leave."

"That's what I told her," Hadley replied. "She seemed really exci . . ." Hadley trailed off at the sound of loud scratching at the screen door.

All three of the sisters' heads swiveled around, listening.

"What was that?" Martha asked.

"I don't know," Hadley replied, holding up her spatula. "It sounds like someone is tearing the door apart."

"Or *something*," Pfeiffer said.

"Maybe it's Old Crow," Martha said, her voice hopeful. "Maybe he's just come by to check on us."

"Why would he be scratching at the door like a maniac?" Pfeiffer replied. "He doesn't have hooks for hands."

Martha's eyes widened, and Pfeiffer knew she was recalling the story their mother used to tell them on camping trips about the man with the hook for the hand who terrorized a couple in their parked car. The story, aptly titled "The Hook," was their favorite, but it also scared them senseless.

"That story isn't true," Pfeiffer said. "It's just an urban legend, Martha."

As the scratching continued, Martha said, "Maybe we better

turn on the news. Just in case there's an escaped murderer on the loose."

"I patched the raccoon door," Pfeiffer said, pointing to the now-boarded-up opening. "At least no hooks are going to be coming through there."

Martha cast a terrified glance at Pfeiffer. "Oh my God. We're all going to die."

Hadley put a finger up to her lips and motioned at them with the spatula to follow her. They tiptoed to the front door and listened for a long moment.

"Do you still hear it?" Martha asked, lingering by the kitchen behind Pfeiffer.

"No," Martha said, releasing a relieved sigh. "Maybe it was just the wind or something."

"Look at us," Pfeiffer scoffed, stepping around Hadley to open the front door. "What would our parents say about us, skulking around here like we're from the city."

"We *are* from the city," Martha protested.

"No, we *live* in the city," Pfeiffer replied. "We aren't *from* the city."

Just then, the scratching started up again, this time more furiously than before, eliciting a scream from Martha. She tumbled back into the kitchen and landed with a hard thump as Pfeiffer jerked open the door.

"Is it a hook?" Martha asked, lying flat on her back.

"There's nobody here," Pfeiffer said, peering out into the darkness from behind the screen door. "Nobody that I can see, anyway."

"Uh, Pfeiffer," Hadley said from behind her. "I think you need to look down."

Pfeiffer did as she was told, and there, on the other side of the now-shredded bottom half of the door, sat a dog. The same dog, she realized, that she'd found sleeping beside the couch earlier that morning.

"I think it wants to come in," Pfeiffer said finally.

"Don't let it in!" Martha shrieked.

"You don't even know what *it* is!" Pfeiffer replied.

"What is it?" Martha pulled herself into a sitting position.

"A dog," Hadley and Pfeiffer said in unison.

"What's the deal with dogs today?" Martha asked.

"It's the same dog," Pfeiffer said.

"How do you know?"

"Come look at it."

Slowly, and with effort, Martha rose to her feet. "Well, I'll be damned," she whispered. "It *is* the same dog."

"And it does look like it wants inside," Hadley said.

"Should I let it in?" Pfeiffer asked.

Hadley shrugged. "Close the door and see what happens."

Pfeiffer closed the door, and sure enough, the scratching started up again. "I think I have to let it in."

"If we want to save the door, we do," Hadley replied.

Pfeiffer opened the door. Without hesitation, the basset hound waddled in, staring up at all three of them as if to say, *Sure took you long enough.*

"What are we going to do with it?" Martha asked, keeping her distance.

"Well, it's just for the night," Hadley said. "And I'm sure if it wants back out, it'll let us know."

"She's not wearing a collar," Pfeiffer said. She crouched down next to the dog. "And now that I'm really looking, she's pretty skinny."

"How do you know it's a girl?" Martha wanted to know.

"Her nipples are practically dragging along the floor."

"All of her is practically dragging along the floor," Hadley replied.

"What is that smell?" Pfeiffer asked, her eyes sliding from the dog to the kitchen. "Hadley, did you leave the stove on?"

"Oh my God!" Hadley dropped the spatula and ran into the kitchen, where the stove was practically on fire. "I forgot about the hamburgers!"

Pfeiffer hurried after her, grabbed a wet cloth from the sink, and threw it over the flames, as Hadley removed the cast-iron skillet from the stove. The dog looked on serenely from the living room, as if nothing were amiss.

"Well, there goes dinner," Pfeiffer said, after they'd managed to put out the fire. "I was really looking forward to that burger, too."

"If your dog hadn't interrupted everything," Hadley continued, "we'd be eating by now."

"*My* dog?" Pfeiffer asked. "It's not my dog!"

As if in protest, the dog barked. It was a deep hound's bark, and it startled them. They all three turned to look at her. She sat down on her haunches and stared at them, licking her jowls.

"Well, I guess at least someone here is going to eat," Hadley said, sighing deeply. She scraped the burned hamburger meat onto a plate and set it down in front of the dog.

"How about I make us some tomato sandwiches instead?" Martha offered, her eyes big as saucers watching the dog devour every scrap of the food on the plate.

"No," Hadley replied, stepping over the dog and going to the refrigerator. "I'll start over."

"Will you make me a veggie burger?" Martha called after her sister.

Hadley turned to face Martha and Pfeiffer, then pointing down to where the dog sat, said, "Sure, but not even that dog would eat the first one."

CHAPTER 13
Pfeiffer

THERE WERE FEW THINGS IN LIFE THAT PFEIFFER ENJOYED more than brushing her teeth. She loved smiling into the mirror once her mouth was sparkling clean, and she loved running her tongue against the slick porcelain veneers she'd paid nearly an entire year's salary for just after she'd become an editor.

As a child, she'd had terrible teeth. A fluoride deficiency from their well water caused her teeth to become chalky, breaking off at the slightest pressure. She'd taken a tiny, pink fluoride pill for years, endured surgeries and braces, but even then her teeth never looked right. Now they were her pride and joy, and even after she lost her job and all of her money, she couldn't bring herself to part with her expensive electric toothbrush and the expensive toothbrush heads it required. The one she was using now was getting a bit worn out, and the thought of living without it made her frown at her reflection.

From the hallway, there was a loud knock on the bathroom

door. "What are you doing in there?" Martha demanded, her voice still groggy with sleep. "Finding a cure for cancer?"

"Brushing my teeth," Pfeiffer said, closing the cap on the whitening toothpaste. "I'll be right out."

"You and your teeth," Martha said when Pfeiffer finally opened the door. "You'd think they were solid gold or something."

"Gold would have been cheaper," Pfeiffer quipped.

"They were expensive, huh?" Martha asked, leaning in for a better look.

"You coulda bought three sets of those for what these cost," Pfeiffer said, gesturing to Martha's chest.

"I don't need three sets," Martha replied. "The one I've got has always worked out well enough. Pretty sure they got me my first record deal."

"They might've gotten you through the door," Pfeiffer said. "But it's your voice that got you the deal."

Martha's face lit up. "Thanks, Pfeiffer." She reached out to hug her sister. "That's really nice."

Pfeiffer allowed herself to melt into the hug before pulling away and saying, "It's definitely your turn to brush your teeth."

Martha covered her mouth with her hand. "Oh my God; I'm sorry."

"Don't use my toothbrush!" Pfeiffer called over her shoulder. "I'll know it was you!"

Pfeiffer waited to make sure the bathroom door was closed before she crept back down the hallway to her aunt's bedroom door. She'd been dying to read the journal. It was all she could do to wait until her sisters were occupied. She crossed the threshold, careful not to step where the lamp had been broken in case there were any pieces of glass still lodged in the floor. She didn't need tetanus on top of black eyes and bumps and bruises from her fall the day before.

She sat down on the bed and reached underneath the mattress to retrieve the journal. She'd made a small dog-ear on the page where she stopped reading, folding it back up as she began to immerse herself in her aunt's words.

Beatrice
February 1, 1948

It snowed all day today. I sat in the living room and, from the window, I watched it fall. It made me wish that I was six years old again, because Daddy would take me outside to play while Mama cooked. Winter is my favorite season, but I'm afraid if I go outside, I might catch a cold before I have a chance to see Will again.

My birthday party was lovely. Everybody said so. I wore the brooch Will gave me. Mama and Daddy didn't even notice, but all of my friends did. Rufus came by later to give me a present and asked about it. I don't think he believed that it was Anna who gave it to me, but I don't care what he thinks so long as he doesn't say anything to Daddy. Rufus said a brooch like this had been stolen from McCallan's Department Store in town. He acted like he thought Anna stole it! Like she or Will would ever do something so stupid. Just because he gave me penny candy instead of a real present is no reason to be so mean.

I spent some time in the kitchen today with Mama, mostly asking questions that vexed her. Mama is such a good cook, and I've never been able to do anything except cause fires in the kitchen. Mama says if I want to find a husband someday, I need to learn how to cook. Today, she taught me how to make a piecrust. Now my hands and dress are covered in flour, but Mama said the pie tasted nice. I told Daddy I'd made it especially for him, but I saved the last slice for Will.

It was nice to see everyone smiling at the table. There hasn't been much smiling or laughing since Charlie and Maryann lost the baby a few weeks ago. I wasn't supposed to know about it, but I overheard Mama and Daddy talking in the kitchen, and when Mama saw me, she turned about as red as a turnip and took me into her bedroom to tell me about God's will and life being precious.

I didn't tell Mama, but I already know how babies are made. Anna's mama told us all about it one night after she had too much gin and Anna's daddy didn't come home in time for dinner. I didn't say anything at the time, but I filed it away for later. I keep a catalog in my head of interesting information that would make Mama pass out cold.

What I don't understand, not really, is how a baby can be lost. How do you lose a baby once you've got one inside of you? I know that what Mama and Daddy meant was that Charlie and Maryann's baby died, but it doesn't seem like "lost" is the right word.

Lost and dead aren't the same thing. Maryann told me later that the doctors say she might never have a baby, and that makes me feel terrible for her and Charlie. Next week Maryann is going to see some special doctor in St. Louis, but nobody is supposed to know about it. Mama says these kinds of things stay in the family, just like when Anna's cousin Louise Parker got pregnant last summer and her mama sent her away to stay with relatives until the baby came. When she came home, she said she'd gone up there to rest, but Anna told me later that she had a baby and that the baby lives with another family in Illinois. It's too bad Maryann and Charlie couldn't have Louise's baby. Of course, Mama says Louise isn't the kind of girl Anna and I should be talking to, so I guess she wouldn't like it if we ended up with her baby.

It's time to turn off my light so Mama and Daddy will think I'm asleep long before I go out to meet Will. He says he's got a surprise for me. Anna says to be careful, but I know what I'm doing. I'm seventeen, after all, a whole six months older than her. Just so long as Rufus isn't snooping around like he does sometimes, nobody will ever know. I'll just have to tell Mama I ate the last slice of pie in the morning and remember to wash the plate and put it back before she comes downstairs. I might not get any sleep tonight, but it will be well worth it to see Will. Maybe Mama will be right, and the pie will make him see that I could be a good wife. I imagine what it's like to

be married to him all the time, but I don't dare say a
word. He says he will take me to the East Coast one
day, and I believe him. Being in love is the best feeling
in the world.

Pfeiffer returned the journal to its hiding place. She wished she could stay upstairs all day and read it, but she knew that her sisters would come looking for her if she stayed too long. She couldn't help but think that her aunt's words would make a great book, and she wished, not for the first time, she still had her job at Henry Brothers. Slowly, so as not to disturb her sister in the bathroom, she made her way down the stairs and into the kitchen, where she was pleased to find that Hadley had thought to buy coffee the night before. Pfeiffer needed coffee like she'd never needed it before because the couch was proving to be a lumpy substitute for a bed. But she knew that if she slept upstairs in her old room with Hadley, she'd end up sharing a twin bed with Martha before the night was over, and her sister kicked like a mule. Pfeiffer preferred lumps to mules.

As she busied herself finding a coffee mug that wasn't cracked or dusty, a sharp knock came at the side door in the kitchen. Pfeiffer glanced around the room. Who would be knocking on their door so early? Old Crow was the only one who ever used the side door—at least, he always had been—and he had a tendency to come inside without so much as an invitation. Often, one of the sisters would find him sitting at the kitchen table when they came out of their bedrooms yawning and still in their nightgowns.

At least this morning she was dressed.

Pfeiffer opened the door a crack, surprised to find that it

wasn't Old Crow at all, but a spindly woman she'd never seen before with wisps of gray hair and a nose like a beak. Without waiting to be spoken to, the woman said, "You seen a dog around these parts?"

"A what?" Pfeiffer asked.

The woman squinted at her. "A dog, girl, a dog. I lost one a mine, been about two nights ago."

Pfeiffer's eyes widened. The dog! She hadn't even thought about it that morning. It had been, once again, sleeping beside the couch. As far as she knew, that's still where it was.

"She's one a them basset hounds," the woman continued. "She's a tricolor. Got them long ears. Practically drags the ground with 'em."

"Actually—"

"And she ain't got a lick a sense," the woman continued, interrupting Pfeiffer. "Follows her damn nose everywhere. Chews outta her pen. Keeps gettin' out and havin' a bunch a babies with one a our other dogs."

"Well—"

"Somebody down the way said they seen her up this direction."

Pfeiffer wondered if the woman was ever going to let her finish a sentence. "She was here yesterday," she said, letting her words run all together so that she could get them out. "She showed up again last night, scratching at the door until we let her inside."

The woman stepped back from the door. "You belong to Bea James?"

Pfeiffer frowned. "She was my aunt."

"We moved here about ten years ago from down south," the woman replied. "Took over my mother-in-law's farm down the road. Past that boy Brody's place. Bea told me 'bout her nieces. Didn't get to go to the funeral. Too much work ta do on the farm."

"I'm sure my aunt would have understood," Pfeiffer replied, one eye trained on the pie safe. "So do you want your dog?"

"Had her down for coffee a few times," the woman continued on, as if she'd never heard Pfeiffer. "Never invited me here, though." She stepped forward again, sticking her head inside the kitchen. "Now I can see why."

"Do you want your dog?" Pfeiffer asked again. "She's in the living room asleep."

"I reckon." The woman sighed. "I figure I'll give her to my brother-in-law. I was gonna shoot her, but she ain't worth the bullet."

Pfeiffer took a step back from the door and from the woman. "You were going to shoot her?"

"That's what I was tryin' ta do when she run off," the woman said.

"No wonder she ran away," Pfeiffer replied, unable to hide the disgust from her voice.

The woman made a move to come inside, but Pfeiffer blocked her with her foot. "No."

"What?"

"No," Pfeiffer repeated.

"If you've got my dog, you best let me inside," the woman replied, her upper lip curling into a menacing smile. "She's my property."

As Pfeiffer was trying to think up a legitimate excuse for keeping the old woman's dog, Hadley stepped up behind her.

"What's going on here?" Hadley wanted to know.

"This woman wants her dog back," Pfeiffer replied. "But she can't have her."

"Why not?"

"She tried to shoot her!" Pfeiffer exclaimed, pushing back on the door as the woman tried once again to come inside.

"You best deal with me," the woman said. "Or I'll come back with my shotgun. Ain't nobody have the right to keep my property."

Hadley stepped away from Pfeiffer and walked to the kitchen table, riffling through her purse. Slowly, she counted out two hundred dollars in twenty-dollar bills. "Here," she said, shoving the money at the woman. "Now she's my dog."

The woman clutched at the fistful of money, her expression caught between anger and amazement. "She ain't worth this much."

"Just take it," Hadley said.

The woman shoved the money into her pocket and took a step back. "Yer aunt had a head full a stump water," she said. "I reckon you two come by it honest."

"Well, I reckon you're not the only one who knows how to aim a shotgun," Hadley replied. Her voice was calm, but there was an edge to it, nonetheless. "Don't make me prove it."

Hadley and Pfeiffer watched the woman stalk away, and then Pfeiffer turned in amazement to look at her sister. In that moment, Hadley looked more like their mother than she ever had before, and Pfeiffer felt herself longing to reach out and hug her.

"Why'd you do that?" she asked.

"You said she was going to shoot the dog," Hadley replied with a shrug. "I figured money would be the only way we'd ever get her to go away."

"That's what Mama would have done," Pfeiffer replied.

"Mama never *had* any money."

"You know what I mean," Pfeiffer replied. And then, wrestling with the words for a moment, she said, "Thank you."

Hadley turned and smiled at her. "You're welcome."

"I'll pay you back."

"No, you won't."

Pfeiffer resisted the urge to argue, but she knew that her sister was right. She wasn't sure if it meant that Hadley knew more than she was saying about Pfeiffer's current state of affairs or if it was because she knew just how terrible Pfeiffer was with money. She decided it didn't matter. Hadley had done something nice for her, and she was going to be grateful.

"I guess we'll need to stop and get some dog food on the way home," Pfeiffer said after a few moments.

"We need to get going," Hadley replied. "We're going to be late for our appointment with Luke Gibson."

Pfeiffer nodded. "Okay," she said. "I'll go get Martha."

THE GIBSON LAW Office was located in downtown Cold River, in a loft above one of the old Laundromats and just across the street from Mama's bar. Pfeiffer nudged Martha as they walked inside the entryway and pointed to the bar. "I can't believe that place is still open."

Martha giggled. "Yeah, it was a dump twenty years ago."

"When were you two ever even in there?" Hadley asked, holding the door to the office open for them.

"You missed a lot when you left us for college," Martha replied.

"I didn't leave *you*," Hadley said. "I left Cold River."

"We were here, too," Martha said. "Remember?"

Mama's, with its dark lighting and bartenders who didn't ask questions, was the perfect antidote to the boredom of life in Cold River. Even then, Martha could drink most men under the table. It was, Pfeiffer supposed, where her sister learned to drink, and drink hard.

"Come on," Hadley prodded. "We're already five minutes late."

Pfeiffer tore her eyes away from the bar and followed her sisters up the staircase. When they got to the door, they were greeted with gleaming oak floors and an austere-looking receptionist sitting behind a large desk. She gave the sisters a once-over before saying in a grainy voice, "You're late."

"Five minutes," Pfeiffer replied.

"Time is money," the receptionist said.

"You can send the bill to our aunt," Pfeiffer shot back.

The woman raised her eyebrows and was about to respond when Luke Gibson emerged from the room behind her and said, "It's nice to see you again." He shook their hands. "Sorry about Lorain," he whispered to them. "She's family."

"Well, we *are* late," Hadley said, giving him an apologetic smile.

"It's not a problem," Luke replied. "I don't have any other appointments today. Please, have a seat."

There were three chairs set neatly beside each other in front of his desk. He sat down and opened a manila folder, licking his thumb to leaf through the pages.

"Did Aunt Beatrice really leave it all to us?" Martha asked, sitting down.

Luke nodded. "What she had left, which isn't much, is yours," he said. "There isn't any money to speak of, with the exception of a few stocks and bonds. But the house and its acreage are to be split evenly between the three of you."

"Did she say why?" Pfeiffer wanted to know.

"No," Luke replied, looking up at them. "But you *are* her only family, and as I'm sure you're aware, your aunt wasn't in the habit of explaining her decisions."

"What if we don't want it?" Hadley asked.

Pfeiffer and Martha turned to look at their sister.

"Well," Luke said, clearing his throat, "you don't have to take it. The estate and its entails would go into probate. We'd of course have to try to find other living relatives."

"There aren't any," Pfeiffer said.

"You don't have to decide anything right now," Luke assured them. "This meeting is purely informational. I simply want to make you aware of the will as it stands."

Pfeiffer looked over at Luke. "Could you give us a minute?" she asked.

Luke smiled warmly. "Of course. I'll just wait outside."

Hadley sank back in her chair and folded her arms across her chest. "It's going to take at least a month to get the place cleaned up," she said. "Whether we sell it or not."

"Let's give it two weeks to see what can be done. We should at least try. And if it doesn't work out, then we can make the decision to sell it. The three of us, together," Pfeiffer said.

"I agree with Pfeiffer," Martha said. "Let's think about it for a couple of weeks. There is no reason to make a decision right now."

"Fine," Hadley replied, her jaw still clenched, clearly unhappy about the discussion. "But I have to be back in D.C. by the beginning of September. Fall is very busy for us."

"It's a deal," Pfeiffer replied, resisting the urge to roll her eyes at her sister.

Martha got up and called Luke inside so that they could tell him about their decision.

"We haven't decided anything," Hadley said, "but we do want to take some time to think about it before we make a decision."

Luke smiled. He had a warm smile that reached all the way up to his eyes, and Pfeiffer found herself smiling back at him. "We'll be in touch," she said, standing up.

"I'm looking forward to it," Luke replied. He put his hand flush against Pfeiffer's back as he walked them out of the office. If any man had touched her back like that when she lived in the city, she would have turned around and used a few of the moves she and Seth had learned in self-defense class. But there was something about Luke's touch that sent shivers down her spine—in a good way.

"We appreciate your time, Mr. Gibson," Hadley said.

As the sisters exited, Luke said, "Pfeiffer?"

"Yeah?"

"I know I told you that your aunt never said or did anything to imply to me the reasons why she decided to leave you her farm," he said. "I can only guess that her reasoning was that you're her only living relatives."

"I know," Pfeiffer replied. "And it makes sense. There really isn't any reason for us to be confused about it."

"But she did write something that I thought was interesting," he continued.

"What was it?" Pfeiffer asked. She took a moment to study him. He wasn't tall; in fact, she could almost meet his eyes without lifting her own. And his eyes were, she noticed, a deep blue rimmed with thick, dark lashes.

Luke took a step back from her and withdrew his hand when he realized she was watching him, a hint of pink rising to his cheeks. "When we drew up the will," he said, "she wrote that it was absolutely imperative that at least one of you three kept the farm. She said it *had* to stay in the family."

Pfeiffer's eyebrows furrowed. "That's strange."

Luke shrugged. "I didn't think much about it at the time. Lots of older people say things like that when they're writing up their wills. Many of them have guilt about even the smallest things."

"But she didn't explain? Not at all?"

"I didn't ask," Luke replied. "I don't make it a habit to ask unless I have to know for legal purposes."

"Are you ready?" Martha asked, doubling back through the doorway. "Hadley is already down at the car."

"Yeah," Pfeiffer replied, adjusting her purse on her shoulder. "Thanks, Mr. Gibson."

"Please," he replied. "Call me Luke."

"Okay," Pfeiffer replied. "Thanks, Luke."

Martha ushered her outside and toward the car. Finally, she said, "He's cute, Pfeiffer."

"He's our lawyer, Martha."

Martha sighed. "He's also a man."

"I realize that," Pfeiffer replied.

"What did he say to you?" Martha asked. "After Hadley and I walked out."

"Nothing," Pfeiffer said quickly, not sure why she didn't want to tell her sister what Luke had said. "He just wanted to tell me he was glad we weren't going to give up on the farm."

"Well, that makes three of us," Martha replied. "Hadley is pissed."

"Hadley's always pissed."

"I don't know," Martha admitted. "It seems different this time."

"She's just anxious to get back to Mark," Pfeiffer said. "It's hard to keep tabs on him from Cold River."

"I guess so."

"What about you?" Pfeiffer asked.

"I don't have anyone to keep tabs on," Martha replied. "Not anymore."

Pfeiffer linked her arm through Martha's. "You can keep tabs on me," she said.

"You aren't any fun," Martha replied. "You don't even know when there's a good-looking man standing in front of you."

"That's not true," Pfeiffer said. "I know very well when a good-looking man is standing in front of me, but I'm not going to throw myself at him."

In front of them, Hadley rolled down the passenger's-side window of the Tesla. "Are you guys coming or not?"

Pfeiffer sighed and got into the backseat of the car, wondering what wrong her aunt could have wanted to right and why Luke Gibson's eyes had to be so goddamn blue.

CHAPTER 14
Martha

MARTHA DROVE DOWN THE NARROW ROAD, LISTENING TO her sisters bicker about the farm. They'd argue about anything, even the grass being green. Hadley would tell Pfeiffer that it was green, and that all she had to do was look at it in order to see that. Pfeiffer would tell her that the beauty of language was that it was possible to get a group of people to say that the grass was blue, and if enough people started saying that, then it would change the meaning of the words "blue" and "green." Hadley would roll her eyes and say that the stupid grass was green. Making up possibilities for changing a word in her head didn't make the grass any less green.

And the grass was, at least for now, green. Martha missed the rolling hills and gravel roads that had been so familiar to her growing up—the roads and hills and sky about which she'd written her first album. There wasn't anything she'd done in the years since that compared to that first album, and she feared she'd spent all of her talent writing those twelve songs. Everything that came after was the product of cowriting with her ex-husband, with the exception of the songs she'd written in rehab, and she worried that nobody would be interested in a song with just her name in the credits.

When she first met Travis, she'd been eighteen years old. He'd been one of the celebrity judges on *Nashville Talent*, a contest in which unknown singers and songwriters could get their first shot at fame. She hadn't survived past the second round, and thus never made it onto television, but Travis made sure to get her phone number before she was booted off of the program. He'd called her about a week later, and the rest was history. He'd helped her find an agent and a record deal, and in exchange, he'd gotten writing credit on the album, even though Martha had written all of the songs herself. From then on, they were a duo. Nothing she'd tried to do since the divorce had been a success, and now there were whispers around Nashville that she never wrote any of her own songs. Travis, for his part, didn't seem to be doing much to quash the gossip. She'd been nobody before him, and she was beginning to feel like she was becoming nobody after him, too.

"Do we want to stop somewhere for lunch?" Martha asked. "I'm not sure what we'll fix if we don't."

"We all need to make a trip to the grocery story if we're going to stay," Hadley replied.

"I'm starving," Pfeiffer said. "Let's go ahead and stop at a restaurant. We can go to the grocery store after."

"Let's go to Cranwell Station," Martha suggested.

Both of her sisters stared back at her in horror. "Why would we go there?" Hadley wanted to know. "That's not a restaurant. It's probably not even still open."

"I heard someone at the funeral mention it—it's reopened. It's a gas station and deli. They said it was pretty good," Martha replied. "It's not that far from the house."

"I'm not eating at a gas station," Hadley said.

Ignoring her, Martha flipped her blinker and turned down the road that led toward the river. "Pfeiffer, I bet they've got pastrami on rye."

"I'm in," Pfeiffer replied without missing a beat. "Come on, Hadley, you can't pretend you're too good for a gas station. You used to eat fried okra from a stand on the side of the road during the summertime until you were fifteen."

"And it gave me food poisoning."

Martha rolled her eyes. "It did not give you food poisoning. Don't try to pretend that you were sick that whole week because of okra. Pfeiffer and I both know you were off drinking Wild Turkey with Brody until all hours of the morning, and that's why you were sick. If anything, you had alcohol poisoning."

"You two don't know anything about it!" Hadley protested.

"We know all about it," Martha continued. "Amanda told me Brody threw up for days and his whole face was green."

With that, Hadley began to laugh. "He never could hold his liquor."

Martha pulled up to a small building whose parking lot was teeming with cars. "This can't be it," she said. "There's nowhere to park."

"It has to be it," Pfeiffer replied, swiveling around in the backseat. "Look, there's the bait shop across the road."

"The food must be good," Hadley replied, looking not a little relieved. "It doesn't look like a gas station at all."

In fact, Cranwell Station didn't look anything like a gas station.

It was set up more like a 1950s-style diner, complete with a neon sign out front. People streamed in and out—some of them in bathing suits and flip-flops, and some of them dressed in work clothes and on their lunch breaks. It was an interesting mix of people, and Martha couldn't help but smile. Only in Cold River.

"It smells delicious," Pfeiffer said. "I can't believe we didn't smell it all the way out at the farm."

"Welcome!" said a woman standing at the door as the sisters entered. She had bright blue eyes and blond curls. She was smiling from ear to ear. "Give us just a minute to get a booth cleared out for y'all."

Martha took a moment to look around. The larger part of the building was dedicated to the deli, and there were several booths set up, all around a large glass counter full of meat, behind which stood a tall man with close-cropped dark hair. The other, smaller part looked like a general store, and out past it were several old-time gas pumps.

"My name is Ava Dawn, and I'll be takin' care of ya today," the woman said, motioning for them to sit down at a now-gleaming booth.

Hadley squinted at the woman, cocking her head to the side slightly. "Ava Dawn?"

"That's me."

"Ava Dawn O'Conner?"

"Well, it was."

Hadley broke out in a wide grin. "Ava Dawn, it's me! Hadley Hemingway . . . well, it used to be Hemingway, anyway. Don't you remember me?"

"Oh my good lord!" the woman squealed. "I almost didn't recognize you! Your hair ain't as long as it used to be! Them highlights you've got look nice!" She turned around from the sisters and called, "Caroline! Caroline, come here! Our old babysitter is in the deli!"

"Well, I don't know how I feel about the 'old' part," Hadley muttered.

Another woman emerged from behind the deli counter, pausing briefly to smile over at the man with close-cropped hair. He smiled back and gave her a peck on the cheek before she made her way over to the booth where the sisters sat.

"Caroline!" Hadley exclaimed, standing up. "It's so good to see you."

"You too," Caroline said, her reply muffled by Hadley's hug. "It's been a long time."

"Is this your place?" Hadley wanted to know. "Yours and Ava Dawn's?"

"Oh, shoot no," Ava Dawn replied. "I just fill in here and there when Noah needs me." She pointed to the man behind the counter, and then whispered, "He belongs to Caroline, but this place belongs to him."

Caroline visibly blushed, but gave the women a Cheshire cat–like grin. "We've been open about a year," she said. "I don't think Noah ever imagined the deli would be so popular. We've had to expand twice."

"I can't believe the Cranwells sold this place," Pfeiffer said. "And let you keep the name."

"They didn't sell it, exactly," Caroline said. "Noah *is* a Cranwell."

Hadley, Pfeiffer, and Martha all craned their necks to get a better look at the man behind the counter.

"Well, I'll be damned," Martha said.

"I was real sorry about your aunt," Caroline said. "My dad said it was a beautiful service."

"We sent potato salad to the potluck," Ava Dawn offered. "Noah's special recipe from Jersey."

Martha smiled. She was glad to see Caroline and Ava Dawn all grown up and doing well—Ava Dawn, especially. She'd just been eleven or twelve when Hadley babysat for them, usually together, since the girls were cousins, but she knew enough to remember that Ava Dawn had a rough go of it as a kid. She'd been as rough-and-tumble as they came, and nobody could match her in a fistfight.

"Thank you," Hadley replied. "And I think I had some of that potato salad. It was wonderful."

"It was," Pfeiffer agreed. "I think I ate two platefuls."

"We'll send some home with you," Ava Dawn said.

"How are your folks?" Hadley asked. "I didn't get a chance to speak to your dad at the funeral, Caroline, but I saw him there."

Caroline's smile faltered ever so slightly. "They're good. Mom was diagnosed with Alzheimer's a few years ago, so, you know, there are good days and bad days."

"Oh, I'm sorry," Hadley said. "I hadn't heard."

"Okay, I know you'll probably think I'm a stalker or something," Ava Dawn blurted. "But, Martha, could I get my picture with you? I just want to post it to my Instagram account."

Caroline shot Ava Dawn a quizzical look tinged with, what looked like, relief for changing the subject. "You have an Instagram account?" she asked Ava Dawn.

"Of course," Ava Dawn replied with a snort. "I ain't behind the times like you are with your damn flip phone."

Caroline rolled her eyes. "Well, excuse me."

Martha glanced around the deli. All around her, people were pointing and whispering in her direction. She tried to ignore it. She already knew what they were probably saying. She could both see and feel camera flashes from phones going off around her, and she wished that she'd taken the time to make herself look better.

Realizing that Ava Dawn was staring expectantly down at her, she said, "Scoot over," shoving at Pfeiffer with her elbow. "Let Ava Dawn in here so we can take a picture."

Pfeiffer obliged, looking only slightly annoyed. "And then could we order?" she asked. "I'm starving."

"Oh lord, I'm sorry," Ava Dawn replied. "Let me get you menus."

As soon as Ava Dawn walked away, Pfeiffer whispered, "I can't believe that a Cranwell actually exists outside of Cranwell Corner."

"He's a good-looking Cranwell, too," Martha commented. "Real good-looking."

Pfeiffer rolled her eyes, but didn't contradict her sister. "The last time I saw this place, it was about to fall in," she said. "Remember when Mom took us fishing that one time and Mary about got pulled down by the undertow, and Jep Cranwell saw us and had to pull her out?"

Hadley nodded. "He was quick to tell us we were on his land."

"He was nice enough, though," Pfeiffer replied. "Let us stay as long as we didn't say anything to anybody about it, since Daddy worked at his store before he and Mama got married."

"Daddy always had a way of making people be nice even when they didn't want to be," Martha said.

"So did Mary," Pfeiffer added.

The three sisters looked at each other for a moment, the

happy memory suddenly tainted by the reality that neither their mother nor their sister was there to share it.

Martha looked down at her menu, tears threatening to spill over. It had been a long time since she cried over her mother and sister—onstage, in fact, the night she won her first Country Music Award. She'd been just twenty-two years old, and when she went to thank her family, she realized at the end that she'd left her sister and mother out, and the feeling of loss and guilt was so overwhelming that she practically had to be carried offstage while the music played and they cut to a commercial. Travis was the only one to know the truth about what really happened, and the next day the Nashville papers all reported that Martha had been so overcome with her award that she was moved to tears and a dizzy spell.

"Martha?"

Martha looked up to see both of her sisters staring at her.

"Are you okay?" Hadley asked. "Ava Dawn has asked you twice what you'd like to drink."

"Oh, sorry," Martha replied, doing her best to smile up at Ava Dawn. "I'd like a sweet tea, please, and when you come back, we'll get that picture."

"I know it's hard," Ava Dawn said, putting her hand on Martha's shoulder.

Martha looked up at her, confused. "What?"

"The divorce," Ava Dawn continued. "I know it's hard. I just went through one myself."

Martha looked up at Ava Dawn. "Oh," she said at last. "Yes, thank you."

"I mean, Roy wasn't no Travis Tucker, but it still sucked," Ava

Dawn said, blowing a piece of her blond hair out of her eyes. "It was like all of Cold River knew before the ink was even dry."

"I found out Travis filed for divorce through Twitter," Martha replied.

"That's awful," Ava Dawn replied, her eyes wide, and then she winked. "Is that why you went to rehab?"

Martha took a breath. "No," she said. "I went to rehab because I'm an alcoholic."

"Oh," Ava Dawn replied. "Yeah, my daddy tried that a few times. Never stuck." She gave Martha a smile and headed off to grab their drinks.

"Don't you get tired of that?" Pfeiffer asked. "I can't imagine how I'd react if people I don't even know kept commenting on my personal life."

Martha shrugged. "I guess you get used to it after a while," she said. "Besides, I know Ava Dawn. She's not a stranger. I watched Hadley change her diapers."

"True," Pfeiffer replied. "But still. I think I'd hate that."

"People are going to comment on your personal life whether you're famous or not," Hadley replied. "I have people I don't even know stop me at the grocery store and ask me how I think my husband may vote on a certain bill, and then expect me to stand there and listen to them while they list all the reasons why their ideas are better than everyone else's."

"That's almost worse," Pfeiffer replied.

"How do you answer?" Martha asked.

"I usually tell them we don't talk about politics," Hadley said.

"But that's Mark's whole life!" Pfeiffer exclaimed. "How can you not talk about it?"

"He doesn't like to talk about work when he comes home," Hadley replied.

"So what do you talk about?" Pfeiffer wanted to know.

Hadley was lost for a long moment, contemplating the question. "Other things," she said.

"Like what?" Pfeiffer pressed.

"I don't know," Hadley said, throwing up her hands. "Regular things, I guess."

"Regular things?"

Martha shot Pfeiffer a warning glance. "Leave it alone," she said.

"I just don't understand," Pfeiffer said. "Didn't you and Travis talk about music?"

"Of course," Martha replied. "But music was basically the only thing we had in common."

"At least you had something in common," Hadley muttered.

Martha looked over at her sister from across the booth. "You and Mark don't have anything in common?"

"I don't know," Hadley admitted. "We used to. We used to have a lot in common. At least I thought we did. But I can't remember the last time we talked about anything other than dinner plans or the name of an important diplomat's wife I need to impress."

"Those are important things," Martha said.

"No, they aren't," Hadley replied, her voice rising slightly.

"I'm sorry," Pfeiffer said, her brow creased. "I wasn't trying to upset you."

Hadley straightened in the booth. "You didn't."

Martha shifted uncomfortably. She didn't like it when Hadley was upset. For her entire life, especially since their mother died, Hadley had been the strong sister. Everyone knew that Pfeiffer hid behind her sarcasm and that Martha was more emotional than a grandmother going through menopause. But Hadley never seemed to be affected by anything. And now she looked like she might start crying—*in public.*

"I've got those drinks," Ava Dawn said, appearing in front of them. She set down three tall and frosty glasses on the table.

"Thanks," Hadley said, smiling her brave smile again.

"You all right?" Ava Dawn asked, handing her a straw. "You look like my cousin Donny looked last week when he found out pro wrestlin' was fake."

Pfeiffer laughed. "Is he gonna be all right?"

Ava Dawn shrugged. "I don't know. His wife had to give him some of her Xanax, and I ain't seen him since."

Martha took a long drink of her sweet tea and then turned on her own brave smile for the flash of Ava Dawn's phone.

Chapter 15

Martha

EXHAUSTED, MARTHA PULLED INTO THE DRIVEWAY AT THE farm and put the car into park. Although shopping on a full stomach had probably been a good idea, it hadn't done much except make her wish they'd gone straight home for a nap.

"Well, at least we have food now," Pfeiffer said. "I don't know how long those rotting cabinets will hold it, but at least we have it."

"The cabinets aren't rotting," Martha said.

"No, that's the porch," Hadley replied. "We are going to have to fix those boards before one of us falls through."

"There's a lot around here that needs fixin'." Crowley stood on the porch, one hand holding his tattered baseball cap and the other scratching his oily head. "Been knockin' on the door."

"Didn't you notice the car was gone?" Martha asked.

"Nope." He scuttled down the steps and took the bag from her hands. "Your aunt never had a car. I keep forgettin' there ought to be one here."

"I forgot you drove her everywhere," Pfeiffer said. "Like *Driving Miss Daisy*."

"Ain't no backseat in a truck," Crowley replied. "But purty much."

"Aunt Bea never had a license," Hadley said. "I always wondered why."

"It were the arthritis," Crowley replied. "She wouldn't say it, of course, but that's what it were."

"Aunt Bea had arthritis?" Pfeiffer wanted to know.

Crowley nodded slowly and then looked around, as if he was afraid Beatrice James might jump out of the woods to scare him quiet. "She didn't like to talk about it, but her hands would shake mighty fierce sometimes. Got worse as she got older."

"It can be hereditary," Hadley offered. "I have it in my knees already."

"Mom and Dad never had it," Martha replied.

"That's because they didn't live long enough to get it," Pfeiffer said.

Crowley cleared his throat and started up the steps. "Did y'all know there was a dog inside?"

"You went inside the house?" Pfeiffer wanted to know.

"'Course not," Crowley replied. "I heard it. I thought at first I was goin' crazy."

"I guess it's ours now," Martha said.

"Well, you ought to let it outside," Crowley said.

"I'll let her outside," Pfeiffer replied. "We just kept her inside while we were gone so she wouldn't run off."

"You get some food for her?" Crowley wanted to know.

"We did," Martha replied. "Stopped on the way home."

"Home," Crowley echoed. "So you'll be here awhile?"

"We'll be here for at least a couple of weeks," Hadley replied.

"But we can't stay here forever," Martha finished.

Crowley nodded. "Me an' Brody plan on comin' by tomorrow morning to help ya get this yard cleaned up," he said. "Yer aunt would never let me do too much outside, but yer lawn could use mowin', and we could get some of these twigs out of the way and clear the garden up. Maybe replace a few a them rotten boards in the porch."

"You don't need to do that," Hadley said.

"'Course we do," Crowley replied. "Won't take no time."

"Thanks," Martha replied before Hadley could respond. "We'd really appreciate it."

"Ain't no problem," Crowley said, but his cheeks warmed with pleasure. "It's been a long time since this place looked right. I'm glad yer here to make it nice again."

Martha wasn't sure anything could make the property look nice again or that two weeks would do the trick, but she didn't say it to Old Crow. He was just trying to be nice, and she knew that he probably missed the farm as much as the rest of them did. She wondered if he missed her mother and sister, too. Without taking the time to think about it, she said, "Would you like to come in for dinner?"

"That's real nice of ya, Miss Martha, but I don't want to put ya out none."

"You aren't putting us out at all," Hadley replied. "Come on in, and we'll fix you something to eat. It's the least we can do."

"It's not much," Martha said. "We're just making sandwiches, but my mother always said sandwiches taste better when there's someone else making them for you."

"Your mother was a smart lady," Crowley replied. "A smart, smart lady."

Martha followed everyone into the house and began to put away the groceries. Despite the situation they all found themselves in, she figured that Hadley and Pfeiffer would agree that this day had been a good one. With both of her sisters in the kitchen with her, unpacking groceries and chatting with Old Crow, it was starting to feel a little bit like old times. She pulled two tomatoes out of a bag and put them on the cutting board Pfeiffer found that morning while she was looking for the drying rack for the dishes. Martha couldn't wait to slice them for her tomato sandwich. When she turned around to grab a knife, however, she stopped.

"Uh, Pfeiffer," she said, pointing at one of the chairs that was pulled back from the table. "Why is your dog sitting there like it's waiting to be fed like a human?"

"What?" Pfeiffer closed the refrigerator and turned around. "I don't know. Maybe she's hungry."

"Feed it," Martha replied. "But not at the table."

Pfeiffer sighed. "Where is the dog food?"

Martha handed her a bag of food from the counter and turned back around to slice the tomatoes. Pfeiffer hesitated for a second and then took a slice of cheese with the bag.

"Hey," Martha said. "That's our cheese. Dogs can't eat cheese."

"Sure they can," Crowley said. "Ain't gonna hurt it none."

"Come on," Pfeiffer said to the dog. "Come on outside and have your dinner."

"This old place is feelin' like a home again," Crowley said, watching Pfeiffer awkwardly pour out dog food for the basset hound. "Yer aunt would be glad about it."

"It's going to take a lot of work to make this place comfortable," Hadley said. "Lots and lots of work. And money."

"Your mama never had much money to speak of," Crowley replied. "She always managed to make this place right pretty."

"And she couldn't keep up with it," Hadley replied. "Not with the money she made."

"We did okay," Martha replied. She looked over at Hadley. She didn't know why her sister said that. Nobody in Cold River had much. But her mother always said that having each other meant more than having money, and for a while, at least, Martha believed her. Now she enjoyed having money, but her mother was right in that not having anyone to share it with made having it all the more lonely.

"Doing okay doesn't pay the bills," Hadley said, refusing to meet her sister's gaze.

"When your mama and daddy first got married, this place was a shambles," Crowley replied. "Took them months to get it cleaned up. And to get the plumbin' workin' again. She ever tell you they had to use an outhouse for the first year they lived here?"

"No," Martha and Hadley replied simultaneously.

"It weren't pretty, let me tell ya. Yer daddy had to fix the plumbin' all by himself 'cuz your mama was pregnant with you, Hadley, and couldn't do anything 'cept sit in the house and sweat like a penguin in Arizona."

"We *have* heard about that," Martha said. "She said Hadley made her sweat like crazy, even though it was the middle of the winter when she was born."

"Ain't a one of ya got children?" Crowley asked.

Hadley took a deep breath and got a look on her face like she was counting to ten. Finally, she said, "No, none of us have kids."

"We've all been busy with our lives since leaving Cold River," Martha said, giving Hadley an encouraging smile. "Kids don't always fit into the plan."

"That's what your aunt used to say," Crowley replied.

Martha wanted to reply but stopped herself when she realized that Crowley looked as if he might begin to cry. She knew he and Aunt Bea were about the same age, and she knew they'd gone to school together for a while before Crowley quit to work on his parents' farm. Crowley stuck around Cold River, but he never married or had any children either. Maybe he thought it was a good thing that she and her sisters were childless. It certainly wasn't something she minded much—not having children. But Hadley . . . well, Hadley was different. She'd always wanted children, and now that she was thirty-eight, maybe she felt like it was too late to be hopeful that Mark would finally agree to the one thing she wanted.

"Martha?"

Martha looked around the room, suddenly realizing she'd gotten lost in her own thoughts. "I'm sorry," she said. "What is it?"

"Do you want this pepper jack cheese for your tomato sandwich?" Hadley asked.

Martha shook her head no, but she found her mouth saying, "Yes."

"I won't tell anyone you ate dairy," Hadley replied. "If that's what you're worried about."

"When I gain twelve pounds before going back to Nashville,

the secret will be out," Martha replied, but she took the cheese anyway. Pepper jack was her favorite. "I need the lettuce, too."

Pfeiffer returned, the dog in tow. They all watched as the dog made itself comfortable underneath the pie safe. "I tried to get it to stay outside," Pfeiffer said. "But it started scratching at the door again."

"Don't you think we ought to give it a name?" Martha asked. "That way we can stop referring to it as *it*."

"I agree," Pfeiffer said. "But I can't think of anything good."

Hadley thought for a minute. "What was the name of the basset hound in that Disney cartoon that Mary used to love?" she asked. "What was that show called? *The Aristocats* or something?"

"That was it," Martha said. "We had to watch that movie every morning before we could do anything else."

"Lafayette!" Pfeiffer said triumphantly. "The dog's name was Lafayette."

"That's as good a name as any," Crowley replied.

"It's a boy's name, though," Martha said.

"I like it," Pfeiffer replied. "But if I never have to watch that movie again, it'll be too soon."

"Me too," Hadley replied. "That was back when we had that old television set that sat on the floor. God, that thing was huge. And heavy. When we got that new one, I insisted the old one go in my and Pfeiffer's room. It lasted about a week before the picture turned all green and fuzzy and we had to lug it back down the stairs to throw out."

"We got a flattened box to put on the stairs to slide it back down," Pfeiffer said. "Mary used the box for like a week after that to slide down the stairs until she got her leg on a loose nail and had to get a tetanus shot."

"She didn't even cry. Mom didn't realize it until she found blood on the box an hour later," Martha said. "She hid under the bed so she wouldn't have to go see Dr. O'Conner."

"And then he gave her a lollipop and a sticker after the shot, and he was her new favorite person. She expected a lollipop every time she saw him. Even in the supermarket," Hadley continued.

Crowley was watching them from the table, chewing the fried bologna sandwich Hadley had fixed for him. Martha caught him watching them, and he gave her a sheepish smile and stood up from his chair. "I think I'll take this and get on back to my place," he said. "I gotta get some work finished while there's still a bit a daylight if I'm gonna be here first thing tomorrow mornin'."

"You really don't have to—" Hadley began.

"I want to," Crowley replied, cutting her off. "I want to, and it's what yer mama and aunt would want me ta do."

Hadley nodded.

"I wish they could see this," Crowley continued, pointing his sandwich at the sisters. "All of ya, back here again. It's been lonely these last years."

Martha turned around in order to avoid letting him see a small tear slip down her cheek. She knew what lonely felt like, and for some reason, the thought of the old man she'd known all her life feeling lonely as well made her feel a sadness she couldn't explain. She pulled out a ziplock bag and quietly fixed him a tomato sandwich. "Here," she said. "For the walk home."

Crowley took the sandwich.

"We'll see you tomorrow morning," Hadley said.

Crowley nodded, his mouth full of white bread and bologna. The sisters watched him go as evening settled around the farmhouse, and it was quiet but not empty, the way all houses in the Ozarks are wont to be on lazy August evenings.

CHAPTER 16
Hadley

THE FIRST AND ONLY TIME HADLEY SNUCK OUT OF THE house was the summer before she turned eighteen. Looking back, she wasn't even sure why she'd done it. If she'd told her mother that Brody wanted to take her fishing in their pond at midnight, she probably would have allowed it. Their mother wasn't the kind of mother who set curfews or had silly rules about certain hours of the night being off-limits—unless, of course, it was a school night. But this night wasn't a school night. There was a whole week before Hadley's senior year began, and there was just something about the thought of sneaking out to see her boyfriend that sent excited chills down her spine.

Brody was waiting for her by the gate, fishing pole in hand. In the other hand, he held a coffee can.

"What's that?" Hadley asked.

"Worms," Brody replied, grinning. "I forgot to go by the bait shop before they closed. Just dug these up fresh."

"Gross," Hadley replied, but she was smiling. "I hope you

didn't wake Amanda up. If she tells Martha I snuck out of the house, Martha will tell Mom."

"They were asleep," Brody reassured her. "Besides, you're safe when you're with me." He set down his fishing pole and can of worms and grabbed her around the waist.

Hadley allowed him to kiss her, slow and deep the way he liked, and then she pulled herself away from him. She never got tired of kissing Brody, or looking at him, for that matter. She'd loved him since they were twelve years old, and she didn't expect that to change anytime soon. "Come on," she said. "I can only stay a couple of hours."

Brody took her hand and led her toward the pond. "What are we gonna do with all the fish we catch?"

"We'll be lucky to catch anything," Hadley said. "And watch out for snappers. They've been all over the place this summer."

"Amanda got bit by one last week," Brody said. "Did Martha tell you?"

"No," Hadley replied. "But she's fourteen. She won't talk to anybody unless it's to tell on one of my sisters or to be dramatic over some boy she likes."

"Amanda's the same way," Brody said. "You know, half the time I don't understand women at all."

"Just half the time?"

Brody threw a worm at her, and Hadley had to dodge it to avoid being hit, catching her foot on a root and falling headfirst into the pond. Brody tumbled in after her, laughing and calling her name.

"Are you all right?" he asked. "You can't drown in this pond. It smells like cow shit."

Hadley splashed him, pulling herself out of the tepid water

and heaving herself down on the bank. "Now I'm all wet. And dirty."

"Still look beautiful to me," Brody said, sitting down beside her.

"Can you believe we're about to be seniors in high school?" Hadley asked, handing Brody her hook for him to bait. "It doesn't seem like we're old enough for that."

"I can't wait to be done with school," Brody admitted. "Dad is driving me nuts about applying for the University of Missouri. He wants me to join his old frat and everything."

Hadley looked over at him, his frame silhouetted in the moonlight. "Don't you want to go there?"

Brody shrugged. "I don't know," he replied. "I don't know if I want to go to college, much less be in a fraternity and get a degree in veterinary medicine. I like animals, but I don't want to cut on them for a living."

"What does your dad say about that?"

Again, Brody shrugged. "I haven't told him."

"Brody," Hadley began, "you have to tell him."

"Why?" Brody asked. "It won't make a difference."

"Why not?"

"Because my dad decided I was going to follow in his footsteps before I was even born," he replied. "If I tell him I don't want to be a vet, it'll crush him."

"But if you don't want to be one, you've got to tell him," Hadley said. "Surely he'd rather you be happy than do something you don't want to do."

Brody laughed, but it wasn't a happy laugh. It was strained. "My parents aren't like your mom, Hadley. They don't even believe I can be happy without doing exactly what's been planned out for me by them."

"My mom wants me to go to community college for the first two years," Hadley said. "I don't want to, though. I really want to take a year off and work."

"And what did your mom say about that?"

"She said it might be more difficult to go back to school after taking a year off, but she'd support me if that was my decision," Hadley said.

"See?" Brody said. "She's going to support you no matter what. You're lucky."

"But if my dad were alive, he might have a different opinion," Hadley said. "And I'd give anything to have a dad to disagree with."

Brody put his arms around her. "I know you would," he whispered.

Hadley felt tears pricking at her eyes. And she nestled her head into Brody's chest, breathing in his scent. He smelled like Tide detergent and chewing tobacco. "I miss him," she said.

"Hey," Brody said, straightening up. "You want my dad for a little bit? I'd be happy to share."

Hadley smiled and wiped her eyes with the back of her hand. "I don't think that would work out too well."

"Why don't we just take off?" he asked. "The last day of school, you know? Let's just leave and go somewhere new. Start a new life together."

Hadley stared up at him. "You mean, leave Cold River completely?"

"Why not?"

"I don't know," Hadley replied. "I hadn't thought about it."

"Well, think about it," Brody said. "We can go anywhere. Anywhere you want to go."

"Does this mean . . . ?" Hadley stopped herself, afraid of what she might say.

Brody turned his whole body so that he was facing her and cupped her chin in one of his hands. "Yes," he said. "It means I want to marry you."

Hadley felt all the air leave her lungs, and she thought for a second she might fall right back into the pond. "Really?"

"Really."

"I can't imagine spending my life with anyone else," Hadley managed to say, her tears now flowing freely.

"I've saved up all my money from baling hay at the Johnson farm this summer. I was planning to buy you a ring," Brody said. "But if you can live without the ring for just a while longer, we could use that money after graduation. Maybe we could put a little more back over the next few months."

"I don't care about a ring," she said.

"Listen, we can't tell anyone," Brody continued. "Nobody. Not even your sisters, okay?"

Hadley nodded. "I won't tell."

"I know," he said. And then he kissed her, laying her back onto the soft earth beneath them, until all Hadley could think about was his mouth on hers and the way the stars shone brighter that night in the Ozarks Hills than they ever had anywhere else.

CHAPTER 17
Hadley

H ADLEY STARED OUT THE WINDOW, CUP OF COFFEE IN hand, at Brody and Crowley. It was half-past six in the morning, and they were already at the farm, unloading the lawn mower and Weed Eater and various other tools they'd need to hack through the jungle that was once the Jameses' front lawn.

She wondered about the last time it had been mowed. It looked like the grass had been growing since the summer before. In front of her, Brody instructed Crowley as he backed the lawn mower off the trailer. He was wearing tight-fitting jeans and a T-shirt, his arms tan and muscled beneath it. She felt a little bit like the heroine in one of those cowboy romance books she knew her aunt Bea used to read, lusting after some man working in her yard, but she couldn't help herself. Most of the men she knew now, including her husband, wore suits every day. It might be fitting for Mark, but there was just something about a man in a pair of Wranglers that Hadley couldn't resist.

"Getting an eyeful, are you?" Pfeiffer observed, coming down the stairs to stand beside her. "You know, say what you want, but Brody is still just as good-looking today as he was twenty years ago."

Hadley allowed the steam from her mug to warm her face and then said, "You'll get no argument from me."

"That's a first."

Hadley gave her sister a sideways glance. "I guess I should go out there and see if they need help."

"Do you miss him?" Pfeiffer asked her. Her voice was so low that it was almost a whisper. "I mean, even a little?"

"Yes," Hadley said, surprising herself with her answer. She hadn't meant to say it, but the words just fell out of her mouth. "It was a long time ago, though. I don't even know him anymore."

"I doubt he's changed that much," Pfeiffer replied.

"*I've* changed," Hadley said.

"Everybody changes," Pfeiffer said. "What I meant was that I bet he's basically the same guy you've always known."

Hadley wanted to tell Pfeiffer that there were certain things that could change a person so much that they were never the same afterward. She figured Pfeiffer already knew that, considering they'd been orphaned. Losing both parents and a sister was enough to change anyone. But there were some things, or rather, the knowledge of things, that could whittle a person down so much that they wouldn't even recognize the person staring back at them in the mirror every morning. Instead, she said, "We were kids twenty years ago. We aren't kids anymore."

"Well," Pfeiffer said, turning away from the window and heading into the kitchen, "he wouldn't be outside with a Weed

Eater, sweating with Old Crow, if he didn't still care about you."

Hadley didn't respond. She knew Brody would say yes to anything Crowley asked him. He'd helped work Crowley's farm baling hay when they were teenagers, and the two were close. She wouldn't be surprised if Brody was helping him pay the bills now that Crowley was older and unable to do most of the farmwork himself. That was just the kind of person Brody was. He was even the kind of person who would be nice to her when he saw her after twenty years of silence, but that didn't mean he still cared for her. He'd never admit it out loud, but Hadley knew he was still angry with her. She knew, because she was still angry with herself.

There was a knock at the door, vibrating Hadley out of her thoughts. Crowley was standing there, a small sack in his hands. "I brought this for yer dog," he said. "Just some meat scraps."

"Thanks," Hadley said. "Would you like some coffee? Just made a fresh pot."

"Thank ya," Crowley replied. "But I can't be havin' too much a that or I'll be runnin' back and forth to my outhouse all day long."

While Hadley and Pfeiffer both tried to mask a response that was equal parts disgust and amusement, another voice echoed from the doorway.

"I'll take a cup," Brody said. "If you're offering."

"Okay," Hadley replied. "Do you want cream?"

Brody cocked his head to the side. "Black, please."

Hadley busied herself trying to find just the right cup for Brody so that she wouldn't have to look at him. Pfeiffer had

THE SISTERS HEMINGWAY   163

stepped outside with Crowley, and now there was no buffer between them. "Thanks for coming today," she said, her back still
turned to him. "It's really nice of you."

"It's no problem," Brody replied easily. "Lucy is over at my
parents' house for a couple of days, or I would have brought her,
and we've got everything covered over at the farm."

"How are your parents?" Hadley wanted to know. She truly
did want to know. Despite Brody's difficult relationship with his
father, his mom and dad had always been nice to her. "I didn't
see them at the funeral."

"They were out of town," Brody replied. "They just got back
yesterday. Now that Dad's retired, they travel a lot."

"So they're doing all right?"

Brody nodded. "They're both just fine. Amanda has taken
over the clinic."

"I never pegged Amanda for a veterinarian," Hadley replied.

"Me either," Brody agreed. "But she's great at it, and now my
father finally has a child he can be proud of."

Hadley stopped what she was doing and turned to face him.
"Oh, don't say that," she said. "He's proud of you."

"You and I both know he's not," Brody replied.

"I do not know that."

"You know what he said to me when I told him I wanted to
buy a farm?" Brody asked.

"No," Hadley said. "I don't know what he said, but I'm sure
you're going to tell me."

"He told me he didn't spend all those years and money in
medical school for one of his kids to go back to the dirt," Brody
replied. "What kind of a lousy thing is that to say? Especially

when we both know the only way he even got through vet school was because my grandfather mortgaged the farm to pay for it."

"Well," Hadley said, "your dad is kind of a jerk."

"You're not telling me anything I don't know already," Brody said.

Hadley turned to the window above the sink and watched Crowley work. She couldn't imagine being as old as he was and still working so hard, but she knew there were plenty of men who were the same way. She supposed if her own father had lived long enough, he would still be working the farm. When she turned back around, she caught Brody staring at her. "What?" she asked, bringing her hand up to her face to check for breakfast crumbs. "What is it?"

Brody gave her a shy grin, the kind he'd given her back when they were still children, and said, "Nothin'."

"Do you like being a farmer?" Hadley asked. "Are you glad you didn't go to veterinary school?"

"You know," he said, "for a long time I didn't know what I was going to do with my life. When Melissa and I were first married, I worked at the auto-parts store in town. Worked my way up to manager. But I hated it, and my marriage was a shambles. My dad reminded me every chance he got that I should have done what he told me to do." He set his cup down and his hand brushed against Hadley's. "There are a lot of things in my life I regret," he said. "But being a father and buying that farm are not two of them."

"I'm glad," Hadley managed to say. She moved her hand away from his and picked up her coffee cup.

"Do you like being a congressman's wife?"

"It's the choice I made," she said.

"But are you happy with it?"

Hadley snapped back around to face him. She examined his face to see if he was making fun of her, somehow demeaning her choices, but she saw no mirth. His face was open, his eyes searching. She thought about telling him the truth. She wanted desperately to tell him everything she'd held inside for the last twenty years, but she couldn't find the words. Instead, she said, "Why do you keep a picture of me at your hunting cabin?"

Brody didn't respond at first, but after what seemed like an eternity, he said, "I guess I better get back out there. Old Crow looks like he could use a hand."

Hadley followed him outside and down the steps to where Crowley was struggling with the Weed Eater. She watched as Brody took the equipment from the older man and told him to have a seat on the tailgate of the truck.

"Take a break," Brody said. "We've got plenty of work to do today. No sense in wasting all your energy before lunchtime."

"I 'preciate you pretendin' I got any energy at all," Crowley replied. "Where's that kid of yourn?"

"She's with her grandparents," Brody replied. "Next week they're taking her to Branson to Silver Dollar City and White Water."

"Sounds awful," Crowley said.

"It will be," Brody replied. "She'll come back sunburned with taffy stuck in her hair, and we'll spend the next three days covered in peanut butter and aloe vera."

Brody sounded annoyed, but the smile on his face gave him away, and Hadley felt herself soften to him the way she used to when he appeared gruff, because she knew his secret, the real person he was underneath the suntanned exterior. She wondered if he really enjoyed being a father. He'd always said he wanted children, but as teenagers, neither one of them really knew what it meant to want a child. Now they were both adults with separate lives, and when Brody turned his smile on her, she felt herself ignoring the girl she used to be, instead turning around to go back inside.

From the porch, Hadley could discern a pair of legs, seemingly hanging from the ceiling. As she stepped closer, she saw they were Martha's legs, and Pfeiffer was standing behind them, trying to push them up into the attic.

"What are you *doing*?" Hadley asked. "Why didn't you pull down the ladder?"

"Because it's stuck," Martha grunted from somewhere above Hadley and Pfeiffer. "I'm trying to get it unstuck."

"You're going to break a rib," Hadley cautioned. "Why didn't you get a chair?"

"This seemed easier," Pfeiffer replied, trying to shrug and almost dropping Martha at the same time.

"Easier than getting a chair?"

"I got it!" Martha shouted. "Pull me down."

Pfeiffer let go of Martha's legs, and Martha came crashing down onto the floor, landing in a tangled heap.

"Are you okay?" Hadley asked.

Martha pointed to where the ladder was now hanging. "It worked," she huffed.

"Why are you two trying to get up there, anyway?" Hadley wanted to know.

Martha stood up and dusted herself off. "I want to see if Daddy's guitar is still up there," she said. "And Pfeiffer wanted to see if there was any of Mom's stuff up there, too."

Hadley sighed. "Fine, but let me get a flashlight."

"I saw one underneath the sink in the kitchen," Pfeiffer said. "It still works."

"Okay." Hadley went to the kitchen and grabbed the flashlight.

By the time she returned, her sisters were already in the attic. Begrudgingly, she climbed the rickety stairs, shining the light so that she could make out any errant cobwebs or—shudder—spiders that were lurking in the darkness.

She found her sisters at one corner, huddled by an old guitar case. "Is that it?" she asked.

"I think so," Martha replied. She flipped the case and opened it up, causing dust to surge around them. "I haven't seen it in years."

"Look at all this stuff," Hadley said, shining the light around the room. "It's like years and years' worth of junk."

"It's not all junk," Pfeiffer replied. "And if it is, I bet a lot of it is our junk."

"I didn't take anything but a suitcase when I left," Hadley said. "I wondered what Aunt Bea did with all our stuff."

"I didn't take anything but my wallet," Martha replied. "And the forty dollars I lifted from Aunt Bea."

"I wondered what she did with it all," Hadley said, sitting down in front of a box with her name labeled on it. "I figured she just threw it away."

"Me too," Pfeiffer said. "I took almost everything with me, though."

"I wish I had," Hadley murmured, lifting one of her yearbooks from the box. "But at the time all I wanted to do was get out of here."

"I came home one day, and all of your stuff was gone," Pfeiffer said. "Your side of the room was just . . . empty."

"Really?" Hadley asked.

Pfeiffer nodded. "It was awful."

Hadley motioned for Pfeiffer to sit down next to her. "I'm sorry," she said. "I wasn't thinking about anyone but myself at the time."

"I know," Pfeiffer replied. "And I was mad about it for a long time."

"*You* were mad?" Martha said. She walked over to where they were, wading through a sea of boxes with the guitar still in her hands. "I was completely alone after the two of you left. How do you think that felt?"

"I had to leave," Hadley said. "I couldn't stay here. Not after . . . not after everything that happened."

"It happened to all of us, not just to you," Pfeiffer said.

"I know that."

"Do you?"

"You two don't understand," Hadley replied.

"Why don't you explain it to us?" Pfeiffer asked, her arms now crossed on her chest.

"It's not that I didn't love you," Hadley said. "But I had to get away from everything."

"Including us?" Martha asked, looking more than a little hurt.

Hadley wished they were having another conversation, any conversation except this one. "Including you," she said finally.

"Well, I'm glad you left," Pfeiffer said, attempting to stand up in the cramped attic. "I mean, why not? We'd lost Mama and Mary. Might as well lose you, too, while we were at it."

"That's not fair," Hadley said.

"No," Pfeiffer replied. "It wasn't fair. You left, and you didn't come back. We were lucky to get a phone call from you on our birthdays. I was sixteen years old. Martha was fourteen. It wasn't fair we had to raise ourselves."

"And it was my responsibility to raise you?" Hadley asked. "That became my responsibility when Mama died? Aren't you the one always telling me that I'm *not* Mama?"

"No, you're not Mama," Pfeiffer replied. "Mama didn't leave because she wanted to."

"We all left," Martha broke in. "We all left when we got the chance, didn't we?"

"That's not the point," Pfeiffer said. "Hadley left first."

"Grow up," Hadley replied.

"Oh, don't worry." Pfeiffer smirked. "I did that a long time ago."

Hadley was about to respond when she heard footsteps downstairs. After a few moments of silence, Brody called up to her.

"Hadley?" he yelled. "Hadley, are you up there?"

"We're up here," Pfeiffer answered.

"Y'all need to come down here, quick."

"What is it?" Hadley asked, finally finding her voice. "There's more coffee in the kitchen."

"It's not about coffee," Brody replied.

There was an odd edge to his voice, something akin to panic, that Hadley had never heard before. "Is everything okay?" she asked, getting to her feet.

"No. Get down here," Brody replied. "There's something . . . there's something you need to see."

"Okay," she said. "We're coming."

"I'm taking the guitar with me," Martha said, almost defiantly.

The three women started down, Hadley still carrying her yearbook and Martha with the guitar. Martha motioned for Pfeiffer to grab the case, and she obliged, rolling her eyes only a little bit.

"What is it?" Hadley asked as she inched down the ladder.

Crowley was in the doorway, pacing back and forth and back and forth. His eyes were wild and he was muttering something to himself.

"What is it?" Hadley asked again. "Did Crowley hurt himself? Should we go to the hospital?"

"No," Brody replied. "We found something, and you need to see it."

"Another dog?" Pfeiffer joked, her smile fading when she realized that Brody and Crowley were not smiling.

"Seriously, what *is* it?" Hadley was next to Crowley, attempting to get him to look at her, but he wouldn't. Instead, he was looking out into the yard, where their work had been halted.

Brody motioned for them to follow. "We found . . . it . . . while we were digging up your aunt's old flower bed. We were going to pull out all the weeds, and I was going to ask you to go get new bulbs later at the greenhouse, but then . . ." He trailed off.

Hadley stopped short at the flower bed, where, next to the upturned earth and glinting into the sun, there were two shovels, two wheelbarrows, two cups of coffee, and one yellowed human skull.

CHAPTER 18
Pfeiffer

PFEIFFER STARED AT THE GROUND IN FRONT OF HER, WON-dering if maybe her eyes were playing tricks on her. She *had* needed glasses, but refused to wear them, afraid they would make her look old. Now she hoped that her eyes really were that bad.

"Is that a . . . ?" Pfeiffer trailed off.

"Skull," Martha finished for her.

"We were digging in the garden," Brody said. "I thought it might be nice to clear it out and start over, since all the plants are dead."

"We have to call the police," Hadley said. "How much . . . did you find?"

"We stopped digging after we found the skull," Brody replied. "It was so dirty we thought maybe it was an animal."

"It's not an animal," Pfeiffer said, taking a step back from the overturned earth. "How long has it been here?"

Brody shrugged. "I reckon a long time," he said.

"Jesus Christ," Martha whispered.

"Look," Brody continued, bending down and gingerly picking up the skull with one of Crowley's red handkerchiefs and wiping at it to reveal what looked like a jagged hole just above where the right ear would have been.

"I don't understand," Pfeiffer said. "How could this . . . *skull* have been here all this time without anybody knowing?"

"Somebody had to know," Brody said, placing the skull back down onto the dirt. "It didn't bury itself."

"Do you think someone in our . . . *family* . . . did this?" Hadley asked. "Do you think this is someone *in our family*?"

They all turned their attention to Crowley, who had yet to say anything. He was staring at the skull, his face pale. He looked up at them but said nothing.

"We need to call the police," Hadley repeated.

"They're on their way," Brody said. "I called them before we came inside."

"What did you tell them?" Pfeiffer asked.

"I told them we found something they need to take a look at," Brody replied. "I told them we might have found a body."

"Might have?" Pfeiffer said. "It's pretty clear that we *did*."

"You want to call them back?" Brody asked. "Tell them there's a dead person in your garden? Be my guest."

"It's okay," Hadley said, placing her hand on Brody's arm. "Thank you for calling them."

Brody took a deep breath. "I'm sorry," he replied. "It's just I expected to find weeds and found bones instead."

"We're all in shock," Hadley continued. "It's okay."

From the porch, Lafayette let out a bark and waddled down

the steps, trotting over to where they all stood. She sniffed at Brody's feet before, to their abject horror, she began to sniff at the skull and, in a move that could only be described as shark-like, grabbed it between her teeth.

"Lafayette!" Pfeiffer screamed. "No!"

As Pfeiffer reached for the dog, she took off, running away from them and toward one of the large oak trees in the yard.

"Give that back!" Pfeiffer said, running after her.

The dog stopped at the tree, plopping down to give the skull a good once-over with her tongue. By the time Pfeiffer reached her, she had one of her teeth lodged in the eye socket and was chewing. Pfeiffer dropped to her hands and knees, attempting to wrench the skull out of the dog's mouth, but Lafayette held tight, and then let go for a millisecond before latching back on, as if she and Pfeiffer were playing a game.

In the distance, there was a crunch on the gravel road as two Ozark County sheriff's deputy cars pulled up to the farm. Two men got out of each car and ambled up to where Hadley, Martha, Brody, and Old Crow were huddled. "We're here about a call we received," one of them said. He was wearing sunglasses, so that nobody could see his eyes. His dark hair was slicked over to one side, and Pfeiffer got the distinct feeling that he thought he might be on an episode of *Miami Vice*.

"Nice glasses, Wade," Brody said.

"Thanks, man," Wade replied, adjusting them. "Got 'em on one of the yard sale pages on Facebook. Thought they make me look more official."

The deputy standing next to Wade rolled his eyes. "So, what seems to be the problem?"

Pfeiffer looked up from her position next to the dog and gave the skull one last pull. Lafayette let go, sending her spiraling backward into the dirt. After a few moments, she held the skull up triumphantly and said, "I got it!"

Over by the garden, Hadley and Martha stood with their hands over their mouths while Brody looked as if he were caught between a laugh and a grimace.

"What's going on?" Wade asked.

Pfeiffer stood up and dusted herself off with her free hand. "This," she said, presenting him the skull. "There's a dead guy in our garden."

All four of the deputies turned to stare at her.

"Well, a dead *person*," she corrected herself. "I don't know if it's a guy or not."

"Are you serious?" Another one of the deputies spoke up. "There's a dead body?"

"We stopped digging after we found the skull," Brody replied. "Mr. Crowley and I were digging up the garden, and . . ." He trailed off and pointed to where the skull was resting in the dirt. "We found that."

"Then the dog ran off with it," Pfeiffer replied. "I had to chase her down. I'm sorry."

"Jesus Christ," Wade muttered, taking off his glasses.

Pfeiffer recognized him immediately once the glasses were off. His name was Wade Pierson, and he'd been in her class in high school. He'd pined after Martha for years.

"What do we do now?" she asked.

"We'll have to call in the sheriff," Wade replied. "He's gonna shit when he sees this."

"I'm going to need everyone to take a step back," one of the other deputies said. "This is now an active crime scene, and we need to treat it as such."

Pfeiffer took a step back, and Hadley, Martha, and Brody did the same. On the other side of the garden, Old Crow stood, still staring into the dirt.

"Come on," Brody said to him, motioning for him to follow. "We need to let them do their job."

"It can't be," Crowley muttered. "It can't be."

Pfeiffer looked around to see if the deputies heard what he'd said, but they were busy back at their cars radioing for help. She wanted to ask Old Crow what he was talking about, but Brody got to him first.

"Are you all right?" Brody asked.

Crowley looked up at Brody as if seeing him for the first time all morning. "I should get home," he said.

"Nobody leaves," Wade replied, heading back toward them. "The sheriff and coroner are on their way."

"I need to get home," Crowley repeated.

"Did you hear me?" Wade asked, one hand on his gun as if Old Crow might bolt any second. "Go on up to the house."

"Cool it, Wade," Brody said, putting one hand up. "He heard you. He's an old man. Give him a break."

Wade scowled at Brody, but said nothing, turning around to face the noise of the sirens creeping closer and closer to them.

Pfeiffer watched as four more patrol cars pulled up, and she had to cover her ears to keep the wailing of the sirens out of her head. She backed toward the porch and sat down next to Crowley.

"You'll sit here for a minute?" Brody asked her. "I don't want to leave him, but I think I need to go out there and give some kind of an explanation."

"Sure," Pfeiffer replied.

Crowley was staring out at the garden, seemingly unaware of the commotion around him. "I need to get on home," he said.

"Brody will take you home later," Pfeiffer said as gently as she could. "But you're going to have to stay here for a little while. The deputies are going to have some questions."

"I don't know nothin'."

"Me either."

Crowley looked over at her as if he just realized he wasn't alone. "Of course you don't," he said. "You weren't even here when this happened."

Pfeiffer raised an eyebrow and looked around to see if anyone else was listening. When she was sure they were out of earshot, she said, "Were you?"

Crowley shook his head. "No," he replied. "I weren't."

"Then how do you know when it happened?"

"I just know," he said, pushing on his knees with the palms of his hands to stand up. Without saying another word, he ambled over to where Brody was standing at the edge of the garden talking to three officers with their pens and notepads out, taking notes.

Pfeiffer was about to respond when one of the officers came over, pen and pad in hand. "Mr. Crowley," he said, "I need to ask you a few questions."

Crowley stood up and put his hands in his pockets. "All right."

"Were you with Brody when the skull was discovered?"

Crowley nodded. "I were."

"Where did you find it?"

Crowley pointed over to the garden. "We was diggin' down purty deep. All of a sudden my shovel hit somethin' hard. I figured it were a rock, so I stuck my hands down in the grass to pull that sucker out."

"And it was a skull?"

"It were."

"And what did you do when you found it?"

"I dropped it on the ground," Crowley replied matter-of-factly. "And backed away, because I ain't interested in holdin' no skull in my bare hands."

"Do you have any idea who the skull might belong to?" the officer asked.

Crowley removed his hands from his pockets and crossed his arms over his chest, and Pfeiffer prepared herself for whatever he might say.

"I don't," Crowley said. "This ain't my property, and it ain't my business."

"Okay," the officer replied. "Thank you, Mr. Crowley."

"Mmm-hmm," was all Crowley said.

Pfeiffer stared at Crowley as the officer turned his attention to her. "And where were you when the remains were found?"

"Uh," Pfeiffer began, feeling her mouth go dry. For some reason, law enforcement terrified her. She thought it might have something to do with driving down back roads with too many boys and too much liquor when she was in high school. "I was in the attic with my sisters."

"And you have no idea who that skull in your garden might belong to?"

"It doesn't belong to me," Pfeiffer replied. "I mean, no, I don't know."

"Uh-huh," the officer said. "And what were you and your sisters doing in the attic?"

"We were looking for Martha's guitar," Pfeiffer said. "Well . . . it was our dad's guitar. But Martha got it after he died, and we thought it might still be up there."

The officer's gaze fell on Martha, who was smiling and touching the arm of one of the other officers as she used her other hand to sign his notebook. "Hey," he said, jogging over to where Martha stood. "Can I have your autograph, too?"

"Sure thing," Martha replied, sending a wink Pfeiffer's way.

Pfeiffer rolled her eyes, but was relieved that she was no longer being questioned. She turned her head to say something to Old Crow, only to realize that he was no longer standing beside her. In fact, he wasn't standing beside anyone. He was gone, taking whatever he knew about their garden and its contents with him.

Chapter 19
Pfeiffer

The deputies had come and gone, leaving yellow crime-scene tape around the garden and a promise to return the following day with the medical examiner to exhume whatever remains there might be. Brody stayed until everyone else had gone, also promising to return as soon as the sun was up.

Pfeiffer caught him outside as he was heading to his truck. "Brody," she called. "Hey, wait up."

Brody turned around, his fingers curled around the door handle. "What's up?"

"Oh, you mean besides a dead body in the yard?" Pfeiffer quipped.

"Besides that."

"Would you go check on Old Crow before you go home?"

Brody cocked his head to one side and said, "You gettin' soft, Pfeiffer?"

"No," Pfeiffer replied, setting her jaw in the way she used to do when they were children and he'd teased her. "It's just that he was acting kind of strange, and I want to make sure he's okay. He left in a hurry without asking the officers or telling anyone."

"Well, like you said, there *is* a dead body in your yard," Brody replied. "I don't blame him for wanting to leave. It's creepy as hell."

Pfeiffer bit at the insides of her cheeks. "I think he knows something."

"About the body?"

Pfeiffer nodded. "How did he react when you found it?"

Brody shrugged. "I don't really remember. I was paying more attention to the skull in his hand."

"He was muttering about how I couldn't know anything about it, because I wasn't here when it happened," Pfeiffer said, the words coming out in a rush. "I asked him what he meant, but he wouldn't elaborate. And then when the officer asked him about it, he said he didn't know anything at all."

"Pfeiffer," Brody began, "the man is almost ninety years old. He'd just had the shock of his life in the middle of a heat wave. I doubt anything he said was making much sense."

"I think he knows something."

"I don't think he knows any more than either one of us, but if it'll make you feel better, I'll go over and check on him on my way home," Brody told her.

Pfeiffer sighed. "Okay," she said. "You'll be back tomorrow?"

"I will."

"Do you think they'll be able to figure out who it is?"

"I don't know."

"Thanks," she said, not knowing where the words came from.

"For what?"

"I don't know," Pfeiffer said, shrugging. "Just thank you."

Brody nodded and climbed into his truck. Pfeiffer watched him pull away and felt for a moment a sense of sadness as the tires left behind a trail of dust on the dirt road. Brody made her feel safe. She supposed that he made her sisters feel safe, too, even though she knew that Hadley would never admit it now.

"Did Brody leave?"

Pfeiffer turned to see Hadley standing on the front porch, her arms crossed over her chest. "Yeah," she said. "He'll be back tomorrow morning."

Hadley nodded.

"Are you okay?" Pfeiffer asked.

"I don't know," Hadley replied. "I mean, this wasn't exactly how I expected the day to go, you know?"

"I know," Pfeiffer said. "I figured we'd be done with yard work and would be getting ready for dinner."

"Did the deputies say anything to you that indicated they might know who it is?" Hadley asked.

"No," Pfeiffer replied. "Do you think it's been here . . . for a long time?"

"I think so," Hadley replied. "Unless Aunt Bea killed someone within the last twenty years and buried the body by herself."

"Why would Aunt Bea kill someone?" Martha asked, joining her sisters on the porch.

"She wouldn't," Hadley replied. "Aunt Bea was the quietest, calmest person I knew."

"Maybe nobody killed anyone," Pfeiffer said. "People used to bury relatives on their property all the time. Maybe that's what this is."

"That could be it," Martha said. "But there was a hole in the skull. We all saw it."

"This is going to be all over the news," Hadley said. "Once people in town get wind of it, it's going to spread like wildfire."

Martha gave her sisters a panicked look. "This is all I need right now," she moaned. "Everybody is going to find out. It'll be all over the Internet, too. I need to call my agent."

"I should call Mark," Hadley replied.

Pfeiffer felt herself becoming annoyed with both of her sisters, and it had nothing to do with the fight they'd had earlier that day. "Is that all you care about?" she asked. "What all of this might mean for you two?"

"No," Hadley said quickly. "But it would be stupid of us not to at least attempt to mitigate the damage."

"The damage has been done," Pfeiffer said. "There is a dead body in our front yard."

"I don't want to think about that right now," Hadley said. "Right now all I want to do is take a shower to wash this day off me."

"Me too," Martha replied.

"You go first. I'm going to call Mark."

Pfeiffer watched her sisters go off in opposite directions—Martha to the shower and Hadley outside to use her phone. She knew that they were right about the need to mitigate the damage of the day. If she'd still been employed with Henry Brothers, she would probably have reacted the same way. But there was nobody for her to call—nobody for her to recount her story to, so instead, she went upstairs to find her suitcase so she could change clothes. She was dusty from the attic and dirty from wrestling with the dog.

She couldn't stop thinking about the way Old Crow had acted when the deputies arrived. She didn't care what Brody said; the man knew something—something he was either too scared or too upset to talk about. Pfeiffer thought about the journal and the way her aunt wrote about Old Crow. It was clear that he had had some feelings for Bea and that she didn't reciprocate. Maybe there would be more in the journal than just flowery writing about a boy that Aunt Bea loved. Maybe her aunt and Old Crow had seen something, something they should not have seen, and maybe her aunt had written it down. When she was sure she was alone, she extracted the journal and began to read.

Beatrice
March 11, 1948

The ground is finally beginning to thaw out, and it appears maybe the snow will let up and make way for spring. Daddy says we shouldn't count on it and should prepare for a snow in April, but I hope he's wrong.

At the dinner table last night, he told Mama that he was going to hire Rufus to help out on the farm this summer. He says Rufus could use the money since his daddy can barely keep all of his family fed. He doesn't think their farm or his daddy's health will last another season.

I told Daddy that Will and Rufus didn't get along too well, considering Rufus doesn't like Will, and Daddy said it wouldn't matter come spring, because after he and Charlie get back from St. Louis in a couple of weeks, he's going to send Will packing.

I thought I would burst into tears right there, but

I kept myself together until I got to my room. I made up my mind to go and tell Will Daddy's plan so that maybe he could figure out a way to make himself invaluable to Daddy, but when I got to his house, I found that I couldn't do it.

I started to think that maybe Will might leave before Daddy had a chance to send him away, and then I'd be left here all alone. I couldn't stand that. When Will asked me what was wrong, I told him Mama and I had a fight, because I didn't know what else to say.

We sat on his bed and he held me until I could stop crying. I got his shirt wet with all my silly tears, but he didn't seem to mind. I love the way he smells— like soap and fresh earth. I didn't want to let him go.

Will gave me a glass of water, and then he gave me a kiss. We'd kissed before, but not like this. This kiss was different. It was hungry. I felt like I'd been starving for years, and I could tell he felt it, too.

I thought for a moment about Mama and Daddy. I knew they wouldn't like it if they knew where I was and who I was with. I thought about Anna, and how she'd be mad at me for not talking to her first, and then I thought about Rufus and how mad I was at him for being so darn good and helpful to my daddy. I know it's not his fault, but right then, I didn't care. I blamed him for losing Will, and there was nothing that could have talked me out of what came next.

After it was over, we lay in the bed for a time. I said I'd love him forever, and he said forever was a

*long time, but that he loved me, too. By the time I
got home, it was almost sunup. I was afraid Mama
or Daddy might be awake, but the house was quiet.
I undressed and tried to go to sleep, knowing that
nothing in my life would ever be the same.*

Pfeiffer turned the page, ready to read what came next, only
to find that there were nothing but blank pages. Even more curious, it appeared as if several of the pages in the journal had been
ripped out, jagged tears evident in the binding.

Pfeiffer sat the journal down next to her on the bed, her
brow furrowed. Why would there be pages missing from the
journal? More importantly, what had happened to Will? Had Beatrice's father, her great-great-grandfather, fired him from working the farm? It was obvious Beatrice hadn't gone on to marry
him or have any kind of a relationship with him after she left
Cold River, so there had to be more to the story. She felt de-
flated, like she sometimes felt after a literary agent sent her
what promised to be a wonderful work of fiction only to have it
pulled out from under her by another sneaky editor at another
publishing house.

What happened to those pages?

When she glanced up, she saw Lafayette sitting in the doorway, staring at her. Unable to be mad at her for her earlier behavior, she beckoned for the dog to come inside. "Come on," she
said. "It's okay."

The dog obliged and plopped herself down next to Pfeiffer.
Pfeiffer began to give her head a scratch. As her fingers ran
up under her ears, she felt something bumpy on the inside—
something very bumpy. When she turned the ear over, she

gasped. There were ticks all over. Hundreds of ticks, it looked like, attached to the dog.

"Oh my God," Pfeiffer said aloud.

She scrambled up and knocked on the bathroom door. "Martha?" she called. "Martha, is it okay if I borrow the car?"

"Mmmflorph," came the muffled reply.

"I'm going to take that as a yes," she said, and hurried downstairs.

Hadley was sitting at the kitchen table and looked up when she saw Pfeiffer. "Where are you going in such a hurry?" she asked.

"I'm going to the store," Pfeiffer replied. "Lafayette is covered in ticks."

"What?"

"There are tons of ticks under her ears," Pfeiffer said. "I don't know how I didn't notice them before."

"I'll come with you," Hadley said, standing up.

"I'm okay," Pfeiffer replied.

"I want to go," Hadley said. "I don't know what else to do besides sit here, and it's driving me crazy."

"Fine," Pfeiffer replied. "Leave a note for Martha, though. I don't want her to freak out when she gets downstairs and realizes we're both gone."

Hadley pulled a pen and paper from her purse and scrawled a note. "Do you have the keys?" she asked.

Pfeiffer held them up for her sister to see. "Where do you think we should go?" she asked. "Walmart?"

"I guess," Hadley replied. "It's getting late. I don't know what else is going to be open."

"I haven't been to a Walmart in years," Pfeiffer said, heading out the door. "It's been since college."

"I go to Costco sometimes in D.C.," Hadley replied.

"You don't have a personal assistant to do that for you?" Pfeiffer asked, getting into the car and raising an eyebrow. "I can't believe you do any of your shopping by yourself."

"I'm a congressman's wife, not a Disney princess," Hadley said.

Pfeiffer ignored her sister and tried to ignore the dirt pile that used to be the garden. Instead, she concentrated on maneuvering out of the driveway and down the dirt road. It was a twenty-minute trip into town, and she had no idea what she was supposed to talk about to Hadley for that long without Martha as a buffer.

"So, did you get ahold of Mark?" she asked after minutes of silent driving in the fading daylight.

"No," Hadley replied. "And I was afraid to leave a message. I mean, this isn't the kind of news you can explain over a voice mail."

"You're right," Pfeiffer replied. "It's not really the kind of news you can explain in general."

"This is going to complicate everything," Hadley said, leaning her head against the passenger's-side window.

"Imagine how the dead guy feels."

"I don't want to," Hadley replied. "Do you think the body has been there since . . . since we were kids?"

"I don't know," Pfeiffer said. "Brody seems to think it's been there awhile."

Hadley shuddered. "Did you call anybody in New York?"

"No."

"Don't you think you need to?"

"Why?" Pfeiffer wanted to know. She kept her eyes focused

forward, afraid if she looked at her sister she might tell her everything.

"Surely someone at Henry Brothers should know."

"It doesn't matter," Pfeiffer replied.

"Why not?"

"It just doesn't," Pfeiffer said, feeling herself lose patience. "I don't have a husband or an agent to keep tabs on me. I don't have to tell anybody anything if I don't want to."

"Fine," Hadley replied, raising her hands into the air.

Pfeiffer sighed. "I don't want to fight with you," she said. "I really don't."

"I don't want to fight with you either," Hadley replied. "It just seems like I don't know how to talk to you without fighting."

"That makes two of us."

"We didn't always use to fight like this," Hadley replied. "Did we?"

Pfeiffer shook her head. "No. I mean, you've always tried to boss me around," she said with a sly grin.

Hadley was quiet for a moment before she said, "Do you really hate me for leaving?"

"I don't hate you," Pfeiffer said.

And it was true—she didn't hate Hadley. She'd resented her, she'd been angry with her, she'd been envious of her, but she'd never once hated her. The hardest part about Hadley's leaving was that it made Pfeiffer feel exposed and vulnerable. Always before, she'd had Hadley, despite her constant protests to the contrary, to protect her and her sisters. Pfeiffer hadn't known how to take care of Martha, and it was a failure for which she'd always feel guilt.

"How can this place be so crowded?" Hadley asked as they

pulled into the Walmart parking lot. "Are there even this many people in Cold River?"

"It's probably the only Walmart for miles," Pfeiffer replied. "I bet people come from all over."

"I kind of miss the little Walmart we used to have," Hadley said. "You know, before it was a supercenter."

Pfeiffer pulled into a parking space and put the car into park. "Remember that year Mama got her income tax return and she let us all go to Walmart and pick out whatever we wanted?"

Hadley grinned. "Yeah, because Martha filled her Caboodle with makeup and then didn't understand that Mama had to pay for what was *inside* of the Caboodle."

"I thought Mama was going to have her hide," Pfeiffer replied. "And seriously, what twelve-year-old girl knows more about eyeliner than her teenage sisters?"

"Martha was an early bloomer," Hadley said. "And I guess you and I were late bloomers."

The fluorescent lights of the Walmart beckoned to them as they entered, and Pfeiffer wasn't even sure where to begin. "Where do you think the dog stuff is?" she asked Hadley.

"It's in aisle thirteen," the door greeter replied, stepping up to them. "Over here on the left side of the store."

"Thanks," Pfeiffer said. She pushed a shopping cart down the middle of the store, with Hadley trailing behind her.

"Does it feel like people are staring at us?" Hadley whispered.

"Kind of," Pfeiffer replied. "Maybe it's because they're wondering where Martha is."

"That could be it," Hadley said. "At least here, I don't have to worry about people coming up to me and asking me about how Mark is going to vote," she said.

"It was pretty genius of him to move to Kansas and establish residency," Pfeiffer said. "Now Kansas can hate him instead of Missouri."

"They don't hate him too much," Hadley said. "They keep electing him. We keep a house in Topeka, of course, and we visit a couple of times a year. I never leave the property for that entire week."

"I was always kind of sad that I didn't ever get the opportunity to vote against him," Pfeiffer replied.

Hadley leaned in close to her sister and said, "I've *never* voted for him."

Pfeiffer let out a burst of laughter so loud that even the people who weren't already staring turned to look at them. She grabbed Hadley's hand and pulled her into the dog supply aisle. As they giggled with each other, Pfeiffer put into the cart some dog shampoo that boasted the ability to kill both ticks and fleas.

"Don't you think she probably needs a collar and a bed?" Hadley asked. "And maybe a toy or two?"

Pfeiffer did the math. There was no way she could afford all of that. "I can come back for it later," she said.

"Nonsense," Hadley replied.

"It's just . . ." She trailed off. She really didn't want to tell her sister about her poverty in the middle of Walmart.

Hadley stared at her for a second before she said, "Don't worry about it. It's my treat."

"You don't have to do that," Pfeiffer said. "Really, it's fine."

"I want to," Hadley said. "If it hadn't been for me, you wouldn't have to be buying anything, anyway."

"But you saved that dog," Pfeiffer replied.

"You can pay me back later," Hadley said. "Besides, it's Mark's money. Doesn't that make you feel better?"

Pfeiffer grinned and considered her sister. She was looking at her in a way that said she understood everything. She felt like she might cry. Clearing her throat, she said, "Thank you."

Hadley waved her off. "What about this?" she asked, holding up a pink-and-gray gingham bed. There's a collar that matches!"

"Hadley? Pfeiffer?"

The women looked up from the dog bed to see Luke Gibson beckoning to them from the end of the aisle. He pushed his cart toward them, a wide smile on his face.

"Oh, hi, Luke," Pfeiffer said. "What are you doing here?"

"Same as everybody else," Luke said. "Selling my soul to a giant and greedy corporation. Did you get a dog or something?"

Pfeiffer nodded. "A basset hound."

"I love those dogs," he said. "I have a beagle named George. He's about out of food, and if I let him run out, he will make me pay for it."

"Can you recommend a good bed?" Pfeiffer asked.

Before Luke could answer, Hadley interrupted them. "I think I'm about out of shampoo," she said. "I'll be back." She gave her sister a wink before sauntering off.

Pfeiffer knew good and well that Hadley didn't need shampoo. And if she had needed it, she wouldn't have bought it at Walmart. All of the beauty products currently in the bathroom at the farm came from someone's very expensive salon. Pfeiffer knew, because she'd been using them.

"So how is everything going?" Luke asked. He nodded his approval at the pink-and-gray bed.

Pfeiffer eyed him skeptically. "You've heard, haven't you?"

"Everybody has heard."

"How?" Pfeiffer wanted to know. "It hasn't even been twenty-four hours."

"Apparently half the town heard it over the scanner," Luke replied. "I heard it from my neighbor Mrs. Sutherland. She called me over to listen to it."

Pfeiffer rolled her eyes. "So that was why everybody was staring at us."

Luke nodded. "As your lawyer, I'd advise against speaking about it with anyone, though."

"This is such a mess," Pfeiffer said. Her face crumpled. She'd been holding everything back for so long that she wasn't sure she could continue to do it for another solitary second.

"Hey," Luke said, reaching out and taking her hand. "It's going to be okay."

Pfeiffer allowed herself to be drawn into him, and she rested her cheek against his white button-up shirt. He smelled like Zest soap, and she breathed him in. She knew it was probably weird to be losing it on the shoulder of a man she hardly knew, but in some ways, not knowing him made losing it just a bit easier.

"I'm sorry," she said, composing herself and pulling away from him. "This day has been more than a bit overwhelming."

"It's fine," Luke said, his eyes crinkling around the corners.

"Do you have hysterical women crying on your shoulder all the time?" Pfeiffer asked. "God, I'm such a stereotype right now."

"Having an emotional response to an emotional situation isn't stereotypical," Luke said.

"You don't even know the half of it."

"I'd like to hear about it sometime," he said. "You know, if you'd like to—oh, I don't know, maybe . . ."

He trailed off when Hadley came racing around the corner, charging full speed toward them. "There's . . . a . . . whole . . . aisle . . . of . . . people . . ." she huffed, doubled over. "They keep following me. Asking me questions about Martha and the farm. I can't . . ."

Luke tore his eyes away from Pfeiffer. "You two go on," he said. "I'll hold them off. I'll use some of my fancy lawyer language and scare them."

Pfeiffer smiled up at him gratefully. "Thanks," she said.

"Come on," Hadley said, grabbing at Pfeiffer. "I am not going to answer any more questions about whether Aunt Bea was a secret serial killer."

"What?"

"I'll tell you about it later," Hadley said, looking over her shoulder. "Let's just go."

Pfeiffer followed her sister, pushing the cart as fast as she could toward a checkout line, the entire time wondering if maybe Luke Gibson really was going to ask her out on a date.

CHAPTER 20
Martha

MARTHA SAT ON THE COUCH WITH LAFAYETTE NEXT TO her, wondering what was taking her sisters so damn long. Hadley left a note telling her they were going to get some kind of dog shampoo, but that had been nearly two hours ago. She hated being alone, and being alone at the farm was no different from being alone in her house in Nashville, except there were decidedly no dead bodies in her yard in Nashville.

God, she wished she could have a drink. The conversation she'd had with her agent hadn't exactly been comforting. He'd told her she should come back to Nashville to mitigate the damage. She told him under no circumstances was she leaving her sisters, and even if she could, she doubted very much that the Cold River Sheriff's Department would appreciate her departure.

Besides, she didn't want to leave. Yes, she wanted a drink, but she knew the urge would have been worse back in Nashville. So instead, she busied herself with an old VHS copy of *St. Elmo's Fire* and gave the dog belly rubs.

Martha jumped when she heard the door slam, and she turned around to see Hadley and Pfeiffer, laden with bags, coming inside.

"What took you so long?" she asked.

Her sisters shared a look.

"Everybody knows about the skull," Pfeiffer said, setting the bags down on the floor by the couch. "Hadley was practically mobbed in the shampoo aisle."

"Great," Martha replied. "How long do you think it'll be before it's all online for the world to see?"

"Well, since it happened on the property of a country-music star and a congressman's wife, it's probably already online," Pfeiffer said. "And there was a truck parked at the bottom of the driveway when we pulled in."

"What?" Martha asked. She turned her full attention to her sister. "Like someone was watching us?"

"I don't know," Pfeiffer replied. "But there didn't appear to be anyone inside."

"I bet somebody got stalled on their way to the river, and they pulled in our driveway rather than leave it in the middle of the road," Hadley suggested. "It looked local—it had Missouri plates."

Martha felt herself relax. "Oh, okay."

Pfeiffer picked up one of the bags and took out a handful of bottles. "Where's Lafayette?"

"Right here," Martha replied, pointing down to one of the couch cushions. "She wanted up."

"She's full of ticks," Pfeiffer said. "Help me get her upstairs to the bathroom."

"Ew!" Martha squealed, pushing herself up from the couch. "Gross."

Lafayette must've known what she was in for, because she jumped off the couch and cowered in the corner while Pfeiffer and Martha coaxed her out with a piece of cheese.

"I'll go upstairs and start the bath," Martha said. "Can you get her up the stairs?"

"Hadley will help me," Pfeiffer replied.

Hadley shot Pfeiffer a look that said she was absolutely not helping her, but she gave in when she saw Pfeiffer struggling at the foot of the stairs.

"You take her front end," Hadley said. "I'll take her back end."

Together, taking the steps one at a time, they got the dog upstairs and into the bathtub, which caused Lafayette to let out the most sorrowful excuse for a bark that any of them had ever heard.

"She sounds like we're trying to kill her or something," Martha said, shaking her head. "You suppose she's never had a bath before?"

"I wouldn't doubt it," Pfeiffer replied, taking the tweezers to a colony of dead ticks on Lafayette's ears. "Look at her."

"She's pretty beat up," Martha agreed. "But she's the sweetest thing. How could someone not take care of her?"

"You didn't see her former owner," Hadley replied. "I don't think she's ever taken care of anything in her entire life."

"In my experience, it doesn't matter what you look like," Martha said. "I once toured with this woman back when I was just an opening act. Anyway, she thought I was a glorified dog sitter for her two Pekingese terrors. She let them use the tour bus as a bathroom, she never cleaned up after them, and she actually left one of them in a dressing room in Poughkeepsie!"

"Why even have a dog if you're not going to take care of it?"

Hadley asked, presenting a towel to Pfeiffer so she could dry the now-soaking Lafayette. "It doesn't make any sense to me."

"People don't make sense sometimes," Martha replied.

Lafayette allowed Pfeiffer to dry her for approximately fifteen seconds before she darted out of the room, and the sisters heard her padding down the stairs. Pfeiffer, Martha, and Hadley looked at each other.

"She's going to jump on the couch!" Pfeiffer said, attempting to get up from the floor, and slipping in the soapy mess they'd created.

"I'll get her!" Martha jumped up, and at the same time so did Hadley. They knocked into each other and landed on top of Pfeiffer, and in the end, the only thing louder than Lafayette's barking was the Hemingway sisters' laughing.

CHAPTER 21
Martha

RACHAEL JAMES HEMINGWAY GAVE HER DAUGHTERS NAMES that would make them stand out from a crowd. At least, that's what she always told them. The reality was that she'd named each of her daughters after one of Ernest Hemingway's four wives, and although most people never noticed, boy, did it make an impression when someone did. Martha's and Mary's names were so regular that they hardly thought about the fact that they were forever linked with a brilliant and womanizing writer from the Lost Generation. However, Hadley and Pfeiffer had a much different experience. Martha always thought this was one of the reasons why Pfeiffer was so literary—it was in her name. She had to be.

Martha had been closest to Mary—both in age and sisterly bond. Most of the time Mary knew what Martha was thinking and feeling, sometimes even before Martha herself knew. She'd known about her crush on Brody, even though Martha would have died before mentioning it to anyone. It was embarrassing, having a crush on her oldest sister's boyfriend.

The night Martha followed Hadley and Brody to the river, Mary found her on the stairway, hastily putting on her shoes.

"Where are you going?" Mary asked.

"Nowhere," Martha mumbled. "Just out."

"Why do you have Mama's car keys?"

Martha stood up so that she could look down on Mary as she spoke. She was almost a whole foot taller than her baby sister, having gone through a growth spurt the summer before. "If you tell Mama, you'll regret it."

Mary looked hurt. "Why would I tell her?"

"Because you tell her everything."

"I do not."

"Yes, you do," Martha replied smugly. "That's why you're her favorite."

"Well, I didn't tell her you like Brody," Mary said.

"Everybody likes Brody," Martha replied, trying to ignore the pounding in her chest.

"Yeah, but you *like him* like him," Mary said.

"I do not."

"Yes, you do," Mary replied. "I see you staring at him when you think nobody is watching."

Martha sighed and sat back down on the stairs. "Do you think Hadley knows?"

"No," Mary replied. "Hadley doesn't notice anything but Brody."

"And you won't tell her?"

"I wouldn't," Mary said. "I wouldn't tell her or Mama or Pfeiffer."

Martha smiled, relieved. "Thanks."

"I think Brody is too old for you, anyhow," Mary said, sitting down next to her sister. "He's eighteen."

"That's only four years."

"But when you're eighteen, he'll be twenty-two," Mary said. "That's old."

Martha felt smug knowing that twenty-two wasn't really that old in the grand scheme of things, but she didn't say it to her sister. "I'm gonna be prettier than Hadley one day," she said instead. "Lots of people think I'm older than fourteen, anyway."

"You're already pretty," Mary replied. "You're just a different kind of pretty than Hadley."

Martha knew that Mary was right. She was a different kind of pretty than any of her sisters. Her sisters all had dark hair and eyes, where Martha's hair was lighter, and her eyes were blue. She was tall like Hadley, but that was where the similarities ended. Hadley was tall and slender. Martha was tall, but full of curves from top to bottom, and boys were starting to notice. Sometimes full-grown men noticed, and she could tell it made Pfeiffer jealous, because Pfeiffer was still waiting for a growth spurt, and people often mistook her for younger than Martha, sometimes even younger than Mary.

"I don't want to be different," Martha said.

"You don't have a choice," Mary said. "And besides, you're a good kind of different."

Martha looked over at her sister. Out of all of them, Mary knew the most about being different. She hadn't even spoken until she was almost four years old, and then she began speaking in full sentences and reading on top of that. Her kindergarten teacher suggested skipping her up not one but two grades. Now twelve, Mary felt much more comfortable talking to adults than to children, and it was no secret she'd read more books than all of the Hemingway sisters combined.

"I better go," Martha said. "Don't tell Mama if she wakes up."

"I won't," Mary replied. "And you better not let Hadley and Brody catch you."

"Who says I'm going to find Hadley and Brody?"

"Just don't let them see you," Mary repeated, rolling her eyes and standing up.

Now, nearly twenty years later, Martha wondered what Mary would have to say about the way things turned out. She wondered what life would be like. She knew the speculation was useless, but she couldn't help it. She let her mind wander to the place it usually didn't wander to—the place where she kept twelve-year-old Mary, her very best friend.

She rolled over in bed, the light on the eighties-era alarm clock glowing 6:03 a.m. Light was finally beginning to peek through the yellowed curtains, and Martha forced herself upright, groaning slightly. She'd never been much of a morning person, and sleeping on a decades-old mattress wasn't helping matters any.

Martha crept out of the room and down the stairs, careful to skip the squeaky step, passing Pfeiffer and the dog sleeping at her feet, and wandered into the kitchen to make coffee. She opened the cabinet to grab the coffee can, and her hand brushed against the almost empty bottle of whiskey. Pfeiffer must've put it there for safekeeping, and Martha felt her heart pound at the thought of pouring just a tiny bit into her coffee cup. She didn't see how a little bit could hurt. After the night she'd had, she doubted anyone could blame her.

She removed the bottle from the cabinet and took one of the freshly washed coffee cups from the drying mat on the counter. As she turned around, she noticed her father's guitar leaning against one of the wooden kitchen chairs. She hadn't remembered removing it from its case, let alone leaving it in the kitchen, but she supposed quite a lot had been forgotten after the discovery of the body in the garden. In fact, she hardly remembered anything from the day before Brody called them down from the attic. Maybe one of her sisters put it there for safekeeping, she thought again.

Martha looked carefully at the old guitar. It was her father's 1967 Gibson Flat Top acoustic guitar. It was the guitar on which she'd learned to play, and she took it out of the case and cradled it in her arms as if it were a baby. Forgetting about the coffee and the whiskey, she took the guitar out onto the front porch and sat down on the top step. The guitar needed to be tuned and it needed a good cleaning, but Martha felt a sense of calm and relief the moment her fingers grazed the strings. Her shoulders relaxed and her mind went blank, and all she could see when she closed her eyes were lines of music.

Slowly, as if moved by the hazy hands of summertime, she began to play. For the first time in a long time, Martha wasn't trying to write a song good enough to sell or get airplay. She wasn't thinking of catchy lyrics. She simply let the music guide her and allowed everything else to fade away. So involved in the music was she that she didn't hear Brody's truck roar up the driveway. She didn't hear him park and get out, and she didn't hear him sit down next to her until she felt his hand tap her lightly on the arm, and her eyes popped open, and she jumped back, almost falling off the top porch step.

"How long have you been here?" she asked, straightening herself.

"Long enough to hear you play that beautiful song," Brody replied.

"It's not anything," she replied, surprised to find that she was embarrassed he'd been watching her. "I was just playing around."

"Well, I liked it."

"Thanks." Martha set the guitar over to her left side. "What are you doing here so early?"

"The coroner is coming to exhume the rest of the body today," he said. "If there *is* a rest of the body. They should be here by eight o'clock."

"I know," Martha replied. "But it's barely seven."

"I thought you all might want me to be here," Brody said. "Might make it easier in case there are more questions, since I was the one who found the body."

"You and Old Crow," Martha corrected him.

"I doubt we'll be seeing him today."

"Why not?"

"Pfeiffer asked me to go check on him last night before I left," Brody said. "He was pretty shaken up when I got to his place. He wouldn't let me inside. He wouldn't talk about the skull. I told him to take a shower and go to bed. Everything looks better in the daylight, you know?"

Martha nodded. "Except that crime-scene tape and pile of bones I'm sure they're going to find," she said.

"Except that."

From the corner of her eye, Martha saw movement in Brody's truck. A little blond head poked up and looked around.

"Uh, is there someone else in your truck?" Martha asked.

"My daughter, Lucy," Brody said. "She fell asleep on the way over."

"You brought your daughter to the exhumation of a dead body?"

"She insisted," Brody replied, shrugging. "She wasn't supposed to be home for two more days, but both of my parents got food poisoning from the new Chinese place in town, and Lucy said she wasn't going to miss her chance to meet you, dead body or not."

Martha grinned. "So you can't tell her anything, huh?"

"Not a damn thing."

Martha watched as a pair of sunburned and skinny legs forced open the passenger's door of the truck, and Lucy slid out, followed by a squat English bulldog with an underbite that made him look like a cartoon character.

"Dad!" Lucy yelled, hurrying toward Brody. "I told you to wake me up when we got here."

"I tried," Brody replied. "You kicked me."

Lucy opened her mouth to respond, and then saw Martha sitting next to her father, and clamped it shut, her face turning as red as her legs.

"Hi," Martha said. "I'm Martha. It's nice to meet you, Lucy."

Lucy gave a sidelong glance at her father and whispered, "She knows my name."

Martha tried to hide her grin as she said, "My sister said she met you at the grocery store the other day."

Lucy nodded fervently. "Dad never told me he knew you, but of course I knew you were from here. I know everything about you!"

"I've known him practically my whole life," Martha replied. "In fact," she said, leaning conspiratorially toward Lucy, "I used to have quite a crush on him."

Lucy wrinkled her nose and looked over at her dad. "Ew," she said. "He's old."

"He wasn't always old," Martha replied.

"But you were married to Travis Tucker!" Lucy exclaimed.

"And how old do you think he is?" Martha asked. "He's almost as old as your dad."

Lucy sat down on the step next to her. "Well, you're too pretty for my dad," she said. "And Travis Tucker."

Martha grinned. "I like her," she said to Brody.

"So is that where the body is?" Lucy asked, nodding toward the garden.

"I guess we'll find out today," Martha replied.

"Dad says I have to stay inside when they get here to dig it up," Lucy said. "He thinks it might *traumatize* me."

Martha shot a glance above Lucy's head over at Brody. "Does he?"

"Yup." Lucy rolled her eyes. "But my friend Ava's grandparents own the funeral home, and my stepdad is a cop. So I've seen plenty of dead bodies."

"Your stepdad has never let you near a dead body," Brody replied. "And just because you've seen an open-casket funeral doesn't mean you're a seasoned criminal investigator."

"Ava's grandma lets us watch when she puts the makeup on them," Lucy said. "It's super gross."

"I need to have a talk with Ava's grandma," Brody replied.

Lucy ignored her father and turned her full attention to Martha. "My friends are going to be so jealous when they find out I got to meet you," she said. "Especially if they see my picture with you in a magazine or something."

"Oh, I doubt they'll see you with me in a magazine," Martha

said with a laugh. "Unless, of course, you come to visit me in Nashville, which you're welcome to do anytime."

"Really?" Lucy squeaked.

"Sure," Martha replied.

"Martha," Brody said.

"Don't worry," Martha interrupted. "I won't let her near any dead bodies."

"No," Brody continued. "That's not it."

"What is it?"

"What Lucy said about pictures made me think of something I saw as we were coming up the driveway."

"What did you see?" Martha wanted to know.

"There was a truck parked kind of off to the side," Brody said. "I thought maybe they were just lost—maybe got turned around looking for the river."

Martha shifted uncomfortably on the step. "But you don't think so now?"

"I don't know," Brody replied. "They didn't turn around after we passed them. They were sitting there even as we pulled up to the house. I could see them in the rearview mirror."

"Shit," Martha muttered. She stood up. "Are your keys in your truck?"

"Yeah, why?"

"I'll be right back," Martha said.

"You're not wearing any shoes!"

Martha ignored him, hopping into Brody's truck and starting it up. She drove down the winding driveway to where she knew she would see a truck—the very same truck Hadley and Pfeiffer had seen last night as they were driving back to the farm from

Cold River. She could see the long lenses of their cameras even before she saw their faces.

"Hey!" she called, rolling down her window. "This is private property!"

The men said nothing but continued taking pictures.

"I'm going to call the sheriff," Martha continued. "Get off my property. Now."

"Come on and smile for us, darlin'," one of the men said. He pulled the camera down from his face.

"I'm warning you," she said.

"You look real pretty this mornin'," the other man said.

Martha resisted the urge to jump out of the truck, grab the camera, and bash it over the man's head. Honestly, had they no decency? Following her all the way to Cold River. She knew someone was paying them to be here, and she knew that they'd take hundreds of pictures before anybody could get there to stop them. Now they had pictures of her unwashed hair and bare face, and wearing no bra and one of Travis's old concert T-shirts.

"Hey!" came a voice from behind the truck. "Hey you, get out of here!"

Martha looked in the rearview mirror to see Brody running down the gravel driveway. He stopped when he got to the passenger's side of his truck and slid in next to Martha. "What are you doing?" she asked.

"Giving them one more chance to leave," he said, opening the glove compartment. He pulled out a Ruger LCP pistol.

"Brody . . ." Martha whispered.

"Don't worry," Brody said, loud enough for the men to hear. "I'm not gonna shoot them. Not unless they force me to."

"We're just doin' our job," the man behind the wheel said.

"Your job is to trespass?" Brody asked.

"Our job is to get pictures," the other man replied.

"Get 'em somewhere else."

With a grunt, the man in the driver's seat dropped his camera and began to back the truck down the driveway while the other man continued to snap pictures.

Once they were gone, Martha slumped down in the seat, rubbing her temples with her fingers. "They're going to have pictures of that," she said. "They're going to have pictures of me half-dressed, sitting next to you, while you pointed a gun at them."

"They were breaking the law," Brody said.

"You pointed a gun at them."

"And they left."

"I want to know how they found me," Martha said. "I didn't tell anybody besides my agent that I was coming here. I haven't used social media since the day I left."

"Somebody in town must've tipped them off," Brody said. "I reckon pictures like that will fetch a pretty hefty price."

Martha nodded miserably. "I hope you're ready to be splashed all over the Internet."

"They'll think I'm your new boyfriend," Brody replied, a mischievous smile on his face. "I'll be your mystery man of the week."

"Yeah," Martha said, putting the truck in reverse and backing up the driveway. "It's too damn bad that you're still in love with my sister."

CHAPTER 22

Hadley

HADLEY STOOD BEHIND THE SCREEN DOOR AND WATCHED Martha pull into the driveway in Brody's truck. Even more curious to her was that Martha was in her pajamas and bare feet. Her hair was wild, and she had a look on her face that she usually reserved for watching arguments between Hadley and Pfeiffer.

"What on earth is going on?" Hadley asked, stepping out onto the porch to greet them. "Where are your shoes, Martha?"

"You were being followed last night," Martha said, stomping past Hadley into the house.

"What do you mean?"

"That truck you saw parked down at the bottom of the driveway was there when Brody and Lucy drove through. Those dumb rednecks were being paid by somebody to take pictures of me," Martha replied.

"Lucy?" Hadley turned her attention to Brody. "Where is Lucy?"

"I'm here!" came a small voice from the side of the house. Lucy emerged with her dog in tow, an old garden hose in her hand. "Ollie was thirsty."

Hadley looked down at the dog slobbering and panting next to Lucy. "That's a dog?"

Lucy nodded. "He's an English bulldog."

"More bull than anything else," Brody said. "He had terrible allergies as a puppy, and the family who owned him brought him in to Amanda to be put down. Amanda gave him to us instead."

"Why would you put a dog down for allergies?" Hadley asked.

"His allergy pills cost a hundred a month. He has to eat grain-free food, and he also has to have drops in his eyes every day. And with that short muzzle he's got, he can't be outside for very long in the summer or he gets too hot," Brody explained. "It's basically like having another child."

Hadley walked over to Lucy and squatted down in front of the dog. "He's so ugly he's cute," she said.

"That's what I think, too," Lucy replied.

"Are you guys coming inside?" Martha called. "Those jerks are bound to come back. I don't want them getting any pictures they don't have to work for."

Hadley followed Brody, Lucy, and Ollie inside, picking up Martha's forgotten guitar as she went. "I thought I heard music coming from the porch when I was in the bathroom this morning," she said, handing her sister the guitar. "It sounded nice."

"Thanks," Martha muttered. "Too bad I can't remember a damn chord of what I played."

"It'll come to you," Hadley replied. "I also found this bottle of whiskey by the coffeepot."

"I think that's our cue to go into the living room," Brody said, taking Lucy by the shoulders and steering her away from the two women.

"I didn't drink any," Martha said, sticking out her chin.

"I didn't say you did," Hadley replied.

"You want to smell my breath?"

"No," Hadley said. "I believe you."

"Doesn't sound like you do."

"I do."

Martha narrowed her eyes at Hadley. "Why would you even say anything, then?"

Hadley shrugged. "I just wondered why it was out, was all."

"I thought about it, okay?" Martha replied, lifting her hands up into the air. "I thought about it, but then I saw the guitar that you left out, and I took it outside on the porch to play instead."

"I didn't leave the guitar out," Hadley replied.

"Must've been Pfeiffer."

"Wasn't me," Pfeiffer said, wandering into the kitchen, Lafayette following close behind.

Martha crossed her arms on her chest. "I suppose it was the dog, then?"

Pfeiffer stopped smiling when she saw the bulldog at Hadley's feet. "What is that?"

"It's a dog," Hadley replied. "I wasn't sure at first either."

"It better not bother Lafayette," Pfeiffer said. "She's had a rough night."

"Don't worry," Brody called from the living room. "He's a lover, not a fighter."

Pfeiffer rolled her eyes and pulled a small tube from one of the cabinets. The minute Lafayette saw the tube, she began to back up, waddling her way underneath the kitchen table, making the same noises she had in the bathtub the night before.

"Come on out of there," Pfeiffer said, dropping to her knees in front of the table. "I promise it hurts me more than it does you."

"What's wrong with your dog?" Lucy asked, sitting down next to Pfeiffer.

"She's still mad about her bath," Pfeiffer replied. "She's clean now, but I need to put these flea and tick drops on her now that she's dry. I couldn't do it last night."

"I don't blame her. Ollie does the same thing when he sees his drops," Lucy replied. Then, rolling onto her knees and elbows, she peered underneath the table. "Come on out, pup. We won't hurt you."

"I can't believe this is my life," Pfeiffer muttered. "Sitting on a dingy farmhouse floor, trying to keep fleas and ticks off of a hound dog."

After a few moments, Lucy wrangled her way underneath the table. "I'll hold her, and you put the drops in," she said. "Quick, before she gets loose."

Pfeiffer did as she was told, and within seconds, the ordeal was over. "Thanks," she said.

"No problem," Lucy replied. "I help my aunt Amanda sometimes at the clinic."

"You want to be a vet?" Pfeiffer asked.

Lucy shook her head. "I want to be a country-music star like Martha," she said. "Or maybe a writer. I haven't decided yet."

"You can be both," Hadley cut in. "Martha writes her own songs, you know."

"I thought Travis Tucker wrote them," Lucy replied. "At least, that's what I read."

"That's what he'd like everybody to think," Hadley said. "But it's not true. My sister has been writing her own songs since she was eleven."

"I write songs sometimes," Lucy said. "Well, it's mostly poetry, but my friend Ava plays the guitar, and we put them to music once in a while."

"That's the best way to start," Martha said. "When I was your age, your aunt Amanda and I used to write songs together."

"Really?"

Martha nodded. "Yep. She's very talented on the piano. Did you know that?"

Lucy looked to her father, who said, "It's true. She took piano lessons through high school. But she stopped playing in college once she decided to go to veterinary school."

"She never told me that," Lucy said. "There's an open-mic night at that bar down by Aunt Amanda's office this Friday. But Dad says Ava and I aren't old enough to go."

"I don't think they'd even let you through the door." Martha laughed. "You're a little young for a place like Mama's."

"I go to school with the granddaughter of the lady who owns it," Lucy said. "Her name is Geneva, but everybody calls her Gin, you know, like the liquor."

"Seems appropriate," Martha replied.

"Anyway, she says her mama and her mama's mama don't get along and one day the bar will be her mama's and she's going to close it down and turn it into a massage place for dogs."

Martha stifled a snort and looked to Brody, who only shrugged and said, "You know Gin's mom, don't you?"

Martha nodded. "I do, and I guess it doesn't surprise me."

All three of their heads turned when they heard a car crunching down the gravel path. The Ozark County coroner's truck pulled into the driveway, followed by the sheriff and two deputies.

"You stay in here," Brody said to Lucy. "Sit on the couch and watch TV or something."

"But I want to go outside with you," Lucy replied, crossing her skinny arms over her chest. "I want to see."

"No," Brody replied. "Stay here."

"Ugh," Lucy said. "Fine." She flounced over to the couch and sat down, the dog at her heels. "This television doesn't work!"

Brody opened his mouth to respond, but Hadley held up her hand. "It does work," she said. "But there isn't any cable."

"Well, then, what am I supposed to watch?"

Hadley walked over to the television and opened the double doors on the stand on which it was sitting. "There are a ton of tapes in here you can watch."

"Tapes?"

"VHS tapes," Hadley said. "For the VCR."

"VCR?"

Hadley ran her fingers down the spines of the tapes and pulled one from the shelf. "What are you, twelve?" she asked. "Have you ever seen *Sixteen Candles*?"

Lucy shook her head. "No."

"It's my favorite," Hadley replied. "It might be a bit old for you, but I think you'll like it."

"Okay," Lucy replied, turning her head slightly to look back at her father. "My dad thinks I should only watch cartoons. He thinks I'm still a baby."

"But you're not," Hadley said with a conspiratorial wink. "Now, here's how the VCR works. You turn it on and put the tape in and press play. That's it."

Hadley started the movie and then sat down on the couch next to the bulldog, both she and Lucy petting him. On the outside, Hadley looked like a put-together socialite with her perfectly bobbed hair and ability to flawlessly match a pair of capri pants to a sweater. But Hadley still remembered the girl she'd once been with a tangled mass of hair and a sense of adventure that would put most men to shame. She still remembered the girl who wanted to travel everywhere, the girl who watched movies to escape their small town, and the girl who would never, ever be caught dead wearing pearls. And for this reason, Hadley suspected she and Lucy had much more in common than either of them realized.

"Hadley?"

Hadley turned around to see Brody standing in the doorway. "Hey, is everything all right?"

"Would you mind coming out here for a second?"

"Sure," Hadley replied. "I'll be right back," she said to Lucy.

"The sheriff has a few questions," Brody said. "They've found more bones. He wants to talk to each of you, and he's already talked to Pfeiffer, and Martha went upstairs to get dressed."

"More bones?"

Brody nodded. "I reckon they're going to find a whole body."

Hadley shuddered. "What could they want to talk to us about?" she asked. "Clearly, we couldn't have had anything to do with this."

"I don't know," Brody replied. "But Pfeiffer was pretty pissed when she left."

"Where did she go?"

"She went to see if she could get Crowley to come over and speak with the sheriff," Brody replied. "I offered to go, but she said she'd prefer to go alone."

Hadley stepped out onto the porch. It was turning out to be a muggy day, with the heat hanging in the air like wet clothes on a line. She wondered if it might rain. What she didn't have to wonder about, however, was which one of the men in uniform was the sheriff. Hadley knew he was the man wearing the ten-gallon cowboy hat and snakeskin boots. She knew this because, like most things in Cold River, the attire of the sheriff never changed.

"Howdy," the man said, tipping his hat to her, and Hadley had to stifle a giggle. "Mind if we have a word, ma'am?"

"Sure," Hadley replied. "Sheriff?"

"Name's Sheriff Tobias Driscoll."

Hadley squinted. "Are you any relation to Coy Driscoll?"

The sheriff nodded. "That's my nephew. But try not to judge me on account of him."

"I wouldn't dream of it," Hadley replied. "How can I help you?"

"Now, I've got a few questions for ya," Sheriff Driscoll said. "They may be a bit uncomfortable, but I'd appreciate ya not cursing at me for askin' them like your sister did."

"I won't judge you based on your nephew, if you won't judge me based on my sister," Hadley replied. She couldn't imagine what kind of questions the sheriff asked that would have made Pfeiffer so upset, but it wasn't unlike Pfeiffer to lose her temper when flustered.

"Now, we don't know how long the body has been buried on your property," Sheriff Driscoll said. "We won't know that for a while, but can you tell me the last time you lived on the property?"

"It was 1998," Hadley replied. "I left the summer after I graduated from high school."

"What month?"

Hadley rolled her eyes back to try to remember. "I don't know. It must've been June. I stayed with a friend in Columbia for a couple months, with her grandparents, until school started up."

"What prompted you to leave so early?"

"I was just ready to leave," Hadley replied.

"But do you have a specific reason?" Sheriff Driscoll asked. "I need you to try to be as specific as you can."

Hadley took a deep breath. "Sir, my mother and sister had just died. I'm sure you remember that."

"I do."

"My boyfriend and I broke up, and I guess I thought anything was better than staying here."

The sheriff scribbled something onto his notepad. "And your boyfriend at the time was Brody Nichols?"

"It was."

"Why did you break up, if you don't mind me asking?"

"I don't really remember," Hadley replied.

"Seems to me that you and that Nichols boy was pretty steady. Wouldn't you remember a thing like that?" Sheriff Driscoll asked.

"A lot was happening at the time," Hadley said. "And it was twenty years ago. We were kids, and kids break up. It happens."

"Mmm-hmm."

Hadley looked over to see if she could read what the sheriff was writing, but it all looked like something Pfeiffer's dog would have pecked out. "Is that all you have to ask me?"

"No, just a few more questions," Sheriff Driscoll replied. "All routine, of course."

"Of course."

"Can you think of anything strange happening while you lived here?" Sheriff Driscoll asked. "Anything—I don't know—out of the ordinary?"

"What do you mean?"

"Did your mama or daddy have any disagreements with anybody? Was there any fightin' that you can remember? Or someone who showed up one day at your house, and you never saw 'em again?"

"I was eight when my father died," Hadley replied. "He was sick for nearly a year before that. I don't have too many memories that don't involve happy times before he got sick."

"What about after he got sick?" Sheriff Driscoll asked.

"Well, he had cancer," Hadley replied, feeling herself stiffen at the use of the word. "He was pretty weak after he got sick, and I don't know what you're getting at. Do you think my parents had something to do with this?"

"What about your mama?" Sheriff Driscoll pressed. "What was her mental state after your daddy died?"

Hadley's nails dug into the palms of her hands. If these were the questions he'd asked Pfeiffer, it was no wonder she'd used colorful language. Hadley was tempted to do the same.

"Ma'am?"

"She just lost her husband and had four little kids to take care of," Hadley said through gritted teeth. "How do you think her mental state was?"

"Was it anything you would have thought to be concerned with?"

"I was eight."

"What about later?" the sheriff asked. "Once you got a bit older?"

"She was raising four kids," Hadley repeated. "Alone. She didn't have a lot of time for much else."

"Raising y'all must've been expensive all alone."

Hadley nodded, confused. "It was."

"I know that your aunt Beatrice James used to help your mama a bit here and there," the sheriff said.

"She did," Hadley replied. "For a long time, it was how we got by."

"But then she quit just a few months before your mama passed."

"How did you know that?" Hadley asked.

"It's my job to know," he replied. "Do you think leavin' your mama all high and dry like that could've made your mama do something desperate?"

"You mean like kill someone and bury them in the garden?" Hadley sputtered. "Of course not. My mother would never have hurt anyone."

"Money problems make people do crazy things sometimes," Sheriff Driscoll said.

"My mother didn't kill anyone," Hadley said. "We always had money problems. That wasn't anything new."

"But how was she keeping up with the farm?" Sheriff Driscoll continued. "Without that money from your aunt?"

"I don't know," Hadley replied.

"I think you do," Sheriff Driscoll said, matter-of-fact. "I think one of you knows something."

"Like what?"

"Like the fact that your mother was planning to move out after you graduated," the sheriff said.

"Where did you hear that?" Hadley demanded.

"Like I said, it's my job to know things."

"I don't understand what this has to do with anything," Hadley said. "My mother didn't kill anyone."

"I'm not saying she did," Sheriff Driscoll said.

"But you aren't saying she didn't."

"I'm not saying that either."

"I think we're done here," Hadley said, taking a step back from the sheriff. "If you have any more questions, I'd be happy to give you the number of my lawyer."

"Oh, I don't think there will be any reason for that," Sheriff Driscoll said.

"I don't think there will be any reason for you to be talking to me again," Hadley said, crossing her arms over her chest. "I will not stand here and listen to you suggest my mother, who died trying to save my sister, by the way, was a murderer. I just won't."

"Hold on, hold on," the sheriff said, extending his hands, palms up, for Hadley to see. "Ain't no reason for you to get upset. It's just like I told your sister. It's my job to ask these questions."

"That may be," Hadley said, turning on her heel and walking back toward the house, "but it ain't my job to answer them."

CHAPTER 23
Hadley

HADLEY WAS FUMING BY THE TIME SHE GOT BACK INSIDE the house. She stopped Martha on her way outside and said, "Don't go out there and talk to that man."

"Why not?" Martha wanted to know. "Brody said he had some questions for us."

"She has to go," Brody said, lightly touching Hadley's arm.

"I know," Hadley said, nodding to Martha and walking into the kitchen. "I just wish this wasn't happening."

"What do you think is happening?" Brody asked.

"I don't know," Hadley replied, "but it's not good."

"What did the sheriff ask you?"

Hadley pulled out one of the chairs from the kitchen table, surprising Lafayette, who'd been sleeping beneath it. "He seems to think that my mother or father may have had something to do with the body we found," she said, sitting down. "I told him that he was wrong, but I don't think he believed me."

"There is no way either of your parents would have killed any-one," Brody replied.

"I know," Hadley said. "But he asked about my mother's mental state after Daddy died, and then he brought up the money trouble we always seemed to have."

"He thinks there's a link?"

Hadley shrugged. "I guess. Maybe. I don't know. He knew that Aunt Bea gave Mama money for years until she stopped just before my mother and Mary died."

"Did he ask why she stopped?" Brody asked, sitting down next to her.

"He didn't have to," Hadley said. "He knew Mama was plan-ning to move as soon as I graduated."

"Did you tell him anything else?" Brody asked.

"No," Hadley said. "I didn't tell him anything."

"Why not?"

"Because it's not his business," she replied. "Because it's not anybody's business, and I'm not going to say anything that could make my mother look even more guilty in his eyes."

"Stealing isn't the same thing as murder," Brody said.

"Don't say that about Mama," Hadley said. "Don't you dare say it."

"Is everything okay?" Lucy asked, appearing in the kitchen.

Hadley looked up, blinking away any tears that were on the verge of forming in the corners of her eyes. "Everything's fine. How's the movie?"

"It's so good," Lucy said, her eyes dancing. "I mean, it's old and it's kind of wobbly, but I love it."

"I knew you'd like it," Hadley said.

"Do you have any more old movies?" Lucy asked.

"Tons," Hadley said. "Do you want to borrow the VCR and a few of them?"

Lucy looked to her father, who said, "We have an old VCR in storage. No need to borrow yours."

"Well, take any of the movies you'd like, then," Hadley said.

"We've got movies, too."

Hadley looked over at Brody, raising her eyebrow slightly. "It's really fine."

"Oh, come on, Dad," Lucy pleaded. "Just let me borrow a few."

"Just go finish what you're watching," Brody said.

"Fine." Lucy sighed. Then turning to Hadley, she said, "I learned how to pause it. That's what took me so long to come in here. There is no remote."

"There used to be a long time ago," Hadley said. "But it's probably stuck so deep inside that couch that we'll never find it."

Lucy grinned. "I'm going to look anyway," she said.

Before Hadley could answer, Martha came through the door, tears streaming down her face. "I'm going upstairs," she said, pushing past both Hadley and Brody. "Tell them I'm not answering any more questions."

"Are you okay?" Hadley asked.

"Did you know Mama was going to move us?" Martha asked. "Did you know?"

Hadley hesitated and then nodded. "Yes."

"Where were we going?"

"I don't know," Hadley said. "I don't know that she ever got that far."

"Why?" Martha asked. "Why was she going to move us?"

"She couldn't make ends meet here," Hadley said, taking

Martha's hands. "The house, the bills Daddy left . . . she just couldn't keep up."

"Even with the money Aunt Bea sent her?" Martha asked.

"Even with that," Hadley replied.

"Why didn't you tell us?" Martha asked.

"What good would it have done?"

Martha sniffed. "The sheriff seems to think Mama had something to do with all of this."

"She didn't," Hadley said.

"How do you know?" Martha asked. "How could you possibly know that?"

"You know that our mother wouldn't have hurt anyone."

"I don't know anything anymore," Martha said. "Right now it feels like my entire childhood was a lie."

"Don't let that stupid sheriff put those ideas into your head," Hadley said. "The sheriff is just trying to scare us."

"Well, he did a damn good job," Martha replied. "Because I'm scared as hell." Then, turning around, she hurried up the stairs, ignoring Hadley calling her name.

CHAPTER 24
Pfeiffer

THE CROWLEY FARM WASN'T MUCH OF A FARM, NOT ANY-more. There was no more livestock save for a few sickly cattle and some chickens, and all that remained of the original buildings was a tenant shack and an outhouse. The rest burned in a fire in the 1970s, before Pfeiffer was born. All that remained of the original house was a stone chimney, and behind it, Pfeiffer knew that she would find Old Crow.

Pfeiffer cut the engine to Brody's old truck and hurried up the crumbling steps of the shack. The door opened before she had a chance to knock, and Old Crow's ragged frame stood before her.

"I reckoned one a you would come," he said, opening the door wider for her to enter.

"The sheriff would like a word with you," Pfeiffer said. "They sent me after you."

"I won't be goin'."

"I don't think you have much of a choice."

"I'm an old man, girly," Crowley replied. "I don't have to do nothin' 'cept die."

Pfeiffer tried not to smile. "The sheriff will come here himself if you don't come with me," she said. "I doubt you want that."

"I ain't got nothin' ta hide."

"I'm not saying you do," Pfeiffer said, taking inventory of Old Crow's meager home.

The shack had only one room, fitted out with a rustic table and one chair. There was a twin bed in one corner and a small kitchenette in the other. There were books on the floor next to the bed and a pair of tatty slippers.

"It ain't much, I know," Crowley said, as if reading Pfeiffer's mind. "But I don't need much."

"It's more than some people have," Pfeiffer replied.

"I'm sure you've yerself quite a place in New York. Quite a place," Crowley said.

"You'd be surprised."

"Would ya like a cup of coffee?" he asked, motioning for her to have a seat at the table.

"Got anything stronger?" she asked.

Crowley touched his finger to his nose. "I've got just the thing, youngin'."

Pfeiffer accepted the glass of whiskey, grateful that the old man didn't judge her for asking for alcohol in the middle of the day. "Thank you," she said.

"Things not goin' so well for ya up there in that big city?"

Pfeiffer shrugged. "You could say that."

"I ain't sayin' it," Crowley said. "I was askin'."

"Things aren't great," Pfeiffer said, taking a swig of the whiskey and allowing herself to enjoy the burn in her throat and chest. "In fact, things are pretty spectacularly awful."

"Ain't a lot better here, is it?"

Pfeiffer shook her head and took another sip. "No. They aren't."

"You ready to hightail it on back?" Crowley asked, pouring them both another glass.

"There's nothing to go back to," Pfeiffer said, realizing too late the words she'd just spoken. "I don't . . . I don't have anything to go back to."

"Nothin'?"

"Nothing," Pfeiffer replied. "I lost my job nearly a year ago over something stupid I did, which, if you know me, isn't surprising. I spent all of my savings just trying to keep up, and when that ran out, I lost my apartment and everything in it."

Crowley sighed. "Do yer sisters know?"

"No," Pfeiffer said. "And I'd appreciate you not telling them."

"I ain't never been one to tell nobody's secrets," Crowley replied.

"Have you been asked to keep many secrets?" Pfeiffer asked.

"I've kept me a few," Crowley replied. "Some of them my own. Every man's gotta have a few secrets."

"Is that why you don't want to talk to Sheriff Driscoll?"

Crowley paused, his glass halfway to his lips. He set it back down again and said, "I ain't never been fond of the law, and I certainly ain't fond of that cross-eyed, beer-bellied redneck, Tobias Driscoll."

"I'm not too fond of him either," Pfeiffer said. "Especially after what he said about my parents."

Crowley sat up straighter in his chair. "What did he say?"

"He didn't really say anything, but he sure suggested that one or both of them had something to do with the body in the garden," Pfeiffer replied. "I think he was just fishing for information, but it was insulting."

Crowley put one of his gnarled hands on Pfeiffer's arm. "Your parents ain't had nothin' to do with that. You hear me? Nothin'."

"I know that," Pfeiffer said. "At least I think I do."

"I know it fer certain, child. I know it."

"How do you know?"

"I just know," Crowley said, draining his glass.

"I don't think that answer is going to be good enough for the sheriff," Pfeiffer said.

"Well, I won't be talkin' to that sheriff, so it won't matter none, will it?"

"Please," Pfeiffer said. "Tell me what you know about what happened at the farm. I promise I won't tell anyone."

"You shouldn't make promises that you can't keep, girl." Crowley stood up and took his glass to the mildewed sink, keeping his back to her.

"But if you know something—"

"What I know is that yer mama and daddy didn't have a thing to do with what happened in that garden," Crowley said, cutting her off. "And that's all anybody needs to know."

"I found the journal," Pfeiffer said suddenly, surprising herself. "Aunt Bea's journal."

Crowley turned around. "When?"

"Just after we got here," she replied, keeping her eyes locked with his.

"And did ya read it?"

"I did."

"And yer sisters?"

Pfeiffer stood up. "I haven't told them. You're not the only one who can keep a secret," she said. "But what I want to know is, how did you know about it?"

"Yer aunt always kept a journal," Crowley replied. "That ain't no secret. She didn't talk none, so she wrote down most a what she wanted to say."

"She used to talk, though, didn't she?" Pfeiffer asked. "A long time ago when you were kids?"

Crowley nodded. "She did."

"And there are pages missing from that journal," Pfeiffer continued. "I'm willing to bet that whatever's in those missing pages explains what happened in the garden, or at the very least explains why she stopped talking."

"If them pages are gone, then they're gone fer a reason," Crowley replied. "Ain't no way to get 'em back now."

"I just want to know if the reason is the dead body in my garden," Pfeiffer said.

Crowley walked up to where Pfeiffer stood, pulling his stooped frame up to its full height. He was so close to her that she could smell the whiskey on his breath and see the bits of tobacco lodged between his teeth. "Go on back to Sheriff Driscoll and tell him I ain't got nothin' to say," he said. "And you tell him if he steps one foot onto my property, his pants'll be so full a buckshot he won't be able to sit down fer a week."

Pfeiffer swallowed. "I'll tell him," she said.

"Ain't nothin' to learn from Old Crow," he said. "Ain't nothin' to be learned from that journal neither."

"I'm going to find those pages," Pfeiffer said. "With or without your help."

"You've been gone from here too long," Crowley replied. "You've fergotten what happens when ya stick yer nose where it don't belong, and you've fergotten that secrets in this town are just like rocks in the soil—as soon as you've dug one up, another one appears. Ya won't find what yer lookin' for here."

CHAPTER 25

Pfeiffer

WHEN PFEIFFER ARRIVED IN NEW YORK CITY, SHE HAD four hundred dollars in her pocket. She'd been due to go home to Cold River after college graduation, as she had no job prospects. Instead, she hitched a ride to the East Coast with three of her English-major friends. By September, she was the only one left. The other three gave up after they couldn't make rent in their cockroach-infested apartment. Pfeiffer, in turn, posted ads for roommates at the shoe store where she worked. It was one of those places that was changing locations all the time, and she never knew if the shoes she sold were stolen, but they gave her a free pair every week with her paycheck, so she didn't complain.

In the end, it was a snarky comment she made about the Twilight series to a book editor at Henry Brothers that landed her her first job in publishing. Five years later, she was shopping at Kate Spade on Fifth and living in her own apartment. Pfeiffer never pretended that her grimy beginnings hadn't led to her ability to spot a bestseller a mile away or her ability to feel the pulse of readers all across the globe. Somewhere along the way, however, she lost herself within her work and began to think she could say and do whatever she liked.

It was a mistake.

A mistake that cost her her job.

The day she lost the job, the vice president of Henry Brothers came into her office and closed the door. She was a tall woman, the vice president, with a nose like a beak and tiny, dark eyes that made her look like a bird. Her name, in fact, was Alexandria Byrd, and people often made fun of her behind her back, but Pfeiffer knew better. The woman might've had eyes and a nose like a bird, but she had ears like an elephant, and she heard everything.

"I received the most interesting email forward this weekend," Alex said, sitting down in the chair opposite Pfeiffer.

"Oh yeah?" Pfeiffer asked, opening the lid to her lunch—egg salad—on her desk. "Was it from digital marketing? They send out some whoppers."

"No," Alex replied, sliding her fingers together. "It was from a literary agent, Dasha Pilar. Do you know her?"

At this, Pfeiffer looked up from her food. "I do," she said. "We've worked on a few projects together, but it's been over a year since she sent me something worth publishing."

"She sent you a manuscript a few weeks ago, correct?" Alex asked. "Written by a debut author?"

Pfeiffer nodded, the egg salad tasting rotten in her throat. "She did."

"And you weren't interested?"

"No," Pfeiffer replied. "There were too many holes in the plot and no way to fill them without a complete rewrite."

"Apparently, none of the other major houses had a problem with the plot," Alex said. "In fact, there is now quite the bidding war over the manuscript."

"That's insane," Pfeiffer sputtered. "Any seasoned editor could see that it needs too much work."

"Would any seasoned editor fire off a rejection email to an agent like the one you sent?" Alex asked. She pulled a piece of paper from the breast pocket of her pantsuit, unfolded it, and slid it across the desk to Pfeiffer.

Pfeiffer looked down at the printed version of the email she'd sent the unknown author's literary agent, an agent she'd known for years, and an email she'd meant merely as a joke. "I'm sorry," she said. "I didn't mean to offend anyone."

"It doesn't matter what you meant," Alex said. "Your literary agent friend sent this around to everyone once the bidding war began. You made a mockery of a novel that is being called the next bestseller, and you made a mockery of this publishing house. You made us a public laughingstock."

Pfeiffer felt herself begin to sweat. It started at the backs of her knees and caused them to stick to her chair. She knew what was coming, but she couldn't bring herself to believe it. "How can I make it right?" she asked.

Alex stood up. "There's only one thing you can do at this point," she said.

"Anything," Pfeiffer replied.

"You need to pack up your office and be out by the end of the day," Alex said. "You'll receive pay for this month, and we'll split your authors among editors."

Pfeiffer stared at Alex, unable to move. Surely this couldn't be happening. She'd been working for Henry Brothers for so long.

She'd brought in bestseller after bestseller. She'd rarely had a book that didn't end up on some kind of list. "Please," she said. "Give me another shot."

"I gave you a shot years ago," Alex replied. "In that shoe store. And I told you then not to disappoint me."

"And I haven't," Pfeiffer replied. "Not in all these years."

"Not until now."

"I shouldn't have said what I said," Pfeiffer admitted. "I shouldn't have said it, and I know that."

Alex didn't move. She didn't unfurl her hands. "I wouldn't have cared if you'd said it," she replied. "In fact, I agree with you. We might have laughed about it over lunch. But you didn't *say* it. You *wrote it down*. Words last forever, Pfeiffer. You should know that by now. Words are our business."

Pfeiffer felt herself close to tears but blinked them away. "I can fix this," she said. "I swear I can fix this."

"You can fix it by leaving without causing a scene," Alex replied. "I don't want this to garner more attention than it has to."

"Does everybody know?" Pfeiffer whispered, looking out through the glass windows of her office. "Has everybody seen the email?"

Alex nodded. "Everybody knows. Everybody has seen it."

Pfeiffer nodded, picking up the lid to her lunch and placing it over the smell that now threatened to make her vomit. "I'll be out as soon as I can gather my things."

"I think that would be best."

Pfeiffer thought about her former boss's words as she drove home from Old Crow's. She thought about what she said about writing words down instead of saying them, and the power those written words have. She knew it then, but she'd forgotten about it in the moment she sent that email to the literary agent. She'd forgotten that she couldn't take them back once they were written and sent out into the world.

She also knew that her aunt Beatrice had used the journal to write her own words, even before her aunt stopped speaking. She'd written something important on the pages that had been ripped out, and Pfeiffer knew without a doubt that someone else besides her aunt had seen them, and she was willing to bet the chicken pox that it was Rufus Crowley.

CHAPTER 26
Martha

MARTHA WAS RELIEVED WHEN THE CRIME-SCENE TAPE was taken away from the perimeter of the garden. She was even more relieved when the Ozark County coroner was finished exhuming the body buried there, and his van disappeared down the driveway for the last time on Friday morning.

The sheriff, for his part, kept his distance from the sisters after asking his initial round of questions, and Martha did her best to stay in the house and out of his line of vision. She'd also stayed out of Hadley's line of vision as best she could. She was still angry at her sister for not telling her and Pfeiffer about their mother's plans to move all those years ago. Martha hadn't known they had money trouble. She'd known that money was tight, but money was tight for everyone in Cold River most of the time. What she hadn't known was that her mother could no longer maintain the farm, and if Hadley had kept that piece of information a secret, she wondered what else she'd kept secret.

What if their mother *had* done something awful out of desperation and Hadley knew about it?

Martha shook those thoughts from her head. Hadley was secretive, but she always had been. Surely, she wouldn't keep a crime like that a secret. She seemed just as surprised as everyone else by Brody and Old Crow's discovery. Besides, it was just like Hadley said—their mother would never hurt anyone. Not on purpose, anyway.

"What are you doing up here in the bedroom?" Pfeiffer asked, standing in the doorway. "You look like you're in a trance or something."

"Just thinking," Martha replied, lying back on the pillow. "I was going to take a nap, but I can't sleep."

"Well, your phone's been ringing off the hook for the last five minutes. Same number."

"Why didn't you come up here and get me earlier?" Martha asked, sitting back up. "It could be something important."

"I thought maybe you heard it and chose to ignore it," Pfeiffer replied. "That's what I would be doing right now if anyone were trying to call me."

"I never ignore my phone," Martha replied. "It just hasn't been ringing a lot lately."

"Well, someone is pretty desperate to get ahold of you."

Martha pulled herself up off the bed and followed her sister downstairs. As they neared the bottom of the stairs, she could hear her phone ringing from its precarious position on the back of the couch.

"Hello?"

There was a crackling and then silence on the other end. After a few moments, Martha could hear her agent's voice. "Mar . . . Mar . . . are you there?"

"Hang on," Martha yelled into the phone. And then, to Pfeiffer, she said, "I swear, this place is a dead zone."

"In more ways than one!" Pfeiffer called after her.

Martha covered the receiver with her hand until she got outside. "Hello? Rodney, are you there?"

"Martha? Can you hear me?"

"I can now," Martha replied. "Sorry. The cell reception isn't great where I am."

"Do you get Internet?"

"I don't know," Martha admitted. "I haven't tried. Why?"

"There's something you need to see."

"What is it?"

There was a pause, and then Rodney said, "There were some pictures posted on a Nashville gossip website today."

"And?"

"And they're mostly flattering," Rodney replied. "That's the good news."

Martha took a breath. Rodney always had a way of drawing out the inevitable. "What's the bad news?"

"There is one of you with a man, and he's pointing a gun at the camera," Rodney replied, sounding miserable. "They're calling you Bonnie and Clyde."

"That doesn't sound so bad," Martha replied. "Everybody in country music loves them."

"Well," Rodney began, "the site is also suggesting that you've hit rock bottom after your divorce and the subsequent death of your aunt, and you're hiding out in the Ozarks to drink with the locals."

"They can tell all of that from one picture?" Martha replied, her tone sarcastic. "Jesus, Rodney. Men were harassing us with cameras on my own property. Everybody around here carries a gun."

"Not everybody points it at paparazzi."

"They'll move on soon enough," Martha replied. "Maybe it'll even boost a few sales of my older albums."

"It might've," Rodney said, "if they also hadn't posted pictures of the coroner leaving your farm amid reports of a body found on the property."

Martha closed her eyes. "Shit."

"I tried to tell you that you needed to come home," Rodney replied.

"I'm sorry," Martha replied. "But you know I can't leave. Even if I were willing to leave my sisters, and I'm not, I doubt the sheriff would let me go. He's been asking some questions."

"Do you need a lawyer?"

"I don't know," Martha said. "I don't think so."

"Is there anything you need to tell me?" Rodney asked. "Wait, don't tell me. I don't want to know."

"God, no," Martha said. "I didn't kill anyone, and nobody I know did either."

"But they found a body in your *yard*," Rodney replied.

"It's been there for a while," Martha replied. "If someone I knew killed whoever it is, and that's a big if, then that person is long dead as well."

"Martha, there's one more thing," Rodney said. "You weren't the only one with fresh, new pictures on that site."

"Travis?" Martha asked, even though she already knew the answer. "Who was he with this time?"

"Missy Lion."

Martha took a deep breath in and then let it out, but it did nothing to dissolve the mix of tears, jealousy, and rage that was boiling up inside of her. "So, while he's out there wining and dining Missy Lion, I'm here in the boondocks hitting rock bottom?"

"That's what it seems like."

"Jesus Christ, Rodney."

"Do I need to come out there?" Rodney asked. "To make sure you won't do anything stupid?"

"No," Martha said. "It'll be fine."

"Are you sure?"

"No."

"You'll call me if there are any more problems?"

"I will," Martha replied. "Or if I need bail money."

Martha pressed end call on the screen and shoved the phone into her pocket. For once, she was glad she didn't have access to the Internet to see the pictures and accompanying story that had been posted. Before she'd come to Cold River, that's how she'd spent her mornings, with a cup of coffee, scanning the gossip columns. She could never decide if she was insulted or relieved when they left her alone.

When she got back inside, both of her sisters were sitting at the kitchen table, eating cold SpaghettiOs out of the can. Despite Rodney's phone call, the sight made her smile. It was something they'd done since they were children. Their mother had been a wonderful cook, but they'd all loved eating SpaghettiOs straight out of the can while watching Saturday-morning cartoons.

"Don't worry," Pfeiffer said, her mouth half-full. "We saved you a can."

"Thanks."

"Who was on the phone?" Pfeiffer wanted to know.

"My agent," Martha replied. "You know the guys Brody and I caught taking pictures of us the other day?"

"Yeah," Pfeiffer said. "Did they get some or something?"

"They did," Martha replied. "They got an especially interesting one of Brody pointing his gun at them while he told them to get off our property."

Hadley looked up from her can. "Brody pointed a gun at someone?"

"Wouldn't be the first time," Pfeiffer murmured.

"Ashby Bean deserved it," Hadley replied. "He was meaner than a snake and twice as slimy."

"Snakes aren't really slimy," Pfeiffer said.

"You know what I mean," Hadley replied, rolling her eyes. "He was going to shoot his own dog for barking at him."

"I would have barked at him, too," Pfeiffer replied.

"I remember that dog," Martha said. "Wasn't he a bloodhound or something?"

Hadley nodded. "And Brody took him and brought him home. When his dad found out, he had to return him."

"And then the dog escaped from Ashby and came back!" Martha finished. "I remember now."

"Brody always has been good to his animals," Hadley said. "It's almost a shame he didn't want to become a vet."

"He's good to his people, too," Martha replied, eyeing her sister. "He's loyal, you know?"

Hadley averted her gaze and said, "So what are you going to do about these pictures?"

Martha shrugged. "You know just as well as I do that there's nothing I can do. They're up for the whole world to see. It wouldn't matter what I say; people are going to believe what they want."

"I know," Hadley said. "The worse the picture, the better the money."

"It's Friday today, isn't it?" Martha asked suddenly, standing up. "It's open-mic night at Mama's."

"Are you going to go?" Pfeiffer asked.

"*We* are going to go," Martha replied. "All of us."

"It's a bar," Hadley told her. "Are you sure you need to go to a bar?"

"You think I'm going to be able to stay out of bars forever?" Martha asked. "Besides, it's either I play music tonight or I drink tonight. I don't have to leave the house to drink. All I have to do is open that cabinet over there."

Hadley sighed. "I guess you're right. And we could all use a night out after the week we've had."

"I can't remember the last time I went out and did anything," Pfeiffer said. "It's been months and months."

"Then it's settled," Martha said. "We're going out. And you're both going to borrow my clothes and let me do your makeup."

Hadley and Pfeiffer exchanged a look.

"I'm not letting you anywhere near my face," Pfeiffer replied.

"Oh yes you are," Martha replied, grabbing Pfeiffer's arm and pulling her up. "Come on. Let's get this party started."

FORTY-FIVE MINUTES LATER, the sisters were upstairs in the bathroom, staring at their reflections in the mirror. Martha regarded her creations proudly, Hadley and Pfeiffer wearing more makeup than an entire Texas beauty pageant. They were showing more skin, too.

"I'm afraid my face will crack if I talk too much," Pfeiffer said through tight lips. "How do you wear this every day?"

"I don't wear it *every* day," Martha said. "Just when I want to be seen."

"We're going to be seen all right," Hadley replied, adjusting the straps on her pink tank top. "I don't like showing my stomach. It makes me feel like I'm trying to rewind twenty years."

"You look twenty years younger," Pfeiffer told her. "Your arms are so . . . toned."

"I work out three times a week in D.C.," Hadley replied. "For what I pay that trainer, they better be toned."

"I should work out," Pfeiffer murmured.

"What?" Martha asked. "You're tiny. You can eat whatever you want."

"So?" Pfeiffer replied. "People still mistake me for a teenager. If I cut my hair off, people think I'm a teenage *boy*."

"I guess nobody is really ever happy no matter how they look," Martha said. "I know I'm not."

"That's Travis talking," Hadley replied. "He never did appreciate you like he should have."

"I didn't appreciate him either," Martha said. "But that's over now, and it's time to move on."

Hadley put her hand on Martha's arm. "I know it's hard."

Before Martha could respond, there was a heavy knock on the front door, causing all three of the sisters to jump.

"Was someone supposed to come by?" Martha asked.

"Not that I know of," Pfeiffer replied. "Unless it's someone about the . . . you know . . . body."

"They wouldn't be here this late," Hadley replied.

Martha followed her sisters downstairs, feeling slightly

wobbly. She was nervous about singing in front of an audience, especially because she had a new song to play that she hadn't told anyone about. She'd been working on it for the last couple of days. She didn't know if, when she finally got up to sing, she'd be able to. She reached the bottom of the stairs just in time to see Hadley open the door to Mark, standing in the doorway, still wearing his sunglasses even though it was getting ready to rain.

"Mark?" Hadley asked. "What . . . what are you doing here?"

"You didn't think it was necessary to tell me that you found a dead body in your front fucking yard?" Mark asked, stepping inside the house and pushing past Hadley. "A simple phone call would have been nice. I had to find out through my campaign manager at four a.m."

"I tried to call you," Hadley said, taking a step back. "You didn't answer. Like always."

"I don't have any missed calls."

"I can't help that."

"This could be bad for my campaign," Mark said, finally ripping his sunglasses from his face. "Please tell me you didn't know anything about it."

Martha studied the man in front of her. He was short; some might even call him diminutive. Martha made a crack about his height at his and Hadley's rehearsal dinner, and Mark responded with a glare so cold she'd been afraid to look him directly in the eyes ever since.

"We were just on our way out the door," Pfeiffer said, taking a step closer to Hadley. "You're welcome to come with us if you'd like."

"You look like you're headed to a hoedown," Mark replied. "Hadley, what are you wearing? You look positively country."

"And you look like you're about to conduct a ribbon-cutting ceremony for the farmer next door's new pigpen," Pfeiffer snapped. "What are you doing here, Mark?"

"I came here to speak to my wife," he said. "I should have known leaving her alone with the two of you for this long would result in . . . this."

Pfeiffer opened her mouth to speak, but Hadley put up her hand. "It's fine," she said. "You and Martha go on. Mark and I will catch up later."

"Hell no," Pfeiffer replied. "I'm not leaving you here with him."

A flicker of gratitude crossed Hadley's face before she said, "Go on. We need to talk, anyway."

"Let's go," Martha said, nodding toward the door.

Pfeiffer sighed. "Fine. But you call me if you need anything, Hadley." She sent a withering glare to Mark.

"Where's my guitar?" Martha stood at the doorway with her hands on her hips. "I put it right here before we went upstairs."

"I don't know," Hadley replied. "I didn't see it when I came down."

"That's so weird," Martha said.

"It's in here!" Pfeiffer called from the kitchen. It's leaning against the chair again."

"I swear that's not where I left it," Martha said. "I swear."

"Whose dog is that?" Mark said from behind them. "Underneath the kitchen table."

"My dog," Pfeiffer replied. "And her name is Lafayette."

"What kind of a name is that?" Mark wanted to know.

Pfeiffer turned her attention to Hadley. "I cannot believe you married him sometimes."

"Let's go into the living room, okay?" Hadley asked Mark. She wanted to keep her sister and her husband as far away from each other as she could.

Martha picked up her guitar and ushered Pfeiffer outside, the two of them rushing toward the car before the sky opened up on them.

CHAPTER 27
Hadley

Hadley watched her sisters leave, wishing more than anything she could go with them. She hadn't even realized how much she wanted to go until she couldn't. She knew that she wouldn't be following along later, and certainly not with Mark.

She turned around to face her husband. "Why *are* you here, Mark?"

"You need to come home with me," he said. "Now."

"Why?"

"My campaign manager says it's best."

"Well," Hadley replied, waving her hands in the air, "if your campaign manager says it's best . . ."

"You agreed to make this as smooth a transition as possible," Mark said. "We agreed."

"That was before my aunt died and left me a rickety old farmhouse with a body buried in the lawn," Hadley replied. "I can't come home right now. There is too much going on."

"I need you in D.C.," Mark replied.

"I can't go to D.C.," Hadley said.

"Think about how it looks if you stay here," Mark said. "Think about what people will say, what the papers will write."

"They're going to write about what's happened whether I'm in D.C. or not," Hadley said.

"I saw that picture of your sister," Mark continued. "The one of Martha with your old high school boyfriend. Have you been seeing him?"

"Is that what this is about?" Hadley asked. "You're worried I might be spending time with Brody?"

"Are you?"

"No," Hadley said. "Well, not really."

"Think about how it'll look if your picture gets taken with him," Mark told her.

"It'll look like a picture," Hadley replied. "Besides, everybody already knows." She paused, swallowing. "They already know we plan to file for divorce after you're reelected."

"The voters don't know!" Mark exclaimed. "And I'm willing to bet you haven't told your sisters either."

"I'll tell them," Hadley said. "When the time is right."

"Just like we'll tell the voters when the time is right."

"I don't care about the voters," Hadley said.

Mark nodded, shoving his hands into the pockets of his suit coat. "I know. You never have. That was always part of our problem. Well, that and the fact that you've always been in love with someone else."

Hadley felt her face grow warm. "Don't act like I didn't try," she said. "I tried. But you were too busy with your campaigns and your donors and other women to care about me."

"We had a deal," Mark said to her, taking a step closer to where she was standing. "We had a contract."

"Marriage is a contract, you're right about that," Hadley said. "But I wasn't a business deal. Marriage isn't a business deal."

"Do you think I didn't know that you didn't love me?" Mark asked. "You never loved me any more than I loved you. But we had an understanding, didn't we? I knew you would never do anything to make me look bad, and you knew I'd provide you with a life away from"—he took his hands out of his pockets and waved them around the room—"all of this."

"I don't want that life anymore," Hadley said, turning away from him. "Our deal was simple. Because I wanted simple fifteen years ago. I wanted, and you wanted, a simple arrangement. But nothing about my life right now is simple."

"You'd rather live in a falling-down farmhouse with someone who doesn't even make enough money in a month to pay for those Gucci sandals on your feet?"

"I don't know," Hadley replied, shrugging. "But I know I don't want to live with you anymore. Not another second of another day."

"I don't care what you do once I'm elected," Mark said. "But you'll live to regret anything you might do before then."

Hadley narrowed her eyes at him. "Go back to Washington, Mark."

"Not without you."

"I'm not leaving."

Mark grabbed her arm, wrenching her closer to him. "Go get your suitcase. Go pack your clothes. Go get in the goddamn car."

Before Hadley had time to react, she heard a commotion

from the kitchen, followed by a growl. Lafayette squared herself between Mark and Hadley, the low sound emanating from her throat causing Mark to let go of Hadley's arm.

"What the . . . ?" Mark jumped back, away from Hadley, kicking his feet at the dog.

Lafayette backed her way toward the door, and Hadley, regaining her sense, followed suit. Together they scurried down the steps of the farmhouse and out into the yard just as the first fat raindrops began to fall.

CHAPTER 28
Pfeiffer

B Y THE TIME PFEIFFER AND MARTHA GOT TO MAMA'S, IT was raining. It amazed Pfeiffer that such a dump could attract so many people on a Friday night. She had a feeling it had to do with the fact that it was easy to hide at Mama's. The parking lot was a general one, and nobody could really tell which cars were parked by patrons headed into the bar and which cars were parked by customers going inside the various other shops around the square. By the time it was late enough in the evening to leave the bar, anybody who might care was already at home, fast asleep with their Bible.

Pfeiffer couldn't help but grin to see that Mama was still behind the counter, just as surly as ever. Mama took one look at her and Martha across the room and nodded, setting two beers out onto the bar.

Martha hoisted the guitar case up nervously. "I don't think I want to do this," she said.

"You'll be fine," Pfeiffer replied. "Look, Mama put out beer for us, just like she used to."

"You're kidding me," Martha said. "How did she know we were here?"

"I was wonderin' when you two was gonna show up," Mama said when the two women sat themselves down on the barstools.

"It's been a while," Pfeiffer said.

"Heard y'all been havin' some trouble out at that farm," Mama replied.

"Where did you hear it?" Pfeiffer wanted to know.

Mama shrugged her meaty shoulders. "Around."

Pfeiffer and Martha shared a look. If Mama knew, that meant everybody knew.

"You gonna play tonight?" Mama asked Martha, motioning to the guitar. "Got a few slots left."

"I thought I might," Martha said. "But now I'm not so sure."

"Honey, you're the most famous person in here," Mama said. "Hell, you're the most famous person in the whole town. You got yer start here. Don't tell me yer afraid of a few locals."

It was true; Martha had gotten her start at Mama's bar. She'd been allowed to play even though she was technically too young to go inside, because she was just that good. She and Pfeiffer weren't allowed to drink in the bar itself, but Mama always let the two girls have a beer before Martha got up to play. Had their mother still been alive, neither of the sisters would have dared to go near Mama's, let alone inside. But the truth was that Mama herself kept them safe when it felt like nobody else could. Mama always made sure they got home, didn't have too much to drink, and Pfeiffer once witnessed her break a man's arm for grabbing Martha's ass after she'd finished playing a set.

Mama, and her bar, got a thank-you in every single one of Martha's albums, and only Pfeiffer, Martha, and Mama knew why.

"Thanks, Mama," Martha said. She pushed her beer over to Pfeiffer. "Can I just get a Diet Coke?"

Mama raised a bushy eyebrow but didn't say anything as she turned around to fill a glass for Martha. "Been a lot goin' on at that farm a yours," she said. "Been hearin' about it all night."

"I'm sure you have," Martha replied, feeling every eye in the place on her back.

"Don't you worry none," Mama continued. "Ain't nobody gonna mention *that* to ya. I'll make sure of it."

Martha shot Mama the most grateful smile she could muster. "You're the best, Mama," she said.

"Do you see anybody you know?" Pfeiffer asked her sister. "It's so dark in here I can hardly see anything."

"Not yet," Martha said, scanning the room. After a moment, she waved at someone. "I think that's Ava Dawn over there."

Sure enough, Ava Dawn came bounding over to them, her curls bouncing through the smoky air. "Hey, y'all!" she called. "Oh my God, Martha, are you gonna play?"

Martha tried to smile, but found it came out as more of a grimace. "Yes, I think so."

"Come sit with us!" Ava Dawn squealed. "Please! It would be *such* an honor."

Martha looked to Pfeiffer, who only shrugged. "Okay," she said. "We'll be right over."

Pfeiffer waved at Mama, who nodded and grunted, "I'll put you on the list, Martha."

The two women followed Ava Dawn over to a table near the

front of the makeshift stage, where a man with dark eyes and a slick, black beard was sitting. He looked rather uncomfortable, and merely nodded at them as they sat down.

"Martha, Pfeiffer, I want you to meet my boyfriend, Haiden," Ava Dawn said. "Haiden, this is *Martha Hemingway* . . . you know, the country singer!"

Haiden smiled at both of the sisters. "It's nice to meet you both," he said. "I apologize if I seem a bit stiff—it's my first time in a bar."

"In this bar?" Martha asked. "Yeah, I can see how that might be a shock to the system."

"No," Ava Dawn said. And then leaning closer to them, she continued, "In *any* bar."

"What?" Pfeiffer asked. "You've never been to a bar before?"

Haiden shook his head. "I used to be . . . a man of the lord."

Ava Dawn slapped his chest and said, "You're still a man of the lord. Don't say things like that."

"I know plenty of men of the lord who can be seen inside Mama's bar on the weekends," Pfeiffer said. "You don't have to worry that you've lost your God credentials over this."

"He used to be the pastor down at Second Coming," Ava Dawn said. "But he met me last year while he was still married, and . . . well, the Baptists don't take too kindly to that."

"No," Pfeiffer said after a long pause, "I don't imagine they do."

"But now he works over at the tractor dealership, and he's such a good salesman that they're thinkin' about promotin' him to assistant manager!" Ava Dawn beamed. "The town has mostly forgiven him, but that don't mean I didn't have to threaten a couple of old biddies in the Walmart checkout before it was all said and done."

Pfeiffer and Martha exchanged a look, and Pfeiffer had to close her eyes briefly so that she wouldn't laugh. "Well, I'm glad it seems to be working out for you," she said.

The music onstage stopped, and a man wearing a faded Cardinals baseball cap stepped up to the stage. He wasn't tall, but his chest was broad, his white T-shirt stretching across his chest in a way that made Pfeiffer's blood flow just a degree or so warmer beneath her skin. "Listen up," he said. "We've got a few more musicians for you tonight, but this one about to get up here is a regular. Please put your hands together for Mandy Wilbanks!"

A woman with a guitar stepped up to the stage and sat down on the chair in front of the microphone. "Thank you," she said. "Y'all know I appreciate it."

At the sound of her voice, Martha jerked her attention away from Ava Dawn and Haiden. "Oh my God," she said, elbowing Pfeiffer. "That's Amanda!"

"I know," Pfeiffer said. "I didn't recognize her at first. That's her married name, isn't it? Wilbanks?"

Martha nodded. "I didn't know she was still singing."

"Me either," Pfeiffer said.

"She doesn't write her own stuff much anymore," Ava Dawn whispered. "But the covers she does are lovely."

Onstage, Amanda dove into a melancholy rendition of "Stay" by Sugarland, and the audience was quiet for the first time since Pfeiffer and Martha arrived. Her voice was powerful but soft, and the crowd stayed quiet until the song was over and she started up with a more lively tune, allowing a few people to push the tables in the middle aside to dance.

"She has great presence," Martha said. "I'm really impressed. I haven't seen her sing since we were kids."

Pfeiffer agreed. "I just assumed she didn't play anymore."

"Lucy said she didn't," Martha replied. "And Brody agreed. They must not know she does this."

"I wonder why she hasn't told them," Pfeiffer said. "She's really good."

"I bet it's because she thinks it would get back to her parents," Martha said. "I doubt she wants them to know."

"Why would they care?" Pfeiffer wanted to know. "She's running the practice. Isn't that enough for them?"

"Oh, her mom wouldn't care," Martha replied, "but her dad thinks this kind of thing is frivolous."

"She's a grown woman," Pfeiffer said. "More than a grown woman! She's in her thirties."

"You don't know her dad," Martha replied, her mouth tight. "He's very demanding. And he never liked Hadley or me very much. He always thought we were wild."

"I guess you kind of were," Pfeiffer agreed. "We all were."

"You know Brody and Hadley were going to run off after graduation, right?" Martha asked.

"What?" Pfeiffer tore her eyes from the stage to look at her sister. "How did you know that?"

"Amanda told me. She overheard them talking about it, and then so did I, once. If we found out about it, I'm willing to bet that Brody and Amanda's dad did, too," Martha said. "I've always wondered if that's the reason they broke up."

"She wouldn't tell us even if we asked," Pfeiffer mumbled. "She won't ever talk about it."

"Talk about what?"

Pfeiffer looked up to see the man in the Cardinals baseball

cap staring down at her. He was smiling at her as if he knew her, his blue eyes dancing all around her face. "Uh, do I know you?"

"Don't tell me you don't recognize me without the dress shirt," he said. He sat down and took off his cap. "It's Luke. Luke Gibson."

Pfeiffer's eyes widened. "Oh, hi!" she said. "I'm sorry. I just didn't . . . well, I didn't expect to see you here."

"Most of my clients think I live in my office," he replied. "So I try not to take it personally when they don't recognize me out in public."

"Hi," Martha said, giving Luke a smile. "I think what Pfeiffer means is that she didn't expect to see a fancy Cold River lawyer at Mama's bar."

"Oh, and she fits in so well?" Luke asked.

"Hey!" Pfeiffer said. "I practically grew up here."

"Well, Cold River looks good on you," he replied. "I'm glad you decided to trade Kate Spade for some denim."

Pfeiffer raised her eyebrows.

"Yeah, I know Kate Spade when I see it," Luke replied. "I have two sisters in St. Louis who live for her stuff."

"Impressive," Pfeiffer replied.

"What are you drinking?" Luke asked, turning her beer around so he could see the label. "Let me get you another."

"Oh," Pfeiffer said, "that's okay, you don't have to."

"She means she'd love another drink," Martha interrupted. "And I'll take another Diet Coke."

Luke nodded and stood up, reaching across the table to ac-knowledge Ava Dawn and shake Haiden's hand. "I'll be right back."

"What is wrong with you?" Martha asked once he was gone. "He clearly likes you."

"He was just being nice."

"Are you really that stupid?" Martha replied. "Or has it just been that long since someone flirted with you?"

Truthfully, Pfeiffer couldn't remember the last time anyone flirted with her. She couldn't remember the last time she'd gone out on a date. It wasn't that she was uninterested, but her work kept her so busy that she didn't have time for that kind of thing. At least, that's what she told herself. Now she really had no excuse, and she knew it.

"Cute, ain't he?" Ava Dawn whispered. "I swear women in town make up reasons to sue their relatives just so they can hire him."

"Seems like an expensive way to meet someone," Pfeiffer replied, but she couldn't help but smile. Luke Gibson *was* cute. There was no getting around that.

"Mama says to get ready," Luke said to Martha when he returned a few minutes later with the beer and Diet Coke. "Mandy's on her last song."

Martha gave Pfeiffer a nervous glance. "I don't know if I'm ready."

"What do you mean you're not ready?" Pfeiffer asked. "You're a pro."

"I haven't played a song live in over a year," Martha said. "And it's been longer than that since I've played a new song. This was a mistake. Let's just go home."

"No way," Pfeiffer replied. "Get up, take your guitar, and go get ready. You're doing this."

"But—"

"No buts." Pfeiffer stood up and pulled her sister along with her. "Besides, if you make me go home now, I guess I'll never know if the cute lawyer is flirting with me."

Martha sighed. "Fine, but if you don't get a date out of this, I'm going to tell him you think he's the sexiest man alive while you're standing right there."

"Just go."

Martha nodded and turned to walk over to the stage. Pfeiffer sat back down and took a swig of her beer, relieved. She'd heard Martha working on her new song for the last couple of days, and it was good. She'd meant to tell her, but she'd never done well with compliments, not even with her own sisters. She made a mental note to work on that. If she'd said something before now, maybe Martha wouldn't be so nervous.

"Your sister is afraid of the stage?" Luke asked. "Seems odd seeing as how she's sold millions of records."

"She's been going through a tough time," Pfeiffer replied. "I'm sure you and everybody else on God's green earth have read about it, which only makes it worse."

"Divorce is a messy business," Luke said.

"Isn't it *your* business?" Pfeiffer asked.

Luke nodded. "It is, but when it's your own divorce, it's not quite as easy to stay neutral."

"So you've been divorced?" Pfeiffer asked, and then immediately kicked herself. "I'm sorry. That's none of my business."

"It's okay," Luke replied. "It was a while ago—just before I moved here. She didn't want to move to Cold River, and I didn't really want her to want to move to Cold River."

"Sounds like it worked out all right, then," Pfeiffer observed.

"In the end."

"I've never been married," Pfeiffer said, wondering why she couldn't seem to shut up.

"Never even been close?"

Pfeiffer shook her head. "Nope."

"And you're not seeing anyone in . . . where is it that you live?"

"New York City," Pfeiffer replied. "And no."

"Good to know."

Before Pfeiffer could ask him what he meant, Amanda's set ended and the crowd erupted in applause. Luke stood up and said, "I'll be back. I've got to go introduce the town superstar."

Everyone turned their attention to the stage when they saw Martha step up. The room hushed, with the exception of a few whistles and shouts of her name. She gave the crowd a shy smile. "Thanks for letting me jump in last minute," she said. "I have to admit I'm kind of nervous to be up here tonight. It's been a while since I was in front of a crowd."

There were more shouts and whoops and a few people moved even more tables so they could stand in front of the stage.

"Most of you know that the last year of my life has been a little turbulent," Martha continued. "I got divorced and lost my record label, and it's been nearly six months since I've had a drink." She held up her glass of Diet Coke. "Lord knows I'd love to have a little whiskey to add to this right now."

Martha strummed on her guitar for a moment before she said, "But I don't want to sing about any of that right now. Maybe I'll be ready to do it soon, but for now, I want to sing a song about my mama. It's new, and I've never played it for anybody before. Would y'all mind to give it a listen?"

This time, the crowd erupted, and Martha's grin widened. "Okay," she said. "Here goes."

The music started, a slow, quiet stream against the buzz of the bar. For a moment, Pfeiffer wasn't sure if her sister was going to sing at all. But then she began, and Pfeiffer couldn't look away.

> *I wish that you could see me now,*
> *Standin' all alone against the crowd.*
> *It doesn't make sense to be*
> *Older now, without you here with me.*

As the song wore on and Martha's voice became stronger, Pfeiffer felt a small tear slide down her cheek, and she feverishly wiped it away. She wished Hadley were there, and at the same time she was glad she wasn't, because she didn't want to have to share this moment with anyone else. She didn't want to have to admit that she still, even after all this time, felt so broken by her mother's and sister's deaths.

She looked around the room, and found that she wasn't the only person crying. Even Mama herself was taking the dishrag she usually reserved for wiping the counters to the corners of her eyes. For the first time in a long, long time, Pfeiffer felt the love she used to have for Cold River swelling inside of her. Everybody in that room knew her, knew Martha. They all knew what the sisters had been through, because they'd gone through it with them. She didn't have to explain her grief to anyone, and it was a feeling only a town like Cold River, only a place like home, could give her.

When the song was over and everyone in the bar was on their feet clapping, Martha mouthed a thank-you to Pfeiffer and then said out loud, "Now, how about I play something else? But before I do, I'd like to see if my friend Mandy would come on up here and play with me. Mandy, are you still out there?"

From the back of the bar, a hand shot up, and Amanda was weaving her way through the crowd and back up to the stage, guitar in tow.

"Now, most of you may not know this, but Mandy and I used to play together all the time as kids," Martha said. "What should we play for them, Mandy?"

Amanda pretended to think about it for a moment, but Pfeiffer already knew what they were going to play. There was just one song they'd ever perfected, and they'd played it constantly one summer. It got so irritating that Pfeiffer had taken to the shed to read her books because of their infernal racket.

"How about 'Strawberry Wine' by the one and only Deana Carter?" Mandy asked.

"You read my mind!" Martha replied, standing up beside her friend. "Sing along if you know the words."

Pfeiffer sat back in her chair, trying not to grimace as the music started up. It wasn't a bad song, but it was probably the only one in the entire world about which she could say that if she never heard it again, it wouldn't be too soon. That's when she noticed someone sitting between Ava Dawn and Haiden, his arm thrown over the two of them—both of them looking annoyed.

"That's your sis up there, huh?" the man said to her.

Pfeiffer nodded. "Yep."

"Pretty famous, I reckon."

"Yep."

"Can't say I've heard much of her music, but she's something to look at," he commented.

"I've heard that a time or two," Pfeiffer replied, rolling her eyes and turning back around to face the stage.

"The name's Reese," he said, calling her attention back to him.

"Pfeiffer," Pfeiffer said. "You look familiar. Did I used to babysit you?"

Ava Dawn let out a laugh and said, "You'd for sure remember him if you babysat him. He was even worse then than he is now."

"Your aunt and my grandmama were best friends," Reese replied.

"Who is your grandmother?" Pfeiffer asked.

"Anna Graham," Reese replied. "Been best friends since they were kids. My grandmama was real broken up about her passing."

"She was very kind to us when we got into town," Pfeiffer said. She was trying to warm to this Reese person, but the shit-eating grin threatening to overtake his face was making it difficult. "Please tell her how much my sisters and I appreciate it."

"I'll tell her," Reese said.

"Thanks," Pfeiffer replied. She meant to turn and focus her attention on Luke, who was making his way back over to their table, but then she remembered something. "Hey, Reese."

"Yeah?"

"Your grandmother and my aunt . . . they were best friends since childhood?"

"That's what my grandmama always said."

"Do you think she would mind if I went to visit her sometime?" Pfeiffer asked.

"I don't see why not," Reese replied. "What for?"

"Oh, just to talk about my aunt," Pfeiffer said. "I have some questions about their childhood that I think only she could answer."

Reese shrugged. "She'd probably love to talk about old times," he said. "She tries to talk about them with me all the time, but I have to admit, I'm not much interested in history."

"Could we go tomorrow?" Pfeiffer asked hopefully.

"I reckon," Reese said. "I'll give her a call in the morning."

"Thank you so much."

"Will your sister be going?" Reese asked, licking his lips slightly.

Pfeiffer fought the urge to roll her eyes again. "No, it'll just be me."

"That'll be okay, too," Reese said.

"I'll go, too," Luke said from behind them. "I do like history."

"Oh, that's okay," Pfeiffer said. "I don't want to bother you."

"It's no bother," he said. "I like Mrs. Graham. She's a sweet lady."

"Great," Reese replied, slightly less enthusiastic than he had been before.

"Why don't we meet outside my law office, say nine thirty a.m.?" Luke asked.

"Will that be too early for your grandmother?" Pfeiffer asked Reese.

"Naw, she gets up at the crack of dawn." Reese chuckled. "Sometimes before."

"Okay," Pfeiffer said. "And thanks again."

"No worries," Reese replied, standing up. "Just put in a good word for me with your sister, and we'll call it even." He winked at her, and then he was gone, disappearing into the crowd and smoke.

"I just saved you an entire morning of being hit on by Reese Graham," Luke said, sitting back down in his chair. "You ought to thank me, you know."

"I can take care of myself," Pfeiffer replied. "I lived in New York City for nearly two decades, and I took self-defense classes."

Luke laughed, and when he did so, a little dimple appeared in the corner of one of his cheeks. "Oh, he's harmless, but he fancies himself a man about town."

"And he's not?"

"Why? Are you interested?"

Luke was smiling at her, as if he was joking, but Pfeiffer couldn't tell if it was a joke or if he was being serious. "He's too young for me," she said. "I'll see you tomorrow morning."

She stood up and walked toward the stage, ready to find Martha and even more ready to go home. She needed to pore over her aunt's journal before meeting with Anna tomorrow, to see if there were any clues that she might know something about the missing pages or about what happened with Aunt Bea's boyfriend, Will. If they were truly best friends, surely she would know something. Pfeiffer just hoped she could figure out a way to ask the old woman questions that wouldn't make her suspicious, as Old Crow had been when she approached him. Maybe it was her editor's brain at work, but Pfeiffer knew there was an end to the story, and she had to find out what it was.

She just had to.

CHAPTER 29
Hadley

Hadley pulled off her sopping cardigan and glanced down at Lafayette. The dog had been following her since she left the house, and she was grateful that she wasn't alone. The rain was beating down on them and showed no signs of letting up, but Hadley soldiered on despite it, determined not to go back to the farm. She knew if they kept walking, she'd eventually hit Brody's property line, and hopefully the house wouldn't be too far back.

She froze when she heard a vehicle coming down the road, fighting the urge to jump into the bushes in case it was Mark coming to look for her. That wasn't his style, though, going after her; it never had been, and when she turned around, she saw Brody's beat-up Ford flying toward her, going entirely too fast for a wet gravel road.

Had she not been so cold and tired, she might have smiled.

Then he drove past her, flinging mud up onto her shoes and legs, and she started cursing and hollering so loudly that Lafayette stopped dead in her tracks. They both looked up as the truck stopped in the middle of the road and backed up toward them.

"What are you *doing* out here?" Brody asked, rolling down the window.

"Shut up and open the door," she said, miserable.

Brody complied, jumping out to pick a soaking-wet Lafayette up out of the mud and into the cab of the truck. "Are you okay?" he asked once they were all three safely inside.

"No," Hadley replied. "Can I come home with you?"

Brody raised an eyebrow but drove on until they got to his house. Hadley almost gasped when she saw it. It was an old farmhouse, although not as old as the one on her farm, but it had been beautifully redone, complete with a screened-in wrap-around porch.

"Do you like it?" Brody asked.

"This isn't the original house," Hadley said. "It can't be. I've been to this farm before, long before you bought it. The original house was a one-story."

"It was condemned," Brody said. "I had to tear down what was left."

"Where did this one come from?"

"A farm over in Shannon County," he said. "I bought the land and moved the house here."

"Why?" Hadley asked. "Why didn't you just build a new one? It would have been cheaper, I'm sure."

"It wasn't about that," Brody said. He got out of the truck and went around to the passenger's side to let Hadley out. "Look at the porch."

"It's the first thing I noticed," she said. "I've always wanted a porch like that."

"I know," Brody replied. He put his hand around her waist. "Come on. Let's get you inside."

Hadley allowed him to lead her into the house while Lafayette plopped down on the floor, exhausted by their excursion. The house was cozy, and not nearly as sparse as she would have expected from a bachelor. There were carpets over the hardwood floors and a couch sitting in front of a fireplace with a television set mounted above it. She saw a dog on the floor in front of the fireplace, snoring with his tongue hanging out, but saw no signs of Brody's daughter.

"Where's Lucy?"

"She's spending the night with Ava," Brody replied. "I'm pretty boring to her now. We're both having a hard time admitting she's getting ready to be a teenager."

"I can imagine."

"Let me get you a towel and a change of clothes," Brody said. "I'm afraid you'll have to contend with an old T-shirt and a pair of pajama pants."

"Thanks," Hadley told him. "Anything is better than being soaking wet."

"And then you're going to tell me what you were doing wandering around at dusk in the middle of a rainstorm with an old basset hound at your heels."

Hadley sighed. She truly didn't know what she was doing. She knew that Mark wouldn't have hurt her, but she also knew that she would have ended up going home with him if she'd stayed. He always had a way of persuading her to do things that she didn't particularly want to do.

"Will these do?" Brody held out a towel, a pair of sleep pants, and a gray T-shirt with the name of the family veterinary clinic across the front. "They're clean."

"Thanks," Hadley replied. "Where's your bathroom?"

"Around the corner," Brody said, pointing.

Hadley nodded and went into the bathroom to change. She could hear him talking to Lafayette as she pulled off her soggy shoes and pants. She was sure the dog was completely traumatized and that Pfeiffer would have a thing or two to say about it when she finally got home. That was when Hadley realized she'd run off without her cell phone. Instead of causing her to be upset, the thought relieved her, because she knew that meant Mark had no way of knowing where she was or getting into contact with her. She hoped he'd be gone by the time she got back home, although she doubted he would give up so easily.

"Are you okay in there?" Brody asked, knocking lightly on the door. "Do you want a glass of water or something?"

"Got anything stronger?" Hadley asked as she emerged from the bathroom.

"I've got my good friend Jack in the cabinet," Brody replied. "Will that work?"

"Perfectly."

"You've never been much of a drinker," Brody said as he pulled down a couple of glasses. "You must be pretty shook up."

"I'm okay now," Hadley replied. "And really, it was nothing."

"What was nothing?"

"Martha and Pfeiffer were going to that open-mic night at Mama's," she said. "And I was headed out with them until my husband showed up."

Brody paused in his pouring of the whiskey. "You didn't know he was coming here?"

"No," Hadley said. "I had no idea."

"I'm guessing it didn't go well."

Hadley sat down on one of the barstools at the kitchen island and said, "Our marriage is over."

"Oh?"

"It's been over for a long time," Hadley said, waving him off. "Don't feel bad about it."

"I don't," he said, handing her a glass.

"I tried calling him the day we found . . . well, what we found, but he didn't answer, because he never answers my phone calls," she continued. "And there was a picture of you in one of the Nashville gossip blogs with Martha. You were pointing a gun or something."

"Martha said that would happen."

"Well, Mark flew here to scold me and demand I come back to Washington, D.C., with him right this very second, and when I told him no . . . well, things got pretty heated."

Brody set down his glass and stared intently at Hadley. "He didn't hurt you, did he? Because I swear to God if he hurt you . . ."

"He didn't hurt me," Hadley replied, feeling slightly warmed by the whiskey and Brody's reaction to her fight with Mark. "But Lafayette didn't like the yelling, and she got between us. That's when I ran outside. I just wanted to clear my head, I swear. I meant to go back, but I just kept walking instead."

"Toward my house?"

Hadley nodded. "Toward your house."

"You can stay here as long as you want to," Brody said, pouring himself another drink.

"I have to go back," Hadley said. "And deal with him."

"I'll go with you."

"No," Hadley replied. "That wouldn't be a good idea."

"Why not?"

"Because you're *you*."

"He knows about me?" Brody asked.

"Of course he does," Hadley replied.

"And he doesn't like it?"

"What husband likes their wife's old boyfriends?" Hadley asked.

"I never cared much about Melissa's," Brody replied.

"I never cared much about Mark's girlfriends either," Hadley said. "But I've never run for office."

"He sees me as a threat to his campaign?" Brody asked, pouring them both another glass. "How is that possible?"

"He's afraid someone will see us together and post a story about it," Hadley replied. "Or worse, take a picture."

"And here you are, sitting in my house after dark, wearing my clothes," Brody said.

"I don't care," Hadley said.

"That's probably just the whiskey talking."

"No," she replied. "It's me talking. I don't care. Our marriage is over, and everyone knows it. We're just putting on a face until the campaign is over, but I'm done doing that, too."

"I'm sorry," Brody offered.

"For what?"

"All of it."

"It's okay."

"We should have talked about things, you know?" Brody said. "We shouldn't have ended things the way we did."

"It wasn't *we*," Hadley replied. "It was me."

"Do you ever wish it had been different?"

Hadley drained her glass. "Every day."

Brody went to pour her another, and she put her hand over the top of her glass and shook her head. He replaced the cap on the Jack Daniel's and said, "Do you remember why you always said you wanted to have a wraparound porch? When we were kids?"

Hadley grinned. "So I could roller-skate all the way around it."

"Come on," Brody said, taking her hand.

"Where are we going?"

Brody led her over to the hall closet and opened the door. After rummaging around for a few seconds, he pulled out a pair of Rollerblades. "These are Lucy's, but I think they'll fit."

Hadley's eyes widened. "Oh, I don't know. I've never used Rollerblades before. And I don't know that I could stay upright now that I've had a couple of drinks."

"You might as well give it a try," he said, handing them to her. "Nobody is going to see you. Not all the way out here."

Hadley took the Rollerblades and followed Brody out onto the porch. She sat down on the porch swing just outside the door and slipped the skates onto her feet. "I'm going to fall and break my neck," she said.

"I'll be right here," Brody assured her. "I won't let you fall."

"Okay." Hadley stood up on wobbly legs. "Does this work just like regular skating?"

"Pretty much," Brody said. "Lucy says it's actually easier."

Hadley lurched forward, grabbing onto the side of the porch for support. "It doesn't feel easier."

Brody took her hand and led her around the porch as she

learned the feel of the blades and the wooden boards beneath them. After a few minutes, she was zipping around the porch with her hands in the air while Brody watched and laughed from the porch swing.

"See?" he said. "I told you it was easy!"

"It's amazing," Hadley yelled. She continued to breeze around the porch, the sound of the Rollerblades and cicadas in her ears. It had been a long time since she'd felt this free, since she'd been able to think about anything else except Mark and the divorce or the farm or anything that didn't make her feel like her heart was going to beat right out of her chest. Right now all she felt was happy. Half an hour later, when she collapsed next to Brody on the porch swing, she leaned into him, exhausted and panting.

"Thank you," she said. "I really needed that."

"Lucy does it when she gets frustrated," Brody said. "She says it makes her feel better."

"It really does."

"It's why I bought the house."

"So Lucy could Rollerblade when she got frustrated?"

"Because after my divorce, I wanted something that made me happy every time I looked at it," Brody said. "It's why I kept your picture, and it's why I bought the house."

Hadley turned her head so that she could look at him. "You bought a house because it made you think of me?"

"I bought the house because I hoped maybe one day you'd come home," Brody said. "I never gave up hope, Hadley."

Hadley allowed him to brush a piece of damp hair out of her eyes, and then she felt his lips on hers, the first pair of lips she'd ever felt on hers, when she'd been thirteen years old. She kissed him back, the hunger inside of her spilling over, until she felt dizzy with want. "I can't," she said, pulling herself away from him, gasping. "I can't."

"I know," he said. And then, more quietly, "Mark."

"Mark," Hadley repeated, touching her lips. "He's still my husband."

"Do you want me to take you home?" Brody asked.

Hadley leaned down and pulled off the Rollerblades. "No," she said. "I don't want to go home tonight."

"You can have my room," Brody replied. "I'll sleep on the couch."

"Are you sure you don't mind?"

"No," he said, leading her inside. "At least I know you'll be safe here."

Hadley took his hand in hers and squeezed it. "I don't love him," she said. She wasn't sure if it was the Rollerblading or the whiskey or both that made her say those words, but in that moment, she had to tell him. It was the truth, and deep down, she knew it always had been.

"I know," he said, squeezing her hand right back. "I know."

CHAPTER 30
Martha

MARTHA FELT LIKE SHE'D JUST WON BEST FEMALE ARTIST at the Country Music Awards. She couldn't remember the last time she felt so good, and all she'd done was play a few songs for a relatively small crowd. But her new song had gone over well, and she and Amanda played together for the first time in years and years.

From the corner of her eye, she saw Pfeiffer talking to Luke, and she grinned. It was about time her sister met someone. She needed someone smart. She needed someone argumentative, someone like Luke, with a lawyer's brain. When he was bending down to whisper in Pfeiffer's ear, Martha felt like letting out a whoop. Instead, she turned around to collect her guitar and ran right into the person standing behind her.

"Oh, I'm sorry," she said, taking a step back. "I didn't see you."

"It's okay."

Martha looked up at the man standing in front of her. She'd

seen him earlier, sitting with her sister at the table, between Ava Dawn and her boyfriend. He was handsome, in a boyish sort of way, but the cocky grin on his face reminded her too much of Travis.

"Excuse me," he said as Martha attempted to sidestep him. "Could I get your autograph?" He handed her a slightly crumpled bar napkin.

"Sure," Martha replied, trying not to sound annoyed. Really, she ought to be grateful. She knew that. "Who should I make it out to?"

"Reese," he said.

The shyness in his voice startled Martha. He didn't look like he was shy. He looked like he took girls like her . . . well, the girl she used to be, home by the dozen. "Okay," she said. "How do you spell that?"

"R-E-E-S-E," he said. "I own all your albums."

"Really?" Martha asked, squinting up at him. "Excuse me for sayin' so, but you don't look like my fan base."

"My best friend Court is a big fan," he said. "He kept playin' that one song, you know, the first single from your first album, and man, I couldn't get it out of my head. Been listenin' to ya ever since."

"Well, thanks," Martha said, trying to ignore the urge to reach up and touch his rust-colored beard to see if it felt as soft as it looked. "I appreciate that."

"I told your sister I didn't know who you were," he continued. "But I knew the minute you walked in. I guess I'm used to savin' face around town. I can be kind of . . ."

"A jackass?" Martha replied with a straight face. "Yeah, you remind me a lot of my ex-husband."

"Travis Tucker?" Reese spat out, as if the words left a bad taste in his mouth. "That fool? I can't stand him."

"Me either, currently."

"He can't sing for shit. I don't give a damn what anybody says, you're a million times better than he is any day of the week."

Without realizing what she was doing, Martha took hold of Reese's shirt and pulled him down to her, laying a kiss right smack on his mouth. His eyes widened, and when she pulled away from him, she couldn't help but giggle at the look of astonishment on his face. "Thanks," she said, trying to catch her breath. "I needed that."

"Hey," he said as she turned to leave, "I'm taking your sister and Luke Gibson to talk to my grandmama tomorrow about your aunt. Maybe you'd want to come?"

"Maybe!" Martha called over her shoulder, too distracted by his kiss to hear much of what he'd actually said. "Good night! And thanks again! Your lips are mighty soft!"

"Do you think everything went okay with Hadley and Mark?" Martha asked nearly an hour later as they pulled into the driveway of the farm. "I see his car is still here."

"I don't know," Pfeiffer replied. "I kind of thought we would have heard from her at some point."

"Me too," Martha agreed. "But I have to admit that I was so caught up in the show, I'm just now realizing it."

"It was a great show," Pfeiffer said. "Truly, it was."

"Thank you, Pi. That means a lot."

"Hey," Pfeiffer said, squinting into the darkness. "Is that Mark sitting on the front porch?"

"Looks like it," Martha said. "I wonder where Hadley is."

"Probably inside packing her suitcase to go home," Pfeiffer guessed. "You and I both know that's why he came here tonight."

Martha got out of the car and followed Pfeiffer up to the house. "What are you doing out here, Mark?" she asked.

"Where's Hadley?" Mark replied. "I thought she'd be with you."

"Why would she be with us?" Pfeiffer wanted to know. "She was with *you* when we left."

"Well, she's not with me now."

Pfeiffer ran into the house, opening the door wide, calling her sister's name. When she was nowhere to be found, she hurried back outside to confront Mark. "What did you do to her?"

"Me?" Mark asked, standing up. "I didn't do anything. She left with that stupid dog. I assumed she was going to find you."

"You assumed she was going to walk nearly fifteen miles in the rain to find us?" Martha asked, her hands on her hips.

"Wait, why does she have Lafayette?" Pfeiffer demanded.

"The damn thing growled," Mark replied. "I thought it was going to bite me."

Pfeiffer's gaze went from alarm to satisfied smugness.

"And you don't have any idea where she went?" Martha asked, ignoring her sister. She was glad Lafayette had been there, too, but she didn't know if the dog had done more harm than good now that Hadley had seemingly disappeared into thin air.

"She went off down the road," Mark replied. "I don't know where she went after she turned right at the end of the driveway."

"You didn't go after her?" Martha asked.

"And let that psychotic animal anywhere near me?" Mark asked. "No way. Besides, I assumed she'd come home with you."

"I know where she went," Pfeiffer replied, her hands on her hips. "I know exactly where she's gone."

"Where?" Martha and Mark said at the same time.

Pfeiffer looked at Martha and raised an eyebrow. "Who do we know who lives just a few miles to the right of us?"

"Who is it?" Mark demanded.

"Brody," Pfeiffer said. "He's our closest neighbor on that side."

"You're telling me Hadley's ex-boyfriend is your neighbor?"

"Yep."

Mark strode into the kitchen and grabbed his phone and keys from the table. "I'm going over there."

"Like hell you are," Pfeiffer said, stepping in front of him.

"Get out of my way, Pfeiffer," Mark said, his jaw tight. "You look just like that damn dog, but I know good and well you won't bite me."

"Try me," Pfeiffer replied.

"Now, I'm warning you . . ."

"I'm telling you this for your own good," Pfeiffer replied, unmoved. "You won't get twenty feet from his house before he shoots you."

"He's not going to shoot me."

"Oh yeah?" Pfeiffer countered. "You see those pictures of him with Martha? Did he look like he was joking around?"

Martha caught the look Pfeiffer was giving her and said, "Oh yeah. You don't want to go causing him any trouble."

"This is bullshit," Mark muttered.

"This is Cold River," Pfeiffer replied.

"I never should have come here," Mark said, beginning to pace back and forth.

"Probably not," Pfeiffer agreed. "At least not without telling your wife."

"Didn't she tell you?" Mark sneered. "We're getting a divorce. So she won't be my wife much longer."

"What?" Martha furrowed her eyebrows.

"We've been separated for months," Mark replied. "But we were waiting until after the election to finalize it. Now it looks like she's dead set on ruining my campaign over some crush she had when she was eighteen."

"Not everything is about your stupid campaign," Pfeiffer replied. "And Hadley would never do anything to ruin it. If she took off, chances are that it was your fault. And I'm guessing the same is true of your divorce."

Martha shook her head. She was having trouble believing what she was hearing. Of all people to get a divorce, she never figured it would be Hadley and Mark. True, she also never thought they were much in love, but she'd learned the hard way that being in love didn't always make a marriage last.

"I don't think you're in any position to be talking about blame," Mark said to Pfeiffer, interrupting Martha's thoughts. "Didn't you lose your job because you couldn't keep your trap shut?"

Martha swiveled around to look at her sister. "You lost your job?" All of this new information was starting to make her head swim.

Pfeiffer was too busy glaring at Mark to answer. "That's none of your business," she said to him.

"Yeah, well, my relationship with Hadley is none of *your* business," Mark replied. "I'm going to go see if I can find a clean hotel room in this shit hole of a town. You tell your sister I'll be back tomorrow."

Martha and Pfeiffer watched him walk out the door, neither one of them moving or speaking until his car had long disappeared down the gravel path. After what felt like forever, Martha said, "Did you really lose your job?"

"Yes," Pfeiffer replied, still staring after Mark. "I wonder how he found out."

"How long ago?" Martha wanted to know.

Pfeiffer sighed. "Nine months."

"Nine months?" Martha exclaimed. "That's longer than I've been divorced!"

"I know," Pfeiffer replied. "I was going to tell you. I was going to tell both of you. But there never seemed to be a good time."

"What have you been doing up in New York that whole time?" Martha asked.

Pfeiffer walked over and plopped down on the couch. "Hiding in my apartment mostly," she said. "But now I don't even have that."

"What happened?"

"I sent a stupid email," Pfeiffer said. "It kind of went viral around the publishing world, and Henry Brothers fired me."

"Pfeiffer, I'm so sorry," Martha said, sitting down next to her. "You should have called me. You could have come and stayed with me."

"You had your own stuff to deal with," Pfeiffer replied. "By the time I realized that I wasn't going to find a job, you were already in the middle of your divorce. Then you left for rehab. I didn't want to mess that up for you, you know? I couldn't throw my own troubles on top of you or Hadley."

"Hadley apparently has a few troubles of her own," Martha replied. "I guess we all do."

"I had no idea about it," Pfeiffer replied. "Did you?"

"No," Martha said. "No idea. Do you think she knows you lost your job? I mean, she knew something was up from the beginning; you've been acting so weird."

"I don't think she knew," Pfeiffer replied. "She would have said something by now. She would have called me the minute she found out and demanded I come and live with her."

"That's kind of what sisters are for," Martha replied. "We take care of each other. Well, we're supposed to."

Pfeiffer looked down at her hands. "I haven't done a very good job of that recently . . . or ever."

"That's not true," Martha said. "I saw you sticking up for Hadley tonight. And I saw how proud you were of me up on-stage. You might not always say it, but I know you love us."

"I do love you," Pfeiffer replied.

"I love you, too," Martha said. "And you can still come and live with me."

"I think I might stay here," Pfeiffer replied. "I mean, it's the only thing I own now, anyway."

"Really?"

Pfeiffer shrugged. "I was thinking about getting a job and writing for a while," she said. "I don't know; it's just a thought."

"I think it sounds like a good idea," Martha said. "You always were a good writer. I never understood how you moved to NYC to write and ended up editing instead."

"Writing doesn't pay the bills," Pfeiffer said. "Unless you're Stephen King or Janet Evanovich."

"I still think you should give it a shot," Martha said. "Everybody said music doesn't pay the bills, and let me tell you, it does."

"Well, of course it does when you're Martha Hemingway," Pfeiffer replied.

"I sometimes wish I wasn't Martha Hemingway."

"Don't say that," Pfeiffer replied. "Martha Hemingway is the most talented woman I know."

Martha pulled her phone out of her pocket when it began to ding. "I got a text from Brody," she said.

"What does it say?"

"It says Hadley is fine," Martha replied. "And there's a picture of Lafayette and Brody's dog, Ollie. Look." Pfeiffer held up her phone to show her sister a picture of Ollie cuddled up next to Lafayette, one of Lafayette's ears in his mouth.

"Who do you think Hadley's cuddled up next to?" Pfeiffer asked, a wry smile on her face.

"I'll give you three guesses," Martha replied. "But as always, the first two don't count."

CHAPTER 31
Pfeiffer

PFEIFFER STOOD IN FRONT OF MARTHA'S HALF-OPEN SUIT-case the next morning, trying to decide if she could steal some of her sister's clothes without waking her. She didn't want to contend with telling her that she was meeting Luke at his office to go and speak with Anna Graham, and she hoped to get out of the house before Hadley, Brody, *or* Mark showed up.

Pfeiffer held up a yellow sundress, just casual enough not to be conspicuous, and turned to the dresser mirror to see how it might look.

"Don't wear that," Martha croaked from underneath a mass of blankets. "It'll make you look washed out."

"What are you talking about?" Pfeiffer asked, whipping around so fast she dropped the dress.

"You can't go meet Luke Gibson looking washed out," Martha said. She sat up and rubbed at her eyes, smearing the mascara she'd been wearing the night before. "Shit. I meant to wash my face."

"How do you know I'm meeting Luke?"

"Because some smooth talker named Reese Graham told me last night," Martha said. "He asked me for my autograph."

"He did?"

"Yeah," Martha replied. "He's kind of cute, don't you think?"

"I guess," Pfeiffer replied. "In that big-truck, Blake Shelton kind of way."

"Is there any other way?" Martha asked.

"Maybe not for you," Pfeiffer replied, grinning.

"So why are you going to talk with Anna Graham?" Martha asked, switching subjects and rubbing dried mascara out of her eyes.

"I just want to ask her a few questions about Aunt Bea," Pfeiffer replied. "Maybe she knows something we don't."

"About what?"

"About the body we found in the garden."

Martha removed her hands from her eyes and stared at Pfeiffer. "You think Aunt Bea had something to do with it?"

"I don't know," Pfeiffer said. "But I do know that Mom and Dad didn't have anything to do with it, and I want to make sure the sheriff knows it."

"Somebody in our family has to have known about it," Martha said.

"And you think it was Mom and Dad?" Pfeiffer asked.

"No," Martha said. "But it has to be somebody."

"That's why I'm hoping Anna knows something. Reese said she and Aunt Bea were best friends as kids," Pfeiffer said, careful to omit the information she'd found in the journal. For some reason she wasn't ready to share it yet. Not without the missing pages.

"Did you know Mom was planning on leaving the farm that spring she died?" Martha asked. "Because Hadley knew, and she didn't tell us."

"I didn't know," Pfeiffer replied. "I found out the same way you did."

"Why do you think she didn't tell us?"

Pfeiffer shrugged. "I don't know. But I guess it wouldn't have made any difference after Mama and Mary died."

"I guess not," Martha said, chewing on a strand of hair. "I don't know. It's too early for me to think."

"Well, can you at least help me pick something to wear?" Pfeiffer asked. "I'm at a loss."

Martha climbed out of bed and rummaged through her clothes. She pulled out a mint-green sundress identical to the yellow one. "Wear this one," she said. "It will go great against your skin."

"Thanks," Pfeiffer replied. "I don't really have much that doesn't look like I'm headed for a business meeting."

"So you like him?" Martha asked. "Luke?"

Pfeiffer felt herself blush and had a flashback to when they were teenagers—this very room, this very same conversation about other boys. "I think I might," she said.

"Well, he wouldn't have offered to meet you at nine thirty a.m. on a Saturday if he didn't like you, too," Martha replied.

"Thanks," Pfeiffer replied. "Are you going to come?"

"And miss the chance to go back to sleep while the house is quiet?" Martha asked. "Hell no. The keys are on the table."

Pfeiffer grinned. "Okay. I'll let you know what I find out," she said, slipping from the room and closing the door behind her.

The quiet of the house was foreign to Pfeiffer after so many years of hearing a busy city bustling outside her apartment. But she could remember waking up early on the weekends, before anyone else in the family was awake, and just sitting outside and thinking. It was the only time she didn't have to worry about arguing with Pfeiffer or Martha, or listen to Mary's incessant questions, or do the list of chores her mother would inevitably present to her. When it was quiet outside, it was quiet in her head, and that was worth more than any Manhattan sunrise.

LUKE WAS WAITING for Pfeiffer when she pulled into the parking lot. He was sitting on the front steps of his law office in a pair of jeans, leather sandals, and another crisp, white T-shirt. The sky above them was dark as she got out of the car to meet him, the rain from the night before never completely subsiding.

"Good morning," Luke said, handing her a cup of coffee. "I took a chance that you'd like it black."

"I do," Pfeiffer said, breathing in the aroma. "Thank you."

"Weird weather we're having, isn't it?"

Pfeiffer looked up at the bruised sky. "Yeah, but that's Missouri for you."

"The weather was a bit more predictable in St. Louis," Luke replied.

"That's the thing about the Ozarks," Pfeiffer said. "We can't decide if we're the South or the Midwest, and neither can the weather."

"Well, you look nice," Luke said, standing a little too close to her.

"Thanks," Pfeiffer replied. And then, for lack of knowing what to say, added, "Where's Reese?"

"He'll be here," Luke replied. "He's always late."

Pfeiffer raised an eyebrow. "Are you two friends?"

"I wouldn't say that," Luke replied. "I was his lawyer a couple years back. He was late for every single meeting we ever had."

"I bet your secretary didn't like that much."

"She did not."

"I think my sister has a crush on him," Pfeiffer said.

"Which one?"

"Martha."

"Well, he's not a *bad* guy," Luke told her. "He just wants everyone to think he is."

Pfeiffer rolled her eyes. "He's too old for that, but I guess I should be grateful he agreed to take us to see his grandmother."

"So you want to tell me the real reason you're going to have a chat with Anna Graham?" Luke asked.

"Real reason?"

"I'm a lawyer," Luke said. "I can tell when someone has an ulterior motive."

"I don't have any motives," Pfeiffer replied, looking down into her coffee cup.

"Doesn't have anything to do with the body they found on your property?" Luke asked. "And the odd request from your aunt that the farm stay in the family at all costs?"

Pfeiffer's eyes snapped up to his.

"That's what I thought."

"Looks like it's gonna rain!" they heard Reese call out, driving up to them with the window to his pickup truck down. "Hop on in."

"I can drive myself," Pfeiffer said.

"Ain't no reason," Reese replied. "Plenty of room up here in the front seat."

Pfeiffer walked around to the passenger's side of the truck and opened the door. The truck was lifted so high up off the ground that she considered taking a running start at it. Before she had the chance to give it a try, she felt a pair of hands on her hips, lifting her up.

Luke was behind her, helping her into the truck. "You got it?" he asked, once she was in the seat.

"Yeah, thanks," Pfeiffer said. She allowed his hands to linger on her waist for just a moment longer before she scooted over and shut the door.

"My grandmama just lives a couple miles away," Reese said. "She said she was *tickled pink* to have you come and visit."

"I'm glad," Pfeiffer said. "I promise I won't take up too much of her time."

"It's not you taking up time that I'm worried about," he said. "I just hope you're ready for the photo albums to come out."

"I like looking at old pictures," Pfeiffer said.

"Might get a couple of me in the buff," Reese replied with a wink.

Pfeiffer ignored him and stared out the window at the passing rows of houses. There had been a time in her life when she knew who lived in every single one of them. Now she wasn't sure if she would recognize half of the people she graduated high school with. When they pulled up to a small, white one-story house surrounded by a wrought-iron fence, Pfeiffer remembered that she'd been there before. "I came here once with my aunt," she said. "To return a serving dish your grandmother brought over after my mother and sister died."

"Her casseroles are the best," Reese said. "I practically live on 'em."

The older woman was sitting out on the porch with a quilt square in her hands. She waved and smiled at them as they approached, standing up to greet them. "I thought maybe Reese overslept," she said. "He has a tendency to do that, you know."

"I set an alarm this morning, Granny," Reese replied, bending down to give her a kiss.

"Was she pretty?" Anna asked.

Pfeiffer almost burst out laughing, but managed to contain herself. "Thanks for having me over, Mrs. Graham."

"Oh, honey, call me Anna," she said. "You're practically family."

Pfeiffer smiled, feeling slightly embarrassed. "Well, thank you."

"Come on inside," Anna replied. "I've already got coffee cake on the table. Would you all like some coffee, too?"

"I'd love some," Luke said.

"How are you, Lucas?" Anna asked. "You're looking well."

"I *am* well, thank you."

"How's business?"

"Booming," Luke said. "There's always someone who needs a lawyer. Even in a little town like this."

"Don't I know it," Anna replied, nodding over toward Reese, who was already eating a mouthful of coffee cake. "You don't know how much I appreciate your help with that one over there."

"All in a day's work," Luke replied.

"Goodness, I hope not," Anna said with a tinkling laugh.

Pfeiffer and Luke followed Anna to the table, where they were told to sit, despite offering to help her serve the coffee. She presented them with china that Pfeiffer hadn't seen in a home in years, and she wondered if her aunt had some stored somewhere as well. It might be nice to have some of the cups for coffee.

"So how long were you and my aunt friends?" Pfeiffer asked after everyone was settled.

"Since we were five years old," Anna replied.

"That's a long time," Pfeiffer said. "I don't remember seeing you at our house while my aunt lived there . . . well, while I lived there for those two years before I left for college."

"I rarely went there," Anna said. "In fact, I haven't been out there since before Bea moved away back in the forties."

"How come?"

Anna shrugged. "I guess it was always easier for your aunt to come here."

"But she didn't drive," Pfeiffer said. "Old Crow had to take her everywhere."

"Old Crow?" Anna raised an eyebrow.

"Sorry. Mr. Crowley."

Anna took a sip of her coffee, leaving a smear of peach-colored lipstick around the rim. "Well, she came into town at least once a month for necessities," she replied. "So she would come by and have coffee. It was just easier."

"Not much except the river out your way," Reese interjected. "Good fishin', though."

"Are you and Mr. Crowley friends, too?" Pfeiffer asked.

"We've never been close," Anna replied. "He's an odd duck. But he was always good to your aunt."

"So you tolerated him."

Anna nodded. "I suppose you could say that." She took an-other sip of her coffee. "Your aunt and I were the exceptions to the friend rule back then," she said. "Your aunt lived in the country, and I lived here in town. Most of the country kids stuck together."

"But you all went to the same school, didn't you?"

"We did," Anna replied. "Most of them, like Rufus Crowley, stopped going at about sixth grade. But your great-grandfather believed that school was important, even for girls. Quite the revolutionary, he was."

Pfeiffer smiled. "I'm glad to know that."

"He was a good man," Anna said. "All the James men were good men."

"I wish I'd known more of them," Pfeiffer replied.

"You come from good stock, honey," Anna said, patting her hand. "Would you like some more coffee?"

"Yes, please."

"Here you are, my dear," Anna said, pouring from the pot into Pfeiffer's cup. "Just like your aunt, no sugar or milk."

Pfeiffer bit at the corner of her lip. She wanted to ask Anna about Will, and about the journal, but she wasn't sure how to broach the subject without sounding obvious or having to answer questions from Reese and Luke. Instead of mentioning either, she said, "Did my aunt ever come close to getting married?"

Anna shook her head. "No, not that I can recall."

"Not ever?"

Anna's eyes flicked up to Pfeiffer. She took a sip of her coffee and then said, "Reese, would you be a good boy and take the rest of this coffee cake over to Mrs. Anderson next door? She's got her niece and nephew for the weekend, and I'm sure she would be grateful for anything she doesn't have to cook. Take Lucas with you."

Reese stood and picked up the cake. "Where's the cover, Gran?"

"On the counter in the kitchen."

"Are you sure this can't wait?" Reese asked, once he and Luke were at the front door. "It's pouring outside."

"You ain't sugar, and you won't melt," Anna replied. "Neither of you."

"Come on," Reese said to Luke. "Let's go before she thinks of something else she needs done in this damn monsoon."

"He's really not so bad," Anna confided to Pfeiffer once they'd gone. "He just needs a bit of reining in every once in a while."

"I'm sure he's not," Pfeiffer replied. "It was nice of both of you to make time for me today."

Anna smiled and set her cup down daintily on its saucer. "Now, my dear, why don't you tell me why you've really come to visit?"

Pfeiffer cleared her throat. "To talk with you about Aunt Bea."

"And what about her?"

"I need you to tell me about Will."

A flicker of surprise registered on Anna's face for only an instant before she said, "How do you know about Will?"

"He was Aunt Bea's boyfriend," Pfeiffer said. "When you were teenagers?"

"Yes," Anna said. "A long, long time ago."

"What do you remember about him?"

"Not much," Anna replied. "He was your great-grandfather's farmhand for less than a year."

"And he and my aunt were in love?"

"How do you know about Will?" Anna asked again.

"Can you tell me what happened to him?" Pfeiffer said,

ignoring the older woman's question. "Where did he go after he left Cold River?"

Anna was quiet for a few moments, running one of her pale pink fingernails across the rim of her saucer. "I don't know."

"Did it end badly between them?"

"She wouldn't tell me," Anna replied. "She wouldn't tell anyone anything ever again."

"Is that why she stopped talking?" Pfeiffer pressed. "Because of Will?"

"I don't know," Anna said again. "One day Will was gone. The next, she and Maryann, your grandmother, were leaving for St. Louis so Maryann could see some kind of fertility doctor up there. Those were a rare thing back then, you know, and Maryann suffered so many losses. They never thought they'd have your mother. Anyway, they didn't come back until after Maryann had given birth, and I never heard Beatrice speak another word."

"Why did Aunt Bea go to St. Louis?" Pfeiffer asked.

Anna shrugged. "I always assumed it was because she was so heartbroken over Will leaving."

"But you don't know what happened between them?"

"Tell me how you know about Will," Anna said. "Nobody knew about him except for me."

"I found a journal," Pfeiffer said. "In her nightstand. It was hidden, and I wasn't looking for it, I swear. She mentioned a boy named Will, a farmhand her father didn't like, but she was in love with him."

"She was deeply in love with him," Anna said.

"In the last pages, she wrote about going to his cabin," Pfeiffer said. "I think they might've . . . might've . . ."

"Had sex?" Anna finished. "It's okay, honey, no need to be embarrassed. I have given birth to six children. I know what it is."

"Yes, well, I think they might've," Pfeiffer replied. "But the journal ends there. She went over there to tell him that her father was going to fire him, only she never told him. And the pages after that have all been ripped out."

"Strange," Anna said.

"And when I asked Mr. Crowley about it—"

"You asked Rufus?" Anna interrupted her. "You asked him about the journal?"

Pfeiffer nodded. "He's been acting like he might know something about the body he and Brody found in the yard. But he won't talk to the sheriff. He won't talk to anyone."

Anna took a deep, ragged breath. "Rufus was in love with your aunt," she said. "Clear until the very end."

"But she didn't love him?"

"She did," Anna replied. "But not in the way he wanted."

"Do you think he could have hurt Will?" Pfeiffer asked. "Do you think that's what all of this is about?"

"I don't know," Anna said. "I never understood their odd friendship, but I do know that he would have done anything for her. He would have done anything to keep her safe."

"Safe from what?"

"Whatever he saw as a threat," Anna replied. Then, reaching out to take Pfeiffer's hand, she said, "Don't underestimate him, Pfeiffer. He may be old, but he's not stupid. Leave it alone and let the sheriff do his job. It will all come out in the wash."

Pfeiffer pulled her hand away from the older woman and said, "The sheriff thinks my mother or father might've had something to do with it. I know they didn't. If finding out what happened to Will can help prove their innocence, I'm not going to stop asking questions."

Anna sat back in her chair as the door blew open and Reese and Luke staggered inside, battered and soaking. "There's a storm headed this way, Pfeiffer," she said. "There won't be anything you can do until it passes. Go home and try to forget about this unpleasantness. It's been nearly seventy years. Another few days won't hurt."

"It's getting bad out there," Luke said. "Pfeiffer, I hate to cut our visit short, but I think it might be a good idea to get home."

"I agree," Anna replied. "But thank you for coming to see me. You made an old lady's day."

Anna was smiling, but Pfeiffer could see the pain in the older woman's eyes, and part of her felt terrible for bringing up old memories. "It was nice to see you again," she said. "Thank you for the coffee."

"You're welcome anytime," Anna replied. "And, Pfeiffer, remember what I said, will you?"

"I will."

Pfeiffer kept quiet on the drive back, watching the rain pour down. She hated rain. She hated any kind of weather that had the potential to do something other than warm her skin or allow her to ski. Rain meant floods. Rain meant thunder and lightning, and sometimes, rain meant tornadoes. That was one of her favorite things about living in New York City—no tornadoes.

Reese drove off in a hail of exhaust, talking about a meeting with a hot blonde, leaving Pfeiffer and Luke standing in the rain.

"Do you want to come up for a minute?" Luke asked, motioning to his office. "Just until it lets up a bit?"

"I thought you said we needed to get home?" Pfeiffer asked.

"Do you really want to argue with me in the rain?"

"No," Pfeiffer said, shaking her head. "Let's go up."

"Do you need a towel or something?" Luke asked when they were inside the office. "I've got some in the bathroom in the hallway."

"Thanks," Pfeiffer said, taking off her wet shoes. "I'm okay."

"Your hair is dripping on the floor," Luke said. He handed her a towel and moved over to his desk, opening one of the drawers.

"It's a little unwieldy lately," Pfeiffer replied. "I haven't had a haircut in months."

Pfeiffer watched as Luke took off his soaking-wet T-shirt and pulled an identical one out of the drawer. She couldn't look away, even though she knew she should. There was a trail of fine, dark hair leading from his chest all the way to the dip in his jeans. For a moment, she forgot all about Anna and Old Crow and the whole reason she'd come into town that morning.

"Pfeiffer?" Luke asked, pulling the dry shirt over his head. "Are you okay?"

"What? Oh yes, I'm fine," Pfeiffer replied, trying to keep the warmth coiling in her core from reaching her cheeks.

"So did you find out anything useful?" Luke asked. "During your talk with Mrs. Graham?"

"I don't know," Pfeiffer replied.

"I know Anna sent me and Reese out for a reason," Luke replied, taking a step away from his desk and closer to Pfeiffer.

Pfeiffer dragged her eyes away from him. "I asked her about a man my aunt was in love with back in the forties," she said. "I found a journal detailing some of it, but the last few pages have been ripped out."

"And you thought Mrs. Graham might know something about it?" Luke asked.

"It was worth a shot," Pfeiffer said. "But she didn't know anything, not really."

"What do you think happened to the pages?"

Pfeiffer shrugged. "I don't know, but I think Rufus Crowley might."

"What does he have to do with it?" Luke wanted to know.

"He and my aunt were friends," Pfeiffer replied. "And he's been acting strange ever since the body was found."

"Do you think that the body is this man your aunt was in love with?" Luke asked.

"I don't know," Pfeiffer said. "I mean, I can't imagine that it's likely."

"How likely is it that there would be a dead body on your property?"

"Good point."

Luke turned toward the window. "Man, it's really coming down out there. I thought it would be letting up by now."

"It's supposed to rain for the next few days," Pfeiffer replied.

"I guess I haven't been paying too much attention to the weather," Luke said.

"I have about six weather apps," Pfeiffer said. "I like to know what's going to happen."

"That seems excessive."

She grinned. "Well, I can be a bit excessive sometimes."

"I'm glad that I saw you last night," Luke said. "I was hoping I would see you around."

"Really?"

"Yeah, of course."

"Why?"

Luke turned around so that he was standing so close to her that she could smell his bay rum aftershave. "I thought it might be nice to get to know you," he said.

"I think I'd like that," she replied.

"What about dinner one day this week?"

Pfeiffer pretended to think about it, but her mind was already coiled around the thought of going on a date with Luke. It was all she wanted to do. "I think that would work," she said finally.

Suddenly there was an intense warbling from both of their cell phones. Luke pulled his out of his pants pocket to look at it. "There's been a flash flood warning issued for Ozark County," he said.

"I better get home," Pfeiffer replied. "There's a low water bridge not far from the farm. If it gets up too high, I won't be able to make it back."

"I'll drive you," Luke said.

"I've got the Tesla," Pfeiffer replied. "I should be fine."

"Sure, if you want to get washed away in the flood," Luke replied. "We can take my truck."

"Okay," Pfeiffer said. "But Martha will kill me if anything happens to her car."

"You can follow me home, and we can put it in the garage," Luke said. "I just live a couple of blocks away."

Pfeiffer considered for a moment telling Luke she'd much rather stay at his place than go home. She had a pretty good feeling he'd oblige, but she knew she needed to go home. There was no telling what had happened since she left that morning, and more than anything, she needed to show her sisters the journal. Maybe together, the three of them could figure out the next step. She never should have kept it hidden from them in the first place.

"Let's go, then," Pfeiffer said. "Before the Cold River rises up and washes us all away."

Ten minutes later, Pfeiffer pulled onto a driveway at the end of a neat cul-de-sac. It was in the older part of town, not far from where she knew Dr. O'Conner lived. She was a bit surprised that the two-story native-stone house belonged to Luke. She expected him to live in something . . . she didn't know, a bit larger, more lawyer-ish. All of the lawyers she knew back in New York lived in brownstones or multi-million-dollar apartments.

"Quaint, isn't it?" Luke asked after he'd guided her into the garage. "It was built in 1910. I bought it from St. Louis before I ever even saw it in person."

"Why?" Pfeiffer wanted to know. "Weren't you scared it would be in awful condition?"

"I already knew it needed work on the inside," he replied. "But that's one of the reasons I bought it. It needed work."

"You like to fix up old houses?"

Luke nodded. "In my spare time. I worked with Brody on the house he's got on his farm now. We refinished all the floors and practically gutted every room."

Pfeiffer stepped from the doorway in the garage and entered a large kitchen with a butcher-block island. To the left was a living room with a rich, leather sofa that sat directly in front of a native-stone fireplace. "I love fireplaces," she said. "I always wanted one in my apartment, but they were never *real*. It's not the same when they're just for looks."

"I agree," Luke replied, close enough behind her that Pfeiffer could feel his breath on her ear. "This is one of my favorite parts of the house. Right here by the fireplace."

Beside the fireplace, a gray-faced beagle looked up at them. He stood up, stretched, and then hobbled over to where they stood.

"This is Crosby," Luke said. He reached down to scratch the dog behind one of his ears.

"How old is he?" Pfeiffer asked.

"Close to fifteen," Luke replied. "He doesn't hear or see much, but he gets along all right. Never misses hearing that treat bag open."

Pfeiffer bent down to pet the dog. He had a sweet face. It wasn't quite as long or droopy as Lafayette's, but she could see some definite similarities. "He's adorable," she said.

"Don't tell him that," Luke replied. "He likes to think he's tough."

"Do you think we'll have any trouble getting back to the farm?" Pfeiffer wanted to know. "I really hate being out in this stuff."

Luke busied himself inside one of his cabinets and said, "I think it'll be fine. My truck can go just about anywhere. Do you want a drink before we head out?"

"Sure," Pfeiffer replied, sitting herself down on the couch.

"Hot toddy okay?"

"Perfect."

Luke carried the drinks over and sat down beside her. "This is my grandmother's recipe," he said. "I can't tell you what's in that rum, but I can tell you that you won't catch a cold for at least a month."

Pfeiffer took a sip and allowed the warm liquid to run down

her throat. "God, I love these," she said. "I bet I haven't had one since I was a teenager."

"A teenager?" Luke asked.

"My aunt used to make them when we were feeling under the weather," Pfeiffer replied. "Looking back, she probably just did it to get us to sleep, but it worked. I always woke up feeling better."

Luke grinned. "My parents were teetotalers. So was my grandfather. We were all raised Church of Christ. Drinking, dancing, and basically having any fun was off the table. But the grandmother that I grew up with was really my step-grandmother. My dad's mother died long before I was born, and my grandfather remarried a woman from Tulsa," he said, and then took a long sip of his drink. "She had flaming red hair and lipstick to match. She smoked and drank and cursed; you know, the big three. You can imagine that she didn't go over well with the family. My grandfather's marriage to her is about the only thing I think I ever appreciated about the man."

"Nobody in my family has ever been a teetotaler," Pfeiffer said. "I sometimes wonder if maybe we had been, my sister wouldn't have become an alcoholic."

Luke turned to look at her. "I don't think it would have mattered," he said. "You and your sisters went through something traumatic at a young age. It makes sense that at least one of you might try to self-medicate to get through it."

"My other sister married a man she didn't love because she wanted to forget," Pfeiffer said. "I guess it took me a little bit longer to self-destruct, but when I did, I went big."

"What happened?"

"I destroyed my career," Pfeiffer said. "And you know, I knew what I was doing when I did it. I even thought about it before I did it, and realized I just didn't care anymore." She turned herself so that she was face-to-face with Luke. "I think that's the first time I've ever said that out loud."

"Are you sorry you let it happen?" Luke asked.

"No," Pfeiffer replied, her voice softer than it had been before. "I'm not."

When Luke leaned in to kiss her, Pfeiffer allowed herself to be pulled in to him. Every ounce of longing, of loneliness, she'd been holding onto for the last twenty years came flooding out, and she didn't even realize she was crying until Luke lifted her up and carried her, her head lolling against his shoulder, to the bedroom.

"We don't have to do this," he said, his breathing hot in her ear. "It's just that I—"

"No," Pfeiffer said, cutting him off. "I want it, too. You don't know how much I want this."

Luke wiped at the tears on her cheeks with his thumb, and then he kissed her again.

Pfeiffer found the hem of his shirt and pulled it up, and then she laid her hands flush against his chest, allowing the warmth radiating from him to warm her, too. Their clothes nothing more than a heap at their feet, Luke took her in, all of her, and Pfeiffer kept her eyes open so that she could watch the way his body responded to hers, the way the dimple in his left cheek flashed when he smiled in satisfaction just before he pressed his mouth onto her neck and her collarbone.

When Luke's hand slid between her thighs and his tongue

traced the outline of one of her nipples, Pfeiffer arched her back, but Luke took his time. It wasn't until they were in perfect sync with each other, when their breath was ragged and their hearts were beating to the same rhythm as the rain coming down outside the window, that they finally became one.

CHAPTER 32
Hadley

H ADLEY LET OUT A SIGH OF RELIEF WHEN SHE AND BRODY pulled into the driveway at the farm and Mark's car was gone. She hoped he got the first flight out of Missouri that morning. She knew she would have to deal with him and the end of their marriage at some point, but she didn't want to deal with it today.

"I can't believe it's still raining," Brody said. "We get flash flood alerts all the time around here, but if this keeps up, we'll be in trouble."

"Maybe it will stop soon," Hadley said. She absently stroked Lafayette, who was nestled down beside her. Ollie, too, had come with them, and it was a tight fit inside the cab of Brody's truck. But Ollie had followed Lafayette all the way out to the truck and whined until Brody lifted him up into the cab of the pickup.

"The forecast says it's supposed to keep up all day," Brody said.

"Is Lucy going to be all right with your parents?" Hadley asked. "Do you need to go check on her?"

"Naw, she's fine," Brody said. "Mom and Dad live up on that hill, so they should be fine. But I'm going to make her stay with them until all of this passes by us."

Hadley knew they were both thinking about her mother and sister, and the last great storm that rolled through Cold River. She wondered if he ever thought about Mary, who was Lucy's age when she died. Sometimes, when the rain came down in sheets and the wind began to howl all around her, it was all Hadley could think about.

They all four got out of the pickup and hurried inside. Martha was sitting at the kitchen table, reading, when they entered.

"I'm so glad you're here," she said, a rare line of worry creasing her forehead. "I wasn't sure if you or Pfeiffer would be able to get back in all of this rain."

"Where did Pfeiffer go?"

"Into town," Martha replied. "She's with Luke Gibson."

"The lawyer?" Brody asked.

"He's our lawyer," Hadley replied. "Well, he was our aunt's lawyer."

"He sat by us last night at Mama's," Martha said, her eyes twinkling. "He really seems to like her."

"So she went in to meet him for breakfast or something?" Hadley asked. "That's kind of an odd date to make—first thing in the morning."

"It wasn't a date," Martha said. "She went into town to talk to Anna Graham about Aunt Bea."

"Why?"

Martha turned around and went over to the kitchen table,

picking up a small, leather-bound journal in her hands. "I think it might've had something to do with this."

"What is it?" Hadley asked.

"It's Aunt Bea's journal from when she was a teenager," Martha replied. "I got curious while I was here alone, and went into her bedroom. I found it under the mattress."

"That's an odd place for it," Hadley said.

"I think Pfeiffer was hiding it from us."

"Why would she do that?"

Martha shrugged. "I don't know, but the last few pages are missing."

"Do you think Pfeiffer took them?" Brody asked, taking the journal from Hadley and looking it over. "Man, this thing is ancient."

"Maybe," Martha replied. "But I don't know why she would do that. Why wouldn't she just take the whole thing?"

"Who knows," Hadley said. "I rarely know why Pfeiffer does anything she does."

"I'm wondering if she thinks this has something to do with the . . . you know, *body*," Martha said to Brody. "I'm not sure how it ties together, though."

"She was pretty convinced that Crowley knows something," Brody said. "I think when she went to see him and he wouldn't come and talk to the sheriff, it convinced her even more."

"That was strange," Hadley admitted. "But Crowley? I can't imagine he'd ever have anything to do with something like that."

There was a loud clap of thunder, and the lights inside the house flickered and then went out.

"I don't like this," Martha said.

"It's all right," Hadley replied. "We'll be fine." She reached out and touched her sister's shoulder. She'd said the words more for her own benefit than anyone else's, but she knew Martha needed to hear them, too.

Outside, a truck pulled up into the driveway, and Pfeiffer and Luke emerged, hurrying up the steps and into the house. Pfeiffer entered first, soaking wet, but her skin glowing a luminous pink that Hadley recognized the moment she saw the way Luke was looking at her younger sister.

"Well, hello, you two," she said, arching an eyebrow.

"It's really getting bad out there," Pfeiffer said, ignoring her sister. "We almost didn't make it across the low water bridge."

"Well, I guess that means we'll all be stuck here for a while," Martha replied.

"I'm going to run upstairs and change my clothes," Pfeiffer said. "Please don't scare Luke away while I'm gone."

"How's it going, Luke?" Brody asked, holding out his hand for Luke to shake once Pfeiffer had left the room.

"Not bad," Luke replied. Turning to Martha, he said, "Martha, we left your car in my garage to make sure it stayed safe."

"I was just about to ask where it was," Martha replied. "Thank you. I would have killed Pfeiffer if something happened to it."

"That's what she told me."

"Thanks for bringing Pfeiffer home," Hadley said. "Were you talking with Anna Graham all this time?"

Luke's cheeks turned pink, the color visible even in the dim light of the room, and he said, "We stopped over at my place and had a drink before we headed out again."

"I bet you did."

Martha looked between Hadley and Luke, a question forming on her lips. "Did I miss something?" she asked.

"Nope," Hadley said, winking at Luke.

"I'm sure we'll be able to get home in a few hours," Luke said hastily, looking as if he were ready to risk the flood to escape Hadley. Then he saw the journal in her hands. "Is that your aunt's?"

"How did you know about it?" Hadley asked.

"Pfeiffer told me this morning."

"Apparently, Pfeiffer told everyone but us," Martha commented.

"I told everyone what?" Pfeiffer asked, coming down the stairs.

Despite being irritated with her, Hadley couldn't help but smile. It was obvious Pfeiffer had put some thought into her appearance, as she'd even applied a fresh coat of lipstick. Her sister must really like Luke, because she'd never seen her try so hard. "You want to explain this journal?" Hadley asked after a moment. "Why didn't you tell us about it before?"

"I was going to tell you both," Pfeiffer replied. "But I wanted to make sense of it first. Then Brody and Old Crow found that skull, and I guess I got a little distracted."

"Do you think this has something to do with that skull?" Hadley asked.

"I think it might," Pfeiffer said. "We all know Mom and Dad didn't have anything to do with it."

Hadley nodded. She did know that. Truly, she did. But at the same time there were things neither of her sisters knew, especially how desperate their mother had been to leave Cold River and start over. There were things they didn't know about that awful day when her mother and Mary died, things she never wanted to tell them.

"Have you heard from Mark?" Pfeiffer asked. "He said last night he was coming back this morning."

"He hasn't come back," Martha replied. "Have you heard from him?"

Hadley shook her head. "No, I was hoping he'd gone home to D.C."

"Maybe he did," Pfeiffer said. "We made it pretty obvious last night he wasn't welcome."

"Thanks," Hadley replied. "I'm guessing he told you."

"He did," Pfeiffer said. "We can talk about it later."

Hadley mouthed *thank you* to her before she turned to everyone else and said, "Why don't you all come into the kitchen, and Martha and I will try to rustle us up something to eat that doesn't involve using power."

"We've still got tomatoes," Martha said. "I can make us some tomato sandwiches."

"Why don't you make the sandwiches and I'll go and see if I can find us some candles," Hadley said.

"I'll go with you," Brody offered.

"Thanks," Hadley replied. "I'm not sure where they are, but they may be in the cellar."

"Outside?"

"Well, we have to go outside to get there," Hadley said, rummaging through the pantry. "Here, we can put a couple of these trash bags on our heads."

"Great," Brody replied, rolling his eyes.

"Hey, you offered."

"Let's just go," Brody said. "I've got a lighter in my truck. I'll grab it on our way."

Hadley ran out the front door and hurried to the back of the house, where the cellar was located. The water on the ground almost covered her shoes, and she almost slipped before Brody caught her by the arm.

"Are you all right?" he asked.

"Thanks," Hadley replied. "I'm all right. This is way worse than it looked from inside."

"My mom just sent me a text," Brody said. "She says they've had to evacuate parts of town."

"Is everyone okay?"

"She says they're fine, but that it's gotten pretty bad around the downtown area. We might need to tell Luke. His office could be affected."

"Okay," Hadley replied. "But first, let's get in here and see if we can find the candles."

Hadley threw open the door, and using the flashlight on Brody's phone, made her way down the steps. It had been years since she'd been in the cellar, and the smell reminded her of opening the door the day of the tornado and seeing her sisters down there, huddled together. She remembered sitting on the damp earth and crying with them, telling them everything would be okay and knowing at the same time that it would never be.

"Where do you keep the candles?" Brody asked. "Hadley?"

"Yeah, uh, I'm not sure," Hadley replied. "I think there's a desk over there somewhere. That's where Mom always kept the candles."

"The candles are over twenty years old?"

"Probably."

Brody sighed and rummaged through the desk until he found four tall, white candles. "I think these will do," he said. "They don't look too bad."

"Great," Hadley replied, taking a last look around the room. "Let's get out of here."

"There are cans of food and jars of jam down here," Brody said. "Did you know that?"

"No," Hadley replied. "I haven't been down here since . . . well, in a long time."

Brody's face fell. "Oh, Hadley, I'm sorry. I didn't even think . . ."

"It's okay," Hadley said. "I know. I wish I didn't have to think about it either."

"I should have gone with you that day," he said. "I shouldn't have let you leave like that, all alone."

"We were eighteen," Hadley replied. "Neither of us had the skills to deal with something like that."

"It doesn't matter," Brody said. "I should have gone with you."

"I don't blame you," Hadley said.

"Don't blame yourself either," Brody replied. "You can't blame yourself for what happened."

"I blame myself for a lot of things."

Brody took her hand. "Don't talk like that," he said.

"I'm sorry," Hadley replied. "I don't mean to dump all of this on you. You've listened to me enough already."

"I want to listen to you," he told her, using his grip on her hand to pull her closer to him. "I don't ever want to stop listening to you."

A smile played at the corners of Hadley's lips. "I've missed you so much."

"I've missed you, too," Brody said. "But we better get back to the house before they start to get suspicious."

"Trust me," Hadley replied. "The second my sisters and I are alone together, I'm going to have some major explaining to do."

"I don't doubt it."

Hadley looked down at her feet, realizing that both she and Brody were standing in water nearly up to their shins. "The cellar is starting to flood," she said. "Look how high the water has gotten since we came down here."

"I know," Brody replied. "Come on." He pulled her up the steps and back out into the rain. "Let's get inside."

CHAPTER 33

Pfeiffer

PFEIFFER LIT THE LAST OF THE CANDLES AND LOOKED
around the kitchen with satisfaction. She knew it was probably wrong to feel happy given the weather and everything else going on, but she couldn't keep her mind off Luke. All she wanted
to do was have some time to sit down and think about their time
together, to savor it, but she knew that right now that wasn't going to be an option. Still, she felt lighter than she'd felt in decades,
and she knew she owed it all to him.

"Pfeiffer?"

Pfeiffer turned to see Luke standing in the doorway. "Hey,"
she said. "Did you get a sandwich?"

"I have to get going," he said, his brow creased with worry.
"Brody said his mom sent him a text about flooding near the downtown area. Now it seems like all the towers are out, because nobody
has any reception. I have to go and make sure my office is okay."

"You can't leave," Pfeiffer said. "The bridge will be washed
out by now."

"I need to at least check," Luke replied.

"But your office is on the third floor."

"I own the whole building," Luke said. "Some of the stuff stored on the bottom floor has belonged to my family for years. I can't let it get ruined if I can help it."

"Okay," Pfeiffer replied, putting down the lighter. "I'm coming with you."

"No way," Luke said.

"Why not?"

"Something could happen."

"Well, if it does, you'll for sure want my help," Pfeiffer said.

"That's not funny," Luke replied, his jaw set. "I'd never be able to forgive myself if something happened while you were with me."

"Ditto," Pfeiffer said. "And if we get to the low water bridge and it's washed out, you'll have no choice but to come back, lest you risk putting me in danger."

"Are you sure you weren't a lawyer in a previous life?" Luke asked.

Pfeiffer resisted the urge to kiss him and instead pulled on her shoes, which were still soggy from their previous trips out in the rain. She wasn't entirely sure she wanted to go with him, but she was entirely sure he would try to cross the low water bridge without her. She wondered what it was about some men that made them think driving in terrible weather was a good idea. Her father had been that way. She remembered him taking to the roads as soon as the first snow fell and her mother worrying until he got home that he was stuck in a ditch somewhere, freezing to death.

"Are you ready?" Luke asked.

"Yep," Pfeiffer replied, not feeling ready at all. "Let's go."

"Please be careful," Hadley said.

"Are you sure you don't want me to go with you?" Brody asked, stepping forward.

"We'll be fine," Pfeiffer said. "Besides, I'd rather you be here just in case something happens."

Brody nodded. "You're right. With the way this water is rising up, I don't know that any house is safe."

"Promise me you'll get my sisters out if it comes to that," Pfeiffer replied.

"I will," Brody said. "My house sits up a bit higher, so we can always go there."

"Who's watching your house?" Pfeiffer wanted to know. "And the farm?"

"I have help," Brody replied. "The animals are safe, and the house will be fine, and if it's not, there isn't a whole lot I can do about it now."

Pfeiffer leaned in and gave Brody an impulsive hug before she said, "Thank you. Keep an eye on my sisters for me."

Brody gave her a mock salute. "Will do."

"We'll be back," Luke said. "And if we can't come back once we're in town, I'll find some way to let you know we're fine."

"Okay," Hadley replied. "Hopefully cell reception will be back soon."

Pfeiffer followed Luke outside and into the downpour, hurrying as fast as her soaking-wet shoes would carry her. She gave a sigh of relief once she'd jumped into the relative dryness of the truck's cab.

"So where should I take you for dinner next week?" Luke asked as he started up the truck's engine. "Assuming all the restaurants don't get washed away."

Pfeiffer grinned, almost able to ignore how cold her feet were in her wet shoes. "How about that Italian place on the way out of town?"

"Bello Italiano?"

"I think that's it."

"I'm impressed."

"With what?"

Luke slid a smile in her direction and said, "Aren't women famous for not being able to make up their minds when it comes to dinner?"

"I'm not most women," Pfeiffer replied. "I will always tell you where I want to eat."

"Good to know."

"I mean," she said, realizing how she'd probably sounded, "if there happens to be another dinner after the first one."

"Oh, I don't think that's going to be . . ." Luke trailed off as they came upon the rush of water that was once the bridge.

"Is that a car down there?" Pfeiffer asked, pointing to the top half of a black sedan, lodged sideways and off the road.

Luke threw the truck into park and hopped out, with Pfeiffer at his heels. "It looks like someone tried to cross from the other side," he said.

"Do you think there's someone still inside?" Pfeiffer asked, squinting through the rain. "I can't tell. The windows are blacked out."

Luke ventured closer to the water, wading in all the way up to his shins. "I don't know," he yelled over the gush. "Maybe I should check."

"You'll get swept away!" Pfeiffer yelled back. She scanned the scene before her, but she knew better than to get too close. A person could be swept away and drown within a matter of seconds.

"There's someone on that tree branch in the water," Luke said, pointing to a massive branch caught up in the current. "Look."

Pfeiffer fixed her eyes to the tree branch, wading slightly closer to the water. The person was holding onto the branch, head down, eyes closed, but Pfeiffer recognized the suit that was clinging to his wet body. "It's Mark!"

"Who?"

"Hadley's husband," Pfeiffer replied, her voice growing hoarse from yelling.

"The congressman?"

"Yes!"

"We've got to get him out of there before he falls off and drowns!" Luke said, ripples of water dripping down his forehead and clinging to his eyelashes.

"I know." Pfeiffer waded even farther into the water, using all of her strength not to topple over. "I think I could reach him if you held onto that tree over there with one hand and onto me with the other."

"No," Luke said. "You won't be able to withstand the current."

"You're stronger than me," Pfeiffer argued. "There is no way I'll be able to pull you both in. "You've got to let me be in the middle."

"What if you get swept up by the current?"

Pfeiffer reached up and curled her hand around his neck, bringing him down to her level. "Just hold onto me, okay?"

Luke nodded, pulling her into him and kissing her hard on the mouth. "Let's do it."

Pfeiffer pulled back, trying to keep herself from thinking

about the fact that Luke had just kissed her, and focusing more on the task at hand—rescuing Hadley's soon-to-be ex-husband from a tree branch in the middle of a flash flood. "Okay," she said, grabbing onto his hand. "I'm going to wade down."

"Be careful," Luke said as she stumbled into the water. "Dig in your feet."

Pfeiffer inched her way toward the tree branch. "Mark!" she yelled. "Mark!"

Mark lifted his head slightly, his face bloodied. There was a gash over one eye, and his nose was bleeding. "Help," he rasped. "Help me."

"Take my hand," Pfeiffer said.

Mark dangled his legs off the branch, one arm holding on and the other reaching out for Pfeiffer. "I can't reach you!"

Pfeiffer stretched farther, until just her fingertips were holding onto Luke. Luke was screaming at her to hold on, and for a moment, she lost his grip and plunged into the water, landing on her back. She felt rocks cutting through her shirt as she was dragged along by the current.

"Pfeiffer!" Luke yelled.

Rolling over onto her belly, Pfeiffer dug her hands into the rocks until she was able to stop herself. She pulled herself up against the current, the water filling her lungs while she gasped for air. Just before she was again pulled under, she felt Luke's hand around her wrist, jerking her up. With Luke's strength behind her, she lunged at Mark, this time grasping his hand. "I've got you," she panted.

Luke pulled at Pfeiffer, who in turn used everything she had to pull at Mark until the three of them were tangled in a wet heap on what was left of the dirt road.

"Pfeiffer, are you okay?" Luke asked, pushing her hair from her eyes. "Are you hurt?"

"I'm okay," she said, pulling herself into a half-sitting position.

Beside her, Mark sat up, coughing and bloody. "Thank you," he sputtered. "I thought I was going to die out there."

"Are you all right?" Pfeiffer asked, looking over at him. "You don't look all right."

"I think my nose is broken," Mark said.

"What happened?" Luke wanted to know. "What in God's name did you think you were doing trying to cross that bridge?"

"I realized it was a bad idea after it was too late," Mark said, holding his middle. "I managed to get out through a window, but the current was so strong, and I can't swim."

"You can't swim?" Pfeiffer and Luke exclaimed together.

"Not very well," Mark admitted. "I managed to grab that branch and pull myself up."

"Jesus," Pfeiffer said.

"We need to get him back to your house," Luke replied. "At least until the water goes down enough to take him to the hospital."

Pfeiffer nodded. "Can you walk?"

"I think so." Mark rolled over onto his knees and heaved himself up with a groan.

Pfeiffer and Luke helped him back to the truck, squeezing him into the middle between them. Mark slumped over on his side, his eyes rolling back into his head.

"Is he going to be okay?" Luke asked.

"He'll be fine," Pfeiffer said. "I'm sure we've got a first-aid kit somewhere, and I doubt he's got any internal damage. He's just in shock."

Luke nodded, his jaw tight as he reversed the truck up the road and turned it around in the soft earth. "Let's just get him back."

Pfeiffer looked out the window in an effort to keep from looking at Mark, whose bloody nose was beginning to make her feel nauseous. In the distance, she saw Old Crow's house, and realized that he was probably alone down there at the bottom of the hill. She also knew that he would be too stubborn to leave if his decrepit farm flooded. "Stop," she said.

"What is it?" Luke asked. "What's wrong?"

"Rufus Crowley," she said. "His house is down there at the bottom of that hill."

"Let's take Mark back first," Luke said. "Brody and I can go down and check on him after."

"I'll go," Pfeiffer said, the door to the truck already halfway open.

"No way," Luke replied. "I'm not letting you go all the way down there by yourself."

"Take Mark back," Pfeiffer instructed. "I'll be fine."

"No."

Pfeiffer could feel the blood trickling down her back from where she'd been dragged along the rocks, and her head felt like it was full of cotton, but she couldn't leave Old Crow by himself, even if she was slightly afraid he might've killed someone and buried them in her garden. "Take Mark back," she repeated.

"Don't you have a lick of sense, Pfeiffer?" Luke asked. "You almost drowned five minutes ago."

"I'm going," she replied. "You can run me over or go back to the house." She slipped out of the truck and into the red mud.

Luke's truck stayed put for a few minutes and then continued down the path toward the James farm. She knew she should have gone back with him and waited, but she'd always been too stubborn to listen to reason.

Pfeiffer trudged down the path toward Old Crow's shack, her feet sticking to the sludge beneath them. By the time she got to the door, the water was up to her shins. "Old Crow," she said, banging on the door. "Are you in there?"

When there was no answer, she pushed on the door, the swelling of the wood making it difficult to open. When it finally did open, water rushed inside, mingling with the water that was already there. Pfeiffer looked around the room for Old Crow and found him sitting on his table, clutching his shotgun.

"I don't think that gun is going to save you from the flood," Pfeiffer said, inching forward. "What are you doing still here? You should have left hours ago."

Crowley turned to look at her, his eyes glassy. He said nothing.

"Why don't you come down from there," Pfeiffer said gently. "You can come to our house until all of this is over."

"I'm not leavin'."

Pfeiffer tilted her head back and looked at the ceiling. "Please," she said. "I know that the last time I was here we didn't part on friendly terms, but you're welcome at our house. It's dangerous for you to be here alone."

"My family's lived here for over a cen'try," Crowley replied. "Ain't no reason to abandon her down 'cuz of a bit a water."

"Your house is flooding," Pfeiffer stated.

"It'll be fine," Crowley said. "Give it time."

"We don't have time," Pfeiffer replied. "The bridge is completely washed out, and if this rain keeps up, your house will be underwater before it gets dark."

"Reckon I'll be underwater with it, then."

"Brody and Luke Gibson will be here soon," Pfeiffer continued. "I don't want them to have to force you to leave for your own good."

Crowley patted his shotgun and said, "Doubt they'll be gettin' too close."

Pfeiffer's back was beginning to sting, and the muscles in her legs ached. Right now she wasn't sure why she'd come all this way to be rebuffed by an old man wielding a shotgun. "You could die," she said.

"I was born on this land," Crowley replied. "I'll die on it, too."

"That's just pigheaded."

"Yer aunt used ta call me that," Crowley said, a far-off smile on his face. "A long time ago."

"Before she lost the ability to speak?"

Crowley looked at her. "She never lost the ability," he replied. "She just decided she was done talkin'."

"Why?"

Crowley's eyes hardened and he turned away from her.

"Never mind," Pfeiffer said hastily. "Please, let's just go."

"Yer aunt didn't kill nobody," Crowley said suddenly. "Don't go thinkin' she did."

"I'm not going anywhere," Pfeiffer replied. "And I didn't say she did."

"You were wonderin' about it, though, weren't ya?"

Pfeiffer shrugged. "I don't know what to think anymore," she said. "I know my mother and father didn't kill anyone."

"No. They didn't."

"Do you know who did?"

"I swore," he said, his voice practically a whisper. "I swore I wouldn't tell nobody."

"Please," Pfeiffer pleaded, the water now to her knees. She watched as objects around the room began to float. "You don't have to tell me. Let's just go."

"She spoke to me," Crowley continued. "Before she died. She spoke."

The revelation was enough to make Pfeiffer stop begging Old Crow to come with her. "She spoke?"

Crowley nodded. "I went to see her. Dr. O'Conner said she weren't long for this life. Said she was askin' fer me."

"What did she say to you?"

"Not much at first," Crowley replied. "She made the good doctor leave the room, and then she asked me for a drink a whiskey. She musta knowed I'd come with it."

Pfeiffer grinned. She hoped that someday she could ask for alcohol on her deathbed. "Is that all she wanted?" she asked. "A drink?"

"She showed me the diary."

Pfeiffer's heart stilled. "You've read it?"

Crowley nodded. "I ain't a good reader," he admitted. "So it took me a while."

Outside, there was a horn and shouting, and Pfeiffer recognized the voices as Brody's and Luke's. "They're here," she said. "Please come with us."

"I can't," Crowley said.

"Why not?"

"This is all I have." Crowley's voice broke. "I can't leave it."

Pfeiffer could hear Brody and Luke pressing against the door to open it further, allowing another gush of water to enter. She felt desperate to get Old Crow out of his house while she still could. "Do you think this is how my aunt would have wanted you to die?" she asked. "Do you think she would want this for you?"

Crowley looked at her, his eyes wet. "No," he said. "She'd be madder'n a boiled owl if she knew."

"Don't you think she'll know if you let yourself get drowned?" Pfeiffer asked.

Brody and Luke came crashing through the door, toppling onto each other as they hurried inside. "What are you still doing in here?" Brody demanded. "The water is up to your waist!"

"I'm sorry," Crowley said.

"Come on," Luke replied. "We have to get you both out of this house."

Crowley nodded, handing his gun off to Brody and allowing Luke to lift him off of the table and carry him through the dense water.

"Pfeiffer," Crowley said. "The desk by my bed."

"What about it?" Pfeiffer asked.

"The missing pages," Crowley replied. "They're in the top drawer."

CHAPTER 34
Martha

MARTHA DIPPED THE BLOODY DISH TOWEL INTO THE warm water in the sink, wondering how one person could have so much blood coming out of their nose. She'd seen a broken nose or two, especially on a few rough nights at Mama's, but this broken nose took the cake.

"The car," Mark was lamenting. "That car was a *rental.*"

"I'd be more worried about your face," Martha replied. "Your face is rented to the people of the state of Kansas."

"Shhhh," Hadley hissed. "Be nice."

Martha shrugged and turned back to the sink. "Do you think they're all right?" she asked. "Do you think Brody and Luke got to them?"

"I hope so," Hadley replied. "I don't understand why Pfeiffer thought she could go and get Crowley herself."

"You know Pfeiffer," Martha said.

"I do," Hadley replied.

"Still," Martha continued, "she should have waited."

"She fell in the water," Mark mumbled. "When they were rescuing me. She fell in the water, and I thought she was going to drown."

"What?" Hadley asked.

"But she got back up," he said. "I think she hurt her back."

"Is she okay?" Martha wanted to know.

Mark nodded absently. "Uh-huh."

Hadley stood up and went into the kitchen with Martha. "I feel like this is my fault," she said. "Pfeiffer would have been back here by now if she hadn't been busy saving my stupid husband."

"Soon-to-be ex-husband," Martha reminded her.

Hadley stopped what she was doing to stare at her sister. "How do you know that?"

"Mark told us last night," Martha said. "Both me and Pfeiffer."

"I was going to tell you," Hadley said.

"Mmm-hmm, right," Martha murmured. "The same way Pfeiffer was going to tell us about that journal?"

"No," Hadley said. "I really was going to tell you, but I guess I was just waiting for the right time."

"I don't think there is ever a right time for that kind of thing," Martha replied. "It's not like Hallmark makes a 'Guess what, I'm getting a divorce' card. If they did, trust me, that's how I would have broken the news about me and Travis."

"It just makes me feel like such a failure," Hadley replied. "I didn't want you and Pfeiffer to think that about me."

"We would never think that about you," Martha said, turning to face her sister. "Ever, and you should know that."

"I know." Hadley sighed. "I didn't want to make things worse than they already are," she said. "I never wanted to make life harder for you. Or Pfeiffer."

"I knew you were going to move out," Martha said suddenly, her voice quiet. "That summer after you graduated—I knew it. We all did."

"You did?"

"Mama didn't know," Martha said. "Not until she found the money you and Brody had been saving."

Hadley stood very still. "She didn't find it," she blurted, unable to hold the words in any longer. "She stole it."

"She was going to give it back," Martha said. "She promised us she'd give it back."

"When?" Hadley wanted to know. "After she moved off with all three of you, and left me and Brody with nothing?"

Martha took her hands out of the water and dried them on the back pockets of her jeans. "Is that what you were fighting about?" she asked. "That day of the storm?"

"You knew about that, too?"

Martha nodded. "Pfeiffer and I went up to my room," she said. "We made Mary leave, because we wanted to talk about boys, and we thought she would tell Mama what we said."

"That explains why she was on the stairs," Hadley muttered.

"You saw her?" Martha asked. "Before she ran off?"

Hadley nodded. "Mama and I were arguing about the money and about the move and about how she thought Brody and I were too young to get married. I told Mama I hated her," Hadley said, nearly choking on a sob. "I didn't mean it, but I said it."

"Oh, Hadley." Martha pulled her sister into her arms. "It's okay."

"No, it's not," Hadley replied, pulling away. "I saw Mary on the stairs. I knew she'd heard everything. I knew Mama hadn't told her about moving, because Mary was going to be so upset. She loved it here more than anyone. And instead of saying anything to her, instead of trying to make her feel better, I ran out the door and drove to Brody's house."

"It wasn't your fault."

"I should have said something," Hadley continued. "Instead, I thought to myself, *Good, now she knows the truth*. What kind of a thing was that to think?"

"We were kids," Martha said. "Mama was the adult, not you."

"I was old enough to know better," Hadley replied, the tears now streaming freely down her face.

"It wasn't your fault," Martha said again. "It wasn't anybody's fault, what happened. The storm was so sudden. You couldn't have known what was going to happen."

"I'm just so sorry," Hadley sobbed. "I'm so sorry."

"I'm okay!" Mark called from the couch. "It's not your fault. Don't cry. I'm okay!"

The front door opened, and Pfeiffer stepped through, holding Crowley by one arm. She guided him inside, followed by Brody and Luke. They brought him into the kitchen and sat him down in one of the chairs.

"Old Crow," Martha said, bending down to look at him. "Are you okay?"

Crowley nodded. "I'm all right, child. I'm all right."

"Would you like some tea or something?"

"Only if you'll add a spot of honey and a drop of whiskey," Crowley replied, a faint smile playing on his pale lips. "And I'd have one of them tomato sandwiches you make, too."

Martha nodded. "You've got it."

"Jesus," Pfeiffer whispered. "Since when did we start running a bed-and-breakfast?"

Hadley laughed, despite herself, and began to dry the tears on her face.

Pfeiffer turned to speak, but her face fell when she saw her sister. "Hadley," she said. "What's wrong?"

"I'm fine." Hadley sniffed. "I was just worried about you, that's all."

"I'm fine!"

"We're all fine," Mark called, still on the couch. "We've established that."

Pfeiffer rolled her eyes in Mark's direction. "I'd be a lot better if I hadn't had to save his dumb ass from roaring floodwaters."

"I'm sorry," Hadley said. "I really thought he'd given up and gone home."

"No such luck."

"Here," Brody said, coming into the kitchen and handing Crowley a folded pair of jeans and a shirt. "I always keep a change of clothes in my pickup. Might be a little big, but at least you'll be dry."

"Thank ya," Crowley replied. "I'm sorry fer makin' all this trouble."

"It's okay," Brody replied. "We take care of each other around here, remember?"

Crowley nodded. "These last few days, I've not been myself."

"These last few days have been unlike any days I've ever had," Brody replied. "It's made us all a little off."

Crowley turned his gaze to Pfeiffer and said, "Did you get 'em?"

Pfeiffer glanced between Hadley and Brody, and then said, "I did."

"You need to read 'em."

"What is he talking about?" Hadley asked. "Read what?"

"The rest of the journal," Pfeiffer replied.

"You had the pages?" Hadley asked.

"I did," Crowley replied. "Read them."

Hesitantly, Pfeiffer pulled out a wad of crumpled papers from her pants pocket. The pages were frayed and wet, but the words were clear.

Beatrice
January 1, 1949

Today marks a brand-new year. So much has happened since I last put pen to paper that I scarcely know what to write. This will be the last time I write in this diary. It will be the last time I speak of Will or what happened that night. It will be the last time I speak until the day I die, and I know this to be true, because if I am ever called to speak again, I know these words will spill from my mouth the way they are about to spill onto these pages.

I feel so far away from the girl I was the last time I saw Will. I'm not that girl anymore. I will never be that girl again.

Last April, Maryann came to stay with us while Daddy and Charlie were called away on farm business for two weeks. She didn't like to stay at the house in town alone, especially as she was preparing to go see a special doctor in St. Louis about her inability to have a baby. Mama and Maryann wouldn't talk about it in front of me. Mama said it was a "delicate matter," and I wasn't to hear of it. Only after Maryann found out my own secret did she tell me hers.

Maryann came to my room one night after dinner to find me in bed, sweating and ill. When she asked me what was wrong, I was afraid to tell her. For the last two months, I'd not received my monthly gift, and I could feel my belly swelling beneath my clothing, despite the fact that I was rarely hungry and eating less.

Despite my shame, she was kind to me and told me she'd felt the same way when her babies were still alive inside of her. I made her swear not to tell Mama, and she promised. She asked me what I planned to do, and I told her Will and I were going to elope while Charlie and Daddy were still gone. I knew that Daddy didn't approve of the match, but I also knew he'd have to accept us if we came back married, and I was carrying his grandchild. It wouldn't be easy, I knew, but it was the only way. Will and I loved each other, and I hoped that Daddy would be able to see that someday.

All that week, Maryann helped me prepare. Will didn't have much money, but he had enough saved up to get us out of Cold River. He'd found another tenant job a few towns over, and we planned to marry and live humbly until the baby came. I was afraid to be away from home, but Will promised me that we'd

*come home again just as soon as we could come back
without making people suspicious of us. I told him
that everyone is suspicious in Cold River, but he just
laughed and held me while I cried.*

*The night we were supposed to meet, I gathered
my things and slipped out of the house without waking Mama. Maryann was supposed to be waiting
for me, but her room was empty, so I went on without
her to Will's.*

*I found her coming out of his cabin as I approached.
She rushed toward me and grabbed me. She told me
Will was gone—that his cabin was empty. She said
she was sorry, but that he must have changed his
mind about us—about me and the baby. She said
sometimes men did these things, even if they'd promised otherwise. She wouldn't let me go inside, for fear
it would upset me and something bad would happen
to the baby. She walked me home and put me to bed,
and I slept for two days without waking.*

*By the time I woke up, she and Mama had a plan.
I was too heartbroken and scared to be upset about
Maryann telling Mama, but Mama never looked
at me the same way after that. Even now, she won't
look at me or speak to me unless I speak to her first.*

*Maryann told me that I would go with her to St.
Louis until the baby came. She said that when we came
home, she would introduce the baby as her baby. She
promised me nobody else would ever have to know—
not Charlie and especially not Daddy. She said it
would be easy to tell everyone her health required her*

to stay up north until the baby was born, as treatment in the city is better than in the country. She said she had cousins with whom we could stay, and she promised me it was the best thing for me and for the baby. God help me, I believed her.

We left the next morning, and Maryann's cousin Ginger met us at the train station in St. Louis. The next months were a blur of doctors and sleep. I remember screaming for Mama when the baby was coming, and I remember holding my sweet baby girl in my arms.

Maryann named her Rachael. She is a beautiful child. I've never seen a more perfect child. She has fine, soft hair and she smells of sleep and milk. I wanted to name her Adeline, but Maryann said it wouldn't be for the best. She called her Rachael, and after she took her into her arms and hurried away with her, I relented. I don't care what her name is, as long as she is safe.

We waited six weeks before returning to Cold River after Rachael was born. It gave me time for my body to heal, and Maryann says because I'm young, I still look almost exactly the same as I did when we left.

Daddy and Charlie were so happy to meet the baby. Maryann has never been so happy, and I suspect this is why they were so keen to accept her without any questions. It took Mama a bit longer to warm up, but Rachael is such a good baby, it didn't take her long. She is the light of our lives now.

I tried to find Will after I came home. I went to the cabin to see if I could make sense out of why he left, and I was surprised to find that everything was the same as the last time I saw him, except that he's gone. All of his belongings are there. I even found the money he'd been saving in the floorboard where he'd hidden it. Daddy says Will doesn't have the good sense God gave him to come in out of the rain, but I know that he wouldn't have left everything he owned. He wouldn't have left me. He wouldn't have left our child.

This is how I know that I should have gone into that cabin the night we were supposed to meet. I never should have let Maryann turn me away. I never should have told Maryann the truth, because I knew how badly she wanted a child. I just didn't know what she would do to have a child—to have my child. I may never know the truth about what happened that night, but I know that I cannot stay here. Will is everywhere, and I cannot bear to look at our child without also facing my betrayal to both of them.

I know that I'll never be able to tell the truth, because if I do, it will destroy the lives of too many people I love. For this reason, I will close these pages and never look at them again. I'll close my mouth and never speak of it again.

For now, for always,
Beatrice

CHAPTER 35
Hadley

Hadley stood behind Pfeiffer in stunned silence. In fact, the entire room had gone quiet, with everyone, including Mark, huddled around the kitchen table like a group of campers huddled around a campfire.

"Did you know?" Hadley asked Crowley, breaking the quiet in the room. "Did you know about this?"

Crowley shook his head. "No," he said. "Yer aunt wouldn't tell me nothing about why she left here, but I always 'spected it had something to do with Will. Then, before she died, she showed me that there diary."

"Why did you rip out the pages?" Pfeiffer wanted to know. "Why did you keep it from us for all this time?"

Again, Crowley shook his head. "I couldn't bear it," he said, his voice cracking. "She was so ashamed. I thought it would be better if you didn't know."

"But you left the journal," Martha replied. "Why didn't you take it all?"

"You 'n Pfeiffer showed up the day I decided to take it," Crowley said. "I heard ya comin' up the stairs. I couldn't hide the diary, so I just took the last pages."

"So that's what you were doing upstairs," Pfeiffer said, understanding dawning in her voice.

"I loved her," Crowley continued. "I loved her all my life. And I couldn't even protect her one last time."

Pfeiffer covered the old man's trembling hands with her own. "This isn't your fault."

"I was happy," Crowley said. "I was happy when Will left. I was happy until it broke Bea's heart."

Hadley felt her own heart breaking for the old man in front of her. She understood his guilt. She wanted to reach out and hug him. "You didn't know," she said to him. "Even Aunt Bea didn't know until it was too late."

"The body . . ." Mark spoke up. "Does that mean the body belongs to this Will your aunt keeps mentioning?"

Crowley looked up at him. "The morning I came to see Bea and Maryann off to St. Louis, there was a wheelbarrow in that garden. Fresh earth, like it'd just been overturned, but I never thought . . ." He trailed off, his voice choked with sobs.

"Jesus," Luke whispered under his breath. "How did nobody realize what happened?"

"People just assumed he left," Brody replied. "It still happens all the time with vagrant farmhands. It wouldn't have been a stretch."

"You knew Maryann," Hadley said. "Did you ever think she could have done something like that?"

"Never," Crowley replied. "But them babies she never got to have took its toll. I was just a child, and I knew it. I suspect in the end, she saw no other way."

Hadley now understood why her aunt had wanted someone to take care of the farm. She must've known that Will, the man she'd loved, was somewhere on the property. She couldn't imagine the pain it would have caused her aunt knowing all these years and living with that knowledge. She couldn't imagine the choice her aunt had to make, giving up her baby and then realizing she'd given him to the person who made that pain a reality. All these years, and they'd never known their aunt was really their grandmother. All these years, and their aunt could never tell them.

Hadley put her hand on Pfeiffer's shoulder and said, "That means Aunt Bea was . . ."

"Our grandmother," Pfeiffer finished.

"And Will was our grandfather," Martha added.

"I'm sorry you had to find out like this," Luke said, running his hands through his hair. "I can't imagine any of this."

Hadley smiled gratefully at him. She was glad he was there with them, despite the fact that she didn't really know him. After all, he'd saved Mark's life and probably Crowley's as well. "At least we found out," she said. "Thank you, Crowley, for allowing us to have this."

Crowley shook his head. "I'm sorry it took me almost drownin' in a flood to realize you girls deserved ta know the truth."

"Well, I guess we're all stuck here now, aren't we?" Mark asked, bruises beginning to form underneath his eyes. "That's just great."

"You want to end up like that rental car of yours?" Martha replied. "There's the door."

Mark didn't reply, instead wandering back into the living room, whining about how much the car was going to cost him.

"We'll have to call the sheriff once we can get this journal to him," Hadley said. "We have to make sure we aren't the only ones who know the truth."

"I can't believe this happened," Pfeiffer said. "I can't believe this secret has been in our family for all these years and nobody discovered it until now."

"We never would have known if it hadn't been for you," Hadley replied. "You didn't give up."

"I just knew Mama and Daddy wouldn't have done something like this. Even if Mama did take the money you and Brody saved. She never would have done something like *this*."

"Hadley," Pfeiffer said, standing up and touching her sister's arm, "I've wanted to tell you so many times that none of this was your fault. But I couldn't. I don't know why. I guess I was angry when you left, and I was angry about Mama and Mary. But it's not your fault. It's not."

For the first time in twenty years, it felt like Hadley could breathe. It felt as if a giant weight had been lifted off of her chest, and the only thing she could do was reach out and hug her sister. "Thank you," she managed to say through her tears.

After a moment, Martha joined them, the years melting away, their faces smooth again. Suddenly there was so much to say.

Hadley released her sisters and took a step back, wiping her eyes with the back of her wrist. "I've missed you two so much," she said.

"We've missed you, too," Pfeiffer said. "More than you could ever know."

CHAPTER 36
Hadley

D R. O'CONNER SQUATTED DOWN IN FRONT OF MARK, WHO was slumped over on the couch, his once clean and *very* expensive suit now covered in clay mud and blood.

"Is it broken?" Mark asked. "It can't be broken. I've got a donor brunch next week, and if I go looking like I just wrestled a cow at a rodeo, they're going to think twice about keeping me on the campaign trail."

"We don't wrestle cows at rodeos," Dr. O'Conner replied, pressing lightly on Mark's nose. "But I'd think you might gather a few more votes from country folk if you had."

From the kitchen, Brody and Hadley shared a look. "Are you going to leave with him?" Brody asked.

"No," Hadley said, surprising herself with the strength of her words. "I'm not."

"That's a relief."

"But I will have to go back," Hadley continued. "For a while, at least, until we can get everything sorted out."

"How long?" Brody turned to her, his eyes darkening. "I lost you once, you know. I'm not aching to lose you again."

"Well," Dr. O'Conner cut in, making his way into the kitchen from the living room. "Your husband's nose isn't broken, but two of his fingers are. I imagine it's from hanging onto a tree branch for dear life."

"So he's going to be fine?" Hadley asked.

"Well, I can't do anything about his personality, if that's what you're asking," Dr. O'Conner replied with a wry grin. "But yes, he'll be fine. I splinted his fingers. And I've told him to get some rest, at least for tonight."

"We appreciate you coming out," Brody said, reaching out to shake the doctor's hand.

"It's no trouble. You're my tenth visit tonight since the rain stopped and the bridges became passable. "I reckon I've got at least ten more."

"What about Crowley? And Pfeiffer?" Hadley wanted to know.

"They're both fine, too," Dr. O'Conner replied. "Rufus is in shock more than anything else, and your sister has a couple of nasty gashes on her back. I stitched two of them up and gave her something for the pain and to help her sleep. Luke and Martha are upstairs with her now. It was a very brave thing she did tonight—saving your husband."

"She saved Crowley, too," Hadley said. "I guess he was just going to sit in his house until he got washed away."

"He's stubborn," Dr. O'Conner replied. "I can't ever remember treating him before tonight, and y'all know how long I've been in practice."

"He's had a rough time lately," Hadley replied, her sympathy for the older man threatening to overflow from her eyes. "He's going to stay with us for a while until we can figure out if his house is salvageable. He doesn't have any family, so we're all he's got."

"You're family enough," Dr. O'Conner said. "I wanted to tell you how sorry I am about your aunt Beatrice. I begged her to call you girls before she passed on, but as you know, she was just as stubborn as Rufus."

"She had her reasons," Hadley said, smiling. "She was stronger than anybody ever gave her credit for."

"I believe it," Dr. O'Conner replied. "If you need me, you give me a holler, and I'll be out as soon as I can, all right?"

Hadley nodded and allowed the doctor to envelop her in a warm hug before he gave them a final wave and disappeared out the door.

Hadley turned to Brody. "Could you give me and Mark just a few minutes?"

"I need to get going, anyway," Brody replied. "We're lucky there's no flooding at the farm, but I need to get home and relieve a couple of the farmhands."

"Okay," Hadley said. "I'll see you tomorrow?"

"You will." Brody leaned down to kiss her, but stopped himself, clearing his throat. "I'll, uh, give you a call."

Hadley went over to the couch and sat down next to Mark. When she'd gotten herself situated, she said, "Brody brought you a change of clothes. He went to his farm about an hour ago to check on things, and brought you a pair of sweats and a T-shirt. I know it's not what you're used to, but it'll be dry and clean."

Mark nodded. "I don't mind dry and clean," he said. "But I don't know how I feel about wearing your old boyfriend's clothes."

"You don't have to if you don't want to," Hadley said. "He was just trying to be nice."

"Everybody here is just so nice," Mark grumbled. "It's like I've fallen into one of the movies you like to watch on that women's channel."

"You better thank your lucky stars," Hadley replied. "Pfeiffer would just as soon watch you drown than save you, but she pulled you out of that creek anyway. You know she had to get stitches on her back?"

"I'm sorry," Mark said, his emotion sounding genuine. "I shouldn't have tried to cross that bridge. But I wanted to talk to you."

"What is there left to say?" Hadley wanted to know. She looked down at her hands and then at her feet, anywhere to keep from looking at her husband. "We've said it all, I think."

"We were good together once, weren't we?" Mark asked. "A long time ago?"

Hadley nodded. "Yes, I think we were. We just lost it somewhere along the way."

"I never meant . . . I never meant to hurt you," he said. "You wanted a husband, and I wanted a political partner."

"You wanted a political maid," Hadley replied. "You wanted someone who was going to stand up there and hold your hand and smile, wearing the latest Marc Jacobs. You wanted someone who didn't mind an empty home as long as the bank account was full. I knew that when I married you."

"But you married me anyway?"

"You aren't the only one to blame for this mess, Mark," Hadley said. "I was selfish, too. I wanted to be someone I wasn't. I wanted to marry someone who wasn't going to demand my emotional involvement."

Mark reached out and gripped her hand, his splinted fingers rough against Hadley's skin. "I'm sorry we couldn't make it work."

"Me too."

"We'll announce our separation when you get back to D.C.," he said. "That is, if you're planning to come back."

"Of course I'll come back," she replied. "We started this together, and we'll end it together."

Mark flashed her his best politician smile and leaned over to kiss her on the cheek. "Where are those clothes? I think I'll go change."

"On the kitchen table," Hadley replied. "The bathroom is upstairs on the left."

Mark nodded and eased himself up off of the couch, groaning slightly. "The flight home tomorrow isn't going to be pleasant," he said. "And I don't even know how to begin explaining the car to the rental place."

"You'll figure it out," Hadley replied to his back. "You always do."

Hadley leaned back against the couch and closed her eyes, relieved that the day was almost over. All she wanted to do was crawl into bed and sleep for twenty-four hours straight. When she opened her eyes, she saw that the dog had made its way over to her and was now resting comfortably at her feet. She bent down and ran her hands along its back, and she felt the same sense of comfort she'd felt as a child—the comfort of knowing she was safe as long as she was here, in Cold River, inside this house.

Just as Hadley felt herself beginning to drift off, Martha came bounding down the stairs, holding out her phone. "You'll never guess what just happened!"

Hadley sat up, rubbing her eyes. "What? Is everything okay? Is Pfeiffer okay?"

"Pfeiffer's fine," Martha replied waving her hands. "She's sound asleep and so is Luke. But guess what?"

"What?"

"My agent just called. Someone at Mama's took a video of my new song and me singing with Amanda, and they uploaded it to YouTube. It already has over a million views!"

"You're kidding!" Hadley exclaimed, startling the dog. "That's wonderful!"

"He's had calls all evening from record labels and from people wanting an interview," Martha continued. "And I have *two* voice mails from Travis."

"Oh," Hadley replied. "Are you going to call him back?"

Martha's brow furrowed. "No," she said. "I know he just wants to talk to me because I'm in the headlines."

"Good," Hadley said. "So what are you going to do now?"

"I've got to call Amanda," Martha replied, sitting down next to her sister. "I think we should write some songs together."

"I bet she would like that," Hadley said. "You always did work well together."

"You know," Martha continued, leaning back against the cushions, "I never thought I'd come back to Cold River. When

I first pulled into town, I couldn't wait to leave again. But now the thought of leaving makes me want to cry."

"I know what you mean," Hadley said.

"Are you going back to D.C.?"

"I have to," Hadley replied. "But I'll be back."

"Because of Brody?" Martha asked.

"Partly," Hadley admitted. "But this is our home now. I mean, I guess it always was, but now it really is. And I want to make sure that we honor our grandparents."

"The grandparents we never even knew we had," Martha replied. "Bless baby Jesus' heart. That's a country song in the making."

"I feel like I'm just meeting Aunt Bea for the first time," Hadley said. "Like we never knew her before, you know?"

"We have to call the sheriff's department," Martha said. "We'll have to show them the journal."

"I called them after you went upstairs," Hadley replied. "They said that they would send someone out, but it could be a day or two since it's not an emergency, and they're dealing with the flood right now."

Martha nodded. "That makes sense, I guess."

"I wish we could have known her," Hadley continued. "Known what she was like before all of this happened to her. I wish her life had been different."

"I do, too," Martha agreed. "But she must have known what she was doing, leaving the farm to all three of us. Leaving that journal for us to find. She wasn't able to tell the truth, but we are, you know?"

"I know," Hadley said, putting her arm around her sister.

"We're stronger together, and I don't want to spend another twenty years figuring that out."

Martha snuggled into her oldest sister, resting her head on Hadley's chest. "Stronger together," she repeated, looking up to see Pfeiffer walking down the stairs, careful, as always, to avoid the squeaky step. "I like the sound of that."

CHAPTER 37
Pfeiffer
One year later

PFEIFFER STOOD IN THE GRASS, HER HEELS POKING INTO soft earth. Hadley and Martha stood on either side of her, all three of them looking down at the black marble stone, new to the old Cold River Cemetery.

"I think it looks nice," Martha said. "I think Aunt Bea would've liked it."

"I think so, too," Pfeiffer replied. "At least now they're together."

Hadley nodded. "I think she would have wanted it that way."

"I think they both would have," Pfeiffer added.

The flood, the worst Cold River had ever seen, was trumped only by the news of the body of a young man found in the James family garden nearly a year ago. The young man, later identified as William Lawrence Mason of Bar Harbor, Maine, was now buried next to Beatrice James. He'd been twenty-five when he died, the orphan son of Pearl and Lawrence Mason. He'd had no siblings, no other family to contact besides Hadley, Pfeiffer, and Martha, his granddaughters.

There were no pictures of him. There were no other memories other than the words written by their grandmother, but Pfeiffer felt a certain connection with him that she couldn't explain. Maybe it was because he, too, lost his parents before it was time. Maybe it was because in some small way, he'd brought her and her sisters closer to understanding their grandmother, the woman they'd always known as Aunt Bea.

Pfeiffer wondered if things might have turned out differently if their mother had known that Beatrice was her mother—if Beatrice and Will had run away together as they'd planned. What would their lives have looked like? Would she and her sisters be alive at all?

Most of the town turned out for their grandfather Will's funeral, and now the sisters were back to see the newly placed headstone. They'd removed their grandmother's and had one made for both of them, together, beside their mother and Mary. The hubbub surrounding the Hemingway sisters and the James farm brought people out of the Ozarks woodwork. Nobody could believe that something so awful had happened right under the town's nose, and nobody could believe that a woman like Beatrice James could have borne the brunt of such a tragedy. Bea's story made it as far as the *New York Times*, and the sisters were still sorting through the piles and piles of mail they got on a regular basis. So far, they'd turned down every single interview request.

The years they'd spent without their father, mother, and sister had been hard, and it wasn't something Pfeiffer wanted to attempt to explain to anyone. She couldn't imagine what it must have been like for their grandmother to lose a child and grand-children she'd never been able to love like a mother and a grand-mother are able to love. What would that love have looked like?

Pfeiffer didn't know the answers. In her three and a half decades on earth, the only thing she knew for certain was that people lived and then they died. But it was the stuff in the middle—the good stuff that she sometimes forgot about—that made the difference in the end. She and her sisters had spent too many years avoiding the stuff in the middle. They'd spent too many years avoiding love and life because they were so afraid of what was going to come next.

She looked down at her grandparents' grave. Pfeiffer hoped that they, the two of them, were together. She hoped that they could see their granddaughters and be proud of them. She had a feeling that they could.

"Are you flying out after this?" Hadley asked Pfeiffer, draw-ing her sister out of her thoughts and nodding to the phone that was vibrating in Pfeiffer's jacket pocket. "That phone has been ringing all morning."

"It's the publishing house," Pfeiffer replied, unable to hide the excitement in her voice. "There's a bidding war over the book."

The book that Pfeiffer was referring to was the first book she'd acquired since opening up her literary agency in Cold River—Heart of the Ozarks Literary. She'd followed up on the tip given to her by the woman at the funeral—the one with the niece named Janice who'd written a book. Pfeiffer had expected the book to be terrible. She hadn't been optimistic in the beginning. However, she'd been pleasantly surprised by Janice, and she'd read the manuscript in one day. It was then that she decided to start her literary agency. If there was one thing she knew, it was how to sell a book, and what she'd found over the last year was that the people in the Ozarks had stories, lots of them, and they wanted to tell those stories. Janice's book, Pfeiffer believed, was going to be the first of many successful books here in Cold River.

"That's wonderful," Hadley replied. "But I hope you're back in time for Lucy's birthday party."

"I will be," Pfeiffer replied. "What about you, Martha?"

"Amanda and I aren't set to record until next month," Martha said. "But the demo we recorded is still in the top ten on iTunes."

"And have you gotten any more calls from Travis?" Hadley wanted to know.

"Not since I blocked his number," Martha replied with a grin. "I don't need him to make music anymore."

Pfeiffer reached out and gave her sister's hand a squeeze. "You never did."

"What about Reese?" Hadley asked, winking at her sister. "I hear he's still got quite a crush on you."

Martha's grin widened. "He's sweet, but I'm not looking for anything serious right now," she said.

Pfeiffer didn't believe her sister for one second, but she knew better than to say anything. She'd heard a few of the songs that were going to be on Martha's newest record. One of them, a catchy tune about an impulsive kiss in a local bar, was clearly about Reese. Pfeiffer guessed she'd just have to wait and see.

At any rate, Pfeiffer was excited to be heading back to New York City. She loved it there, and it would always hold a piece of her heart. But her home, her true home, was the farmhouse, the same one in which she'd grown up, and the same one where she'd been spending every waking moment when she wasn't writing, restoring it with the help of her sisters. Martha, for her part, was splitting her time between Nashville and Cold River, and Hadley had arrived for good just last month after her divorce was final. She'd been spending most of her time with Brody and Lucy. Lafayette also divided her time between the James farm and Brody's farm, as she couldn't go too long without her bulldog companion.

As they stood there, Martha's brow furrowed, and she appeared to be deep in thought. "Hey, you know how when we first got here, my guitar case kept getting moved around?"

Hadley and Pfeiffer both nodded.

"Well, it kept happening for weeks after the flood. Every time I went to look for it, it was in a different place."

"Are you sure you weren't just forgetting where you put it?" Pfeiffer asked.

"Yes," Martha replied. "I would put it in odd places just so I wouldn't forget where I left it."

"That's weird," Hadley said.

"That's not the weird part," Martha said.

"It's not?"

"No," Martha continued. "What's weird is that after we buried Grandfather Will, it stopped disappearing."

All three of the sisters turned to look at the headstone.

"Maybe he was trying to tell you something," Pfeiffer said.

"I thought you didn't believe in ghosts," Martha teased, giving her sister a mischievous grin. "Isn't that what you told me once?"

Pfeiffer shrugged. She didn't know for sure if she believed in ghosts. All she knew was that this time last year, she thought that her life was over. She thought that she'd never be whole again, and now, looking at her sisters, she knew she'd been wrong. Loss didn't require that she lose herself, and sometimes it took a voice from the past to show a person just exactly where they needed to look.

ACKNOWLEDGMENTS

IT IS WITH SINCERE AFFECTION AND ADMIRATION THAT I'D like to thank the following:

Priya Doraswamy—thank you for being the lovely calm in all of my storms. I owe you so much.

Lucia Macro—for always knowing exactly where I'm headed, even when it's clear I have no idea the direction.

Matt and Jude—for guild nights.

My mom and dad—for always telling me, "We can fix this," when I was out of duct tape.

The Vicious Biscuits—for video chats and belly laughs and completely unexpected friendships.

Emma and CW Hunter—for being Nikki's parents and for loving me, too.

About the author

About the book

Insights,
Interviews
& More . . .

Meet
Annie England Noblin

Courtesy of the author

ANNIE ENGLAND NOBLIN lives with her son, husband, and four rescued bulldogs in the Missouri Ozarks. She graduated with an MA in creative writing from Missouri State University and currently teaches English for Arkansas State University. Her poetry has been featured in such publications as the *Red Booth Review* and the *Moon City Review,* and she coedited and coauthored the coffee-table book *The Gillioz "Theatre Beautiful."* ᴄ͛

A Walk in the Woods with an Old Friend

By Annie England Noblin

The old dog went to visit the old woman every day. Her paws beat the gravel each morning as she plodded along toward the farmhouse. Sometimes she'd stop to sniff a bullfrog or take a drink from the mossy pond on the edge of the pasture, but mostly she stayed true to her mission and nosed open the front door at 9 a.m. on the dot.

On these mornings, the dog found the old woman in the kitchen, and the dog sat patiently at the woman's feet until the sausage gravy was ready. Then the two would sit—the woman at the table and the dog on the rug—and eat their breakfast together. Afterward, the woman read the newspaper while the dog rested her weary paws from the morning's journey. After all, two miles was a long walk for an elderly basset hound. Long gone were the days when she might've chased a rabbit or a raccoon. Long gone were the days when her ears perked up for much of anything. Well, anything besides the old woman's sausage gravy.

When the weather was warm and the sky was clear, the woman spent her afternoons hanging laundry on ▶

3

A Walk in the Woods with an Old Friend
(*continued*)

the line outside. The dog liked these days best. When the woman was done hanging the laundry, she would sit on the porch and watch it blow in the wind. Sometimes the old woman strolled out into the woods behind the house, walking stick in one hand and a book about birds tucked under one arm. The dog trailed behind her, occasionally picking up the scent of a woodland creature she was too lazy to chase.

Today, the old woman was dressed for walking, but she had no walking stick or book about birds. Instead, she was carrying a small knapsack, slung over one shoulder. She nodded her head toward the forest, and the dog followed her. They walked for a while, deeper into the woods than the two of them had ventured ever before, and the dog started to worry that the woman might become too tired to walk home again.

Eventually, the dense forest gave way to a clearing. Just beyond the clearing was the largest tree the dog had ever seen. It stood feet above all the others. It was so tall, in fact, that it appeared all the other trees were bowing down, in awe of its presence. The woman, too, knelt down in front of the tree, and the dog, curious about it all, sat down beside her.

The woman pulled the knapsack off

her shoulder and sat it in front of her. Opening the flap, she reached down inside and pulled out a wooden box. The dog, hopeful that the box might contain a treat, began to wag her tail and whine, but the woman shook her head and put her finger to her lips. The dog complied, lying down on her belly, stretching her front paws out so far she could almost touch the tree with them.

The woman opened the box and pulled out two pictures. They were old and slightly yellowed, but both of the girls in the pictures had sparkling eyes that the dog recognized—they were the eyes of the old woman, younger eyes, neither clouded with age. The woman set the pictures down at the base of the tree and then clasped her hands together. The tree, for its part, began to sway slightly in the wind, as did the other trees, as if they somehow knew the old woman brought them an offering.

The woman looked up at the tree, her eyes wet with tears. Then she lowered her head again, and the dog rested her chin on the woman's lap. The dog had always known the woman to be alone. She had no family to speak of, and she rarely had visitors with the exception of an even older man who lived down the road. But somehow, these girls with their beautiful eyes must be related. ▸

A Walk in the Woods with an Old Friend
(continued)

The dog wondered why they never came to visit her.

"They're gone," the woman said.

The dog looked up, her ears raised slightly. Had the old woman just spoken? The dog wasn't sure. She'd never heard the woman's voice before. The dog cocked her head to one side.

"The storm took them," the woman continued, her voice cracked and thin with age. "This forest took them."

The dog rested her head back on the woman's lap, and closed her eyes when the woman began to stroke her head.

"My granddaughters will be here soon," the woman said. "Will you look after them for me?"

The dog licked the woman's hand.

"Don't worry," the woman replied. "I'm ready to leave this earth. I've been here too long already. I'm tired."

The two sat there at the base of the tree for a long time, listening to the sounds around them, listening to the trees sway in conversation with each other, listening to the birds and the squirrels and the Cold River just beyond them cutting its path through the Ozarks Hills. Everything was alive, and everything had a story to tell, if only someone stayed long enough to listen.

Finally, the old woman stood up, placing the box back into the knapsack, the pictures still nestled onto the soft earth. "Come on," the old woman said to the old dog. "It's time to go home." ∽

Behind the Book

I can pinpoint the day I decided my next book needed to have more than one female main character. I was in my office at the university where I work, having a text conversation with my two best friends. I'd been friends with these women since high school. We lived hours (and for one of us, an entire continent) apart, but we carried on our daily conversations as if we'd just had lunch together. We were each discussing something happening in our lives, basically having three separate conversations, when I realized despite the fact that our lives were intertwined, we were each the main character in our own lives. We shared our stories with each other, and in this way, we pushed the narrative of our individual experiences forward.

That's when I decided that I wanted my next book to have three narratives. Additionally, I was ready for a challenge. I'd already written three books—*Sit! Stay! Speak!*, *Just Fine With Caroline*, and *Pupcakes*—that had a single female protagonist. It was fun, but I worried that my readers would get bored or begin to think that I was a one-trick pony, the kind of writer who could write one thing. Rather, a writer who could write from only one perspective. I wanted to challenge myself while providing a different kind of book for my readers, which is how I came up with the characters of Hadley, Pfeiffer, and Martha.

Around that time, I was also reading lots of historical fiction (my favorite genre). I was stuck in the 1920s with the Lost Generation—Zelda and F. Scott Fitzgerald, Ernest Hemingway, Gertrude Stein, and Ezra Pound. I was reading biographies of their lives, their writing, but also historical fictional accounts of their lives. When I first began writing *The Sisters Hemingway,* I'd just finished reading *The Paris Wife* by Paula McLain, and I was on to *Hemingway's Girl* by Erika Robuck. I have to admit that I'm not a fan of Ernest Hemingway—neither his writing nor who he was as a person— but at the same time, his personal life fascinated me. His four wives fascinated me, especially Pauline Pfeiffer, Hemingway's second wife. She grew up in Piggott, Arkansas, not far from where I grew up. I wanted to honor them in some way, and so I decided to name the main characters after them. I guess it's just my way of saying thank you for making history interesting. ∼

Reading Group Guide

1. Rachael made the greatest sacrifice for her daughter. To what extent has this sacrifice formed the grown-up personalities of her other daughters?

2. After Pfeiffer loses her job, she seems to lose her identity. How much of your own identity is tied to what you may do for a living?

3. Each of the present-day sisters left Cold River and "never looked back . . ." until now. In what ways does the place you grew up influence the person you are today?

4. Aunt Beatrice chose never to speak out loud, but we learn about her through her diary entries. At one point she says that "Maryann says all women ought to have a secret or two . . ." Do you agree or disagree with that statement? Why?

5. Do you think Beatrice ever regretted her decision to take care of the three sisters?

6. Pfeiffer states about Brody that "Everybody changes," but also tells her sister Hadley that "I bet he's basically the same guy you've always known." Do you think she's right about him? Do you think this holds true for most people, or not?

7. At one point it's said that the sisters had spent too many years forgetting about "the good stuff in the middle" between living and dying. Avoiding love and life. Why is it sometimes easier to be angry in silence than to talk and face the truth?

8. Do you think there was a ghost? ∾